THE
TIGRAN
CHRONICLES

Published by Serenity Mountain Publishing
Springdale, Arkansas

THE TIGRAN CHRONICLES
©2020 by Meg Welch Dendler
All rights reserved

www.megdendler.com

First Edition

ISBN: 978-1733645096

Cover design by Kelsey Rice.
Interior design by Serenity Mountain Publishing.

This is a work of fiction. Names, characters, places, and incidents either are the product of the author's imagination or are used fictitiously. Any resemblance to actual persons, living or dead, events, or locales is entirely coincidental.

"Those who cannot remember the past are condemned to repeat it." (George Santayana)
I've got news for Mr. Santayana: we're doomed to repeat the past no matter what.
That's what it is to be alive.
Kurt Vonnegut

Also by Meg Welch Dendler

At the Corner of Magnetic and Main

Meg's Books for Young Readers

Bianca: The Brave Frail and Delicate Princess

Cats in the Mirror Series
Why Kimba Saved The World
Vacation Hiro
Miss Fatty Cat's Revenge
Slinky Steps Out
Kimba's Christmas

And the Companion Books to the Series
Max's Wild Night
Dottie's Daring Day

To Andy ~ & Laura

THE TIGRAN CHRONICLES

by
Meg Welch Dendler

Meg W. Dendler

SERENITY MOUNTAIN PUBLISHING

Springdale, Arkansas

Chapter 1

The bolt on the door of the attic room clicked, locking her in. Taliya plopped down on the tidy single bed in the corner, and her striped tail lashed back and forth across the bedspread. *My new home.* This depressing room was as far from home as Hitler was from Gandhi. Home smelled like flowers and fresh grass, mountain air, and pine trees. The attic hideout smelled like dust, stale air, and sadness. There was a little window up near the ceiling, but it didn't look like it was meant to open. Not like that would be allowed anyhow. It would provide some natural light during the day. How long before she would see the sky again, feel the sun warm her furry face? At least the passing of sunlight would give her some sense of day and night within those four solid walls that could

1

keep her safe—keep her trapped. She tried to take a deep breath and let it out slowly, but it felt impossible. *How can you breathe without any trees?*

A dull thump sounded in the hallway, and Taliya swiveled one black furry ear, the white spot on the back almost facing front. Had there been a change of plans? The hackles on her neck rose. Was Marla coming back? Or had the Enforcers found her already? She held her breath for a full minute, but there was no more sound from the hall.

All clear. For now.

There was a short while before sunrise and the silent time began. It already felt like an eternity since she'd slipped out the back door of her home in the Ozark Mountains on Thanksgiving Day, her mother close behind her in the dark woods. When Mother had pressed her forehead against Taliya's, she could smell the salt of her tears and the deep grief radiating from her. Following the instructions of the masked human—masked so she could never identify him, even if tortured—Taliya climbed into the enormous hatch of an old shipping truck that was waiting in the dark. She was shocked the thing could still run, even if it had been adapted for solar power. The roller door closed behind her, was chained shut, and she'd wondered if it would be the last time she ever saw her forest home or her family.

Taliya had lugged her suitcase to the front of the vehicle, weaving between boxes and crates of merchandise, following the dim light from a secret compartment at the front of the truck. She stepped inside, closing the door behind her and throwing the latch. The tiny room held an electric lantern, a pillow and blanket, a portable toilet, a box of food, and jugs of water. There was also a stack of well-worn books—that classic series about dragonriders on a planet called Pern and the ones about the Queen of the Tearling. Taliya was surprised someone had found actual paper books. They were rare now, and her family was proud of their own collection of classics. She had a few tucked in her suitcase for the days of solitude ahead.

Whoever was driving the ancient truck had gotten underway immediately, and they'd rattled and clunked along dirt roads for hours until Taliya finally felt the tires humming smoothly on one of the recycled-plastic fabricated roads. They were on the highway. She'd napped on and off and even slept soundly a few times, barely able to stretch out fully in the little compartment, trying not to let her thoughts wander to the dangers surrounding her. She read a bit. It was odd to be completely free from technology of any kind. At home they had a media wall, but not all the virtual reality that went with it. Her parents had insisted they keep things simple, but she always had her tech pad somewhere nearby. Besides surfing the interwebs, she used the pad to video chat or jot notes to her friends. Of course, she hadn't been allowed to bring any of that with her, nor would she have it in her hiding place. Technology was easily traced.

The truck had stopped several times at checkpoints along the road, and once a vigilant Enforcer actually opened the back roller door to search the contents of the storage area. Taliya barely breathed until she heard the door close and the chains restored around the lock. He had not discovered her secret compartment, but the next one might. What if they had dogs to scent her out? Each time she felt the vehicle stop, her heart had raced uncontrollably, and she prayed to the gods no one would find her.

It felt like maybe three days before the truck ground to a halt and didn't start moving again. *We're there*, she'd concluded. It was a few more hours before the chains were removed and she felt the vibration of the roller door being lifted. Clankings and footsteps came closer through the truck itself, but she didn't dare open the door to her hidden room. Enforcers might have been the reason for the stop. She waited, wrestling to keep her breathing calm and even.

When the latch flipped up and the door to her room opened, there were two masked human males and an unmasked female on the other side. *Helpers, not Enforcers.* It was hard for Taliya to rise and walk after being contained for so many days, but they were patient. The brunette woman, pretty for a human, took charge of her suitcase.

The truck was parked inside a warehouse. It was dark except for some dimly lit lanterns, so she couldn't tell exactly how large the space was. The echoing of even slight noises suggested it was enormous. Metallic dust tickled her nose.

The moment she was out of the truck, the men closed and rechained the back door, climbed into the cab, and started the engine. With the headlights off, they pulled up to one of the walls. The woman raised it from the bottom, like a garage door, and the truck drove out into the darkness. After closing and locking the section of wall, the woman looked back at Taliya, put her hands on her hips, and sighed.

"I'm Marla," she said. "You're under my care now. I can't possibly lug you and your bag up the stairs. Are you strong enough? We have a little time to rest, but I don't want to risk it."

Taliya wanted to laugh at the image of the woman trying to carry her, but she was too exhausted. Marla was tall and stocky, but Taliya guessed she weighed over a hundred pounds more than her new friend and stood at least a head taller. Lugging was not an option.

"I can make it."

"Good," Marla said, picking up the suitcase. "It's up two flights, but you can collapse once you are tucked away and safe."

She had followed Marla up one long flight of stairs, through a storage room that was above the high ceiling of the warehouse, and up another flight. On the third floor, there was a long hallway from the stairs to the far side of the building with three doorways along it.

"This area used to be living quarters for the management team many decades ago," Marla said, "and now it's storage space for the factory. I'm the office manager, so I live on site, but down on the first floor, near the entrance. No one should have any reason to come all the way up here, even if they are in the storage room."

Marla had opened the door at the far end of the hall, ushered Taliya inside, put the suitcase on the bed, given her instructions on when to be silent and when moving around was safe, assured her she'd be back with food later, and then locked Taliya in.

Now Taliya didn't feel like resting at all. It was done. She was in hiding. Hours and days and weeks and probably even months of resting lay before her. Opening her suitcase, she pulled out a stack of photos. Taliya sifted through the smiling faces of her family—unique markings of spots and stripes she would never forget.

"It will help you remember what life is supposed to be like," Mother had said, handing her the stack of images as she packed to leave. "It will help you remember why you are staying silent and hidden instead of fighting. You must survive. Whatever happens, *survive*."

She turned back to her suitcase and pulled out the stack of books from home that was tucked in the side. Something to do during the silent time. It had all been explained to before her escape, and Marla had repeated the instructions. Sleep or read during the day. Or stare at the walls. On top of the stack was the book Mother had insisted she read: *The Diary of a Young Girl* by Anne Frank. Taliya had heard of it before, of course, in her history lessons, but she'd never bothered to read it. It was written during World War II, over two hundred years ago.

"Read this first," Mother had said. "It will help you to remain hopeful." The glint in her golden eyes meant she was serious and not to be questioned or challenged.

Taliya sat on the bed, closed her own golden eyes, and curled her fluffy tail around her waist, holding that image of Mother's face in her mind. *I won't forget. I won't.* Who knew when or if they would ever meet again.

Taliya would hide. She had promised. But Mother had gone to fight. Maybe she would find Father among the soldiers, if he was still alive.

The clock by the bed said 6:00 a.m. One hour left. After 7:00, no movement was allowed, except during the noon lunch hour. She could use the bathroom then since the activity of the employees downstairs could cover any creaks in the floorboards, but she'd have to tiptoe carefully and wait until later to flush. No matter how isolated she was, someone might hear. Anyone in the storage room would be right below her.

She pulled the stack of calendars out of her suitcase and set them on the bedside table. Calendars for three years were printed out and ready so she could keep track of the date. Three years. She couldn't even begin to consider three years in that stuffy room.

She rose and paced—small, measured steps—the claws on her furry toes poking out of the front of her sandals but not long enough to click on the bamboo floor. *One, two, three, four, five, six, seven.* Turn. *One, two, three, four, five, six, seven.* Turn. Back and forth she paced across the floor, like her ancestors had done in zoo cages. She'd seen the videos. Back and forth. If there was earth below their paws, they had trod a sad, permanent bare path into it. *One, two, three, four, five, six, seven.* Turn. *One, two, three, four, five, six, seven.* Turn. *One, two, three, four* . . .

She paused in the middle of the room, stretching her arms up toward the ceiling. Even extending the claws from her fingers, she couldn't touch it. But almost. At seventeen years old, she was fully grown and stood six foot five inches tall.

So what does that make it, maybe ten feet high? She sighed and dropped her arms. *Have I ended up in a cage after all?* A cage fourteen feet by roughly eight feet wide.

No bars, but she was just as certainly trapped as she would have been if Enforcers had shown up at their peaceful home in the country and dragged her away. She wondered what they would do when they arrived at the family compound, which they inevitably would, and found the lair empty. Would they torch it for spite, or would her home be waiting for her when this nightmare was over? Without Father and Mother, would she ever want to return?

Survive. That was the only thing that mattered. Survive until the war was over. Survive until she could walk free.

Taliya sat down on the bed again and picked up the assigned book: Anne's diary. She knew it was about a girl who had hidden from those who wanted to kill her. People called Nazis, who wanted to see Anne Frank dead or locked away. Anne had gone into hiding—like she herself was now—from people who hated her for something she was, not for anything she'd done. How did the story end? There wasn't much else to do, so she'd find out pretty soon.

Taliya set the stack of books on top of the calendars on the small table by the bed. Some were educational. Some were just for fun. At least there was a dim lamp to read by. The brightness didn't reach to the corners of the room, where dark shadows lurked, but it was enough for her needs. Her feline eyes could see easily with only the faintest bit of light. If the lamp was any brighter, it might be noticed through the window by someone passing by, though she couldn't imagine who would be looking at a window three stories up above the warehouse. Enforcers, maybe.

Before the silent time, she could change from her traveling clothes, wash, and unpack her few belongings into the small dresser across the room. She laid a furry hand on the bright-blue tunic in her suitcase—her favorite. Probably best to save that for a day when she needed cheering up. This was not that day. She wouldn't be defeated or depressed that easily.

Stay focused.

9

She was safe. She hoped her twin brothers, Tuscan and Tyler, had arrived at their destinations as well. *Only five. So young to be torn from your family.* Separate trucks had come for them before she'd left home. Separate places for all three of them. If one was discovered, the other two would still be safe. That was the plan. She didn't know where they'd gone, so she could never be coerced to tell. She shuddered at the flash in her mind of a violent image from a media broadcast. Enforcers could torture it out of you. Everyone can be broken eventually. Everyone. Her tail puffed at the thought, and an anguished tiger-like moan escaped her throat.

Taliya pulled her dirty tunic over her head and shook it out in front of her. She hoped there was some way to get laundry done. She hadn't thought to ask about that. Washing clothes in the sink was certainly possible but not her first choice, though maybe it would give her something to do in the night when she could be up and about. She ran her clawed fingers through the white fur on her stomach. A quick shower might make her feel more settled. It had been far too many days without a proper bath, and the aroma of stress on her fur was pungent. *I smell like a wild animal.*

She rose from the bed and counted her steps across to the bathroom. *One, two, three, four.* That closet of a room held the shower, sink, and toilet. Towels and some necessities were laid out for her. *It could be worse. I could just have buckets.* She ran some water in the sink basin and splashed it on her face. Droplets stuck to her orange-and-black striped fur and dripped from her black whiskers and protruding nose, cool and refreshing, even if the water held the distinctive salty odor of a city—processed from the oceans to meet the needs of a large population.

Glancing up into the mirror, she grinned and checked her teeth. They could use a good brushing. Her fangs were yellow, and her mouth felt as fuzzy as her body. There would be no dentist trips for who knows how long. She had packed a second toothbrush, for when the first wore out. Taliya would brush her teeth, take a shower, and get ready for bed, just like any other night of her life. That's what would keep her from going crazy and using her claws to hang from the ceiling like some cartoon cat. Routine.

She had to survive. There weren't many tigran left. Certainly not many walking free. Tigran were one of many government-funded genetic experiments, creations they were now ashamed and afraid of. What had they expected when they'd started mixing wild animals with human beings?

Scientists had enjoyed pushing the boundaries of their knowledge and understanding since time began. At least it seemed that way to Taliya, based on what she knew of human history. And they often didn't stop to consider if the next step was the wisest choice. Just plow ahead. Discover. Create. The creating part, that's where the biggest troubles seemed to come from. What was the line from that old dinosaur movie?

"Your scientists were so preoccupied with whether or not they *could*, they didn't stop to think if they *should*."

Cloning dinosaurs—enormous, lethal eating machines. It was easy to see how that was a dumb idea, but if some scientist had actually figured out how to clone a dinosaur, Taliya didn't doubt they would do it. Maybe they had. There could be dinosaurs hiding in some secret government lab at that moment. Being intelligent and being wise didn't always run on the same track. The creation of her whole species might well have been some similarly huge error of judgement. The Enforcers and their supporters clearly thought so.

From the first man who captured a wild tiger and somehow thought this was a creature that needed to live as a captive in his home, that was the beginning of nothing but suffering and death for Taliya's ancestors. Caged. Bred willy-nilly for profit. Pet the adorable cub—precious little tiger baby—but don't think too much about how he was stolen from his mother just days after his birth or what happens in a few weeks when he is no longer safe to pet. Auctioned off to some human who thought a tiger in his backyard would be delightful. Or just shot to make way for more cute cubs. Sold for parts, like an automobile. Bones ground up for medicine that didn't actually cure anything.

What genius thought of the first crazy hybrid? Some scientist? Or maybe just a guy who discovered a way to make more money from the big cats he owned.

"What if we find a way to breed a tiger and a lion together? What would that look like? How much would someone pay to see it?"

The logic couldn't have gone much further than that. Did the creators worry about the health of such an unnaturally bred creature? Doubtful. What did it matter?

"We can call them ligers!" Or tigons, depending on the sex of the parent lion and tiger.

Ligers and all the mixes that came from that interbreeding—like the li-liger, li-tigon, or ti-tigon—were interesting-looking creatures, but they weren't ever quite right. Not natural. The DNA didn't match properly between the two species. Often, the poor animals just kept growing and growing until their hearts couldn't take it. Massive and majestic and beautiful, yes. Necessary? No. Healthy? Rarely. And they were usually sterile or produced sickly cubs because nature has ways of correcting mistakes. But it didn't stop with tigers and lions. Designer big cat hybrids like the jagulep, the pumapard, or even the lijagulep could be created for the right price.

Frankencats. Someone along the way had called them that. If only they'd known what kind of insane crossbreeding was to come.

The tigran were the most successful of the government-sponsored genetic experiments that had been secretly going on since 2040. Human DNA was combined with the DNA of tigers to form a soldier that was massive in size, superior in strength, and more durable and efficient than mere humans. But the need for soldiers was soon eclipsed by the need for workers: builders and rescuers.

The most devastating of the predictions for a warming climate had been held off by the invention of high-efficiency machines to clear carbon from the air and destroy it, but it wasn't enough to avoid decades of catastrophic storms, earthquakes, volcanic eruptions, fires, and rising ocean levels. Words like "bomb cyclone" and "fire tornado" were part of routine news reports. Two new levels were added to tornado and hurricane categories. Earth became so consistently and systematically ravaged that human life was reduced to recovering, rebuilding, and surviving. Coastal towns were wiped off the map, swallowed by the rising oceans. West Nile, malaria, and revived strains of diseases—escaping from melted Arctic ice—claimed victims in the millions. Crops failed, and food production became the sole focus of rural communities less impacted by flooding. Art, literature, technology, and cultural advancement came to a standstill in the battle to survive— meeting the basic needs of food and shelter for the billions of humans on the planet.

In response to the ongoing disasters and recovery, tigran were pulled from the laboratories and put to work. Strong swimmers, tigran were the first responders when devastating floods hit. Besides being immune to mosquito-borne illnesses and many other diseases, their sense of smell was keener than

14

any rescue dog, and they were as intelligent as humans, able to make life-saving decisions that dogs could not. And tigran were strong, able to help clear debris after storms or rebuild what had been destroyed. One tigran could do the work of ten strong men.

The human population was leery of them at first, but as generations went by, the value of tigran made them honored members of any community. Tigran families lived among those they protected and supported, rebuilding neighborhoods and helping to protect them from future disasters. By the start of the twenty-second century, tigran were deeply entrenched in life all over the planet.

As the devastating storms and natural disasters became less frequent and what remained of the humans adjusted and adapted to the new conditions on the planet, the value and the importance of the tigran waned. Tigran stepped outside of government jobs and took on careers, just like the humans around them. Tigran remained separate, not breeding with humans—there were strict laws about that—but they lived amicably alongside them.

That harmony was disrupted in 2138 by an ambitious young politician, Drimavil Kerkaw, who based his entire campaign for the Senate seat of New York on returning the tigran to government labs, where they belonged. His single-minded focus on the danger of allowing "wild animals" to roam freely stirred up the population, and many forgot all the tigran had done to save the human race. Kerkaw's power and influence only grew over the years, and by the time he was elected president, many tigran had removed themselves from big cities. They gathered in rural areas and set up their own communities. Finally, a federal law was passed that tigran could no longer live free. As government property, those who refused to return to the labs or live in a zoo as an "ambassador of the species" were to be terminated.

In October of 2172, the Gathering began—the roundup of tigran that Taliya and her brothers were hiding from.

After spending her shower time pondering the inhumanity of humans and the fate of her species, Taliya hung up her towel carefully and brushed her fur well until it was nearly dry. Some tigran had rough, spiked tongues like a cat, but she did not. With fresh pajamas, dirty clothes tucked away in a corner, teeth brushed, she was ready to settle in for the long hours of silence ahead. Fortunately, she was exhausted. And she was part tiger. Sleeping for the next twelve hours wouldn't be a problem. There was no noise from the warehouse and factory yet, but she wasn't sure how much she would ever be able to hear from her small attic room.

She clicked off the lamp and rolled onto her side, wrapping her tail around her. It only took a moment to fall into a deep sleep, feeling relatively safe, finally, after so many days of worry. Whether that was a false assurance, only time would tell.

Chapter 2

S he dies? Anne Frank dies?! How in the world did Mother think this book would be encouraging if on page one, before the diary even started, it says flat-out that Anne was captured and died in a concentration camp shortly before the end of WWII? What kind of hope was that supposed to inspire? Taliya was grateful she'd waited a couple of days to start reading Anne's diary and opted for one of her favorite books instead. That had been much more soothing, but she'd finished it quickly and moved on to Mother's assignment. *Way to brighten my mood, Mother.* Or was the purpose of the book simply to elaborate the second point Mother had stressed over and over.

1) Survive.

2) Don't let them catch you.

Her fate would probably be the same as Anne's.

Taliya shifted carefully on the bed. There were no springs under the mattress. They had been removed and replaced with a flat board to avoid any chance of squeaking or noise, but she still worried the floor might sense her movement and react. It didn't. She stared at the bathroom door and counted the notches in the wood. Again. She'd only been there for three days, but it already felt claustrophobic and suffocating and never-ending.

After the workers downstairs had cleared out for the night, Marla would arrive, knock three times, unlock the door, and give her food on a tray. *Not much different than being caged and fed by a keeper*, Taliya thought. Marla's arrival was the sign the coast was clear. The toilet could be flushed. Taliya could take a shower and move around and get some exercise. Even when she felt the vibrations stop—the low drone of the building when the machinery was in operation—she was not to let her guard down until Marla arrived.

Marla would return roughly twelve hours later, before the workers clocked in for the day. She would collect the old food tray and bring dinner or breakfast or whatever you wanted to call it in the flipped-upside-down world in which Taliya now lived. Once Marla left in the morning, there were around thirty minutes for Taliya to make limited noise. When the clock tower struck seven o'clock, those seven bongs that Taliya had already learned to dread, the silent time began.

The instinctively wild part of Taliya's DNA felt like it was being strangled in that attic room. Trapped and locked away. The time of silence during the daylight hours when she could barely move was the worst. No one but Marla knew she was hiding there. If anyone were to hear a strange noise and come to investigate . . . then Taliya would learn what it really meant to be trapped and caged. If she was lucky. When she pondered the alternative, which she had done each and every day since her arrival, the attic didn't seem that bad.

A portion of her genetic makeup was nocturnal, but when tigran lived in close contact with humans, they pulled from that Homo sapien part of their heritage and slept during the night. Very "civilized," as that kind of lifestyle was often called, living as much like the humans as possible. Left to her own devices and forced to be silent during daylight hours, Taliya found it was easy to fall into a different rhythm: sleeping during the day and active at night.

When she awoke that day—long before the clock struck five o'clock in the evening, signaling the closing of the warehouse and the departure of the workers—Taliya had started reading the book Mother had insisted on: Anne's diary.

Anne Frank was a saucy teenager, and she was also forced to hide or face being sent away or possibly killed. Unlike Taliya, the others in the office building knew Anne and her family and other Jews were hiding in the upstairs rooms. They didn't have to be silent every moment of daylight. They also had a larger space.

Would I rather have a bigger hiding place if it meant having to share it with seven other creatures? From Anne's constant journal entries about one stupid fight after another between the occupants of their attic annex, Taliya thought it wasn't worth it.

She'd also determined that Anne was either a massive drama queen or a massive pain in the ass. The girl seemed to be in trouble most of the time and filled with overwhelming angst about insignificant things. The fact that she called her diary "Kitty" was enough to make Taliya dislike her, though in the 1940s Anne could hardly have known what a slur that word would become—how tigran would be rudely labeled as Kitties. She could forgive Anne that lack of foresight.

But the horrible things Anne said about her mother? Taliya flexed her claws, thinking about the passage she'd just read where Anne wanted to give her mother a good shaking because her mother's critical words and dirty looks "pierced her like arrows."

Could Anne's mother really be that nasty and horrible? Or was Anne really a melodramatic, spoiled girl? It had to be one or the other, didn't it? Or maybe it was just somewhere in the middle and everything seemed over-dramatic and over-amplified because they were stuck together for months and months and terrified they'd be discovered any day. And they would be, in the end. Taliya already felt frayed around the edges after three days. How would she hold out if the war went on for years and years like World War II had?

What will happen if this war is lost? she wondered. *Then what?*

Anne's next entry talked about the horrible things happening in her world while she stayed hidden. Families torn apart. Women returning home to find their houses locked and their children gone. Everyone waiting for the conclusion of the war or for death to come and end their suffering. People being shipped off to slaughterhouses like herds of diseased, unwanted cattle. That was quite a visual image, and the stories were eerily familiar to Taliya.

She closed her eyes and could easily imagine truckloads of tigran, chased with whips and forced into dirty buildings where they would be caged or killed. Most of the uncivilized tigran in the United States, those living a wild life away from humans, had already been eliminated. She'd seen it on the news. The government had been proud to report that accomplishment. Dangerous wild animals had been removed from the forests. Of course, those tigran had never harmed a single human, a fact no one mentioned.

Taliya had studied the Holocaust in school, like everyone else. She'd seen photos of the concentration camps, but she'd never understood how one small group of humans had convinced so many other humans that some of their species were so undeserving of life that they should be systematically slaughtered. Jews marched to their death—the young and the old, the sick and the pregnant. Anne called the Nazis the cruelest monsters ever to stalk the earth. Taliya wasn't sure that was true. History was full of horrors, but the Nazis were right up there with the worst of them. Yet what had the Jews ever done to Hitler or his family or his friends or his country to deserve such treatment? It hadn't made any sense when she studied it in school, and it didn't make any sense now.

Anne and the Jews had Hitler. Taliya and the tigran had Kerkaw. She felt her hackles rise at just the thought of him. No one had worried much when he'd arrived on the scene as a senator, but his agenda had been carried out swiftly after that. He was sneaky and devious and knew how to perfectly guild his plans for domination in the cloak of respectability and government responsibility. Martial law had been declared back in 2140 in response to the environmental crises—though many humans didn't think the rules and rights laid out in the Constitution applied to genetic atrocities like tigran anyhow. Once he was elected president, Kerkaw had free rein to do as he pleased. It was easy to rally the religious fanatics that had sprouted during the last hundred years. God had not created tigran, so eliminating them was a no-brainer. Once President Kerkaw had convinced the politicians that tigran were dangerous and unnatural and should be restricted or destroyed, new laws and regulations were passed, and the disappearances began immediately.

The Enforcers worked efficiently, though they also worked quietly so the size of the genocide wasn't felt by humans. Taliya's village was far out in the woods. Reaching them would take a while. Her family hadn't worried at first. It seemed impossible that someone wasn't going to step in and stop it all before it knocked on their doorstep. An entire species was being exterminated! Within a week of the first city-wide Gathering, most of those communities were decimated and Taliya's mother had begun to make plans.

Fortunately, there were humans who were horrified by this injustice—and saw it as part of a larger conspiracy to regulate and rule their society. With martial law and emergency powers, President Kerkaw had already imposed curfews and restricted trade with other countries. Elections were suspended. Presidential decree after presidential decree dictated life in the United States. Some welcomed the sense of order and structure after so much chaos, but others grasped the bigger picture. The government held a firm and unyielding grasp over the country. Those who disagreed with government policies tended to disappear without a trace. Battle lines had been drawn months before Kerkaw's genocidal plans for tigran were implemented. They and other "abominations" like them were just one item on his agenda. It was merely the tipping point that set off the first laser-gun blast and began the first skirmish—a human who tried to protect a tigran neighbor.

Humans and tigran had lived together harmoniously for decades. When Kerkaw and his Enforcers began the cleansing of the cities, some humans resisted and stood shoulder to shoulder with the tigran. They fought to save them, but time after time they died for their efforts and the tigran were either shot or caged, regardless of the battle waged on their behalf. Protests became riots, and riots became skirmishes, and skirmishes became battles, and battles became another civil war in America: the government of Kerkaw and his allies against those who opposed them. Backing and aid came from other countries—who supported not only the rights of the people but still admired the tigran and found the ongoing Gathering horrific—but there was no assurance of how long that would last.

Anne's writing about the Christians who jeopardized their lives to hide her and so many others made Taliya think of Marla and the masked men, whoever they were. Those humans had risked so much, right down to their own lives and freedom, to help her family escape, to keep them fed and hidden. Maybe that was how wars like this were won in the end, by all the helpers and those who resisted oppression of their fellow man—or other living beings. Taliya had underlined a section about that in Anne's diary, where she wrote that it would probably be impressive one day to learn how many kind people had been willing to shelter the Jews, how many good humans there were in the face of such evil and injustice.

People like Marla. Taliya was grateful to find that a few good humans could make all the difference when the rest of their species seemed to have gone off the rails and lost their rational capacities. As long as those few good ones remained, there was hope.

The warehouse was Marla's home. She lived in an apartment there, probably a room much like Taliya's. What would Taliya have done without a human like Marla, who was willing to risk everything to hide a tigran and continue to supply her with food and necessities for possibly years to come? *Thank the gods for humans like Marla.* And there were so many others. The ones with the masks who drove the trucks. The humans who had taken in her brothers, and everyone involved in carrying out their escape as well. If they were willing to make these risks to help the tigran, then there was still good in the race as a whole. It had become harder and harder to believe that in the last few years. *Humans are inherently destructive,* Anne had written, *and have an urge to rage, murder, and kill.* Taliya knew that couldn't be true because there were good humans, humans who were helping.

Taliya vividly remembered the day her father had left. Once the Enforcers were done in the cities and began invading peaceful villages—areas where tigran lived alone, away from humans—Father knew he must go to their aid. Resistance armies were forming, and he would join and fight before the battle reached his family. Maybe it could be stopped. Maybe the government officials would see the injustice of their decision and change their minds.

The clock tower chimed, and Taliya counted. Six. It was already six. Where was Marla? The building was normally cleared out quickly once the bells struck five, and Marla came as soon as she felt it was safe.

Taliya's chest clenched, and a sudden panic welled up inside her. She hadn't really thought about what would happen to her if Marla failed to show up. If Marla was caught. She had water that wouldn't run out, but no food. Maybe she should start to stash away bits here and there. Just in case.

The floorboards in the hallway creaked, and Taliya held her breath.

Tap, tap, tap. Three solid raps at the door, warning Taliya that Marla was about to enter. A very polite system, Taliya thought, though it wasn't like she could open the door in welcome if she wanted to. When it was locked with the key, no one could get in or out. Short of overpowering Marla and escaping, she was stuck in that attic room. Taliya couldn't choose to run off, if that crazy thought entered her head—not like she had any clue where she was or where else she could go.

The bolt clicked, and Marla swung the door open. The delightful smell of cooked beef and spices filled the room as she crossed and set the tray down on the bedside table. Then she sighed and turned to Taliya.

"I'm sorry to be so late today, but a few of the workers insisted on staying to finish a project. The weapons we make here supply both sides of the war. It's all very strange to me."

She moved like she might sit down next to Taliya, but then she hesitated, wrung her hands for a moment, picked up the morning tray from the end of the bed, and headed for the door.

"Thank you," Taliya said. "I hope someday I can repay you. I know how dangerous this is."

Marla hesitated at the doorway. Then she turned and faced Taliya squarely, looking her in the eyes. Taliya realized this was the first time she'd done that. It had to have been the first time because if Taliya had ever looked that closely at Marla's eyes before, she would have seen the truth. Taliya whoofed in shock.

"You can repay me by surviving," Marla said. "The building is clear. I'll see you in the morning."

Marla shut the door behind her and clicked the bolt into place. Taliya listened as she walked quietly down the hallway toward the stairs.

One thing was suddenly crystal clear. Taliya no longer needed to worry about Marla or her loyalty and determination. Marla had an agenda of her own. The color of her eyes told its own tale—that glint of gold.

Marla was most assuredly not 100% human.

Chapter 3

Anne wrote in her diary that she had ants in her pants. It took a moment for Taliya to realize that Anne didn't mean that literally. Not that insects had crawled into her pants because she was in one place for too long. Ants in her pants. It brought quite a visual image to mind. Taliya would have to remember that one to use with her squirmy brothers the next time they were all doing schoolwork together . . . if they ever sat down to work together again. She'd probably know that feeling well herself the longer she had to be still for half of each day. It was definitely not in the nature of any tigran to be indolent. The wild side of their DNA made them a very active species, when it didn't demand they nap.

Anne also wrote about wishing for the end, for it all to be

over, so then at least she would finally know if they were the victors or the vanquished. Knowing how the story ended, Taliya knew Anne would have her answer before long. *Vanquished. You will be among the vanquished, poor girl.*

It had been a week now. Taliya had kept track of the days on her calendar. A week of solitude and no news of her parents or her brothers. No news of what had become of their home. She had created a schedule, a routine and rhythm to her days, that helped keep her moderately calm.

6:00 am Marla arrives with a meal. Eat immediately. Mark the day on the calendar.

6:30 am Last trip to the bathroom and any other activities.

7:00 am Settle in to sleep as long as possible. Silent time begins.

12:00 pm Lunch hour in the warehouse. Chance to use the bathroom, quietly.

5:00 pm Awake to sound of workday-end bells.

5:30 pm Marla arrives with a meal. Visit and eat at leisure.

6:30 pm Calisthenics, yoga, and exercise.

8:00 pm Shower and clean up. Do laundry.

9:00 pm Read and complete school studies.

10:30 pm Nap and rest period.

12:00 pm Wake up to midnight clock tower chimes.

12:15 am Write in journal or write letters to family/friends for later.

1:00 am Read for pleasure, finish studies, or play cards.

4:00 am   Any other activities that make noise. Light stretching and exercise.

5:00 am   Read until Marla arrives with the next meal.

If she had trouble sleeping during the day, she could always read then as well. As long as she was quiet, she could stay awake all day, but sleeping helped pass the hours quicker.

After a few days, Marla had started staying longer on her evening visits. While Taliya ate, she would update her on the war and the world outside of her attic room. One evening, Marla brought a deck of cards with her and taught Taliya how to play solitaire without a computer to set up the game. It wasn't that complicated, once she got the hang of it, and it gave her something else to do to stave off the claustrophobia that Taliya was sure would overtake her any day.

As they had been spending more time together, Taliya noticed little clues about Marla's true heritage. She might be passing for human, but it was obvious she was not as human as her employers thought she was. There was no way a mixed breed (illegally created) would have been allowed to manage a factory the size of the one Taliya was hiding in. These days, Marla wouldn't even be allowed to walk free.

That evening, when Marla arrived and sat down with the tray—a sure sign she was planning to visit for a while—Taliya got up the courage to ask. She reached over and touched Marla's hand, tracing her own clawed fingers over the well-trimmed nails of her friend. She'd noticed them when Marla taught her solitaire but had been hesitant to ask.

"It must be hard to keep them so flat, like human nails."

Marla froze for a moment, then she sighed. "Yes. My mother taught me some tricks. It's one of the first things I learned to hide, though they have always been more like human nails than tigran claws."

"Does anyone else know? Know what you're hiding?"

"No one," Marla said, looking at her with those golden-glinted eyes. "The people who work here think I'm shy, but most of them wouldn't notice my eyes like you did. I could tell the moment you really looked at me that you knew, but most humans don't understand the difference. Those of us further down the mishmash of the genetic line are rarely talked about because then you'd have to acknowledge how we got this way, where we came from. And no one wants to talk about that."

"Without fur or obvious signs, you can pass yourself off as human."

Marla looked down at the floor, and her cheeks flushed.

"I'm not judging you," Taliya said. "Just putting the pieces together."

Marla straightened her shoulders and looked up again.

"Yes, I pass for human, but it's not because I'm ashamed. When I was born and looked so . . ." She waved a hand, motioning to her body. "My parents hatched a plan. Once I was grown, I could leave the village and pretend to be human. Then I'd be safe from the dangers they already felt coming. I left home five years ago, when I was eighteen. It's a normal time to be on your own, so no one questioned it."

"Both of your parents couldn't have been tigran."

"No. My father was human, but my mother was a white tigran. There's something about that specific strain of DNA that doesn't mix well, and the human won out in my case. But we don't know if it's permanent."

"You mean you might show signs as you grow older?"

"No one really knows. Or at least no studies have been published about it. It's not like we can go around asking scientists. They'd execute my parents for their crimes against nature and lock me up before I had my full question out."

Taliya nodded. The right scientist would take one look at Marla's eyes and lose his mind. She'd never see the light of day again. Marla passing for human reminded her of something from Anne's diary. Peter, a young man hiding with Anne's family, was determined to pretend to be Christian when the war was over. If Jews were persecuted, he would pretend not to be one. How simple that idea was. Hide in plain sight and pretend. Of course, he wouldn't survive and never got to test his theory, and it wasn't one that was helpful to Taliya. She could never look like anything but a tigran. Under her fur, her skin was orange and white with black stripes, just like a tiger's. No amount of shaving could hide the truth.

"I should get going," Marla said and rose from the bed. "The streets have to be clear by nine o'clock, and I still need to go to the store."

"Curfew is at *nine* now?"

"The Enforcers are getting bolder and bolder. Anyone found on the streets after curfew is usually just shot on sight. Tigran or human, it doesn't matter. They don't even bother trying to catch or imprison you. Too much paperwork."

Taliya's tail puffed instinctively. It was hard to imagine how desperate the situation was becoming outside of her little attic room. How long could she stay hidden and not fight back? Marla picked up the breakfast tray and headed for the door, and Taliya swallowed the dozens of questions she still had. Maybe it was safer not to know the answers.

"Thank you for dinner," she said instead. "Again."

"You're welcome. Enjoy your wild and crazy night," Marla said with a smile.

It was the first time she'd seen Marla smile. No fangs. Her teeth were perfect. Too perfect. *Cosmetically changed, maybe?* That would have been a huge risk, but not as huge a risk as walking around with tigran fangs.

"I'll try to keep the partying down to a minimum," Taliya said and smiled in return.

Did Marla flinch at the sight of my teeth? She couldn't be sure, but Marla scooted out the door quickly and threw the bolt before anything more could be said.

Three more weeks had passed. Taliya marked the days on her calendar. She heard gunfire in the streets most evenings after dark now. Who was stupid enough to defy President Kerkaw's reign of terror? Or was the battle coming closer? So far she hadn't heard any explosions or obvious sounds of large-scale warfare, but that didn't mean it wasn't close at hand.

Marla no longer stayed to chat, but delivered Taliya's meals quickly. She seemed fearful to be out of sight and away from her apartment for too long. There was no link between Marla's family and hers, so there was no reason the Enforcers would suspect the office manager of anything. Who would think she was hiding a teenage tigran in the attic? Nobody. At least Taliya hoped so.

Along with meals, Marla brought library books to read and some printed-out pages of genuine news, when she could smuggle them in from friends around town. She couldn't risk searching certain words or doing dark interweb searches on the office computer. Enforcers would have been at the door before she printed anything out. The extra food was easy enough to include with her own groceries, and winter coats had large, deep pockets that carried items to keep Taliya from going stir-crazy. Or at least more stir-crazy than she already was. She had thought the size of the room and the locked door would be her undoing, but what was even worse were the days and days and days of nothing to do or accomplish. When she could be up and active at night, Taliya had worn a smooth area in the bamboo boards of the attic floor. Pace and turn. Pace and turn. Add a huff at the end of each line when the frustrations tried to settle in.

Taliya stretched out on the bed and flipped back through Anne's diary, looking for a section she had underlined. Anne wrote about her nerves fraying from the silence. Sundays were the worst for her, and she wrote about feeling like a songbird whose wings had been ripped off yet kept hurling itself against the bars of the cage, hoping for freedom. Taliya knew exactly what she meant.

Taliya also related to Anne's fears of being discovered—of someone coming in the night and ripping her from her bed and throwing her into a dungeon alone, without her family. The waiting was horrific, with nothing else to distract you. For Taliya, every little noise, every extra-loud crash of machinery that managed to reach all the way up two flights to her little room made her jump in terror. Maybe it would be better if it was noisy all the time, so the actual presence of some sound wouldn't stand out so much. *It's so terribly quiet, I can hear my own heartbeat.*

Any time Marla chose to stay for a few minutes was a wonderful break in the routine because there were only so many hours even the most devoted bibliophile could spend reading, though Taliya was determined to stay up on her studies. When the war was over and life returned to normal, she would be ready to join society again.

When the war was over. It was something to cling to.

It had become difficult to imagine the tigran would ever be allowed to live in peace and freedom again. What would be the end result of all the fighting and death? What would "normal" look like in a year, two years? They might change some government policies, but would they be able to change the hearts of humans who feared and hated them? It seemed like too large a task. She avoided thinking about what the end of the war would mean if Kerkaw's troops won.

Taliya tried to make Anne Frank's prayer of hope and joy a part of her daily routine. "Thank you, God, for all that is good and dear and beautiful." She would cling to that. Even if she couldn't see out a window and look at the beauty of the world, she could close her eyes and remember her home and their forest and how glorious it all was. If the Enforcers had taken a torch to it out of spite, she knew the forest would restore itself and new life would grow.

Taliya had never been taught about a single, omnipotent God the way Anne talked about having someone to pray to. Being inherently Indian, most tigran leaned toward Hinduism and dharma, looking to many different gods to intervene in their lives. Could Anne's God perform miracles? He didn't save Anne or most of her family. That didn't seem like a miracle worker to Taliya.

Taliya hoped her friends and their families had escaped and someday they could read the letters she wrote them from her attic room. She thought of Anya, her best friend by far. Anya's pattern of stripes and spots filled her mind's eye. Was she even still alive?

Taliya had found herself dreaming about her brothers quite often. Some dreams were pleasant. They were running through the fields around their lair and tumbling in the grass together as young kits do. But there were other dreams. Dreams of them being torn from her arms as bombs exploded all around. Dreams of them in cages. Of her in a cage. Unable to reach them. Unable to help. Humans with whips and electric prods. In a zoo, naked and caged like animals, where humans jeered at them and threw stones between the metal bars. Nightmares based on a true possible future.

Near the end of Anne's diary, after everything she had seen and experienced, Anne wrote her infamous line about, in spite of everything, still believing that people are truly good at heart. Taliya checked the date on the journal entry. Three weeks. In three weeks Anne would be captured and sent to a concentration camp, where she would die in a few months. Did she hold to that belief, that people are truly good at heart, when she was actually face-to-face with the worst humanity has to offer? Anne might have died of a disease, not a gas chamber or any direct assassination, but she was still treated so horribly. Her father was the only one from those hidden rooms to survive. So sad. Would it have been better to die right there on the doorstep of the annex rooms?

Taliya suspected her mother would think so. *Don't let them capture you.* Over and over she had stressed it. A quick death must be the preference over a life of pain and captivity. But didn't staying alive at least offer some future hope? Wasn't surviving also a goal? Taliya set the book aside and curled up on the bed, hoping she never had to make that choice.

When Marla arrived that night, she hesitated at the door before leaving.

"Tomorrow is Christmas Eve," she said. "Did your family celebrate?"

"No," Taliya admitted. "Not really. Sometimes we got each other little gifts, just to keep up with the world around us."

"My father is Christian," Marla said, "so we did it right up over the top. Maybe I can find some treats at the store. Supplies are becoming more and more limited. Chocolates are pricier than beef because of all the import taxes."

"Don't worry about it," Taliya assured her. "You're giving me the gift of *life*. That's enough."

Marla had managed a chocolate truffle for each of them as a Christmas treat and some sparkling water to drink on New Year's Eve. She was still able to afford meat, so they'd enjoyed a simple beef stew for dinner. The streets were oddly quiet when the clock struck midnight. No fireworks. No celebrating. Curfew had not been lifted, even for that night. Taliya wrote her parents a letter, wishing them a Happy New Year, unsure if either would ever see it.

Chapter 4

Day 45.

Taliya never thought she'd be sick of reading, normally a favorite pastime, but it had never been her only possible form of entertainment. She was poking her way back through Anne's diary again, since Mother had thought it was so important. *If Anne writes one more sappy line about stupid Peter and rubbing their cheeks together, I'm gonna to throw this damn book across the room.* With everything that was going on in her world, how had renegade Anne gotten so sidetracked by a boy? It made Taliya gag. Page after page after page of gushy bluck. It probably wasn't meant to be read all at once—in one sitting, like Taliya was doing—but it was still nauseating. Taliya's mother had gotten an updated, unabridged version of Anne's diary, and it contained far more personal information than was really necessary. Way, *way* more.

At seventeen and basically a grown tigran, Taliya had never had feelings even remotely that lovey-dovey for a male. And Anne's parents were clearly idiots. How in the world were they allowing Anne and Peter hours of alone time in the dark with nothing else to do? Taliya didn't care how honorable a male was, her mother would have never allowed such nonsense. But they let Anne share a room with a grown man for years, so clearly they were either totally clueless and naïve or just plain stupid. Or desperate. But couldn't that old man have shared with moody Peter instead?

As Taliya pondered those pointless things, she heard the six o'clock morning bells and set the frustrating diary aside. But Marla did not arrive.

By six fifteen, Taliya had begun to pace in her well-worn track. Marla had never missed a morning. The warehouse was open and busy every day. Even though each employee was allowed to select a day during the week for time off, Marla still made a show of being there daily for opening and closing time. Her employers must have thought she was very diligent.

At six forty-five, Marla still hadn't knocked on the door. Wherever she was, she probably wouldn't risk coming up to the attic now. Taliya used the bathroom and made sure she was ready for the silent time.

She sat down on the bed and carefully opened her suitcase,

where she had stashed snacks. Taliya always suspected there would be a time when Marla might be sick or it might be dangerous for her to venture up to the attic. She had squirreled away enough food to keep contentedly fed for a few days. Nuts and dried fruit and crackers, things that wouldn't spoil quickly.

It was nearly seven o'clock when Taliya finished eating and lay down for her day of sleep. She thought of Marla again briefly, but it was too soon to worry. The long hours of silence lay ahead. She heard the clock chiming as she drifted off.

Being part tiger, sleep came easily and soundly, and Taliya dreamed of home. She was walking through the forest on the edge of the clearing, crunching leaves underfoot. Her tail swayed gently behind her, relaxed and content. The air smelled of evergreen and soil and flowers. Stepping out into the clearing, she saw her family homestead, just as she remembered it. A field of green grass and the cottage, built in the ancient way with logs and a thatched roof. No protective habitat dome for them. Father had been a history teacher at the tigran school and knew all about the lives of the early pioneers. The homestead had started out as an experiment in building log houses, but it had ended up as a refuge. When Father and all the tigran at the school were dismissed, they had moved to the property deep in the Ozark Mountains, and many other tigran had followed suit, making a spread-out village of sorts. There was no one to bother, and no one to bother them. Only the glint of solar panels on the roof gave away the fact that it was not a homestead from the 1800s.

Taliya heard the shouts of her brothers and turned to see them playing kickball on the far end of the clearing, blurs of black and white and orange. Then Mother stepped out of the main house, a basket of laundry under her arm. Taliya watched as she hung each wet item on the line to dry, like the old-timers had done. Mother looked up and spotted her. Taliya chuffed a greeting, and Mother returned the chuff—a soft whooshing sound. Taliya felt a deep sense of peace fill every inch of her furry being.

A scuffling and a clunking noise woke her, breaking into the lovely dream. Senses immediately on alert, Taliya shifted her ears. Another shuffle came from the hallway.

Marla?

She turned her head to check the clock. 10:00 am. It took her another moment to register that the factory below was quiet. No hum. No vibrations.

The bolt on the door clicked, and Taliya felt adrenaline rush into every limb.

There had been no knock.

Marla always knocked.

Taliya sat bolt-upright on the bed. The door was unlocked, but it didn't open. There was silence from the hallway. Her heart pounded in her chest, and her whiskers twitched and shifted, trying to sense a change in the air. A trace of a whisper reached her sensitive ears, and the fur rose all along her spine.

Definitely not Marla.

Mother had prepared her for this moment—what to do if she was found. "Don't let them take you." She had been clear and unflinching in that one directive. "I know we've spent your entire life training you to restrain your wildness and behave in a way that humans consider appropriate, but if an Enforcer comes through the doorway of your hiding place, let it all go. You are as much predator as you are human. Do what you must to escape. *Whatever* you must. Don't let them capture you."

Taliya instinctively rumbled in her throat, and her heart raced, pumping more adrenaline through her system. If whoever was on the far side of that door had anything to do with the Enforcers, they would bust through with little concern for whether she came out of the attic room dead or alive.

She pulled her legs up under her on the bed and crouched there, claws extended, ready to spring. Closing her eyes, she flared her whiskers and focused on the door and what lay beyond. It was a skill she hadn't tested since playing hide and seek with her brothers. She could hear the heartbeats pounding in anticipation and the rapid breathing of three, no four humans. Then she opened her eyes, dilating her pupils to let in more light, darkness taking over the golden hue.

The door flew open, and four men rushed through, all in the distinctive black-and-red uniforms that meant only one thing: Enforcers. Somehow they had found her, and there was no turning back. They were good-sized humans, but not as large as her, not by a hundred pounds. All of her senses on alert, she determined that one held a pistol and two others had ropes and metal mesh nets.

Do they hope to take me alive? For a split second, she considered cooperating. Staying alive, even in captivity, was an option. Then she thought of Anne, who died of some stupid disease in some nasty camp not long before the war ended. No. She was a tigran. She would not go peacefully to wallow and die behind bars.

Taliya bared her fangs and released the scream of a growl she had forced down for too many weeks. Rage flowed through her, and the growl became more of a ferocious hissing gasp—in and out, over and over. Noises she didn't even know she was capable of making. Her ears rotated backward, showing their distinctive white spots as a warning.

Fear. She could feel the fear radiating from the two guards with the nets. They reeked of nervous sweat and terror. *Don't bother with them*, instinct told her. *They may run or back down. They haven't come here ready to die trying to catch you.* She wouldn't worry about the fourth guard yet either, though she sensed he was quite determined.

She turned her attention to the alpha, the man with the gun. No fear there. Only determination and anger. Hatred. Pure, unadulterated hatred. It wafted from him in waves. She aimed her growl/hiss directly at him, not slacking its intensity, and his eyes narrowed. The gun clicked in readiness, but he didn't raise it. Not yet. The moment he did, the battle would begin. Every hair on her body was spiked as she crouched on the bed, the growl/hiss pattern continuing, in and out, fangs bared, as she stared the alpha down. He would take the lead.

Taliya had been raised to be civilized, taught to behave like a human and maneuver through life in a human way. She had never killed so much as a rabbit, but she knew, in that moment, she would rip all four of them to shreds without a flicker of remorse. She could sense the exact location of the arteries in their necks, and her fangs throbbed with the rhythm.

The alpha spoke without moving. "Taliya Sharma, Tigran Generation 11, you are under arrest for resisting Article 25 of the genetic oversight code."

By the book, then. Giving me fair warning.

She raised the volume of her in and out growl/hiss, flattening her ears against her head and curling her lips as far as they could go, throwing another rage-induced scream into the mix. The two frightened guards took a step back.

Then it began.

The alpha moved ever so slightly, probably deciding it was best to just shoot her and be done with it. Without even consciously planning it, Taliya leapt, knocked him flat on the ground, and locked her jaws around his throat, her fangs finding their mark. Quick and decisive. Not giving the prey time to react or struggle. The gun fell from his grasp and he made a faint gurgling sound, but he couldn't move under her weight.

Taliya tasted blood as the alpha's life swiftly pumped out of him, red liquid pooling around his head in a rapidly increasing circle. Without releasing her bite, she sensed the two scared guards backing into the hallway. The fourth one surprised her and lunged for the gun. With a rending tear, Taliya ripped her jaws free and turned her gaze on him. Blood dripped from her mouth and splattered the floor. She snarled and hissed, spraying more blood in his direction. His eyes were wide, and she felt terror emanating from him.

He lifted the gun, but he was too slow. Far too slow. Taliya launched herself onto him, mauling his throat the same way. As they landed, she heard a shot. It was muffled by her body, but the weapon had fired. A pinprick of pain in her chest distracted her—maybe the bullet had grazed her. She assured herself he was dead before releasing him.

Then she rose, eyes locked on the two remaining guards. They hovered in the hallway, ropes and nets hanging loosely at their sides. Baring her bloody fangs, she screamed with every ounce of her being. Both men ran for the stairway, shrieking like little girls.

Her heart was pounding so intensely, she couldn't decide if she should let them escape. Which would make her own route easier? It was hard to focus, and the doorway in front of her suddenly wobbled and wavered. She staggered out into the hallway, but there was no sign of the guards. Using the wall to brace herself, Taliya worked her way toward the stairs.

I'm going to have to sneak through the warehouse and get the hell away from here somehow in broad daylight. I should pack my things and some food. Gods, I have to change. I'm covered in blood. Is Marla downstairs? Does she know the Enforcers are up here?

Reaching the end of the hallway, she looked down and saw the two guards standing at the bottom of the staircase, watching her. She bared her teeth and growled again, but they didn't run. They just watched her, expectantly. Then the staircase roiled like a wave between them. Her eyes slipped in and out of focus, and her heart pounded in her ears, slower and slower. She reached her hand up under her tunic, searching for blood that didn't come from a human, but she wasn't shot. Her finger caught on something small. A tiny barb stuck through her skin. She pulled it out and examined it.

A tranquilizer? Terror gripped her, and her mother's words echoed through her hazy brain. *Don't let them take you. Don't let them take you. Don't let them take you.*

Her eyes lost focus completely.

They want me alive.

Then her world went dark.

Chapter 5

Taliya forced her eyes open, but nothing changed. Wherever she was, it was pitch black. Try as she might, there wasn't even enough light for her feline eyes to see by. One sniff told her it wasn't her attic room. Dank. Wet and sour. Disgustingly musty. Concrete. Maybe a basement prison cell. Was she happy to still be alive? The throbbing, searing pain in her head made it hard to ponder philosophical questions like that.

She was stretched out on a canvas cot, and there was a soft blanket over her. It was a small kindness in what could only be a bad place. Something to be grateful for. She tried to sit up, but her head screamed. A pillow. She had a pillow too. Her aching head was grateful, even if the rest of her was growing more and more suspicious by the second.

The last moments before she'd passed out weren't very clear. Enforcers had found her. A gun going off. She remembered that, but she didn't feel wounded anywhere. She lifted her tunic and rubbed a hand across her chest, where the gun had been pressed as it fired, but the fur was smooth and unmarred. She focused deeper and felt a tiny sore spot on her ribs. An insignificant wound. Then she remembered. *Tranquilizer gun, not a real one. I was drugged.*

That was the only weapon the guards had brought with them. They never meant to kill her, just drug her and bring her to wherever she was now. That made her feel some regret for killing two of them, but not much. Her mind raced at the possibilities of what they wanted her alive for. Nothing good she could imagine.

She didn't smell blood on her fur or clothing, and her mouth tasted bitter from the drugs but generally clean. A stranger had bathed her and changed her clothes. She tried not to dwell on that.

Close by, someone coughed. Every sense went on full alert. She'd been so focused on her body that she hadn't seriously surveyed the area. An analytical sniff led her to another creature on a cot across the room. Another tigran. The odor of her species was unique. He—yes, definitely *he*—was pretending to be asleep. His breathing gave him away.

She took another minute to fully scan the area. A small draft came from the lower part of one wall, probably the door. She could smell large pieces of metal, maybe furniture, but no food. Random dripping sounds led her to a water source fairly near her head. She considered what her next steps should be, assuming her head ever stopped throbbing enough for her to stand up.

The tigran across the room shifted position. She froze, ready to defend herself if she could.

He chuffed quietly. A greeting of friendship.

She chuffed in return without even thinking about it. Instinct.

"Try to rest," he said. "They gave you some strong sedatives. It'll be a few hours before you're rid of it all."

"Where am I?"

"I'll explain everything in the morning. You're not in any danger. If they wanted you dead, you'd be dead. Try to sleep."

"They only had a trank gun. They wanted me alive."

"Then you can consider yourself . . . fortunate. Go back to sleep. You're safe for now."

She wanted to fight it and ask more questions, but her thoughts swam.

I failed. I didn't fight hard enough. I didn't fight well enough. Safe for now. Safe for now.

She slipped back into unconsciousness.

A bright light roused her from restless dreams. As her eyes adjusted, she tested the state of her poor head. The throbbing pain had eased. One glance around the room confirmed her suspicions from the night before. A cell. Concrete walls. A door with a small window near the top and an open slot along the bottom. *That must be for shoving trays of food in for us.* She'd seen a prison movie or two in her lifetime.

Her cellmate still lay on his cot, flat on his back with his arms behind his head. He was awake and staring at the ceiling. Definitely a tigran, but not what she'd been expecting.

"You're white," she said, her voice cracking. "A white tigran."

He turned to face her, bright-blue eyes meeting her golden ones.

"Yes," he said flatly. "I am *rare* and *unique*."

He most certainly was. She'd never seen anything like him. For starters, he was massive. Male tigran were generally large, but Taliya estimated he was at least a full head taller than her. Seven feet tall, at least. A few black stripes lined his face, but his fur was mostly white. He was wearing a tunic and pants, so she couldn't be sure. *Rare and unique, indeed.*

"That explains why you're being caged, but why do you think they wanted me alive?" she asked him.

"Are there any white tigran in your generations?"

"Yes," she said, "though I've never met them. Two uncles on my mother's side. And a cousin somewhere on my father's side."

"Well, there it is, then. White mutant DNA on both sides. They must have been looking for you quite intensely."

"What do you mean by that?"

"There's a better chance to produce white tigran offspring if there are white tigran in your genetic line. Trying to bring out the mutation is tricky work. In the old days, they used to breed siblings, or mothers to their own offspring, to create white tigers. Things are more civilized now."

"Are you saying someone is *breeding* white tigran? That doesn't make any sense. They want us all dead."

"Maybe. Unless there's money to be made from it. Humans are obsessed with us. Zoos and private facilities will pay top dollar for a white tigran to put on display. Private collectors will pay even more."

Taliya let that settle in. Did any of the other excuses for wanting to rid the earth of tigran mean anything at all? Or was it all a massive stunt to get control of the species and make a profit from it? Did their rights as part human mean nothing? She knew the answer to that and snorted. It still didn't explain what they wanted with *her*. There was nothing special about her. She was just one tigran out of thousands. One with a white fur mutation etched in her DNA. Her chest clenched, and she gasped as blood rushed to her face and her tail puffed.

"My name is Kano, by the way. Kano Rama."

"Taliya. I'm Taliya Sharma," she whispered.

"It's nice to meet you. I have a feeling we'll be together for quite a while."

It was too horrible to consider. Her heart pounded in her already-tight chest. She knew the answer, but it was too revolting to say out loud. Kano was not so hesitant.

"Let's hope we're successful," he said as he sat up on his cot. "That's the only way they'll keep us alive."

Before Taliya worked up the courage to ask Kano any specific, uncomfortable questions, the cell was unlocked and the door clanked open. Two stocky, heavily armed guards clomped in—electric prod sticks clacking at their waists, powerful high-capacity laser guns in their hands.

"Behave, Taliya," Kano said as she leapt to her feet. "It will all be easier that way."

Her head swam, not totally clear of the drugs, but she willed herself to stand firm.

One of the guards stepped up to within inches of her and sneered—his crooked, stained teeth close enough to her face to be purposefully obnoxious, breath revolting. She was tempted to laugh at his intimidation tactics while not even tall enough to be face-to-face. She was also tempted to permanently scratch off his smug grin. Wisdom told her to behave, like Kano said, but she'd already let the rage out once. Now it simmered right at the surface and was hard to control. She growled and showed her own teeth, turning her ears back in warning.

"Don't underestimate that one," the second guard said, holding his gun at the ready. "She'll rip your throat out before you even know she's twitched."

My reputation has preceded me. Was that a good thing or a bad thing? She glanced over at Kano, and his blue eyes shot her another warning. She nodded in response. *Fine. I'll behave. For now.*

Her feet were shackled together with slight room for walking, and her hands were clamped into a long metal bar behind her back. Then a metal collar was secured around her throat and a thin electric wire was looped over her neck. The first guard held up a control device with a red button.

"Just in case you take it into your pretty furry head to nip at anyone, kitty. You so much as think about moving the wrong direction, I'll zap you unconscious. You understand?" He waited until she nodded. "Too many zaps, and it's lights out for good. Colonel Narlin would be mighty upset if we had to kill you after all the effort to get you here."

Staring her in the eyes, he carefully attached a chain to the collar around her neck like a leash, giving it a quick yank. She grumbled deep in her throat, and he flashed the control device at her again and grinned.

Stay calm, Taliya. He's itching to press that button. Figure out what's going on before you worry about how to escape. Stay calm and pay attention.

As the guards directed her out of the cell, she glanced back at Kano, still sitting on his cot. There was a slump in his shoulders that hadn't been there before. *He must have done this shackled walk himself.* Her tail thrashed, but there was no point in getting tortured into submission. She'd heard stories that went far beyond electric zapping wires. Kitties could be taught to obey the rules. Or forced to. Neither of the guards gave off even the slightest whiff of nervousness. They knew they were in control and had the power and the tools necessary to keep it that way. Swallowing her pride, she shuffled out into the dank concrete hallway. The cell was closed and locked behind her.

She started counting doors as they made their way down the dim corridor, but she gave up when the number reached into the thirties. Did every cell house a tigran? A pair of tigran? Or was it just an Enforcer prison for anyone who refused to obey their stifling laws?

They finally came to an elevator that lifted them up and out of the smelly dungeon-like area. The doors opened to the outdoors and a field covered with knee-deep snow. The sunlight was blinding, and even the guards hesitated a moment to let their eyes adjust. Taliya inhaled the freezing but clean, fresh air—her first breath outside in nearly two months—and assessed the situation. The elevator was housed in a small concrete shack, and it looked like that was the only way in or out of the underground cells. It certainly made escape complicated. There were mountains in every direction. Not Arkansas hills and swells, but serious mountains topped with snow. The ground was cold under her bare feet, but at least the pathway was shoveled.

The guards led her along a sidewalk for about a hundred yards and then into a towering white building that looked more like it held offices than a prison. She couldn't see them, but there must have been solar panels or wind collection wands on the roof. The style was older, not construction of the last fifty years. Something abandoned the government had claimed and updated for its own purposes.

Inside the security doors, it looked even more business-like—beige walls and carpets and cheap wood doors. Fake potted plants and beige plastic chairs were scattered along the hallway outside the office doors. Everything clean and pro-fessional. A barely distinguishable hum she didn't recognize buzzed through the air. Human ears might not even register it. They passed a woman at what was probably a security desk. The guards both gave her a polite nod while she scanned the prisoner with cold eyes. It took every ounce of Taliya's self-control not to hiss at her.

Finally, they stopped in front of a massive wooden door. One of the guards knocked, waited a second, and then opened the door, leading her inside. It was a large office or meeting room with a fancy desk at the far end, two sofas near the door in a cozy seating area, and a large oak conference table filling the middle of the room. Three middle-aged men were sitting at the table and turned to face her as the guards closed the door, left her leash to dangle, and took positions behind her.

"She's not white," one of the men at the table commented with a frown.

"I told you," another said, "she has the mutation on both sides of her family."

"White offspring are never guaranteed," the third added, standing up and coming toward her, "even if both parents are white. The odds with this one are still good."

While the other two men wore stylish suits, this third man was in a military dress uniform—lots of bars and stripes and colorful medals on his chest—and he reeked of self-importance. Taliya kept her eyes on the other men and tried to ignore him as he finished walking around her, eyeing every inch. He stepped back and stared her in the eyes, though he was an inch or two shorter than her.

"My name is Colonel Narlin, and I'm responsible for your case, Taliya."

Fabulous.

"That white fur mutation in your blood is the only reason you're still standing and not in some mass grave."

She shoved down the growl and hiss that fought to escape. Now was not the time, though her conclusions about their plans for her had clearly been right. Horribly right.

The first man flipped open a file on the tabletop computer and slid the image up on a white-board wall with a flick of his wrist. Taliya glanced up to see the photo from her government ID along with pages and pages of details about her family.

"Taliya Sharma, age seventeen, Generation Eleven of the Tigran Experiments," he read. "Has spent her whole life on the remote family compound in Arkansas."

All three men crinkled their noses, like they smelled something bad.

"It explains how she was overlooked, even before the Gathering began," the second man said.

"Taliya," Narlin said, "do you understand that you are government property?"

This "ownership" was the basis for all the trouble facing her species. The government had taken over the tigran and many other genetic experiments from the military decades ago, but only as a formality and to keep some regulations in place on what could be done and what couldn't. What was "ethical." Or so they claimed as laws and bills and restrictions passed through the legislature one after another. The government was tricky that way. Slip in with good intentions until the time suited them to ride roughshod over policy and rules they had put in place themselves. She was not a citizen with any rights whatsoever. She was government property. Struggling to keep her hackles from rising, she nodded. Yes, she understood.

"And yet, you were hiding from us," Narlin said.

He moved around behind her, catching the top of her tail between two fingers and running them along the length, dragging every inch of it between them. One of the men at the table snickered. Alarm bells went off in her brain, but she didn't flinch or shift her eyes in the slightest. Surely some rules still applied, even in that godforsaken place. Sexual activity between species was absolutely forbidden, on pain of death. This military man was just trying to intimidate or provoke her. At least she hoped that's all he was up to. He ran his fingers slowly along the fur of her arm as he circled around to the front again. He paused, standing far too close, inspecting her face carefully.

"It's hard to believe you were responsible for the violent death of two Enforcers. Such lovely, perfect features."

He stroked her black whiskers, ran a finger down her orange-and-white striped cheek, onto her neck, over the metal collar, and across her shoulder, all the while holding her gaze with his cold brown eyes. If he wanted to rile her, get a violent reaction, it wasn't going to work. She wasn't going to give them a chance to discipline her, though if he touched her sensitive whiskers again, she didn't know how she'd control herself.

But if this important military officer wanted more, as his deliberate and unwelcome touches suggested, she had a problem. A serious problem. She was suddenly more aware of the shackles around her feet and the bar securing her clawed hands behind her back, making her nearly helpless. Nipping off his fingers crossed her mind. She could still bite—and get zapped into unconsciousness for it.

He broke eye contact and moved toward the table, inspecting her file on the wall. The other two men sat silently. They reminded her of the two scared guards back at the attic room. *Lackeys.* They were not the heart and brains of this operation. That knowledge might come in handy later.

"Now that you are here with us," Narlin continued, "all of that running and hiding nonsense is of no consequence. I can understand your desire to flee. Animals run when they know they're being hunted, and they will attack when cornered, like you were."

He turned back to her and tipped his head, possibly considering what approach to take for whatever he had up his sleeve.

"You seem like a reasonably smart tigran, Taliya, so I won't mince words. Can you handle that?"

She nodded. *Quit screwing around and get to the point.*

"Good. I have been entrusted with providing our country's zoos and private collectors with at least six white tigran kits in the next two years. Even more over the next ten years." He paused and leaned against the table.

Ten years? It took her a few seconds more to grasp it all. Her eyes narrowed, despite her efforts. *Kits. His job is to produce kits.* It was nice to have it all flat-out stated, but the shock of that clarity was more than she'd expected. Her hackles rose from neck to tail. None of this had anything to do with the Gathering. This was about money and profit and, gods help them, breeding tigran kits. White ones. The brutality, inhumanity, and barbarity of it made her head spin. Despite all the civility of her life, she was now nothing more than an animal in a zoo breeding program. One that had to be illegal. It had to be.

"Good girl. I can see you understand."

Narlin strode back over and stopped only inches from her face. Her fingers flexed involuntarily, and her claws extended and retracted. She sensed the guards behind her shifting and at the ready.

"When you arrived," Narlin said, starting to circle her again, "besides getting you cleaned up—you naughty kitty, you—we ran some tests. You are quite fertile. You could have produced several rounds of kits by now. Yet you are still . . . intact."

He smiled as he took a seat at the conference table and swiveled the chair toward her, like he had performed that particular exam personally. Her stomach flipped, and she desperately hoped not. It had been bad enough to imagine that some stranger had bathed her, but her gorge rose at the simple announcement that she had undergone a very detailed and invasive exam. *I'm nothing more than an animal. A lab rat, to be poked and prodded.* At least she hoped that was the approach the strangers had taken and that Narlin was nowhere near any of it.

"Kano clearly holds the white DNA in his blood," he continued, "as do you. With several kits produced each year, our odds are very good of securing at least one or two that are white. Possibly more, if we're lucky."

"So," Taliya finally spoke up, "my job is to produce as many kits as possible with Kano." Saying it out loud made her skin crawl, but she wanted to be sure all the cards were on the table. "You will then take those kits and sell them or put them in a zoo."

"Precisely," Narlin said. "You *are* a quick one."

"And if I refuse?"

Taliya had thought Narlin's smirks were nasty up to that

point, but she immediately realized he could take it to another level.

"Well, that wouldn't bode well for your brothers."

Taliya whoofed with rage and shock before she could stop herself. That was the ace up his sleeve, and he'd played it with scalpel-like precision.

"Where are they?" she asked, clenching her jaws to avoid snarling. *Calm. Stay calm.*

"They are safe, here at this facility. Too bad they're a boring orange. And so timid and scared. Not very exciting. But they will stay safe and fed and be well treated." He rose and stalked toward her. "However, if you refuse to cooperate, well . . ." He tipped his head and waited.

She nodded. His implication was clear.

"Does Kano realize what's expected?" she asked, though his comments in the cell made it clear he knew what his job entailed.

"Of course. He's been waiting over a month for a suitable mate. Waiting for *you*. There was no point in bothering with the breeding program if we couldn't be at least remotely sure of producing some white kits. Otherwise, what's the point of making more tigran? That's just a waste of resources. While we have been getting to know each other, Kano has been moved into your permanent quarters. I understand that the damp cells are not conducive to breeding. You two will be provided more comfortable rooms here in this building, as long as you remain part of the program."

"And my brothers?"

"As I said, they are here. After a while, maybe we can arrange a brief visit."

One of the men at the table looked down at his hands.

Narlin is lying, and he knows it. But is it about the visit or their safety?

"That's enough for now," Narlin said with a wave. "Take her upstairs."

The guards spun her around and marched her out of the office without a pause.

"Have a pleasant night, Taliya," Narlin called from behind her.

Laughter from the three men echoed into the hall before the office door closed.

Chapter 6

After shuffling her into an elevator and whisking her up twenty flights, Taliya's guards finally stopped outside one of many doors along a stark-white hallway with gray concrete floors. There was a grated opening at the top of the door, and she could smell that Kano was already inside. One of her guards produced a set of key fobs. He punched a code into the keypad next to the door, then unlocked a massive bolt.

The door swung wide to reveal a living room with beige walls and carpet and two brown, puffy, comfortable-looking sofas in a very civilized seating arrangement facing the media wall. The room smelled recently cleaned and sanitized, no scent left of who lived there before them. Kano sat on a couch, his furry bare feet up on the coffee table in a lounging position, watching a nature special of some kind. He muted the sound and turned to face them, expressionless.

A guard chuckled and shoved her inside. "Here's a present for you, Kano," he added with a snort.

Despite the chummy way the guard spoke to him, she could feel the waves of hatred and rage emanating from the white tigran. Kano smiled, an action that showed his fangs, and stood up. She'd been right. He was quite a specimen—a full head taller than her, broad shouldered, chest muscles visible under his tunic. His tail lashed as he walked over to them.

"Do you suppose we can remove those nasty restraints from my gift?" Kano said. "She can't escape from here."

The guard with the keys shook his head and handed Kano a single key fob, though he did remove the hotwire around her neck.

"There's more she can do than just try to escape. You can open this present all by yourself."

Kano made eye contact with Taliya, and she bristled her whiskers at him.

"You never know," the guard continued, "you may want to use cuffs on this kitty, now and then."

Taliya let her hackles rise, laid her ears back, and growled low in her throat. Both guards flinched, then pretended they hadn't. Kano tipped his head at her, closed his hand around the key, and looked at the guards.

"I think I can handle this dangerous monster from here," he said.

The guards laughed and made delighted hooting noises as they exited.

Men. Revolting.

Taliya heard the lock engage and the massive bolt thrown into place. The door might be white and inviting, but it was a prison door all the same.

"Let us know if you need any help with her," one of the guards called from the hallway.

Taliya could hear them both snickering and whispering as they clomped toward the elevator. Kano sighed and moved back around to face her. He held up the key and chuffed quietly. She did not return the greeting, and his eyes narrowed.

"Don't bite," he said.

"Don't give me a reason to."

Kano raised one shoulder in a resigned shrug and began unlocking the shackles around her neck, wrists, and ankles. She rubbed the sore spots on her wrist bones, and he tossed the restraints and the key fob in a corner near the door.

Without looking at her he said, "You and I will have no use for those."

He walked over to the sofa and flopped down. When she didn't move, he patted the seat next to him. She chose a spot on the other sofa instead and sat cautiously. A herd of bison stampeded silently on the media wall.

"Taliya," he said, looking over at her, "it's time to put things into perspective. We are both alive."

She shrugged and leaned back on the pleasantly soft cushion.

"Narlin has my little brothers, or so he says. He claims they're both still alive and cared for. At least for now."

"Ah," Kano said, leaning back on the sofa and stretching his arms out along the top. "Leverage. It's mightier than the sword, as they say."

They sat silently for a full minute. Taliya wondered about Tuscan and Tyler, so young and vulnerable. She wondered where her parents were. She desperately wondered what Kano was thinking. He finally leaned forward, resting his elbows on his knees, and she looked up into his blue eyes. She hadn't noticed before, but his whiskers were white, almost translucent, and his nose was pink. It was hard to be afraid of a creature whose nose was bright pink.

"I know what's expected," he said. "They told me the moment I arrived. I'm breeding stock. That's the one and only reason they didn't shoot me in the street when they brought the Gathering to my city. How old are you, Taliya?"

"Seventeen."

He whoofed and sat back on the couch again.

"Seventeen?" he said, raking his fingers through the ruff of mane on the sides of his head. "Gods almighty. *Seventeen?*"

"Yes, seventeen. What of it? I'm an adult, though Mother always insisted we live to human civilized patterns. If I were older, I never would have gone into hiding. I'd be out there with my parents right now, blowing up as many Enforcers as I possibly could!"

He dropped his head into his hands, and she watched his claws extend and retract.

"I'm not saying you're a kit," he mumbled. "Well, maybe I kind of am, but not like you think." He looked up at her. "Does Narlin know you're only seventeen? When he paired us together, did he know that?"

"He said I'm old enough to breed. For a tigran, eleven is old enough."

"Yes, biologically, but . . ."

They sat in silence again for a minute. Kano growled and stood up, pacing between a small kitchen area she hadn't noticed before and the sofa. He finally stopped behind her.

"Can I assume that you've never . . . That at only seventeen, you've never . . . ?"

She couldn't see his face, but she imagined he was feeling as uncomfortable as she was.

"No," she admitted. "There has never been anyone. We lived very remotely, in the mountains. There was a small village and some other tigran. But no."

He growled to himself again. It was clearly the answer he'd been expecting, but she still felt uneasy. She'd been prepared to die. She'd been prepared to be captured and held captive. But nothing had prepared her for this disgusting situation.

No one from the outside can possibly know about this. I would have read something about breeding programs. There would be articles, interweb postings. No one knows. No one is coming to help.

"What do you plan to do?" he finally asked her.

"Do?"

"You understand what they want from us?"

"Yes," she said. "They want kits. White kits."

"Exactly. And they haven't had any success using laboratories and petri dishes. They haven't been able to create viable embryos. If they had, you'd be alone in your cell and they'd just stick one right in you and let it bake."

She flinched at the bluntness, but she knew he was right.

"White tigran sperm is apparently quite ineffective if removed from the source," he said. "Nothing artificial or scientific works. They expect us to create kits the old-fashioned way."

She understood, in theory, but it hadn't all come together and sunk into her brain in one piece until that moment. She and Kano. They were expected to breed. Together. She was suddenly very aware of him standing behind her. The rapid beating of his heart. His maleness.

"I know," she whispered. "I understand what they want."

"And?"

"And what?" she said, turning to face him.

"Do you plan on cooperating?"

Her skin prickled. Would he force her if she said no? The shackles were all in a pile by the door, though he'd said he wouldn't use them.

"Cooperating with Narlin, or cooperating with you?"

"I suppose it's one and the same." He moved around and sat back on the sofa facing her. "Taliya, there's no way out of here. I've been over and over it. Unless help comes from outside, we're stuck here together. From what I've overheard, they have funding for this program for ten years. *Ten.*"

He waited for her to respond, but she didn't know what to say.

"If we don't cooperate?" she finally asked. "What then?"

"They kill us. You know that. They kill us, kill your brothers, burn the bodies, and move on. We're science experiments that can turn a profit. Nothing more."

"And the part of us that's human? The part of our offspring that's human?"

"You know they don't care about that. They see animals. Nothing else matters."

"Is it better to be dead than go along with what they have planned? How am I supposed to go through bearing and birthing kits, over and over and over again, only to have them taken away?" She clutched at the cushion, desperately wanting to leap up and run anywhere but there. "What monster thought this up?"

"Kerkaw, of course."

"Kerkaw," she growled. The mastermind of every woe and problem her species faced.

"Taliya," he said, reaching out and touching her for the first time. She allowed him to take her hands in his. "Why did you go into hiding?"

She took a deep breath and blew it out. "So I could survive."

"And that's what your parents would want you to do. Survive. And help your brothers to survive. They'd want you to do what you have to do."

She looked into his eyes and slow-blinked. *Whatever I have to do.*

He chuffed quietly at her, and she returned the chuff. They were in this together, and they would have to figure out how to survive together. She knew what should come next, but she didn't have any clue how to begin. He seemed to sense a shift in her body.

"Don't worry about that now," he said, squeezing her hands gently. "We have time. Why don't you go get cleaned up, get the smell of that dungeon out of your fur. Your suitcase is in the bedroom. This isn't such a bad place to live. An old condominium from back in the days when there was skiing around here, though I imagine the bolts on the doors are new. I'll make us something to eat. We can watch a little TV. We have some time."

She sighed. For the moment, at least, he wasn't going to force himself on her and get things underway.

"Kano, how old are *you?*"

He sat back on the sofa and picked up the controller.

"Twenty-six."

She hoped that was old enough to know what he was doing. Hopefully more than she did. She nodded and left him with his nature show on the wall.

Besides the living room and small kitchen area, there was a bedroom and bathroom. One bed. The space was decorated in a tropical forest theme, with wallpaper covered in rain forest trees and parrots and butterflies. The bedspread and pillows were deep browns and greens. Did they think she'd be friskier if she felt like she was in a jungle?

Humans are so weird.

She'd never been in a rain forest, that was for sure. Her home was all pine trees and maples and oaks, with not a parrot in sight. Maybe a skunk or a bobcat. Possibly a bear, if you went for a really long hike. The colors they'd chosen were soothing at least, compared to the blinding white that blanketed the outside hallway.

Better than that dank concrete dungeon, she admitted to herself.

Her suitcase was waiting for her on the bed. She clicked it open. Everything seemed to be there—her books, calendars, journal, letters, family photos, even the deck of cards. She picked up Anne's diary. It had been preparing her for hiding and possibly a prison-like concentration camp. Not this.

Taliya smiled, despite herself. Anne might no longer be helpful, but she'd read a book about her new reality too. Mother encouraged the classics.

Forced breeding. Nothing but a handmaid. Bring on the long red gown and the white winged hat.

Her ability to produce white kits was her only value now.

Nolite te bastardes carborundorum, Taliya. Don't let the bastards grind you down.

Chapter 7

She did feel better after a shower, but Taliya's stomach was churning and every nerve in her body was on full alert. There was nothing in any of Kano's actions that made her think he was going to take advantage of her, but being locked in a prison cell with a male tigran—no matter how pretty a cell or how fabulous a tigran—left her agitated and anxious. She used the handheld dryer to finish blowing the water from her fur and then pulled on her favorite blue tunic. She'd been saving it for a day when she needed cheering up. This was certainly that day. Looking in the mirror, she realized the blue of her tunic was the same blue as Kano's eyes and smiled at the thought.

At least he's not some old creepy guy, like Narlin. As far as tigran went, Kano was a remarkably handsome one. *Definitely good breeding stock.*

Smoothing the tunic over her human-like breasts and hips, she sighed. She and Kano were stuck together for ten years, if all went well. She was going to have to enter into some kind of relationship with the male tigran if they were going to survive and stay sane through what lay ahead, unless the war was won by the right side. Of course, the war could end tomorrow and they'd have no way of knowing about it. The television news outlets would only report what Kerkaw wanted them to. The government owned the networks as surely as it owned Taliya and Kano. Marla had helped her keep up on the progress of the war to some extent, but now there was no way to know what was truly going on.

Marla. She hadn't stepped out of the immediacy of her situation to consider what had happened to her friend. *Was that how they found me?* Did the Enforcers finally recognize the tigran passing as human for what she was? Had they caught Marla and forced her to tell? *But they found my brothers too, and Marla didn't know anything about where they were, for that very reason.* Could it be the war was so far lost that no tigran could remain hidden?

She huffed, ran her claws through her whiskers on each side, pulled on slacks to match her tunic, snapping them in place around her tail, stuck her feet in her slippers, and shuffled out to where Kano was watching two polar bears playing in the snow on the media wall, though he had reduced the size of the video image.

It must be a historical documentary. They've been extinct in the wild for two hundred years.

"Ah, feel better?" he asked, noticing her standing nearby.

"Yes, some," she admitted.

"I made you a little snack. When was the last time you had something to eat?"

"I have no idea. I'm not even sure what day it is or where on earth I am."

"You are in Colorado, deep in the mountains. I think. And it's Thursday, January 10th."

She nodded in thanks. It was odd how comforting a little thing like knowing the date could be. She'd lost a full day, nearly two, since they captured her. Probably best not to think about that. He handed her a plate from the little table next to the couch with crackers, bits of meat, some dried fruit. She took it and sat down next to him.

"I'll cook more for dinner," he said. "I'm actually a pretty decent cook."

"That's good," she said, popping a few bites of meat into her mouth. "As much as Mother tried, I'm not very useful in the kitchen. I can do dishes, though, like a pro."

"Excellent," he said with a chuckle. "We'll make a good team, then."

A team. That's surely what they were. In it together, wherever that led.

She felt his eyes on her, and the nervous flip of her stomach returned. It took extra effort to swallow her mouthful of food. He must have sensed her tension because he looked away and back at the images on the wall, which now showed penguins huddled together against the brutal Antarctic wind.

"Nothing is going to happen today, Taliya. You can relax," he said. "I'm sure they won't begrudge you a day of rest."

"How will they know?" she asked, then felt overwhelmed by her own naivete. This place wasn't an apartment or a home, it was a prison cell. There were sure to be cameras and monitors, even if she didn't readily spot them. That hum she'd detected when the guards first brought her in the building still hovered in the air.

"I haven't located anything," Kano said, "but there's sure to be some kind of equipment to monitor us. The buzz of it is all over this facility." He looked at her and raised one stripe of an eyebrow. "To *listen* to us."

She nodded. *Be careful what you say.* It made her wonder if some of their earlier conversation was more for Narlin's ears than her own.

"Enjoy some TV," he said, setting the remote next to her. "I think I've finally gotten it adjusted to the right size for how close the sofas are. I'll get dinner cooking, then grab a quick shower." He stood up but paused and turned back to her. "Do you know when your most fertile time will be this month?"

She gagged on a piece of fruit. Kano seemed amused, but he expected an answer.

"No," she finally gasped. "I don't have the faintest idea."

"Did your mother ever talk to you about these things?"

"Not really. Did your mother talk to *you* about it?"

"No, but my wife did. When we were hoping for a family."

"*Wife?*" Her arms went limp, and she nearly dropped her plate. "You're married? What am I doing here with you if you're married?" It had never occurred to her there could be a wife in the middle of this mess.

"She's dead," Kano said flatly and headed for the kitchen. "Don't worry yourself about that."

"I'm sorry," she mumbled, not sure what else to say.

"Thousands of tigran are dead. It's rather a fact of life these days."

She nodded, but still felt uncomfortable. *Kano knows what it means to be in love. He knows how to have a relationship. I must seem like a silly girl to him, just a kit who was hiding out instead of helping to fight.*

"We can set up a calendar and track your cycles," he continued, as if the already bizarre conversation hadn't taken a dark turn. "As long as you're regular, there are some standard guidelines we can follow to help things along."

"Okay," she said, hoping he knew what those guidelines were.

"Are you regular, dates you can count on?"

"Yeah."

"Good."

She pursed her whiskers, but Kano seemed nonplussed. He clanked around in the kitchen for a moment before pulling a casserole dish out of a cupboard and setting it on the counter.

"For the first month at least, we should be making daily and consistent efforts," he said casually. "If only for a good show of being cooperative with the whole program."

"Daily . . . Consistent?" But her thoughts were mostly stuck on *daily.*

He sighed and turned around, staring at her. "Taliya, please tell me you at least understand what's going to be required to ensure you get pregnant. You do know how it works?"

"Yes," she said, feeling the skin flush under her fur. "Of course."

He nodded. "Sometimes conceiving is easy as pie, but other times it's not. Let's hope for easy and quick."

"Quick," she mumbled. "Yes, *quick.*"

He had already moved on to the refrigeration unit, sorting through what they had available.

"According to the guards, they'll deliver food items twice a week, but preparing it is up to us. Looks like chicken and vegetables tonight. It's safest to cook poultry, if you don't mind. Who knows where this has been before it got here." He started putting a meal together without waiting for an answer.

"Cooked is fine. We always cooked all of our meat. Father said it was more civilized."

"Ah, *civilized.*" Kano grimaced. "Act like humans, and they will treat us like humans. It was a nice philosophy."

"Not so nice if this is where we've ended up."

"We're still alive. That's all that matters for now. And we'll do what's required to stay that way. Yes?"

"Yes," she said, knowing what he wanted to hear. "Yes!" she shouted to the ceiling and whoever might be listening in.

"Your brothers are counting on you."

"I'll do whatever it takes to keep Tuscan and Tyler safe."

"Good," he said with a nod, turning on the oven.

Do they know the bargain I'm making for their lives, or are they just being held in the dungeon like common criminals? And what about Kano? Why was he willing to be part of this program without any fight? Maybe it was keeping him out of the dungeon. If he'd been married, maybe he was just happy to take a relationship and sex however he could get it.

"Kano."

"Yeah?"

"Why are you going along with all of this?"

"The same reason you are," he said.

"They're holding your brothers? They have leverage on you?"

He stopped for a moment, his shoulders tensing, but he didn't turn around.

"They have leverage on everyone," he finally said, roughly clunking the full casserole dish into the oven and slamming it shut.

True to his word, Kano made no advances toward her that night. She'd changed into her pajamas in the privacy of the bathroom, though she wondered if even that room was really private from the prying eyes of the Enforcers. Knowing what was on the long-term agenda, it seemed silly to fuss about sharing the one bed.

"Do you have a side you prefer?" he asked as they stood at the end of the huge bed.

"I used to sleep pretty much in the middle of my bed, but it wasn't nearly this large. And in hiding, I only had a single bed. I've never really thought about a side before."

They looked at each other, and he chuckled nervously. Waves of anxiety radiated from him, a very distinct smell, and she suspected hers was the same, if not stronger.

"I've been on an army cot for over a month now," he said, "so I suppose it doesn't matter much to me either."

"You take that one, and I'll take this one," she suggested, indicating the space directly in front of each of them. "At least for tonight."

They both climbed in under the covers—Taliya on the right and Kano on the left—and attempted to settle in. She was grateful their captors had given them a tigran-sized bed. Even Kano could stretch out and not have his feet hang off the end of the mattress. He clicked off the lamp, and they lay next to each other in the darkness. Her eyes adjusted, and she noticed a faint light coming in from a long, narrow window opening at the top of what must be the outside wall. Too small to climb through. Besides, they were twenty stories up.

"Do you snore?" he asked.

"I don't think so," she said with a laugh. "There's never been anyone to notice. What about you?"

"Sometimes," he admitted, "though mostly when I sleep on my back. I'll try not to."

She felt him shift in the darkness, rolling away from her. His tail brushed against her leg and then came to rest on the bed between them. She rolled to face the wall and let her tail settle next to his. He sighed.

"Taliya?"

"Yes?"

"It's nice not to be alone, even if the rest of it is horrible."

"Yeah," she agreed. "This is the first night in a long time I've felt really safe."

"You are. They need us, so we're secure for a while."

But at what cost? She sighed as well. It would be nice to rest in absolute peace, without worrying about agents busting through the door at any moment. She hadn't realized how tense her sleep had been until that threat was gone.

Light snoring came from the other side of the bed. Then a snuffle and snort as Kano shifted into sleep. She matched the rhythm of her breathing to his and closed her eyes.

It really was much better, not being alone.

Chapter 8

When Taliya awoke, the other side of the bed was empty. She rolled on her back and stared at the ceiling, letting all the details of her new life fall into place. The apartment/ cell was clean and homey, and it seemed like they were going to be treated with some level of care. As long as they produced kits—kits that would be taken away from her as quickly as possible, while they were still cute. A shudder ran down her spine and made her tail puff. The sound of metal pans clunking together came from the kitchen, and the aroma of bacon frying snuck into the bedroom. Her new partner was making something for breakfast. *My partner.* It felt like she had awoken from her drugged state in the warehouse attic to discover she'd missed her wedding. For all purposes, she suddenly had a husband.

I guess I should be grateful he's kind and appealing. Could be worse. Could be much worse.

"Taliya," Kano called from the kitchen, "breakfast will be ready in five minutes."

She chuffed in response and rolled out of bed. There was no pretending to sleep with another tigran around. He'd probably heard her breathing change from the other room. Staggering through her morning routine, she emerged from the bedroom dressed and ready for whatever the day had in store. Kano served up plates of fried bacon and eggs on the little kitchen island as she sat down on a stool that made it into a table of sorts.

"A civilized breakfast," he said, but she felt the heavy sarcasm in his words.

Footsteps passed by the cell door, and both of them froze, twisting their ears to listen closely. Whoever it was—a man wearing heavy boots and carrying a high-impact laser gun from the sounds and smells she caught through the grating—kept on walking. A subtle reminder that their apartment was still a prison.

Kano cleared his throat. "There was a note on the floor this morning, probably slipped through the opening at the top of the door. Narlin wants to meet with you in his office at eleven."

Taliya struggled to swallow a mouthful of eggs. She stared down at her plate, sadly marveling how a simple statement could put her off her meal so entirely. Even bacon, and she adored bacon.

84

"It's probably nothing," Kano said. "Don't get too worked up about it. I imagine we'll be meeting with him more than we might like. Finish your breakfast so you can stay strong and healthy. Lots of good protein."

She glanced up at him, wondering about the odd comment, and he shifted his eyes to a far corner of the room and then back to her. *He's found the surveillance system.* She gave him a slight nod of acknowledgment and struggled through finishing her meal. *Big Brother is watching you,* as Mother often said of the government. Something from an old book she'd read.

A few minutes before eleven, there was a firm knock on the cell door. They had both settled in for some quiet reading time, though she'd found it hard to focus on more than a line at a time. Kano looked up from her copy of Anne Frank's diary and smiled weakly.

"Just keep your eyes down and say 'yes' a lot," he whispered. "There's nothing to be gained by being difficult."

And much to be lost, she thought. *Behave, Taliya.*

She set her book aside and walked over to the door. It had been polite of them to knock, but it wasn't like she could actually let them in. Maybe they'd learned it was not wise to startle tigran. She could hear key fobs clunking together before she'd even made it across the room. The bolt clicked free of the lock, and the cell door swung open. Two massive human·males in full Enforcer uniforms were waiting for her. At six foot five herself, it wasn't often she felt intimidated by humans, but this was one of those times. She had been correct about the heavy boots and the laser guns, which each man held across his mid-section, but the wafts of determination she sensed radiating from the guards left nothing to her imagination. They meant business.

"Taliya Sharma, your presence has been requested by Colonel Narlin. You will come with us now."

She nodded, hearing Kano shift uneasily on the sofa behind her.

"Do you require shackles?" the guard asked, nodding at the restraints still sitting in a corner of the living room. "Or will you cooperate?"

"I'll cooperate," she said, struggling to keep her hackles down and in check. "I understand there's no point in fighting or trying to escape."

"Good," the guard said, shifting just slightly but clearly pleased.

He must have been warned about what happened in the attic. He came ready for a fight.

He looped a hotwire loosely around her neck, his breath reeking of garlic.

"Any move you make to run or harm a human will be met with immediate force. Then you'll be sent back to the dungeon for a week, which will delay your objective. Colonel Narlin would not like that."

Well, we must keep Narlin happy, at all costs. She choked the words down and simply nodded instead.

The guard moved to the side and motioned for her to step out of the apartment. With a brief glance back at Kano—his face full of worry, black lines drawn tight in his white fur—she left the safe feeling of their cell and walked between the guards toward the elevator. She'd been too confused and drug hung-over to notice details when she arrived, but now she caught the alarming number of video monitors in the hallway. Here, they made no attempt to hide the fact that every move was being watched. She counted the other doorways along the hall. Twelve more units, six on each side, before they reached the elevator. Did each apartment house another pair of creatures, held captive and forced to reproduce? Were they all tigran, or were there other species as well? She'd never seen any feline/ human mix but a tigran, though she'd heard about them. She couldn't smell anything but the guards and the concrete of the walls. The air was over-purified, nearly without scent. Was that on purpose, to cover up who else was there?

Turning around in the elevator, she stared down the long white hallway, the bleakness of it all settling in her heart, until the doors closed and the lift moved downward with a slight jolt. Floor after floor sped by invisibly. So many. Offices? Or more prison chambers like hers?

The elevator slowed and settled on the ground level, where Narlin's office waited. It felt like an eternity before the doors finally opened, the guards breathing heavily on either side of her. They were ready to act if she made a false move. Once the doors swished aside, the guards grasped her firmly by the arms, one on each side, and guided her toward the office from the day before. The door was open, but the guards hesitated at the threshold, waiting for instructions.

"Ah, Taliya dear," Narlin said from across the room, like he had been waiting to have high tea with her. "Come right in."

The guards released her arms, but they stayed close and alert. Narlin motioned to the couch at the side of the room, and Taliya obediently followed him there and sat down at one end. The guards moved into positions behind it, close enough to touch her. Narlin ignored the men and sat next to her—like it was just the two of them in a private meeting. He was in full military uniform again, so it felt anything but informal.

"I hope you had a good night's rest," he said, smiling.

"Yes, thank you." All of her senses shifted into a higher gear. The smile was out of place, and she couldn't translate his body language. Every inch of him made her skin prickle. It was more than just the stink of his probably expensive cologne.

"You and Kano are settling in comfortably?"

"Yes, thank you."

He frowned, seeming annoyed by her answers, but she wasn't sure what he was expecting her to say.

"We want you both to be comfortable, you know," he added. "Comfortable and . . . productive."

"We understand what you expect," she said carefully.

"Good. And Kano is right, we would like to give you a bit of time to become accustomed to each other."

She nodded. He'd clearly been listening to their conversations.

"However," he continued, "the scientist who examined you upon your arrival says these next few days are your fertile period. I know you're inexperienced, but you do understand how all of this reproduction works, don't you?"

"Well enough, I think." *Please don't let him explain it!*

"Good," he said, but his body language and the odors coming from him were sending her messages she couldn't interpret.

He has some kind of monitors in the room. He clearly knows what went on and what didn't last night. I doubt he would consider any of it productive.

"Seventeen," he said with a smile. "Not too young at all. Definitely fertile. Kano mentioned a calendar, and that's an excellent idea. We will provide you with one that's already filled out, with the days most likely to produce successful fertilization marked for you."

Fabulous, she thought, fighting down a snarl and simply nodding instead.

"There are no rules, however, about making as many attempts as you like all month."

There it was again, that creepy smile that made her skin crawl. *He's hoping for what, exactly? That we hump like animals while he watches on some hidden monitor?* Weird wafts of testosterone flooded from him. A growl formed in her throat, and she coughed to stifle it.

89

"Kano is a remarkable tigran, isn't he?" Narlin said.

"Yes, he's very kind."

"Good. Then there should be nothing to hinder the success of your pairing. You are both healthy. We expect excellent results from you two."

She nodded, not sure what else to say.

"Ah," he added, looking toward the door. "Here they are."

Her nose brought her a message of hope. Her brothers. Two guards escorted the twins through the door, and she leapt to her feet. Her guards stepped forward nervously, but Narlin waved them away. With a shout, her brothers ran to her, and the force of their hugs launched her back onto the sofa.

"Taliya!"

They chuffed and snuggled into her neck, ignoring her hotwire and theirs as well. With gentle hugs and snuffles, she assured herself they were in good health. Their fur wasn't as glossy, but they were otherwise fine.

"You should see our room upstairs, Taliya," Tuscan said. "We have a 3-D media wall and tons of games the system can play. Even CG glasses and hologram projection."

"And they bring us the best food," Tyler said. "Though they don't like us to have too much candy."

"Candy isn't good for you," Taliya said, imagining the room where her brothers were living. *They're not in the dungeon,* she assured herself. *They're in this building and being cared for.*

She glanced over at Narlin and wanted to smack the smug

look from his face—with her claws extended. He had her, and he knew it. She would do whatever it took to keep her brothers safe.

"Can we come visit you in your room?" Tuscan asked.

"Maybe another time," Narlin said, looking straight into Taliya's eyes.

She got the message. If you are good, they can visit you. If you are not . . .

"I'm glad to see you're so happy," Taliya said, trying not to clench her jaws. Her brothers couldn't know the big picture of the situation, and she would keep it that way as long as possible. "Enjoy yourselves, but behave."

"We will," they said together, just like they would have at home with Mother admonishing them.

Tyler snuggled closer to her and whispered, "I miss Mother. I wish she was here."

Her heart raced. Maybe they were just putting on a good show for Narlin too.

"I know," Taliya whispered back. "Remember what she said the last time you saw her?"

"Survive," her brother said with a sigh. "Just survive."

"Yes," Taliya said. "And that hasn't changed one bit. That's your number-one job. Survive."

Her brothers nodded, clutching at her tunic and the orange fur on her arms. She chuffed into the tops of their furry heads, unable to miss the aroma of fear now radiating from them.

They chuffed back into her chest. *Don't cry, Taliya. Don't let him see you cry.*

"That's enough for today," Narlin announced with a lazy wave of his hand.

The twins' guards stepped in to collect their charges. The instant the guards moved, the boys let go and jumped to attention in front of her. Their eyes met hers, the smell of fear from them growing stronger. They understood enough.

"Goodbye for now," she said. "Be good and eat your vegetables."

They smiled at her, showing their tiny fangs, and turned to leave with their guards.

"I love you," she called after them.

"We love you too," they said in unison, glancing back over their shoulders, like so many times before in her life.

She forced down the tears that threatened again. *Not now. Not in front of him.* Narlin reached over and grasped her hand. It took everything in her not to extend her claws.

"So you see, my dear Taliya," he cooed, "they are being cared for, just as I promised. As long as you cooperate, they will stay that way."

She nodded, unable to say anything. He turned her hand over and ran his thumb along the furless palm, and another round of male hormones hit her sensitive nose. She couldn't control her hackles, but she hoped her tunic hid the worst of it. The word *cooperate* suddenly felt more loaded than before.

"Kano has had a mate before," he continued, still stroking her palm. "He knows what to do. Let him take charge. Your best chances for success are right now. There's no time for hesitation. No more delay."

His breathing and heart rate increased, and he dragged his thumb slowly but firmly across the middle of her bare palm, leaning in a bit closer, like he was smelling her fur.

Gods help me. He's imagining it.

He released her hand and stood up. No more needed to be said. She understood. He would be watching and waiting, and no more delay would be acceptable. At a dismissive wave from Narlin, the guards took her by the arms—more forcefully than necessary, she thought—lifted her from the sofa, and led her out the door and back toward the elevator. When the lift door slid open, Kano and two guards were inside.

Why isn't he in the room? What's wrong?

He slow-blinked his blue eyes to assure her all was well. He was having a meeting with Narlin too. She watched him saunter toward the office, his tail swaying casually behind him. The guards, each a foot shorter than him, seemed unconcerned, though he did have a hotwire around his neck. *He's been here for a while. They trust him.* Her guards led her into the elevator as Kano turned to enter Narlin's office.

"Here's the white tigran of the hour now," she heard Narlin say in greeting.

She could imagine the conversation. Just get it done. Use

the shackles we left you if necessary. She choked down a growl as the lift slid shut.

The guards deposited her back in the apartment. She considered trying to read or watch TV until Kano returned, but her nerves kept her pacing like her caged ancestors. *What tactics does Narlin use on Kano?* It certainly couldn't be the sexually threatening style he'd applied to her at both of their meetings. She shuddered at the memory of Narlin's touch on her palm and shook her hand to erase the feeling. Did Kano need any threatening? After all, his part in the whole scenario was a rather pleasant one. Screw the virginal tigran. Sit back and wait for the results.

What was it about having sex with virgins that males found so alluring? It was generally uncomfortable, if not painful, for the female. She would definitely not be bringing any tantalizing skills to the situation. Were Narlin and Kano laughing it up right now at her expense? Kano had been remarkably casual in his approach to the office. No fear at all. Or was that just male posturing? She paced back and forth, fretting over what was happening downstairs and what it would mean for her.

One answer stuck in the front of her mind as absolutely true. She and Kano were expected to get things underway. There would be consequences for her twin brothers if they didn't. Narlin hadn't been subtle with that threat at all. Apparently, she was fertile now. Right at that moment. Any more postponement of the breeding agenda would not be tolerated.

"That's all we are to him," Taliya mumbled to the floor. "Animals, to breed for profit."

She hesitated and looked up at the corner that apparently held a surveillance device. There was a speaker for the media wall there, but she didn't notice anything else. Not like she'd know what to look for. Kano had seemed sure. From her conversation with Narlin, it was clear he was listening in somehow. She smiled in the direction of the speaker, showing her fangs. *Yes, I know you're there.*

Boots clomped in the hallway. The massive bolt thunked, and the door swung open. Kano stalked in, hotwire gone, not making eye contact with her as he passed and headed to the refrigeration unit. He had a cold bottle of ale in his hand before the entrance was bolted again. He popped the top and drank half of it down, wiped his mouth and whiskers with the back of his hand, claws extended, and then turned to face her. His shoulders slumped. Setting the bottle down on the counter, he walked over to her, stopping only inches away, their bodies almost touching. He took her gently by the shoulders so she wouldn't back up and whispered in her ear.

"I'm sorry."

"I know."

"If I don't . . . If we don't . . ." His voice cracked, and she felt his whiskers on her cheek, could smell his anxiety and anger. "If we don't *break the ice*, Narlin says he will find another male to get the ball rolling."

He sighed but didn't release her shoulders or move his head from next to hers. She was grateful because her legs went a bit weak. *Break the ice.* There was more than her lack of experience that made it awkward to just flop into bed with a male she barely knew. *Narlin doesn't care about that. Another male?* So much for all of their concerns about producing a white kit. Or would that other male use some protection to avoid fathering a kit? Who would they send? Would it be a tigran or a human? Narlin himself? Her hackles rose at the thought. There were strict laws, but Father had mentioned many times that rules mattered little to men in power. Men like Narlin. She sensed he would set those laws aside for a chance to get his hands on her. She shuddered a deep sigh, and Kano squeezed her shoulders in response. He rested his head against hers for a moment, then he stepped back and looked her in the eyes, still holding her in place by the shoulders.

"We can make it dark in the bedroom," he said, "and use the covers to conceal as much as possible. I promise, I'll be careful. You don't need to be afraid."

Right now? He must have felt the tremor run through her because he nodded slightly.

"Narlin says we have an hour," Kano said. "After that, he will take matters into his own hands."

Probably quite literally. Another tremor ran through her, and her tail lashed. They would have to chain and shackle her from head to toe if Narlin thought he was getting anywhere near her. Or would he enjoy that even more?

96

"Have you ever been swimming in a cold lake?" Kano asked, looking down at her and holding her gaze. "It's easier to just jump in than to fuss and fret about it too much."

She caught his meaning. This would be her life now. Their life. For many days and weeks and months and probably even years to come.

Best to plunge in and get it over with.

Chapter 9

Taliya adjusted her eyes to focus on the ceiling in the dimly lit room. As promised, Kano had kept the required act as hidden, brief, and painless as possible. Practically pain-free, actually, though *uncomfortable* described more than just that single part of the event. The whole thing was one big uncomfortable deed. But now it was done. With the covers up to her chin, she lifted her tunic—she hadn't bothered removing it for the brief festivities—and rested her hands over her stomach, raking her claws gently through the white fur there. Had they been successful already?

Kano hadn't moved since he'd rolled off her onto his side of the bed, covers up to his chin as well. He cleared his throat. With a chuff and a chuckle, he pulled the covers up over both of their heads and turned to face her.

"Are you okay?" he whispered in the dark.

"Yes," she said, rolling toward him and chuffing a laugh back. "I'm fine." It seemed odd to be laughing in that moment, but there was a surreal ridiculousness to it all. "I suppose that will shut them up for a while." *And keep Narlin away from me.*

"Somehow . . ." Kano hesitated. "Somehow I think Narlin will be disappointed with our obedience. He seems quite fascinated by you. Quite illegally so."

"I've noticed that myself."

"Have you?" Kano shifted next to her, and a deep rumble vibrated the mattress. "If he ever touches you, tell me immediately."

"Well, he's already touched me, but not in the way you mean, I think."

The rumbling grew louder, and she worried whoever was watching them might hear.

"Kano, it's all right. He's just trying to threaten me, make me feel uncomfortable. Maybe even trying to get me to react so the guards can punish me. We have to ignore it."

She reached out and found his hand. His claws were extended, pressing into the fabric of the sheets. At her touch, he relaxed a bit, then velveted his claws completely.

"I know men like him," Kano said. "They'll always find a way to get what they want."

"Well, he wants kits. That may be underway already."

"Let's hope that's all he wants."

They lay there quietly, in the dark under the covers, for another minute.

"I'm starting to smother," she finally admitted.

"Me too."

"And I'm hungry," she said, squeezing his hand.

"So many things to do today. Get you pregnant. Keep you fed." He tried to laugh but didn't quite accomplish it.

"Well, you've done your part on the first of those," she said, swishing her tail over to wrap around his leg. He reached down and pulled it through his fingers, rather like Narlin had done at their first meeting, though it felt completely different when Kano did it. A pleasant tingle ran up her spine.

"I guess food is next then," he said, pulling the covers from both of their heads, careful to leave her mostly concealed.

"You go ahead. I'll be there in a minute."

He slipped out of his side of the bed, pulling his pants on as he stood up. In a moment, she heard the media wall start up, with canned laughter from some comedy show, and cabinets opening and shutting in the kitchen. Not knowing where the cameras might be, she slipped out of bed like he had, sweeping on her slacks in one move, and headed for the bathroom.

The light blinded her for a moment. She splashed some water on her face and grabbed a towel. Staring at herself in the mirror, she didn't notice anything different. Same pattern of spots and stripes on her face: black and orange and white. Black whiskers. Tall rounded ears. Golden eyes. But there was human there as well in the shape of her head and the set of her jaws, despite the tiger-like extended nose. *Not human enough.* Still an experiment. Still government property. And now she was part of a whole new program.

Will we produce a white kit or not? She would avoid thinking about the consequences of failure.

After that first time, the ice had indeed been broken. Taliya and Kano agreed their best hope for any sense of peace was to ensure she became pregnant as quickly as possible, and they left nothing to chance. Over the next two days, they slipped back under the bedspread several times, often much longer than technically necessary. In contrast to the perfunctory efficiency of their first time, they began to explore more, enjoy more. She'd grown accustomed to the unique smell of his fur and the taste of his kisses.

On the morning of the third day, Taliya woke to sunlight peeking in through the small window slit in the bedroom. Kano was snuggled up against her back, one arm under her head and the other clasped firmly around her waist, his tail wrapped around one of her legs, like he was worried she might try to escape in the night. She smiled at that thought. First, escape, in general, appeared impossible. Second, trying to get away from him specifically was no longer in her thoughts.

101

She'd reached the conclusion that he was quite a spectacular male tigran, and a white one to boot, and she was quite lucky to have been paired with him. Not only could he cook, he was kind and funny and sweet. Lingering wildness, among other things, often made male tigran aggressive and territorial. She hadn't seen any signs of that in Kano, except maybe the territorial part when it came to her. *Is that really such a bad thing?* She could feel his soft breath on her neck and the warmth of his fur directly on hers. She tried not to let her thoughts wander any further than that. At that moment, she was cared for and safe.

Before his breathing shifted into wakefulness, he pulled her closer to him and nuzzled his face into her neck. His very presence made her tingle all over. Uncertainty surrounded them, but one thing had become crystal clear to Taliya: Kano's wife had been a very fortunate tigran.

"Good morning," he mumbled, his tail dragging lazily down her leg.

"Good morning," she whispered back.

The arm around her middle shifted, and he settled his hand over her stomach. Sensing his thoughts, she rested her hand on top of his.

"If there's not something magical going on in there right now, it's not for lack of effort," he said.

She laughed, wondering if he was inclined for another try, but he simply patted her belly and rolled over and out of bed.

They had established a routine of yoga and exercise to begin each day, staying fit and ready for whatever might come if the war reached them. It would be too easy to become apathetic and lazy, lulled into stupidity by their captivity. Tucked under the covers, they had agreed to keep each other alert and prepared.

Then came showering and grooming. Neither of them had the ribbed tongue of a tiger, so there was much washing and brushing involved. Taliya had to admit it was nice to have someone care for the parts she couldn't easily reach.

Breakfast was next, eggs and bacon and lots of protein. She crunched on a grape or two, but fruit never really felt natural to her. It was considered civilized eating, so she did it. Kano popped a grape into his mouth and made a sour face at her. She slow-blinked at him in return.

The guards had left them alone for the last two days. She assumed those in power were pleased and content to let them get down to business. And they certainly had, just like normal tigran in the flush of a new affair. Now she felt more of a calm between them. As far as the duty part of it, they had accomplished their mission. Those few days had been her most likely time to conceive for the month. It would be at least a week before they would discover if they had been successful.

After breakfast, they settled at opposite ends of the sofa, each with a book, but Taliya found her thoughts distracted. What would his interest in her be now that the required

103

physical activity was done? They were stuck with each other, but was there more to it? She'd heard her friends fuss and bother over the attention or inattention of males, but there had never been one in her life she cared for enough to go through those emotional gyrations herself. Now? She knew her feelings for Kano went far beyond necessity. All she had to do was meet his bright-blue eyes and she went all gooey inside. It was quite ridiculous, but it was the fact of the matter.

After sitting that way for thirty minutes—Kano reading and Taliya attempting to—he sighed and closed his book. Flopping on his side, he reached over and gently grasped her tail, wrapping it around his arm. Then he lay there contentedly with his eyes closed. She shut her book and stared down at him, focusing on holding her tail perfectly still. There was no necessity for that kind of contact. Nothing productive about it. *He just wanted to touch me.* The tenderness and simplicity of his attention made her chest tight with joy and excitement and feelings she didn't have a name for.

After a minute or two, he opened his eyes and gave her tail a gentle tug, making sure he had her attention. Catching her gaze, he smiled.

"Want to watch a movie?" he asked.

"Sure. Not much else to do."

He chuffed a laugh, and she felt her skin flush.

"I might need a little time off from the other options," he said, wrapping her tail tighter around his arm. "But maybe later."

She swatted at his ear playfully. "That's not what I meant."

He didn't seem convinced, but he released her tail and sat up.

"I'll find something silly, so we can have a good laugh."

That was a perfectly lovely idea. The movie industry hadn't accomplished much during the darkest years—and actual movie theaters were few and far between—but digital records remained of nearly every film ever created, including ancient black-and-white ones. That didn't mean every movie would be available to them in their prison cell, however. Kano used the controller to flip through screens and scroll the options. Nothing political or controversial available, most definitely. All very correct and government approved. He stopped on a movie that could only be categorized as RomCom and clicked to select it—a very silly, smushy love story. He adjusted the wall-sized image, tossed the controller on the sofa, and stretched out, resting his head in her lap.

She froze for a moment, then she let her arm settle along his side. They had clearly shifted into a relationship that was much more than required.

Six days later, there was a knock at the cell door while they were cleaning up after breakfast. Though it wasn't entirely un-expected, they both froze in anticipation. The bolt clacked, and the door swung open. Two guards entered, fully armed, followed by a woman in a white lab coat pushing a machine on a rolling cart in front of her. Taliya's tail puffed, and she heard Kano's heart race next to her.

"Would you rather do this in the bedroom or right here on the sofa?" the woman asked without introduction. "It will need to be an internal exam at this early stage."

Kano growled, but Taliya resisted reacting.

"Don't we just need to do a blood or urine test?" she asked.

"No," the woman said. "What's the point of that if we can confirm visually and be sure? Much more accurate."

"I would prefer the bedroom, then," Taliya said. "Without the guards observing."

The woman glanced at the guards, who hadn't moved, and then back at the two tigran.

"I'm not sure I'm comfortable with that," she said.

"What would be the point in attacking you?" Taliya said. "You have come to do your job, and we'd never get past the guards. I have no wish to die today. Let's just get this done with some dignity."

The woman seemed to consider this, though Taliya doubted the scientist was remotely worried about the dignity of her patient.

"Fine," the woman finally agreed. "But they will stand next to the bedroom door. Just out of sight range. If either of you do anything to worry me, they will be called on."

"I understand," Taliya said.

Kano nodded slightly, and she hoped he would keep his protective instincts in check. The woman pushed the machine into the bedroom, and the tigran followed her. The guards shut and locked the cell door and took up positions outside of the bedroom, though Taliya didn't sense any real concern from them. Based on the many other cells the building contained, an exam like this was probably quite routine.

"Remove your pants and lie down," the woman said as she fussed with items on the medical cart.

Taliya obeyed, and Kano sat down on the bed near her head. She looked up at him, fear and worry flickering in his blue eyes, especially as the woman came toward them with a long white wand covered in goo. It didn't take a huge jump of logic to understand the purpose of the wand for an internal exam. Taliya flinched, and Kano nearly stood up to stop the whole process.

"No, it's fine," she said quietly to him. "Stay with me."

Kano nodded, settled down, and took one of her hands. Taliya tried to remain calm and still as the doctor unceremoniously inserted the cold wand deep inside of her, pushed it up as far as it would go, and began to poke buttons on the machine. All was quiet for a few seconds, then she heard the woman make a clucking noise with her tongue. Looking over at the screen, Taliya had no idea what all of the images and blinking lights meant. Kano looked over as well, and he whoofed, interpreting something she didn't understand.

"Well," the woman said, "Colonel Narlin will be very pleased."

Taliya felt a rush of energy. "I'm pregnant?"

Kano squeezed her hand and looked into her eyes. "You are, but—"

"Twins," the woman interrupted.

"Twins?" Taliya said in wonder.

"It's very common in tigran," the woman said. "See here." She pointed at the screen, tapping one little dark circle area and then another. "Two little tigran." She quickly removed the wand, making Taliya gasp, and started packing up.

"Twins," Taliya said again.

Twins, like her brothers. Then a lump settled in her stomach. Twins she would have to give away and send to be part of some zoo, or worse. Kano seemed to be pondering the same conclusion.

"It's too early to tell if the embryos are white or orange kits," the woman said, "not without the chance of doing damage. We won't know that for another month or so. Your full gestation time should be around one hundred fifty days, though twins often arrive early. Longer than a full tiger, but much shorter than a human. Very efficient for our breeding program."

Kano jumped in with the question Taliya couldn't voice.

"What if they're orange?"

"Colonel Narlin will recommend terminating the pregnancy, I'm sure. That's the logical conclusion. Then you can try again for more successful results in a month or two instead of waiting through the whole cycle."

So clinical. So matter-of-fact. Waves of anxiety radiated from Kano. He stood and stalked across the room, dealing with his feelings alone for the moment.

Two kits were growing inside of her. Kits that belonged to her and Kano. But not really. They all belonged to the government, who could do with them as they liked. She understood enough about genetics to know that the fur color of those two tiny beings had already been determined. Their fate already sealed. White, and they would live. Orange, and they would not.

Taliya used the cleaning wipe the doctor had left next to her, swung her legs off the bed, and slipped her pants back on as she stood.

"Congratulations," the woman said. "I'll be back in a month to do another check."

Taliya and Kano stood, rooted to their spots, until the guards and the lab-coat woman left and they heard the door clunk to lock behind them.

"Well," Taliya finally said. "That's what everyone was hoping for, I suppose." She had expected to be more excited, to feel more successful.

Kano turned to face her, and she was shocked to see his eyes were wet with tears.

"I can't protect you," he whispered. "I can't protect *them*.

What can I do? There's nothing. I can't."

She went to him and let him enfold her in his arms.

"They're going to take these kits from us," he said hoarsely. "Our kits. Yours and mine. Hell, they could take *you* away from me tomorrow if they felt like it. My job is done. There's no need to keep us together if Narlin doesn't feel like it. And there's not a damn thing I can do about any of it."

Chapter 10

The next thirty days dragged by like nothing Taliya had ever experienced before, even hiding in the attic room. Kano's fears they would be separated had been wrong, at least for the time being, but the wait was excruciating—the wait to find out the fate of their kits.

Food was delivered by guards twice a week. Once a week, a guard picked up their laundry and returned it later in the day, fresh and clean from some unknown quarter of the facility. Kano had discovered a small closet off the kitchen with a vacuum and cleaning supplies, and keeping their cell tidy occupied some time.

Stacks and stacks of books arrived, once their reading habit was observed. They were also given gaming glasses and access to all the virtual and holographic media that her brothers had raved about. Taliya hoped these were acts of consideration or kindness, but Kano saw it simply as a way to keep them quiet and appeased. Their indolence made them easier to control, keep in line. Content captives were more compliant than anxious ones. One blessing was that neither of them had been called to see Narlin. Taliya guessed he was busy threatening and manipulating other creatures in the building. Sad for them, but good for her. She wasn't sure she could handle dealing with him in her present state of mind.

While they were in limbo, waiting for the future to be decided, Kano and Taliya spent an inordinate amount of time watching the media system. The censors had been busy, making sure media considered "inappropriate" or "controversial" had been blocked. Taliya found most of her favorites had been removed. Kano joked that this was an interesting commentary on her specific taste. Some days they found themselves watching an entire old comedy series, from beginning to end, one episode after another. It was a good distraction from the reality they faced.

After poking through the selections one afternoon, they came across a movie with a title so ridiculous they had to watch it: *The Guernsey Literary and Potato Peel Pie Society*. Who in the world would eat a potato peel pie? Taliya loved that it was about a writer. Anything involving books was always on the top of her list. But then they were shocked to find scenes of war. World

War II, clearly, because there were Nazis and the town was being occupied. Seeing the horror of that war depicted so intimately took her breath away. Taliya found she was clutching at the sides of the sofa while the character Elizabeth stood up to the invading troops and shouted "Shame!" into their faces.

But some of it was too much to bear. When it came to the children being evacuated—taken from their parents and sent away—Taliya could barely see through her tears. She knew what it meant to be the one running, but she hadn't for one minute considered what her mother must have gone through, sending all three of her kits away with strangers. Not knowing where any of them had gone. Knowing they would not be together for months or even years. Knowing she might never see them again.

Taliya reached for the remote to pause the movie, just so she could recover a bit and enjoy the love story that was really at the heart of it all, and Kano's chest shuddered. He was crying too. That was all it took to open the gates and set the sobs free. She snuggled into his arms and cried for all the kits in hiding. For all the ones who had been found. For their own kits and the horrible future that faced them. They were so exhausted after that, they simply cuddled up and took a nap on the sofa.

When they awoke a few hours later, the movie was no longer available, no matter how she searched. Taliya glanced up at the corner of the room where Kano was sure there was a surveillance monitor. Someone had seen their reaction and removed it while they were asleep. He nodded his head, agreeing with her assessment of the situation without words needing to be spoken. Taking the remote from her, he clicked on a silly cartoon about a panda bear who fights with karate. They both sat and faced the media wall, but she doubted he was really watching any more than she was. Captives. They were captives, and the powers that be were not going to let them watch anything that stirred up that kind of emotions. Strong emotions could lead to dangerous actions.

Back in her real life in her real home on the family compound in Arkansas, Taliya would have immediately ordered a copy of the book the potato peel society movie was based on and read it on her tablet in one day. It was always more fun to read the book. Maybe someday she'd get the chance and find out how it ended. After the war, if the government hadn't destroyed every copy of it by then.

She ached to know what was going on out in the world. Where her parents were. If they were safe or even still alive at all. She tried to watch the silly panda movie and laugh when it would be appropriate, but her heart wasn't in it. Kano pulled her in close, tucked under his arm.

"We should study that panda bear's moves," he said, "but then they might remove this video too. No reason to let us learn karate."

She chuckled and rubbed her face against the fur of his chest. He didn't bother to put on a shirt most days now. What

114

was the point? It was just the two of them in their little love-nest prison. Snuggled into his warmth, she felt herself drifting off to sleep again. One benefit to her pregnancy was that she slept longer than usual, which helped the time go faster. Even with two naps during the day, she still felt groggy and lethargic most of the time.

"It will pass," Kano had assured her. "At least you're not having any nausea or sickness. I've heard that's rare with tigran, but you never know. I'm glad you're only sleepy."

She thought sleepy was a kind word. Perpetually exhausted was more like it. But she definitely wasn't sick. If anything, she was famished most of the time she wasn't sleeping. The size of their food delivery had been increased, no doubt based on the surveillance observations of her new eating habits, and Kano chopped and sautéed and created lovely meals for her to devour. The two kits growing inside her never seemed satisfied.

Then the day came, one month after the first visit, that the white-lab-coat female scientist and two guards arrived at their door. She had a different machine on her cart this time—very complicated and official-looking—along with several ridiculously long needles and a variety of terrifying sharp tools.

She's ready for anything. Ready to terminate these kits, right here and now.

Taliya gawked at the sight of the scalpels and strange knives, and Kano growled. The woman stepped back, and the guards moved their guns to a more ready position. Taliya turned to

Kano and noticed his fangs were bared. She placed her hands in the middle of his chest and chuffed at him calmly. The next few minutes would be hard enough without him being dragged away to cool his heels in the dungeon.

"I need you," she whispered. "I need you here with me."

He cleared his throat and stood taller, but she still felt his rage. Luckily, humans didn't notice such things. As long as he kept his outward demeanor polite, they would never know the difference.

"Have a seat on the sofa," the woman said. "I'll be drawing a tiny bit of fluid from each embryonic sack to test the DNA."

Taliya looked up at Kano, and he nodded once. It was what they'd expected. She moved to the sofa and sat, not sure what would happen next. The woman pulled her cart of equipment close and settled in on the armrest next to Taliya, where she could reach the tigran and her cart at the same time. The first item she grabbed looked like a man's razor, and Taliya shifted uncomfortably, which made Kano take a step closer and the guards act even more nervous. The woman paused.

"It's easier if we shave a patch of fur," she said.

"It would help if you could explain what you're doing," Kano said between clenched jaws, "instead of just coming at my mate with sharp instruments. We have instinctive reactions to being threatened."

The woman leaned away from Taliya, which made the tigran want to laugh, but the situation was too fraught for that.

116

"Yes," the woman said with a nervous flutter in her voice, "I suppose you're right. Many of our guests have been through this process several times. I forgot you two are new to it all."

Taliya looked up at Kano, and she couldn't read the expression on his face. Was he humored by the word "guests," or was he wondering how many others this woman was visiting and for what purposes? White tigran were quite rare. There had to be more going on in the huge building than just breeding for white kits. Before she could think more about it, the woman lifted the razor again.

"Hold still, please. I only need to clear a small spot on your abdomen."

Taliya pulled her slacks down lower around her hips, and the woman removed a four inch section of the white fur on her belly. *You call that small, you bitch?* She knew it was wrong to hate the woman so much. The scientist was just doing her job, but she hated her anyhow. The razor-wielding scientist was there to determine if the kits would survive. There was nothing pleasant about any of it. The woman swabbed the bare patch with some brown liquid that stung and then tingled oddly.

"That should numb the area just a bit," the woman said, "so you don't feel the needle as much."

Next came the giant needle and a wand rather like the one the woman had inserted in Taliya a month earlier.

"This will help me find each embryo," the scientist said,

indicating the wand, "and then I will use the needle to draw a small amount of fluid. It won't harm the kits, as long as you hold still. Do you understand?"

"Yes," Taliya said with a nod. "I need to hold very still."

The woman looked at Kano. "Why don't you come stand behind her and hold her shoulders, just to help when she might be instinctively inclined to react."

He paused for a moment, as if unsure whether she was making fun of his earlier comment or being serious.

"Please, Kano," Taliya said, reaching out to him. "It may be quite hard not to jump when a needle is stuck in my stomach."

He responded to her immediately, moving around behind her and resting a hand on each of her shoulders.

"Close your eyes," he suggested. "Put your head back and try to put it out of your mind."

She frowned, but she lay her head back and closed her eyes. The needle itself was the least of what was racing through her mind, and there was no way she could quiet all of it.

"Can't you give her some kind of sedative for this?" Kano asked.

"We try to avoid sedatives. There are too many variables that are unknown with your species, and we don't want to harm the kits. Of course, if we terminate the pregnancy—"

Kano growled again, and Taliya reached up to cover his hands with hers.

"Well," the woman said, "let's see what we're dealing with before we worry about that."

Taliya kept her eyes closed, but she felt the woman press the ultrasound wand on her small belly pooch, shifting it around to find the right spot, and then the pressure of the needle being inserted. Kano made a noise in his throat and pressed firmly on her shoulders. The needle didn't hurt, but it definitely felt weird and made her want to pull away. She focused on breathing calmly, in and out, and on moving as little as possible in the process.

"Okay, now inhale and hold your breath for the count of twenty," the scientist said.

Taliya obeyed and imagined that needle poking at her tiny kits. She held her breath long past twenty, just in case. At a relaxing of Kano's hands and an easing of the pressure from the needle, she opened her eyes. The woman was already transferring the fluid from the needle into a small vile, which she then inserted into the complicated-looking machine. She set the first needle aside and picked up a second one.

"Now for the other kit," she said. "We can get that sample while the first is still processing."

Taliya closed her eyes, leaned her head back on the sofa, and the woman repeated the steps. Once the second vial was inserted for processing, the woman used the wand to check on the embryos with the ultrasound.

"Good. Everything looks fine."

The machine beeped, and Taliya and Kano both froze. The woman typed a few keys and then smiled.

"Kit number one is a *white* tigran," she said. "Excellent!"

Taliya flushed, realizing the woman's excitement had nothing to do with either of them. A white kit was money in the bank for her or the people who funded her. Kano patted Taliya's shoulders and then came around to sit on the sofa next to her. She leaned into him, but it was hard to be terribly excited. *At least the kit will be allowed to live. That's a start.*

The machine beeped again, and the woman pulled up the results. This time, she did not smile.

"Orange," she said and turned to face them. "I was hoping for identical twins that would share the exact DNA." She started packing up her supplies.

"So what happens now?" Kano asked before Taliya could form a thought.

"That will be up to Colonel Narlin," the woman said. "We have no use for an orange kit."

Taliya felt Kano tense and put a hand on his knee as she sat up.

"*We* certainly *have use* for an orange kit," she said. "Would he allow us to keep it?"

The woman gave a snorting laugh, like that was an irrational idea. Then she paused and looked Taliya up and down critically, taking her all in, and seemed to come to some conclusion.

"The first option is whether to allow the orange kit to continue at all. It is possible to terminate one embryo but not the other, but there are risks for the one we want. The more stan-

dard process is to allow both kits to be born and then eutha-
nize the orange kit immediately. It is quick and quite painless."

Taliya nodded, but disgust swirled in her stomach. *Painless
for you, maybe, you self-righteous—*

"However," the woman continued, "if Colonel Narlin de-
cides to let both kits come to term, he may be persuaded to let
you raise the orange one. If you use the right tactics."

She winked and smiled at Taliya in a way that made her
already unsettled stomach flip over completely. *Right tactics?*
She hadn't been out in the world much, but she had a pretty
good idea what the woman was hinting at. Colonel Narlin
could be convinced to let her keep her own kit, hers and
Kano's, but at what price? The woman didn't say more, but
she really didn't need to. Narlin had made his interest clear
from the first moments they met, but Taliya had thought he
was mostly trying to intimidate her. Maybe not. Maybe he had
been setting the stage for the inevitable negotiation to come.

Kano shifted next to her, but she didn't sense any unusual
level of anger in him. *He hasn't put it together yet,* she concluded.
In time, he'd remember the threats about getting the mating
underway and Narlin's offer to personally help move it along.
Kano was a sharp tigran. He'd get there soon. She hoped the
woman and the guards were gone before then.

"That's all for now," the scientist said, standing up and
pushing her cart toward the door. "It may take a few days for
a decision to be made, but I will advise allowing both kits to
come to term. It's the safest way."

Taliya rose, ingrained civility making her want to see their guest out. Then she stopped, noticing the guards looked suspicious. Kano reached up and held her hand, and they both watched as the woman wheeled her cart into the hallway, followed by the guards.

"We need to head to Nineteen-A next," the woman said before the cell door was closed and locked.

"Just one more stop in her day. That's all we are," Kano said, standing up and wrapping Taliya in his strong embrace.

Two kits. One white and one orange. In any other tigran household, they would host a party to celebrate. In their cell, Taliya and Kano were left with nothing but sorrow.

"Do you think we can convince Narlin to let us keep the orange kit?" Kano asked.

Taliya buried her face in the fur of his neck. "Not *we*. Just me. I can . . . make a deal with him."

"Just you?"

Kano hesitated, then she felt it—his fur rising and rage flowing from his body. He grabbed her by both shoulders and pulled her free so he could look her in the eyes.

"You're not serious. That can't be what she meant. I know he made those threats back at the beginning, but . . . He wouldn't dare."

"Wouldn't he? Do you really think a human male like Narlin is the least bit worried about laws? There's nothing legal about anything in this building."

Kano released her and sat on a stool at the kitchen island, every muscle in his body tense.

"Actually, it may be me who can make a *quid pro quo* deal with him," he said quietly. "When I arrived, I got the feeling Narlin had some special plans for me that had nothing to do with breeding kits."

"What kind of plans?"

"He seemed to have a particular interest in me that . . . that would never in a million years have led to white tigran kits. That flew in the face of several different laws."

Taliya covered her mouth and sat down on the sofa.

Kano grumbled and then cleared his throat. "He never came right out and said anything. It was just the way he acted. Standing too close. Touching me when there was no reason to be touching me. He'd call me up from that dungeon, on the pretext of giving me updates about finding my new mate. Finding you. But he never really seemed to have anything specific to tell me. And he spent a lot of time commenting on how tall and strong I was. What a perfect specimen of a white tigran I am. It sort of made sense. I was basically supposed to be used for stud services, but there was always something more about it that I couldn't quite set my claw on. Some quality to the way he talked, touched me, circled me like prey. I dreaded going to see him, even though it offered some break from the dungeon, a bit of fresh air."

Taliya nodded her understanding.

"At one point," he said, "I got the distinct feeling he was trying to bargain with me."

"Bargain about what?"

"I got the sense that, well, I'm not sure exactly what he wanted, but he kept talking about this room, where we are now, and how nice and comfortable it was. How they could go ahead and move me up here instead of waiting for you in that awful underground cell. I'm sure I was supposed to understand something that I didn't. There were always guards there with the two of us. We were never alone. I was a bit feistier when I first arrived, and everyone was concerned about what I might do, given the chance. Rightly so. My capture was bloodier than yours." He stared at the wall for a second, maybe remembering, and frowned.

"I think he knew better than to say outright what I'm pretty sure he was suggesting. He talked about private time together and how he wanted to get to know me better. Again, the words themselves weren't wrong, it was the way he said them, the look on his face, the feeling I sensed from him that I didn't recognize at all. There I was, probably a foot taller than him and weighing two hundred pounds more, with claws and fangs, and he was freaking me out. I've never been close friends with a human before, so I could have been misreading things. I don't know. But when I didn't say or do what he wanted me to, he would get angry and have me thrown back into the cell. It was all confusing and frustrating as hell. I suspected the whole story about finding me a mate and being part of a breeding program was a lie, and all that he wanted was me, for his own personal amusement. Like a pet or a toy. And I wasn't playing whatever game he had in mind."

She could feel the anger rising from him in urgent waves.

"You said he touches you," Kano said, "but not in the way I was worried about. All that stuff I described, that's what he does with you, isn't it."

"Yes."

Kano leapt up, his stool toppling to the ground behind him.

"I should have known. It's like when he'd call me up from the dungeon just to toy with me, isn't it?"

She nodded, trying to remain calm as Kano's agitation grew.

"I just assumed," he said, "if he was interested in me, he wouldn't be interested in you. Stupid. I was so stupid."

"He clearly either likes both males and females, or it has nothing to do with sex at all. As you said, it's more about the game and winning. Making us feel vulnerable and uncomfortable. If I can use that interest to make a deal with him, I have to try."

He sat down next to her, his hands clasped in front of him.

"You can't make any deal with him," he whispered. "Possibly I can, but you just can't." Despite his quiet voice, she could sense his agitation—tense, wound, and ready to spring.

"I can," she said with determination. "Of course I can, though it's a revolting thought. My biggest concern is whether or not he would honor his word when the time comes and the kits are born. Is it worth the risk if it could save the life of one of the kits? And allow us to keep it?"

"No," Kano growled deep in his throat. "You are my mate. I won't allow it."

Taliya wanted to laugh, but she sensed he was completely serious. He rose and paced for a moment, probably sorting through their options. She was about to say something to calm him down when he froze in place, every hair along his spine standing up, tail puffed.

"Kano?"

Instead of answering, he grabbed a barstool from the kitchen island and threw it across the room with a roar Taliya had never heard from any creature before. Then he seized the other stool and bashed it into the floor over and over and over, bits of it flying in the air and primal sounds ripping from his throat. Frustration and anger enveloped their prison cell. Finally, he hurled the broken stool into the wall and crumpled down on his heels, his breath coming in a growl/hiss pattern that she did recognize—the sound of her rage when the Enforcers broke into her attic room.

Her heart racing, she waited until the growling stopped and his breathing returned to normal, then she rose to go to him, to help him understand what she had to do, but he stood and faced her, his eyes filled with emotions she didn't recognize.

"You are *mine*," he said, pulling her into a rough embrace, "and I will not let some human male paw all over you and . . . No."

Before she could respond, he led her to the semi-privacy of the dark bedroom to make sure she was clear about to whom she belonged.

Kano's explanation of their bond was thorough and extensive, leaving Taliya with no doubt their pairing was more than just forced or convenient. She stretched languidly and rolled herself out of bed, taking a shower before getting dressed and going in search of a snack. The kits were demanding a meal, but Kano was still snoring gently. She left him to nap and headed for the kitchen.

Before she made it across the living room, she noticed a beige envelope on the floor in front of the door. It was the same color as the carpeting, so she'd almost missed it. She froze and held her breath before finally stepping over to retrieve it. Mostly likely, it was a summons from Narlin, eager to discuss the future of her kits. Had they been watching all of the drama that unfolded after the scientist left? She picked the envelope up and saw a message scrawled on the front: **Open away from watching eyes.**

Hmmm. Not official-looking at all. But who else would be dropping notes through the slot?

She wandered casually over to the refrigeration unit, opened the door, and stood there, pretending like she was considering what to eat while blocking her body from the monitor with the door. She tore open the envelope and read the note inside.

The war is coming to you. Soon. You already have friends inside. Freedom is at hand.

Clutching the note to her chest, she tried to breathe normally. She slipped the note into her pant pocket and pulled some items from the cooler. It took everything in her power to sit down and snack normally, like she hadn't just read life-altering news. Every fiber of her wanted to run and tell Kano, but she didn't want to do anything that would call attention to her or her actions. Now that she was pregnant, she doubted they watched every one of their movements. She hoped they hadn't seen her pick up the envelope. *Be calm. Be normal. Be patient.*

Once her snack was done and cleaned up, she sauntered into the bedroom and climbed back under the sheets. Kano stirred at her arrival and laughed when she pulled the blankets up over their heads.

"I've had a nap," he said, "but I'm not sure I'm that rested."

She chuffed at him and then caressed the side of his face, playing with his ruff and whiskers for a moment, knowing how excited he would be about the strange letter.

"There was a note by the door," she said, attempting to control the nervous energy she was sure he could sense, "and it wasn't from Narlin."

"Who was it from?"

"Here." She pulled the note out of her pocket. "It says the war is coming to us, that we have friends already inside here somewhere, and that freedom is at hand."

"Freedom is at hand?" He took the note, but it was too dark under the covers to read it, even for his tigran eyes. "Could it be genuine, or some trick?"

"It seems genuine. What could be gained from trying to trick us like that? It would only make us agitated and anxious, maybe even rebellious. What would the Enforcers have to gain from that?"

"So maybe it's true. Maybe we're winning the war and the battle will come to us soon. Someone does know about this place."

It was hard to translate all the feelings she felt wafting over her. He was excited and happy but . . . hesitant, possibly even scared.

"I'll read it while I'm in the shower," he said, "and then let the water destroy it."

"Good idea."

He rolled out of his side of the bed and headed for the bathroom, the note hidden in his massive hand. She flopped the covers off her head, stared at the ceiling, and clutched the slight bulge of her belly with both hands. If help really came soon, they could escape with both kits. She lay there, hoping and mulling it all over, until Kano returned from the bathroom.

He pulled on some clothes and sat down next to her. With a smile, he rested his hand on top of hers.

"If they hurry, we may be able to save them both," he whispered.

She nodded and smiled at him. With a gentle pat to her tummy, he got up and headed for the kitchen.

"The three of you are probably hungry again," he called behind him.

"I could eat," she said with a laugh. He didn't need to know she'd already had a snack.

While he clunked around in the kitchen, she stared at the ceiling, expectation washing over her. Someone knew they were there. Someone was coming. *Hurry. You need to hurry.* She sent her wishes out into the universe, out onto the fields where battles were raging and hopefully both of her parents were fighting their way to her.

Chapter 11

Taliya was certain there had never been two more perfect kits in the entire universe. One orange and one white, just like predicted. With one cradled into each arm against her furry chest, she couldn't tear herself away from staring at the absolute delight of their stripes and spots and tiny little noses and dainty whiskers. The white kit stirred and began to nuzzle around, wanting to nurse. Taliya started to adjust him, but a pair of hands wrapped around his little body and pulled him away from her.

"No need for that," the female scientist said, putting the kit into an incubator next to the bed.

Taliya wanted to protest, ask for more time, but nothing came out. She watched in horror as the woman tucked in the white kit and closed the side of the incubator.

"As for that one." The woman frowned before taking the orange kit from Taliya.

"No!" she finally forced out, but the scientist ignored her.

Without a flinch, the woman tossed the kit into a garbage can in the corner with a resounding thud. Tiny yelping wails filled the air.

"No!" Taliya screamed again, willing herself to leap up and save them, but she couldn't move. It felt like her body was encased in concrete.

"Give it four weeks, and we can hope for another set of twins," the scientist said as she wheeled the incubator from the room. "Maybe they'll both be white next time."

While the cries of her newborn kits echoed through the cell, Taliya threw back her head and screamed. At first, nothing came out, but slowly she found her voice and screamed louder and louder and louder and . . .

"Taliya?"

Kano's voice sounded far away. He had to hurry!

"Taliya, wake up."

With a gasp, Taliya opened her eyes to find the pink nose of her mate only inches from her in the dimly lit room.

"It was just a dream," he said. "I'm right here. You're safe."

Tears burst to her eyes, and she buried her face in his warm chest. He probably thought it was another recurring nightmare about being captured and killing the Enforcers. She'd welcome that one compared to the new dream that was firmly centered in the reality of the future.

If she hadn't been sure before, she was positive now. Whatever it took, she would protect her kits.

The note at the door in the morning was official and from Narlin. Guards would be there at eleven to collect Taliya—and only Taliya—to discuss her "situation." Her skin crawled at the prospect of what that conversation might involve. Help was coming, and she needed to do whatever was necessary to keep both kits alive until then.

The guards arrived a few minutes before eleven, and she left with them while Kano sat on the sofa, radiating anxiety. They had agreed she would try to stall Narlin, but she was still worried Kano would try to stop the visit and tangle with her escorts. As she walked down the white hallway, the guards clomping along on the concrete floors, she wondered if it was better to know help was coming or might it just cause her more problems. What if she counted on rescue, but it never came? Or came too late? The elevator swooshed her down twenty floors to Narlin's office, where he was sitting and studying some charts and graphs on the display wall. She wasn't sure if it was a good sign or not that he was only dressed in a casual military camo outfit that day. He turned at the sound of her entering.

"Taliya dear," he cooed, like they were old friends.

He rose and stalked toward her, arms extended like he might hug her. One of the guards flinched, and she felt disgust waft from him. At least someone else noticed the bizarre way Narlin behaved. He clasped her shoulders, and the guard shifted into fear and gripped his gun tighter. Maybe he suspected she would react. She gritted her teeth but did nothing else, no matter how much she wanted to simply sink her fangs into Narlin's pale white throat. There was too much at stake. Too many lives besides hers to consider. The hotwire around her neck was the least of her concerns.

"We're all thrilled with the test results," Narlin said, still not releasing her shoulders. "A white tigran kit on your first attempt. Very exciting!"

He finally released her, took the remote for the hotwire from the guard, and headed for the sofa. She followed obediently, like on the last visit.

"Carl and Stan, you're dismissed," Narlin said without looking back. "Please wait outside the door. And close it behind you."

Both guards stiffened, but one turned and headed out the door. The second hesitated. Taliya looked back and didn't like what she saw in his brown eyes. Being asked to leave was bad.

"Carl?" Narlin said. "Is there a problem?"

Carl paused for a moment, then he stood tall, gun across his chest.

"No, sir. No problem. Just worried for your safety. This one's been known to kill."

He's lying. He's angry. Disgusted. Taliya could feel it hitting her in waves. *Don't leave*, she wished to his mind.

"I'm sure my dear Taliya and I will be just fine. I have the remote for the hotwire. We're simply going to have a private chat here on the sofa."

Her stomach churned, and she looked to Carl again. He frowned and pursed his lips, but then he turned and left the room, shutting the door behind him.

"That's better," Narlin said. "Come sit with me, my lovely Taliya, and let's discuss the future of your kits."

She did as she was told and sat down just out of reach, folding her hands in her lap and wrapping her tail tightly around one leg. Narlin picked up a lap tablet and typed in some codes. The background hum—a sound that filled the facility constantly—was silenced. Its absence ached in her ears. He had turned off the surveillance monitors and listening devices in the room.

"And now we are completely alone," he said.

Her chest tightened. One of her hands strayed to her belly, instinctively protecting the bulge there. *Do whatever it takes to keep them safe. Help has to be coming. It just has to be.*

"Dear Taliya," he began and scooted a bit closer to her, "we have a big decision to make. We really only need one of your kits. The white one. You understand that, don't you?"

"I know that's how you feel about it, yes."

"So my concern is how we handle the fact that there is an

orange kit as well. That little one is just kind of in the way, don't you think?"

She clenched her hands together. "The doctor indicated that attempting to terminate the orange kit would likely be harmful to the white one. That seems like a risky solution."

"Indeed, we have found that to be true," Narlin admitted in such a casual way that she suddenly felt that option was not really on the table. He wanted something else.

"So I hope we won't attempt that," she said. "Not if it's risky."

"Agreed." He patted her clenched hands. "No surgery for our sweet Taliya." He smiled at her, and his hand shifted down onto her leg, pressing firmly with one finger as he traced along the inseam of her pants, down to her knee. "Everyone should be happy with that decision. Does it make you happy, Taliya?"

"Yes," she said, attempting to discreetly shift away from him as he inched closer to her.

"So both kits will come to term and be born. But then we'll need to decide what to do with the orange one." He leaned back a bit to meet her eyes. "Normally, in this situation, the orange kit is euthanized at birth. Quick and simple."

She tried not to react, but her eyes and her whiskers betrayed her. Narlin seemed pleased, like he had gotten the reaction he hoped for.

"Of course," he said, "special arrangements can always be made."

"What kind of special arrangements?" she asked, already suspecting and dreading the answer. It was only the specifics and details that needed to be spelled out. One of the oldest negotiations in the world. Sex in exchange for money or goods—in this case, her own kit.

"It could be arranged for you to keep the orange one. You and Kano." He smiled, attempting to be coy or something she couldn't quite place. "I'm sure that would make Kano happy. He's lost so much already."

She nodded.

"And I'm sure you possess a maternal instinct that would make you desire keeping your kit, even if it's useless to me."

"Of course," she said, struggling to keep her hackles down and the growl growing in her throat contained.

"But everything in this world has a price, Taliya," he said, running his finger back up along the top of her thigh, resting it precariously close to territory she wanted him nowhere near. "If we agree that you and Kano will be allowed to keep and raise the unwanted kit, at an expense to this facility for its care, I might add, you and I will need to come to an arrangement of sorts. I'm a busy man, and there are many guests here, so it doesn't need to be elaborate."

It would take only a second. My fangs in his jugular. One swipe of my claws across his neck. It would be over before he knew what hit him. Instead, she nodded for him to continue. He sat back on the sofa, allowing his arms to rest along it. Kano did that often.

It was sexy when Kano did it. Narlin only made her stomach swirl with nausea.

"You will need to come to me," he said flatly. "Willingly. More than just cooperatively." He ran a hand through his hair and then across his chest, and she couldn't miss the lust radiating from him. Male hormones running amuck. "You will need to be interested . . . . Enthusiastic."

Hearing it so bluntly made her swallow hard to keep from vomiting all over him. It wouldn't be enough to just let him do what he wanted. She would have to pretend to enjoy it, be excited about it.

"That's against the law," she finally said. "Punishable by death. For both of us."

He waved one hand in a pish-posh motion. "Laws and rules don't really apply here, Taliya darling. You're in a government facility. We make the rules and laws. I'm a full-bird colonel," he said, tapping an eagle pin on his uniform. "If I want to side-step regulations, I can simply say it's for the good of science and research. Nobody really cares."

And it won't be the first time, she suspected. *Definitely not the first time.* How many female prisoners had he put in this position? Forced into pregnancy and then coerced into his bed to protect her offspring.

"How can I be sure you'll keep your word when the kits are born?" she said as calmly as she could.

"Well," he leaned toward her and smiled, "I suppose you're just going to have to trust me on that one."

Not as far as I could throw you, she thought, and then she imagined exactly how far that would be. Into the wall. Splat. Crashing through the frosted glass window across from them. Narlin bleeding and crawling down the hallway to the guards for help. Guards who would kill her. Or just lock her in the dungeon for a bit, to save the white kit inside her. Maybe punish her brothers or Kano instead. She sighed.

"I need to think about it," she said. "Can I have some time to consider your offer?"

He shifted. "Not for long."

Does he know help is coming?

"Your paunch will become more and more pronounced each day," he said. "A fat tigran is not an appealing prospect. I'm sure you can understand that."

She flared her whiskers and felt the tip of her tail start to beat against the base of the sofa. *Stay calm. Don't let him rattle you.*

"How about a week?" she said. "Seven days from now."

He tipped his head and scanned down to her stomach. "That should be fine," he said. "Seven days shouldn't make too much of a difference. I've heard that pregnancy makes females extra frisky. That would be worth waiting for." He grinned.

He knows I'm stalling but I'll agree in the end. What choice do I have?

"Don't mention this to Kano," she said. "He wouldn't understand, and his territorial instinct is very strong. I'm sure you don't want to keep replacing barstools. Leave this all between the two of us. He never needs to know."

"If that's what you feel is best," he said with a smirk.

A secret. More leverage.

"Go on now," he said with another wave of his hand. "I have more important business than this orange kit waste of resources nonsense. Go tell the guards you're ready to return to your room."

She stood and walked toward the door, struggling to keep her body calm and poised.

"I'll send the guards for you in seven days," he said to her back. "Seven. That will be the end of it, one way or the other."

She paused and then nodded, not turning around.

"That's all then," he said. "Go on."

She opened the door and found the guards casually waiting for her, like they weren't expecting trouble from the room at all. They probably knew about her brothers and her kits. Knew she had too much at stake. Carl looked at her with what could only be pity.

How many, Carl? How many females have you watched go through this? How many times have you taken them to his office and stood guard outside while they did what they had to? The look in Carl's eyes answered: many, many, many times.

"Let's go," she growled.

She barely noticed anything during the walk back to her cell. *Seven days. Please hurry. Get here before then.*

The guards returned her to the room and locked the door behind her. Kano had clearly been pacing the whole time she was gone. She could hear his heart racing.

"What happened?" he said, rushing to her at the door.

"They're not going to attempt to terminate the orange kit."

"That's all he had to say? Nothing more?"

"Yes," Taliya lied, struggling to control any twitch or emotion.

"Thank the gods," he said with a huge sigh of relief. Then he hugged her to him so tightly she yelped a little bit. He laughed and released her. "I'm glad they're being practical about it. Are you hungry? Who am I kidding? You're always hungry these days. Two kits to support. I have something ready for you." He headed for the kitchen and started to set up the plate he had laid out there.

She joined him, sat at the island, and attempted to nibble on the treats he provided. Her stomach was still churning and not remotely interested in eating. She realized he was watching her closely. Things she could hide from a human, she couldn't hide from him.

"It's not that simple, is it," he said. "They're going to take them both away, so what does it really matter."

She reached for his hand across the island. "We have some time," she whispered. "If the war gets here before the kits are born, none of this will matter. They're letting them both live for now. That's all we needed."

He nodded, and she left it at that, letting go of his hand. She could imagine the rage he would fly into if he really knew what had happened in that office. There would be no force on earth to keep him from killing Narlin, not short of being killed himself. As much as she wanted to protect her unborn kits, she needed to protect her mate from himself. A strange look had come over his face.

"What?"

He moved around the island until he was close enough to touch her. He leaned down, put his hands on her arms, and whispered in her ear.

"Taliya, if the war gets here and we're freed . . ." He paused, uncharacteristically hesitant. "I'd like . . . I hope . . . When this is over, I hope *we* are not over." He rested his head on her shoulder and sighed.

His declaration and touch filled her with warmth and joy, much needed after the morning's disgust. She wrapped her arms around his waist and pulled him in close between her legs.

"I do too," she admitted.

"It's not just about being forced together anymore. I can't imagine my life without you now. I need you." He leaned back to face her. "You're my mate. I want it to stay that way. Us. Together."

"The two of us and our kits," she said with a smile. "Together."

He tensed a bit at that, but then he quickly relaxed again. Maybe he hadn't considered the fact that he would have to raise two kits in whatever world was left over after the war, assuming the war was even over just because they were freed.

"All of us, together," he agreed.

Chapter 12

The next week reduced Taliya to tears on a daily basis. She felt like a walking disaster zone. Just the sound of Kano chewing made her want to throw something against the beige walls of their cell. He wrote it off to hormones and kept her plied with naps and snacks—and ate sitting a bit farther away from her.

In contrast to her frenetic moods, Kano behaved like they were on the verge of escape any day. Now that they'd come to an agreement to stay together as mates outside of the bizarre breeding facility and there was the promise of rescue, he'd relaxed to the point it no longer seemed like they were captive at all. He helped her keep her balance when they did yoga, the roundness growing at her core making the whole thing extra tricky, and flopped on the sofa to watch TV like they were living in an apartment or on vacation.

The TV news never reported anything but the victories of Kerkaw's army, but both of them knew that wasn't to be trusted any more than any other government propaganda.

"What if they don't come in time?" Taliya whispered one afternoon as they lounged in their pajamas, watching the news program that took over every feed for an hour each day.

"Don't lose hope," he whispered back, keeping his voice lower than the TV so no one listening in could hear. "Whoever got the note to us, it must be someone inside here. A guard, maybe."

Taliya thought of Carl, who'd been so anxious about her private meeting with Narlin. He was the only guard to ever express anything but hatred. If it was Carl who was going to rescue them, he needed to get to it. She couldn't see any other way of avoiding Narlin's bargain. She only had two more days to stall, then she would have to deliver or suffer the consequences. Narlin would not like being turned down. Her compliance was assumed. If not, there would definitely be consequences beyond losing her kit. Would he really even let her keep one when it came down to it? She doubted it. But if she said no to the demands he had thrown down, what then? What would the punishment be? For her. For Kano. For her brothers. Maybe for all of them. Men like Narlin did not like to have their wishes denied, no matter how illegal and reprehensible.

"We have weeks now before we need to worry much," Kano said and reached over to rub her now very round belly.

In response, the two kits inside of her wriggled. Taliya gasped and sat bolt upright.

"What?" Kano jumped up too.

"They moved!"

Kano smiled. "Really?"

He started to put his hand back on her stomach, but she shook her head.

"I don't think you can feel it yet, but there was definitely something there. Like little butterflies flitting around. What a strange sensation."

She settled back on the sofa, and Kano leaned over to rest his head on her lap, facing her middle.

"Hello, little ones," he said tenderly.

Taliya felt her heart lurch, and she burst into tears. Again.

Please hurry. She sent out her plea to the universe. *Not just for me. I can survive an hour or so of whatever Narlin has in store. It's revolting, but I'll survive it.* But Kano? If he ever found out, would he be disgusted and turn away from her? Would he get himself killed to get even with Narlin? *I'm not really sure what Narlin will do about the orange kit, but I'm positive, if I cooperate, he'll make sure Kano finds out. I can feel it in my bones. Having me won't be enough. He has surely watched video footage of us together. Moments like this, right here. Us, all cozy and bonded. He'll want to rub it in and watch Kano react. It would give him an excuse to do something horrible.*

146

She hesitated. *Though Narlin wouldn't kill him. They need him even more than they need me. They need our kits.* She ran her fingers through the short mane on the side of Kano's face, and he sighed, snuggling into her lap. *There are many, many things worse than death. Please keep us safe from all of it.*

The night of the sixth day, Taliya couldn't sleep. Even the kits draining her energy wasn't enough. She lay in bed, staring at the ceiling, hoping for a miraculous rescue. Narlin would call for her in the morning, and she would have to go. Enthusiastically.

She swallowed firmly to keep from throwing up. It made her skin crawl just to have him touch her. Look at her. She thought back to their first meetings, when he'd been more subtle about his advances. That had been bad enough, but she'd had so little experience with males of any species at that point, she hadn't really understood the full impact of what he was suggesting.

Now she knew. Her face flushed, and she sat up quickly, not sure she could stop the gagging this time. Narlin didn't just want to invade her, have sex with her. He wanted . . . She wasn't really clear on what it was he wanted except to be cruel. Surely he could get sex wherever it was that unmarried men got sex. Was he even single? She had no idea. He was important in the human world. Partners couldn't be that hard to come

147

by. What about her interested him so much, especially if he felt the same way about Kano? Was it just a tigran fascination?

Flashes of intimate moments with her glorious mate raced through her mind. Wonderful moments. A glimpse of Narlin attempting any of it—demanding any of it from her—was too much. *What kind of monster manipulates another living being in such a horrible way?*

In a moment of clarity, she finally understood. It wasn't about the sex or where body parts went. It wasn't about pleasure and intimacy. It was about the horror, the terribleness of it. He wanted to break her, spirit and soul. He wanted to see her, the murderous tigran beast, submissive. Yielding to him and under his power. The sex part was just a vehicle to make it happen.

If she agreed to the whole of what Narlin was demanding, he would own her, more than the government could ever claim to. And after all that, would he really let her keep the orange kit, allow it to survive and live with them in captivity? She doubted it. At least not without more convincing. And he would still take the white one, no matter what.

She swung her legs over the side of the bed, both hands clutching her middle. Before the facility, she hadn't considered whether she ever even wanted kits of her own. She'd never expected to care this much, this quickly. They weren't even born yet, and she knew she would die for them. Maybe it was just instinct, but she knew it without question. If she would die for them, she would certainly submit to Narlin for them. She would do whatever it took to make him happy. Resolution settled within her, and she breathed deeply for the first time that week.

She would buy them time. Time for their heroic rescuers to arrive and free them all. When Narlin called for her in the morning, she would be washed and dressed and ready. She would pretend to Kano that everything was fine, that it was just a normal meeting with that disgusting human, and then she would do whatever was necessary.

Kano stirred next to her, possibly sensing her anxieties. She lay back down carefully and pulled the sheets up. Responding to her movements, Kano rolled toward her and snuggled her into his arms, the length of his body wrapping around hers. Taliya let herself be swallowed up in the warmth of his fur and the security of his embrace, and sleep finally overtook her.

There was a note waiting by the cell door when they left the bedroom in the morning. Kano picked it up before Taliya could reach it.

Be calm. There's nothing he'll suspect about a note from Narlin, unless that disgusting letch wrote something he shouldn't have. She struggled to control her breathing while Kano read the note. *Even Narlin wouldn't be fool enough to put his intentions in writing.*

"Narlin requests the honor of your presence at eleven this morning. What is it about that guy and eleven o'clock?" Kano tossed the note on the kitchen island.

"Maybe it's just the time slot for meeting with us specifically," she said casually as she picked up the note. *Did he really use those words: honor of your presence?* No, he hadn't. Kano was feeling sassy. It was just the standard warning notice to be ready for a guard to pick her up a few minutes before eleven.

"Do you think you can keep stalling him?" Kano asked.

She nodded and sat down at the island. "Yeah. I'll stall him."

Kano seemed pleased with that and set about the business of getting breakfast ready.

"Do you want your eggs fried or scrambled?" he asked, pulling a container from the cooler. When she hesitated, he laughed. "Maybe I'm asking the wrong tigran." He bent toward her belly. "Kits, how would you like your eggs this morning?"

Taliya forced a laugh at his sweetness, but it was hard to concentrate on eating. Only the aggressive demands from the kits gave her any appetite at all.

"They say fried would be lovely," she said. "And lots of bacon."

"At your service," he said with a flourish of the spatula.

As Kano prepared breakfast, Taliya fingered the edges of the note. Her determination from the wee hours of the night was quickly fading. Maybe she should tell Kano, let him be part of the decision. It impacted him, in more ways than one.

She knew that never in a million years would he agree to what Narlin wanted, what she was planning to do, but maybe he would know a way to get around Narlin. Was there someone higher up who could step in? Kano had been there a month longer than she had. It was possible he knew things she didn't.

"Who does Narlin report to?" she asked casually. "Does he have a boss in all of this nonsense? Someone must have assigned him the job of producing white kits."

Kano shrugged one shoulder without turning around. "I don't know. He's the only official sort of person I ever talked to. He met with me as soon as I arrived and told me why I was here. Why I was still alive." He paused and turned to face her. "He seemed to already know about you, somehow."

"What do you mean?"

"Since my wife was gone, he told me they had already selected a specific mate for me to improve the chances of producing white kits. Someone with the white DNA mutation in her genetic line. But they didn't capture you for over a month."

He turned back to the stovetop as Taliya processed that information. Of course the government would know all about her genetic history. They would have files and records all the way through her Generation: Number 11.

"Do you suppose they went looking for me once they had you captured?" she asked.

It had never occurred to her that she had been targeted specifically. All tigran were being rounded up. She was just one of thousands in America. Well, maybe hundreds at that point. She must have escaped just before they arrived.

"I guess it was around when you went into hiding," he said, placing her breakfast on the island in front of her.

Had that been the reason for the rush? Her family had put some plans in place before, but the actual night of the fleeing had been sudden. Thanksgiving Day. Unexpected. Mother had just announced that the helpers would be there in an hour. Her brothers had been whisked off just as quickly, without warning. *Did Mother know they were coming for me? Did she know about all of this?* Taliya poked at her eggs. *I wish she'd warned me.*

But would it really have made all those weeks of hiding any easier if she'd known the Enforcers were looking for her specifically? How could she even have imagined this place and what went on here? It would have been too complicated to explain to the naive Taliya who'd left her home that night over three months ago. Would she have behaved any differently when the Enforcers arrived if she knew they wanted to take her alive? *I'd have killed them all,* she thought with a low growl.

Kano stopped his cooking and looked over at her questioningly. "What's wrong?"

"Nothing. Not really. Just processing the idea that my mother might have known about this setup and what went on here, that they wanted me for breeding, and never told me."

"You think she should have?" he asked, sitting down next to her with his own plate.

"I don't know." She smiled and took a bite of egg. "I probably wouldn't have believed her. I mean, come on. Who out in the world would believe the government was secretly breeding a species they claimed to be trying to destroy? It's all too crazy."

Kano nodded. "I didn't really believe it when I arrived." He paused, took a few bites, and then played with his eggs uncomfortably.

Neither of them spoke for a solid minute.

"I'm sorry I can't protect you more," he said. "From this place. From Narlin."

"Kano, I came to a conclusion last night. The things that Narlin says and does, they're all about power and control. Nothing else. He just wants to feel dominant over creatures that are bigger and stronger than he is."

Kano nodded, then he frowned, his whiskers flexing and the black dots on his forehead shifting downward between his blue eyes.

"Why were you thinking about any of that *last night*? Has something happened?" He reached over and picked up the note, considering it in light of their conversation and not looking pleased. A growl rumbled up from his throat, followed by a snarl and a hiss. "Taliya? What do you know about this meeting today?"

Before she could answer, there was a knock on the door. They both froze, and she looked at the clock.

"It's only nine? What could that be about?"

153

The door swung open, and they both turned to face it. Two guards entered, and Taliya recognized Carl as one of them.

"Narlin is ready for you, Taliya," Carl said, his face contorted in anger.

Kano rose. "Why don't I come with her this time?" he said, surely sensing Carl's emotions and knowing this was no ordinary meeting. "If there are any decisions to be made about the kits, I'd like to be part of it."

Carl's face contorted even more, which Taliya didn't think possible.

"No," Carl said flatly. "Just Taliya."

A tremor ran down her spine, and Kano turned toward her, reading her reaction.

"What's going on?" he growled.

"It will be fine, Kano," she whispered. "I'll handle it. Don't do anything to get yourself hurt or punished. Promise me."

His hackles rose, and he grabbed his plate, smashing it against the kitchen wall with a tiger-like roar that terrified her. The gun-toting guards even stepped back in surprise.

"No!" he roared at her. "You are staying right here!"

"Kano, please."

She tried to grab him, but he broke free and stalked over to the guards, who took another step back, unsure of his intentions.

"I'll go," he said. "Leave her here and take me down to Narlin instead. That will make him even happier. Whatever she has agreed to—"

Carl stood his ground. "Kano, don't do this. Taliya is the one he wants to see. Only Taliya."

Kano stared the guard down, fists clenching and unclenching, claws slipping in and out.

"Please, Kano." Taliya moved to stand behind him. She gently placed one hand on his back against the crinkle of his raised fur. "Don't try to fight this. It won't help."

He turned to face her, eyes flashing. She could feel his heart racing and the rasping in his breath. He was more than just angry. She sensed fear and frustration simmering under all the rage that was visible to the guards and cameras watching the scene unfold.

"If you try to stop this," she said quietly, "they will just lock you up and take you away from me. Don't give them an excuse to separate us until the kits are born. Together, remember?"

She felt his posture slacken some, and he nodded.

"Why are you here so early?" she said to Carl, looking around past Kano. "I'm not ready yet."

"Narlin said your visit needed to be moved up. He has other things to see to later. You can come as you are now. It won't matter." His voice trailed off at the end, and his eyes shifted away from her in what seemed like shame. Then he cleared his throat and set his shoulders in a strange way that Taliya couldn't interpret.

"Kano." He waited until both tigran were facing him before continuing. "Maybe Narlin will want to see you later, but there are visitors arriving this afternoon. A large group of visitors. Narlin wasn't expecting them to arrive today, so he will be quite busy."

Something about the intensity of Carl's eyes struck Taliya as odd. It reminded her of what Kano had said about his talks with Narlin. The words were nothing special, but something about the way they were being said led her to think there was more to it. She sensed a deep emotion radiating from Carl. What was it? Fear? Maybe. Excitement? Definitely. The guard was terrified but highly anticipating those afternoon visitors. If Carl was their inside source, and the visitors had him excited . . .

Kano slipped his hand into hers and squeezed. She looked up into his eyes and saw the fire there. He had read the message the same way she had. Help was coming. Today.

Should I pretend to be sick? How can I stall?

Carl watched the two tigran and said, "I am under orders to bring Taliya without delay. Narlin will not hear any excuses."

The other guard started to move forward, ready to deal with resistance to the order. She squeezed Kano's hand and then let go, stepping away from him and past Carl.

"We'd better get going, then," she said, taking the hotwire from the other guard and putting it over her head.

Kano made a sharp noise behind her, something rather like a whimper, and she turned back to him.

"It will be all right. Stay here. I'll be back soon."

Without waiting for him to respond, she stalked out the door, the guards double-stepping to catch up and flank her after locking the door behind them. As she marched down the long white hallway, Taliya heard the crashing of dishes, pans being slammed into the wall, and the screams of a tiger—a sound of unbridled rage. Whoever was watching the monitors was getting quite a show.

She couldn't worry about Kano now. It was game time.

Chapter 13

It was all good and well to believe help was coming—was literally on the way—but it did her no good that morning. Unless Carl had some miracle up his sleeve, she was going to be locked up alone with an expectant Narlin. Refusing him, planning on rescue to save them from his wrath, was a massive risk.

How far am I willing to go to resist him? She imagined sinking her teeth into his jugular, warm blood dripping down onto her fur. Raking her claws across his pale, pathetic, furless face, scratching the smug smile off him. As enchanting as all that would be, doubt circled in her mind.

But what if I'm wrong? What if rescue wasn't what Carl was talking about at all?

Was that a chance she was willing to take?

When they exited the elevator, Carl and the other guard led her in the opposite direction of Narlin's office. She hesitated for a second and looked back at the normal route.

"Narlin has a special, private meeting planned for you today," the other guard said in such a gleeful way that Taliya had no doubt he knew exactly what was on the agenda. Carl made a noise in his throat that reminded her of Kano's small growls of annoyance and shifted his shoulders uncomfortably as she turned to follow them.

They both know. They're both fully aware of what's waiting for me, and they're taking me anyhow. How many times have they made this sad walk with some female prisoner? She paused that thought and reconsidered. Clearly, Narlin wasn't limited in his lecherous designs. If victory and submission were really the endgame, Kano would be a more satisfying conquest. Would he rather have Kano?

They stopped in front of what looked like every other office door along the hallway. The second guard knocked three times, and the door swung open before he'd pulled his fist away.

"What took you so long?" Narlin snapped, faced flushed. "I sent you up there fifteen minutes ago."

"Apologies, Colonel Narlin," Carl said. "We were earlier than she'd expected, and Taliya was still completing her breakfast. I knew you'd want to make sure the kits were cared for and that their mother was provided the necessary nutrition."

Narlin tugged on the tunic he was wearing, probably annoyed but knowing he shouldn't contradict that logical statement. He wasn't in uniform. Taliya suspected that was a very bad sign for her. Private suite and casual dress—this meeting was off the books, and no one would know about it except these two guards. Her throat tightened, but she forced her body to relax and look at ease.

"Sorry," she said. "The kits are demanding when it comes to food."

"Fine," Narlin said, though he seemed calmed by the fact that she didn't look angry or threatening.

"There isn't much time for this appointment, Colonel Narlin," Carl said. "We anticipate the arrival of our visitors within an hour or two."

That definitely caught Narlin's attention, but she wondered if the comment was meant for him or if it was really a coded message to her.

Maybe I don't have to stall for that long. But how long? He's going to be in a hurry. The repulsive thought came to her that at least it would be quick. If she couldn't hold him off, at least the deed would be done in haste. No chance to linger. Part of her was surprised he hadn't just let it go, stopped worrying about her, in the face of what must be armed forces headed their way. He was one determined son of a bitch, and he wasn't going to be easily dissuaded. She shuddered at the thought, and Carl shifted next to her.

"Are you ready, Taliya?" Narlin said. "Don't walk through this door if you're going to give me trouble."

The second guard snickered, and Carl shot him a dirty look.

"I'm here, aren't I?" she said, knowing that didn't exactly answer his question.

He nodded to the guards, and the second one shoved her roughly through the door. She felt rage flow from Carl as she staggered into Narlin's arms.

"Now, now," Narlin said, catching her and helping her gain her balance, "don't damage the merchandise. This lovely tigran is carrying a priceless white kit. Well, not *priceless*, I guess, but worth more than either of you earn in a lifetime."

He glared at the guards and then slammed the door in their faces.

"Right this way," he said, bowing and motioning toward a massive bed.

Looking around the room, Taliya realized it was barely even private quarters. No kitchen. No media wall or technology or surveillance hum at all. Just a couple of chairs, a sofa, and the bed. A door in one wall to a bathroom stood slightly ajar. *This isn't even his room. It's just a place he can bring prisoners for his "special" meetings.*

Narlin pulled his tunic off over his head, revealing a pasty chest covered with only a smattering of black and gray hair. He was fit enough for a middle-aged human, she supposed, but nothing compared to her Kano. When she didn't move, he walked over to the bed and sat down, patting the gaudy red bedspread next to him.

"Come join me, and let's complete the negotiations for your kit's life, shall we?"

Surprised by this bluntness, she didn't make a move toward him.

"Taliya!" he barked, startling her. "I don't have time for coyness. Get over here or get out."

Stall. I have to stall. "You took me by surprise, sending the guards early. I didn't really have a chance to prepare." He looked unimpressed, but she thought of another tactic she could try. "I didn't have a chance to finish discussing your offer with Kano."

Narlin straightened up. "You've told Kano about this?"

It was hard to determine if he was scared or angry about that turn of events. Some humans were a tricky lot to interpret, especially when they were so used to lying that fabricating a new one didn't even register in their conscious. Mother had called them sociopaths. She'd advised Taliya never to trust what you intuit from a diseased human. Watching Narlin now, she understood, but he was clearly disappointed. She could read that in the slump of his shoulders. So she'd been right that he would hold whatever happened as more leverage over her—visit again or I'll tell Kano. *Well, that ship has sailed.*

"What did Kano advise you to do?" he asked.

She sensed another wave of emotion from him but couldn't translate it.

"As I said, we didn't have time to finish discussing it, but he was . . . well, it sounded like he was furious when I left. Yelling and smashing things. You should watch the video footage from our room."

He flinched at that. So she poked at the topic a bit more.

"He offered to come to this meeting instead of me."

Narlin flushed red from his waist to his scalp, and she knew she'd found a weakness. Maybe Kano was right. *And you're second choice, Taliya dear.* Maybe it was an inclination for males, or maybe it was just the desire to cow a creature as impressive as Kano into submission—not about sexual preference at all. Dominance over her wouldn't be nearly as exciting. Tigran were stronger than humans, but Narlin was a decent specimen. Without the fangs and claws on her side, it was a reasonably fair fight. But against Kano?

"Kano is a remarkable tigran, in every way," she said, observing his reaction. "I'm grateful to have been paired with him. It has certainly made the experience more enjoyable."

A blast of testosterone hit her, and Narlin's nostrils flared in his still flushed face. If she could just switch his focus long enough, she might be able to weasel her way out of this.

"Why didn't you let him come in your place?" Narlin asked, clenching his hands in his lap and radiating agitation.

"Your guards wouldn't allow it. They said you wanted me, and only me."

He hesitated and glanced at the clock, seeming to consider if there was a way to adjust his plan.

"Of course," she said, "Kano would gladly have come in my place. Or maybe have joined me in the negotiations. He is a very devoted mate."

She couldn't miss Narlin's reaction to the idea of Kano joining them, could all but watch the wheels in his demented brain sorting through the risks and benefits of taking the time to call for Kano and renegotiating. He sighed.

"Sadly, there's no time for that. Maybe next time."

Next time? "As I understood it, this was a one-time deal. Once. I was to come to you, here, like this, *once*. But hearing you say things like that makes me wonder if I can trust you to hold up your end of the bargain. What possible guarantee can I have that you would spare one of my kits and let me keep it?"

Narlin apparently felt the morning's activities slipping out of his control. He rose and walked back to her at the door.

"Taliya, what guarantee would you want? You know it would be impossible to put anything in writing." She stood like a statue as he placed his hands on either side of her arms, taking her in. Eyeing her up and down. He hesitated at the obvious bump in her midsection, but it didn't seem to deter him. "You'll just have to trust me," he said with a sly smile. "It will be an agreement between the two of us. Yes?"

"No," she said before she'd even really considered it. "No deal."

He dropped his hands, and his smile was replaced with a glower. "No?"

"No. I don't trust you, and we do not have a deal. Please return me to my cell."

It was a huge risk, refusing and counting on rescue to protect her, but it was also true that she didn't believe his promises.

He huffed and paced across the room. "So you don't care about your kits at all? There's no instinctive maternal behavior in your tiger genetics? Even an animal will die protecting her kits."

"If I knew it would save them, I would do anything, but I don't believe you."

Her heart pounded in her chest, and the kits inside of her fluttered, sensing the adrenalin rush in her system. If Narlin wasn't careful, her fight or flight instinct might kick in, and flight was not in her nature. Her claws extended and retracted involuntarily as he paced in front of her, probably considering what threats to make. She was going to have to control herself. Unless help arrived—and she could be sure of it—there were still others to consider. Kano. Her brothers. Her unborn kits.

Narlin stopped in front of her and suddenly stepped up and grabbed her roughly around the waist in a weird hug. Her arms were pinned, but she could easily free them. Instead, she waited for his next move. He buried his nose in the fur of her neck, ignoring the hotwire, and inhaled loudly.

"You smell fabulous," he mumbled.

She turned her head away and did not return the compliment. He smelled as sour as most humans, but with an even sicklier sweetness. Her skin twitched with the desire to kill him, get him off her, no matter the cost. He leaned back and looked her in the eyes. He had to look up at her, which would have been humorous if it wasn't for the rest of the fiasco. *Is he trying to woo me? Be sexy?* He must have sensed her resistance, the tautness of her body, and his face shifted.

"Oh, Taliya," he said, releasing her and taking a small step back. "I don't really need your consent. It would be more fun that way. More enjoyable for both of us. But you can just lie there like a lump if you must. Once you walked in this door, the die was cast. Wouldn't it be more pleasant if you cooperated?"

"The guards brought me here. That was not a choice."

He shrugged one shoulder and walked back to the bed. Flipping back the bedspread, he motioned grandly.

"Come here and lie down. We're running out of time."

Still, she didn't move, and she watched as his entire being shifted into anger and frustration. Alarm bells went off in her head. An angry human was a dangerous human. They rarely made smart decisions when they were angry.

"You have ten seconds," he said, "to get your furry ass over here."

"Or else?"

He tipped his head and smiled—or a terrifying facsimile of a smile.

"As they say, there's more than one way to skin a cat, my kitty friend."

He stood, opened a drawer in the bedside table, and pulled out a long black rod with two metal prongs on the end. Once he'd made sure she'd seen it, he pressed a button on the rod and an electric current crackled between the two prongs. Her skin tingled at the charge in the air.

"There are ways to even the odds when wrangling an animal," he said. "I have the remote in my pocket, but that hotwire is too strong. It could knock you unconscious. This is a good old-fashioned cattle prod. If it could make six hundred pounds of stupid bovine behave, I'm sure it can work on you."

He smirked at her and ran the current through the rod twice more. Panic roiled in her stomach.

"Maybe I should add," he said, "that you need not be conscious, if it comes to that."

That got her hackles up, and the seriousness of his threats really struck home.

"If you use that on me, I could well lose these kits. Both of them."

He shrugged and stepped toward her. "Then you'd just make a couple more in a week or two."

The change from his preoccupation with the white kit struck her as odd until she realized the breeding program was likely about to come to a grinding halt. If the guests arriving soon were who she suspected they were, he no longer gave a rat's ass about her kits. He was going to rape her, conscious or unconscious, before the war kicked in his door.

She took a step backward toward the exit. Maybe Carl would be ready to help now.

"Bad kitty," Narlin said. "It's locked, but if you make any noise to worry the guards, I will have no choice but to make you be quiet. Which way is this going to go?"

Never in her life had she been at such an impasse. She could not let him use that electric prod on her. The risk to the kits was too great. He might no longer care about them, but she still did. *Do I really want to let him knock me out and have no control over what happens?* Not knowing what took place did have its benefits, but she wondered if she had seen the limits of his depravity. Would he become a bit unhinged if allowed free rein over her unconscious body? *Would he intentionally hurt the kits when I couldn't stop him?* In her gut, she thought he might. She held up her hands, like he was holding a gun on her.

"Fine," she said. "I'd rather remain conscious. I won't give you any trouble, but I'm not going to be *enthusiastic* either."

He lowered the cattle prod. "I can live with that."

Her stomach flipped at just the thought of his disgusting, pale, furless body rubbing up against hers, but she knew there was no getting out of what lay ahead. She nodded and walked toward the bed.

"You will need to remove all of your clothes," he said. "I don't want any impediments."

Her tail lashed and she stopped. *How can I do this? How can I . . . let him win?* If she hadn't believed that was Narlin's main objective, it was certainly clear now. How much pleasure could there be with a partner who had quite literally promised just to lie there and not participate at all? He just wanted to claim this one victory, log it as a conquest, before he had to run for the hills. She couldn't imagine him standing and fighting in the battle to come. That brought a fantastic image to mind: Narlin fleeing in terror before the rebel army.

"Get your clothes off, Taliya," he said in choppy, growling words, sounding a bit like a tigran himself. "Now!"

She spun to face him and threw a growl/hiss back at him in return, fangs bared. That interrupted his bravado, and he took a step back. But then he smiled and tapped the cattle prod against his free hand.

"Oh, so this is going to get interesting, is it?" he said, spinning the cattle prod like an old-time cop with a nightstick, clearly relishing the prospect of violence. "Kitty wants to play?"

She swallowed the bile that was building up in her throat and extended her claws. Her parents may have raised her to be civilized, but she'd already let her wild nature loose once.

"This is no game, Narlin."

"Oh, pretty girl, that's where you're wrong. It's been a game since the moment I heard they'd captured you. We'd been hunting you for weeks, but once you were under my power, there was no other conclusion than this moment right here. I was rather hoping you gave Kano a difficult time. That would have been delightful to watch. Or to help . . . resolve. Of course,

I've watched you two together many, many times. But right now, you're mine, one way or another."

As they squared off against each other, Taliya felt a vibration under her feet. Narlin didn't seem to notice it, and she tried not to let it distract her, but there was definitely something happening somewhere around the building. Eyeing Narlin for any sign of movement, any indication of attack with the cattle prod or the hotwire, she dug her claws into the carpet and felt for other clues. The vibrations reminded her of a large machine, like the old-style pickup trucks sometimes used on the dirt roads near her home. Or larger merchandise transports, like the kind she'd escaped in. Whatever it was, it was growing stronger.

It's them. The army. They're here.

She blinked slowly and then focused on her foe. Her claws extended fully with a pop she felt along both arms—a solid Wolverine snikt, like in the old comic books—and she growled deep in her throat before spitting another hiss/growl/hiss. Narrowing her vision to only what was in front of her, she prepared for attack. It might have been her imagination, but Narlin shifted and seemed to reconsider.

"If anything happens to me, Taliya, you and everyone you love will pay."

The vibrations under her feet grew stronger, and there was a rumbling boom from somewhere outside the building. Narlin hesitated. Nothing about his body language had changed, but there was a distinct aroma of panic in the air around him.

"Time's up," she said. "There's only one creature in this room who has anything to pay for."

Another booming explosion echoed from outside the building, and the *schwep* of laser gunfire sounded even closer, possibly inside. Narlin turned to check the door, and that was her cue.

House cats are notorious for playing with their prey— enjoying the chase as much as the victory, rather like Narlin had been. Skilled hunters count on one effective and incapacitating strike, quick and decisive. If the prey can react or try to defend itself, the hunter could be hurt as well. Despite her human DNA, Taliya had the instinct of thousands of generations of tigers in her blood. Seeing her chance, she didn't falter or fuss. Taliya was no house cat.

Before Narlin could turn back or even noticed a twitch from her, she leaped and made one swipe of her claws across his hairless neck—raking bits of skin free, muscles and tendons snapping under her claws before she spun away. Jetting sprays of blood sailed through the air, and the cattle prod thudded to the ground as she crouched just out of range.

Narlin stood there for a moment, blood flooding down his chest and a shocked look on his face, arms dangling limply. With each heartbeat, new squirts of blood erupted from his gaping throat. Then his eyes rolled back in his head and he crumpled to the floor sideways, rolling onto his back. She kicked the cattle prod out of reach and hovered over him, watching the blood seep into the beige carpet in a dark circle around him. His eyes stared blankly at her, and the tangy odor of his blood assaulted her senses—along with the distinct aroma of urine.

"Can you see me, you son of a bitch? Game over, Narlin dear."

Focusing on his heartbeat, she waited until she heard it slow, slow, slower—the arterial spray of his life force growing weaker and weaker—and then stop. The color had already left his face, and she knew it was over.

Narlin was dead.

But it was too soon to let the adrenaline stop. She used the bedspread to wipe her hand and claws clean of skin and blood, but that wasn't enough to get his smell off. She rushed to the bathroom and scrubbed her hands vigorously in the sink with soap. Then she pulled the hotwire over her head, threw it on the bed, and stalked to the door to lean her ear against it.

The sound of gunfire continued, with scattered booms, maybe bombs, but what immediately caught her attention was the sound of running boots thumping on the carpeted floors. Should she wait or try to escape on her own? She needed to find her brothers. That was her first goal once she figured out how to get out of the disgusting liaison chamber. She felt around the edges of the door for any weaknesses. It opened in, toward her, so sheer force, slamming into it, wasn't going to work. She ran her hands along the pegs in the hinges, but they didn't budge.

A thud vibrated through the door, and Taliya jumped back. Another thud and then the crash of the lock giving way in a shower of splinters that made her leap aside.

Carl stood in the doorway, gun leveled.

Chapter 14

Carl scanned the room and spotted her. Then he noticed Narlin's body on the floor in a wide circle of blood. Taliya braced herself. What if she'd been wrong about Carl?

"Well done," he said with a smile, lowering the laser gun. "Sorry about busting in. I didn't know the code for this room. You and Kano got my note?"

She nodded, relief tingling through every hair on her body.

"Good. Then you know what's happening."

"Are they really here? Is this the end of it?"

A boom vibrated the floor and the walls around them.

"It should be the end of this facility at least. We need to get you out of here. Dying in friendly fire at this point would be quite a waste."

She followed him through the door and then both paused, scanning the hallway.

"I need to get my brothers," she said, her heart racing, pounding in her head. Another explosion rattled the glass in the windows and vibrated up her spine.

"Don't worry about that," Carl said. "They'll get everyone in the cells, but we need to be clear of this part of the facility. This is where they'll be focusing the attack—on the offices and Enforcer's quarters. It's definitely not safe here for long."

Movement caught her eye, and she spun to react, claws at the ready. It was another guard, but Carl seemed to know him and remained calm. He was escorting a creature she'd never seen before—another feline/human species experiment like her, probably a lion mix, with tawny fur from top to bottom. She was wearing green slacks and had a matching tunic clutched across her bare furry chest.

"All clear on your end?" Carl asked the other guard.

He nodded a quick affirmative. "Knocked him out. Let the troops figure out what to do with him."

"This is Dan," Carl said, motioning to the other guard. "You can trust him. Dan, this is Taliya."

Dan gave her a quick nod, and then the body on the floor in the room behind them caught his eye.

"Well, Taliya, guess they won't have to worry about Narlin." Dan glanced at her and then the creature next to him. "This is Kallie."

The two females made eye contact for a moment, but Kallie quickly dropped hers to the ground. Taliya touched her arm gently and then drew her back into the privacy of the room while the guards assessed the situation. Kallie gasped at the sight of Narlin on the floor, then used her tunic to cover her mouth and block the stench from her sensitive nose.

"Slip your top on," Taliya said. "We need to be ready to run."

Kallie did as she was told, but she trembled from head to toe and kept glancing over at Narlin's body.

"It's all right," Taliya assured her. "He's long dead."

Without warning, Kallie grabbed Taliya in a hug that took her breath away.

"Have they come for us?" she whispered. "Are we really going to be free?"

Taliya gave her a strong hug in return. "That's what Carl says. But we need to get out of here before we're caught in the battle."

Kallie nodded and pulled away, smoothing her tunic over her flat stomach. With a tentative smile, she reached over and put a hand on Taliya's bulging belly.

"Kits?"

"Yes. Two."

"Oh, such blessings. And they will be free now."

Taliya let that idea wash over her for a moment, but she didn't want to get too ahead of herself. They were far from in the clear.

"Do you have offspring we need to locate?" she asked Kallie.

"No, no. Liran are sterile. They could never correct that defect. The only liran that exist are the ones they've created. That's why they use us like they do. A rare and special treat."

Taliya felt her skin crawl. Of course, that's why Kallie was in this part of the facility, half dressed. Why the sight of Narlin terrified her. Some other human had been abusing her. And it sounded like it wasn't the first time. Taliya glanced over at Narlin, tempted to slash him up a bit more.

Kallie laughed weakly. "I've never been so happy to see the colonel in all of my life. I love what you've done with him. Much better."

The females exchanged smiles as Carl peeked in through the door. "Ready?"

They both nodded and followed him out as another explosion rocked the building. Taliya had to actually check her balance, and her sensitive ears rang. *That one was close.* Carl and Dan both pulled out large orange bandannas and took turns tying them onto each other's upper right arm.

"If you see a guard with one of these," Carl said, "it should mean you can trust them. They're with the rescue operation. But be careful. The Enforcers may figure that out quickly and set themselves up. Use your instinct."

Carl headed back toward the elevator, and they all followed. Taliya noticed an odd look exchanged between Kallie and Dan, but she didn't have time to worry about it.

"We've already got two guards down in the dungeon to handle things there," Carl said as they jogged along. "Our job is to clear this administration side and get you out to safety. As far as I know, you and Kallie are the only ones over here today. Most of the military leaders have already run off since we had the intel on this attack."

Why did Narlin stay? Taliya wondered as they hustled down the hallway. *Was he so desperate to conquer me that he risked death or capture?* She winced and picked up the pace, hoping there were more humans like Carl and Dan and fewer like Narlin and whoever had been pawing at Kallie.

The guards hesitated at the elevator. They mumbled something between themselves that Taliya couldn't hear, her ears still ringing from the explosion. Dan headed for a door a dozen yards away, and the others followed. He used a pass card to open the door and revealed a flight of stairs.

They must have decided the elevator was too dangerous with explosions going off all over the place.

The guards thundered up the steps without explanation, and the females padded on bare feet after them to the next level, where the pass card allowed them onto another office floor. Taliya hated the idea that there were so many humans, so many possibly violent humans, who had been taking advantage of the creatures in their cells.

"Stay here," Carl said as another explosion sounded outside.

Taliya and Kallie waited near the door to the stairwell as

Carl and Dan hurried in opposite directions to check all of the rooms on that floor. They didn't find anyone, though Taliya did enjoy watching them kick in a locked door here and there. The guards met back in the middle.

"All clear," Dan said. "Let's get these ladies out of here."

Kallie giggled at the term, and Taliya smiled, despite the anxiety of the situation. They all raced back down the stairs to the main floor, and Dan opened the door slowly, clearly ready for any trouble that might be waiting. Assured it was safe, he led the group to the outside exit. He swung the door open, gun at the ready, and a wave of freezing air washed over them. How long had it been since she'd smelled outside air? Inhaling deeply, Taliya hoped for the odor of trees and earth. Instead, she was blasted with the acrid smells of artillery and the vile stink of panicked humans, but among all those odors was also the familiar smell of tigran. She glanced at Kallie and reached over to take her hand. Kallie squeezed hers in return.

Deciding it was safe, Dan and Carl flanked the females and rushed them through the knee-deep snow, across the open field between the building and forest surrounding it. All four of them slogged along as quickly as they could. Taliya desperately wished she had a gun. Many a warm summer afternoon had been spent at the shooting range of a neighbor, and she was an excellent shot. But she wouldn't even know for sure who was friend or foe around them at that moment. Carl seemed to have a plan, so she tucked in close to him.

Before they had gone far, they met two more guards with orange wraps on their arms. One of them said something to Dan, but Taliya couldn't hear it through the series of explosions and gunfire behind them. She and Kallie both ducked down. The motion turned Taliya so she was facing back toward the main building, and she gasped at the stream of creatures being led out by four rebel guards. Tigran, like her. Liran, like Kallie. Some that must be a kind of mix with a leopard or other spotted cat, maybe fifty of them. She didn't see any young ones. Her brothers weren't there. She didn't recognize any of the tigran. And she didn't see Kano's distinctive white coat or any other white tigran. Was he the only one they had?

She jumped at a hand on her back, but it was only Carl, getting her up so they could move along. Kallie was now sobbing, so Taliya wrapped an arm around her to support her steps as they staggered along, creating a trail in the snow. Taliya was grateful it wasn't too deep, though her bare feet were freezing and her pant legs were sloppy and wet.

"My sister," Kallie choked out. "I didn't see my sister."

"I didn't see my mate or my brothers. There must be more than one group. Just keep moving until we get to wherever they're taking us. It'll be okay."

She wasn't at all sure it would be okay, wasn't sure there was more than one group, but having Kallie collapse or run off looking for her sister wouldn't help any of them. They should consider themselves lucky if they made it to safety without accidentally being shot or blown up.

Dan and Carl hesitated. Several guards, no orange to be seen, blocked their path.

"Step away from the prisoners!" one of them shouted.

Dan and Carl squared their shoulders and leveled their guns. Taliya yowled, hissed, and yowled again, not even sure why except for the rage she felt flashing in the air around her.

"It's over, Stan," Carl said. "Get out of here before you get shot."

"I should say the same to you," Stan said. "Leave the prisoners and run. Unless you want them for yourselves. Looks like some prime specimens you have there. Either way, you've proven yourself to be a shit of a traitor, so I may as well shoot you now and get it over with. Kerkaw will never let you see another day of freedom in your life."

Dan and Carl did not run or make any move to abandon them, and Taliya hugged Kallie close to her. She could feel footsteps all around. Smatterings of gunfire. Soldiers were running from side to side and back again, mostly with orange tied on their arms. Seemed to be more friends than foes, though several were dead in the snow, bloodstains spattered around them.

At the sound of shots close by, she turned back in time to see all four opposing soldiers twitch and fall to the ground, though neither Dan nor Carl had fired. Behind the now either dead or badly wounded soldiers was a group of tigran, all armed and looking very proud of themselves.

"All right, then," Carl said with a nod to the tigran. "Forward we go."

They ran, circling around the fallen men and the bloody snow, and didn't stop until they reached the shelter of the forest around the facility, where a military setup awaited. Carl passed Taliya and Kallie into the hands of two female tigran in rebel army uniforms, then he and Dan headed back out onto the battlefield. A soldier stepped out of the trees near them and aimed a rocket launcher at the forest on the far side of the building. With a *shewp*, he fired the artillery into the air. Moments later, the ground shook with the impact blast of the shell as the soldier loaded another rocket.

"It's okay now. It's okay now," Taliya heard one of the tigran saying to Kallie, pulling her attention away from the battle. "I think she's in shock," she called to someone up ahead, a human doctor with a bright-red cross on her uniform. They led Kallie away into the trees.

"I'm Sonya," the other tigran said to Taliya. "You're safe now."

"I'm Taliya," she said.

Sonya's gaze shifted down to the bulge under her tunic. Taliya reflexively clasped her hands across it.

"Guess we should get you to medical as well, yes?" Sonya said.

"I think the kits are fine. I feel fine. I need to find my brothers."

"How many?"

"Two. Twins. They're only five."

Sonya considered this, glancing around at the variety of other species.

"I haven't seen any groups of young ones like that yet," she said. "We started at the top floors, where the older captives were, so they could help us with the rest of the escape. I'm sure we can reunite your family once they're freed."

"My mate, then. I should find him."

"Where was he being held?" Sonya asked.

"We were together, on the twentieth floor. But I wasn't with him when the attack began. I was down on the main floor."

Sonya stiffened at that news and growled in her throat. Taliya shrugged.

"That doesn't matter now," she said. "I took care of him when I knew help was here."

That seemed to please Sonya immensely, which made Taliya smile.

"My mate's name is Kano. He should be easy to find. He's white."

"White? A *white* tigran?"

"Yes."

Sonya considered this and then glanced at Taliya's middle again.

"We need to find him and get you both the hell out of here. You're too valuable for them to give up without a fight."

"Taliya!" A familiar voice called from somewhere behind her.

Both of them turned and saw Kano running toward them, snow flying around him, blue eyes fierce. Taliya rushed to meet him and leaped into his arms.

"Oh gods," he whispered into her furry neck, clutching her to him. "I'm sorry. I'm sorry they didn't get here in time. But I think we're safe now. You're safe."

"I was able to stall," she assured him, meeting his eyes. "I was able to fight."

"Fight?"

"He's dead, Kano. I slashed his throat wide open and watched him die."

He sagged in her arms, relief flowing from him. Certainly relief for her, but most likely relief over the end of Narlin as well. Kano carried his own baggage of that repulsive human.

"They want us to leave," she said. "Now, before we can be recaptured. I hate to go without my brothers, but Sonya says they'll find me and get them to me. The young ones haven't come out yet."

Kano hesitated. Swallowed hard. "I can't leave until that happens."

"Taliya! Let's go!" Sonya called.

They turned and saw her climbing into a huge military transport vehicle, much more modern than the old truck that had secreted Taliya to her hiding place weeks ago. It was ready to whisk them away. Taliya grabbed Kano's hand and headed for Sonya, but Kano pulled her back.

"I can't. Not yet," he said.

"Why not? Sonya knows how much the humans want us and our kits. We've got to get away from here."

"You go now. I'll catch up with you wherever we're headed."

She froze. "You said we were going to stay together. Us and the kits. You said—"

"It's not that. You're my mate. I promise I will find you. There's nowhere they can hide you that I won't find you. But I can't leave until the young ones are free."

She stared into his eyes, trying to understand, wanting to go, hearing Sonya calling for them to hurry.

"Taliya, I *can't* go yet. I can't leave . . . I can't leave without my daughter."

Chapter 15

Taliya whoofed, the shock of what Kano had said rippling through her. *Daughter? What in the hell is he talking about?*

"I'm sorry I never told you," he said, taking hold of both her hands, her claws extended in shock. "I didn't know if it would ever matter."

"How could it not matter that you have a daughter somewhere in this horrible place?" Taliya's knees nearly buckled under her. "Is she white? Gods, are they breeding her?"

He shook his head. "She's too young. She's only two."

"Two?! Two years old and alone in this place?"

"They have a nursery, for the kits. Narlin threatened many times to sell her, and he could have, but I don't think so. He said she was still here, that I could see her when our first white kit was born."

He'd said they had leverage on him, she just never imagined it was that bad. Brothers were one thing, but a kit? A little daughter? The strain of that was too much for her to really imagine. She rested one hand on her belly, knowing well what she was capable of to protect two kits she'd never even met.

"And yes, she's white," he added. "She's the proof I can produce white offspring."

"And she's terribly valuable."

"Yes. I can't leave without her. Not until I see she's safe and can be sure she gets away before someone else gets ideas. We don't know these soldiers. Think of the value of a white tigran kit who's too young to fight and easily manipulated or tricked. Anyone here could have designs on her for any number of reasons, some of which I try not to think about. I have to wait for her, but you go with them now. We'll catch up. I'll try to find your brothers as well."

"No." She shook her head, looking back at the tall building. "We'll stay together. I won't leave without my brothers. And you won't leave without your daughter. We're a family, and I won't risk not being able to find each other again."

She could see he wanted to argue but knew she was right.

"Taliya!" Sonya called again, giving a hand to the last of the creatures loading into the truck. "Let's go!"

Taliya led Kano over to Sonya and the waiting transport. She could see Kallie inside, flanked by two liran females who were soothing her with hugs and quiet words. Hopefully one of them was her sister.

"Take this group without us," Taliya said. "We're going to wait for the young ones."

"Are you crazy?" Sonya said. "Things are going our way now, but it could turn at any time."

"All the more reason for us to wait," Kano said. "We need to see them with our own eyes and be sure they make it to safety. We can't just run off and abandon them."

An explosion echoed from the far side of the building, making all of them turn and stare. More creatures and guards ran across the field, but there were still no young ones.

"Suit yourself," Sonya said, frowning. "This transport is leaving."

Taliya and Kano backed away as Sonya gave an order into her com. Kallie looked up, and her eyes met Taliya's. She lifted her tawny hand in a small wave, and Taliya raised her orange one in response. They'd only had a few minutes together, but their shared stories were a link Taliya knew she'd never forget. Not for the rest of her life.

Taliya felt her heart jolt as the door closed and the transport elevated and whooshed off, but she knew she'd made the right decision. She and Kano headed back over to the area where new waves of rescued creatures were arriving. She spotted Carl, loading up with ammunition.

"Are you going back in?" she asked him.

He nodded without looking up from his task. "We have three more floors to clear before Kerkaw has a chance to get reinforcements. We aren't that far ahead of him."

Kano growled in his throat, and Carl looked up.

"Ah, you two found each other. Good. Now get the hell out of here while you can."

"Not without our little ones," Kano said. "Let me help. Give me a weapon, and I'll go in with you. That's why you rescued the adults first, isn't it?"

Carl slipped a large clip into his gun and adjusted the laser sighting feature, aiming at the ground so a red dot reflected on the snow. Then he considered Kano.

"I know you want to help, but you'd only be a liability. We'd have to worry about you being hurt or captured along with trying to herd dozens of scared and confused kits."

Kano's hackles rose, but Carl stood firm.

"I know you want to see her for yourself," Carl said, "know she's safe, but I can't let you go back in."

"You know about his daughter?" Taliya said.

"The guards know everything that goes on in this place," Carl said, standing up and shouldering his gun. "Everything."

She flushed at the look in his eyes on the last word.

"If you hadn't ended him," Carl said, holding her gaze, "I would have, and not nearly so quickly."

He nodded sharply at Taliya and then turned to join the group of guards with orange on their sleeves, ready to head back inside in rotation with a group that was running across the snowy field toward them now. Still no one she recognized.

She'd almost grown numb to the sound of explosions and

gunfire, but the ground rocked with several blasts close to them. Kano instinctively drew her behind him with one arm.

"The Enforcers won't want to hurt the building if they can help it," Kano said. "There's too much equipment and medical records and experiment data to risk losing it all. A guard told me that's why they're keeping the building between us and the battle."

She hoped he was right, and she hoped that held true.

The most recent arrivals gathered around where they stood, and Taliya found herself next to a creature that could only be some mix between cheetah and human—distinctive spots and black lines marked his face, tracing from his eyes and around the sides of his mouth. She wondered if this experiment could run at super speeds, like his ancestors.

"Where are the young ones?" the cheetah-like creature asked as he bent over to catch his breath.

"Not out yet. Do you have offspring here?"

"Yes," he said. "Five of them."

Her tail thrashed as she tried to imagine having five kits to worry about—out in the world, with humans trying to abuse, capture, and kill them. It was beyond what she could wrap her thoughts around, though she knew she'd better get a handle on it quickly. With her brothers, Kano's daughter, and her own two unborn kits, that made five. Five young tigran she would be responsible for, at least until she reunited with her parents. *Assuming they're still alive.* She desperately wished she could go back to the beginning of fall, before any of this disaster had started. Go back and prepare herself more. *But how do you prepare for this insanity?*

A medic handed her a pair of insulated booties, a blanket, a flask of water, and a plate of cooked meat. Taliya glanced up, bleary-eyed.

"Eat this," the human female said. "You've got a long journey ahead. You're pregnant, yes?"

Taliya nodded slightly and stared at the plate, not sure what she was supposed to do with it. *Am I in shock now too? Is this what it feels like?*

"I'll take care of it," Kano assured the woman, wrapping the blanket around Taliya's shoulders. He led her over to a small table and chair in a medical aid area, sitting her down and putting the plate in front of her. "Eat this and drink all of the water. Keep yourself and the kits strong."

She obeyed mindlessly and finished the food in front of her while Kano dried her bare feet on the blanket and tucked them into the booties. He'd had enough warning to prepare with warm boots and clothes before his escape, but she'd had to run as she was.

"Kano," she finally whispered. "So many little ones. How are we going to manage it?"

"We just will," he said firmly. "Like every other family before us."

She nodded, but she wasn't remotely convinced. Young ones

died all the time because there wasn't enough food. Parents gave their children away because they couldn't care for them and wanted to give them a better life. The reality was settling in of surviving in a world where the war was still going on and an army wanted them dead or back in captivity. Where would they live? How would they provide for themselves, much less the young ones escaping right at that moment or waiting in her belly?

"Taliya," he whispered, taking her hand, "we don't have to figure it all out right this second. Our side, our army, has a safe place to take us. We'll gather your brothers and my daughter, and we'll go with them. Then we'll worry about what comes next."

"Maybe we'll find my parents there."

"Or someone will know where they are. If they're fighting, they could be anywhere in the country right now. We'll take care of your brothers until we find them."

"Okay, okay," she mumbled, pushing away the empty plate. She did feel stronger after the meal, but her mind was still whirling. Shouts from the group closer to the building caught her attention, and Kano leapt to his feet.

"They have them!" he yelled and raced off before she even realized what he was talking about.

It took her a moment to translate the scene through the haze of her own thoughts. *The young ones. The kits are free.* She threw off the blanket and rushed to follow him, catching up at the edge of the crowd where eager parents and rescue workers waited. At first, it was a sea of tiny furry bodies, mostly tigran. She didn't spot her brothers, but one tiny white tigran was being carried by a soldier. Kano made a strangled noise.

"Papa!" the little white tigran squealed.

It was Carl who carried the kit, and Kano embraced his daughter. The little one wrapped her limbs around him and mashed her face into the fur of his neck.

"It's okay now, kitten. It will all be okay now," he whispered to her as he rubbed her back.

Before she even saw them coming, Taliya's brothers smashed into her, clutching her around the middle. She bent down and gathered them into her arms. When they finally released her, she was surprised to see not a tear in their eyes. *Such brave boys.*

"Can we go home now, Taliya?" Tyler asked.

"Not home. Not yet. But we're going away from here. There are transports to take us away."

The boys looked around, and Tuscan nodded slowly.

"There's so many tigran," he said. "And so many others, I don't know what to call them. I didn't know there were so many here."

"It's overwhelming," Taliya agreed.

She looked around too, taking in the mass of young and old creatures all mingling and enjoying their reunions. The cheetah-like creature was surrounded by little versions of himself, hugging in relief. She felt a hand on her middle.

"You got fat while you were here," Tuscan said, patting her very round stomach.

"Not exactly," she said.

Of all the things she'd worried about, how to explain to her brothers about having a mate and expecting kits hadn't crossed her mind. Kano joined them, his daughter still plastered to him, face buried, and they all headed for the safety of the medical tent. Once they were inside, Taliya knew it was time to explain things to her brothers.

"Boys," she said, "I would like you to meet Kano."

The twins stared up at the massive white tigran in awe.

"I've heard quite a lot about you two over the last few weeks," Kano said. "Pleased to finally meet you."

"This is Tuscan," Taliya said, putting her hand on the top of his head.

"Hello, Tuscan," Kano said, extending his hand.

Tuscan stood up tall and shook Kano's hand. Taliya sensed he was frightened of Kano, but Mother had taught them good manners.

"And this is Tyler." She patted the top of his head, but he brushed her off and shook Kano's hand as well.

Taliya squatted down to look her brothers in the eyes. "Kano and I have been together here since I arrived."

"Like Tuscan and I were in a cell together," Tyler said matter-of-factly.

"Sort of like that." She cleared her throat. "But more like Mother and Father living together. Kano is my mate now."

She watched as the boys considered this, looking up at Kano and then back at her. They might be young, but they were old enough to know how things worked. Tuscan looked down toward her stomach again and frowned. Tyler followed his lead, and they both stiffened, tails puffed and ears laid back.

"Yes, I am expecting kits. Two of them. Kano and I are expecting them together."

It was hard to read the variety of emotions wafting from her brothers, but she clearly sensed their possessiveness of her and anger at Kano.

"Boys," she said. "Kano and I are together now. I am choosing to be with him, and he with me. There is nothing to be angry about or try to protect me from. Do you understand?"

They nodded sharply, but she didn't think they were convinced. She stood to face Kano, and he smiled weakly.

"Give them time," he said.

The white kit snuffled and finally removed her face from Kano's fur. Taliya caught the gaze of her bright-blue eyes and smiled.

"Hello there."

She had never seen a more beautiful tigran in her life. The kit was *pure white*. He hadn't mentioned that. Would she develop stripes later, or was she something even more than a white tigran? Her pink nose wiggled at the strange odors all around them.

"This is Aliania," Kano said. "Or Ali, for short."

"Hello, Aliania," Taliya said, going for a more formal greeting of the frightened kit—though scared wasn't necessarily what she was sensing. It was more sadness. Flat, cold, dull, soulful unhappiness. Deep grief.

Soldiers approached, and the group turned to meet them.

"Can we check the young ones, please?" said one of the soldiers with a medic's red cross on his uniform. "Just to make sure everyone is free of any tracking devices."

"Tracking devices?" Taliya said.

The medic shrugged one shoulder. "They can be easily removed."

Taliya nodded. "Go on, boys. I'll stay where you can see me."

They were hesitant, but they obeyed. Another soldier scanned a wand quickly over Taliya and Kano but then said they were clear and walked away.

"Mine's right here," Tyler said, pointing to a spot behind his left ear.

A lump settled in her throat. What other horrors would she learn about in the days to come? Kano surrendered Aliania to another medic, who took her gently with reassuring words. She started to check the kit over on the spot, looking into her eyes and ears while chatting with her about silly things like how cold it was and the sounds of the birds around them.

Taliya realized she could now hear the birds in the trees. The gunfire and explosions had ceased. No one on their side of the battle seemed concerned about it, and that must mean they'd been victorious. She sighed and turned to Kano, who was watching his daughter intently.

"She looks fine," Taliya said reassuringly.

"Yes," he agreed. "Though I knew they'd keep her healthy. She's terribly valuable. I worry more about her little soul. She's been through so much."

"Has she asked about her mother?" Taliya said, suddenly terrified she'd learn that his mate was actually still alive, regardless of what he'd said.

"No, she won't ask for her." Kano shifted uncomfortably and stared at his daughter, wiggling in the medic's arms as they removed a tracking device from behind her ear. "When the Enforcers came for us, my wife did not surrender our kit like they wanted her to."

"I'm sure," Taliya said, imagining she would have done the same thing.

"They wanted us all, especially as a mated pair who could produce, well . . ." He motioned at the white kit. "But my wife resisted. She clawed and bit and did everything in her power to keep them from Aliania. None of it mattered." He looked at the ground, grief pouring from him. "A frustrated soldier stabbed her. He wasn't supposed to, but he got tired of fighting or was scared of being hurt. He stabbed her, watched her die, and took Aliania away from her. I was already shackled. There was nothing I could do to save either one of them."

Taliya reached for his hand, and he squeezed hers in return.

"Ali won't ask for her mother," he said. "She knows she's dead."

They waited in silence for the kits to be returned to them, holding hands in the busy medical tent. Taliya had never asked about what happened to his wife, and now she understood why he hadn't shared the story before. Not only was it horrible, it was wrapped up in the capture of a daughter he hadn't wanted her to know about. A little white kit who must have been desperately missing both of her parents. A kit who needed a mother.

When the medics were done with the young ones, they insisted on giving Taliya a quick physical as well. Now that the battle was over, no one seemed to be in a rush to leave. Before sending her on her way, they did an ultrasound to check on the pregnancy. Kano and the kits gathered around and watched the screen until the clear shapes of one, then two very tiny tigran appeared.

Taliya's heart leaped, watching them squiggle and wiggle—though she could only feel it as small movements so far. The whole group listened to their rapid heartbeats. Aliania eyed the monitor, but Taliya wasn't sure if she was old enough to really understand what she was seeing. Taliya didn't know much about two year olds. It was going to be a steep learning curve.

"Does that make us uncles?" Tuscan said.

"It sure does," Taliya said. "But you will have to promise to be good and kind uncles, not uncles who help them get into trouble."

Tuscan and Tyler eyed each other and smiled. She was pretty sure they would begin making plans to be the latter kind of uncles as soon as they were alone.

"Everything looks perfect," the medic said, turning off the machine. "I can't tell anything about what color they are from this testing."

"We already know one is orange and one is white," Taliya said, pulling her tunic back down over her belly.

The medic paused and gave her a small, sad smile. Taliya wondered how much this human knew about the activities of the facility he had just helped free.

"It's all right," Taliya said. "This may not have been my life plan, but I'm not sorry to be carrying them now that we can be free."

The medic looked up at Kano, who was holding Aliania while she sucked her thumb and cuddled into his chest.

"Regardless of how all this started, we're mated now," Kano said. "We just need to get away from here and somewhere safe, where no one can get their hands on any of my offspring."

The medic looked back at Taliya and smiled. "Well, many pregnancies are unplanned. It's still the start of wondrous things. Now, let's get you all on the next transport. Everyone's getting ready to clear out."

Soldiers milled around casually, not on guard at all, as the group followed the medic back out of the tent. Carl sauntered up, the first time Taliya had ever seen him so calm and without a gun.

"Hold on a second," he said. "They'll want to see this."

He pointed toward the building behind them, and Taliya heard garbled shouts—commands being issued and repeated, though she couldn't see anyone in that area. Several small explosions sounded, then several more, and the ground rocked underneath her.

"Wow!" Tuscan shouted, nearly falling over.

With a creak and a groan, the tall building where they had all been held captive shifted to one side and then began to collapse in on itself. Floor after floor disappeared, starting from the bottom. Waves of dust and debris flew into the air, and the smell of explosives and concrete assaulted her nose. Taliya wondered if anyone had removed Narlin's body, but she hoped they hadn't. It was deeply satisfying, imagining it all tumbling down on him. Within seconds, there was nothing but a pile of rubble left behind. Dust burst up from the direction of the dungeons, and a crater sunk into the ground where they had been buried. Cheers rose up from the humans and various creatures still in the field, and Carl patted Kano on the back.

"We thought they'd fight harder to recapture the site," Carl said, "but they just ran and let us have it."

"Is that a good sign?" Kano asked him.

"We're really not sure," Carl said, "at least as far as the whole war goes. But it's a good sign for you and your family, isn't it?"

"Oh yes," Taliya said, pulling her brothers closer to her.

"They probably have backups of all the files for the experiments," Carl said, "but they lost billions of dollars of research and equipment and specific genetic sampling. One of our hopes when we destroy facilities like this is that the losses will be so great the government won't bother restarting the programs."

"Wait," Taliya said, "there are more like this place? I thought this was the only one."

"Oh no," Carl said. "This is the fifth location we've demolished. We assumed all of the tigran were being eliminated when they were captured, or put on display in zoos. But when the information about the breeding programs was leaked, we quickly realized how widespread it was and how many species were involved. Once we gained access to some government satellites, we were able to start looking for potential locations beyond the first one we found in Texas. That one was mostly just research and testing, creating new species, some that can only survive in sea water. Things the government insisted it had stopped doing decades ago."

"How could this go on without being noticed?" Kano said.

"The media news only reports what Kerkaw allows them to, and who would really know to go snooping besides them?"

Taliya and Kano locked eyes. For all those weeks they had

assumed they were unique in their crazy situation, but they were just a pair among dozens, maybe even hundreds.

"One good part of it, though," Carl said, "is we're finding individuals alive that everyone assumed were dead. You're fortunate that your brothers were brought here with you, Taliya, instead of shipped off to another facility."

"Narlin needed them to get me to cooperate," she said flatly.

"Ah," Carl said, acknowledging the logic of that. It was clear he knew exactly what she meant and all that it entailed between her and Kano—and her and Narlin.

"Let's get you all on the next transport," Carl said. "There're some portable bathroom facilities over there." He motioned to the right of the field. "And then you can load up. There's a small bathroom in the truck bay, but you'll only want to use it if necessary. It'll be a few hours before we stop for a break. Our first destination today is the temporary camp we have at the Standing Rock Reservation. That's about twelve hours away."

"Are we in Colorado?" Kano said. "It seems like it, but I could never be sure."

"Yeah. We're outside of Denver. The isolation of this area made it possible to hide the facility."

Colorado. She sighed. *So far from Arkansas. So far from home.* Their makeshift family was still basically captive, but at least now they were in the care of the good side of the war. So many humans she was supposed to trust. Humans who were fighting Kerkaw, but probably for their own reasons that had nothing to do with mixed-species creations and breeding. President Kerkaw had set up a system of government that infuriated many humans for their own loss of rights and liberty. Their agendas might not have anything to do with saving tigran.

"Get yourselves on that transport over there, and I'll see you at base camp," Carl said, watching the troops start shifting, preparing to make sure the area was clear. With that and a quick nod of his head, Carl was gone and enveloped in the mass of humans wearing green army camouflage with orange cloths tied to their sleeves.

"Okay, kits," Kano said, "let's hit the bathrooms and get ourselves on that truck."

Taking Tyler and Tuscan each by the hand, Taliya and Kano led their group to the facilities and then over to where the trucks were loading. They lifted the three young ones up and in before climbing in themselves. Aliania was hesitant to let go of Kano for very long, and Taliya didn't blame her. They all sat on the floor of the truck with their backs against the wall, damp and snowy pant legs stretched out in front of them. There were other tigran, a couple of liran, some species she didn't know, and soldiers, the last of the fighting force, all sitting around them with the same dazed look they probably had on their own faces. Taliya could smell the sourness of fear and stress from every creature.

As the back door on the transport was closed and secured, Taliya tucked her brothers under her arms, one on each side, and then reached over to hold Kano's hand. Aliania was curled up in his lap, like a tired white kitten.

"What happens now?" Taliya said.

"I have no idea," Kano said with a sigh. "There's some kind of military camp, maybe? We can't just run off into the world. We'd be captured again or shot on sight by Enforcers."

"We can't go home, can we," Tyler said—a statement of fact, not a question.

"Not yet," Taliya said.

The warmth of the inside of the truck enveloped her, and she rested her head against the wall. She hoped they would be safe where they were going. She hoped her parents would be there or someone would know how to find them. Above all, she hoped they didn't separate her from Kano or the kits from the two of them. If they stayed together, it would be easier to face what was ahead.

Carl said they were heading to a reservation. If anyone on the planet could understand the plight of the tigran, Native Americans certainly could.

Chapter 16

The transport was comfortable enough, even sitting on the floor, and the five of them tried to rest as it zipped along. Aliania fell asleep curled in Kano's lap, and the twins had stretched out on the floor on each side of Taliya, keeping their feet firmly in touch with her body, tails coiled around her legs. She leaned her head on the wall behind her and tried to sleep, but her mind was too occupied, trying to figure out the next hundred steps for their group. Since she didn't know what was waiting for them at the next stop, it was hard to wrap her head around more than fuss and bother and fret. Kano's body was tense, and she sensed he was doing some of the same worrying. Probably on alert for danger as well. Taking a moment to consider the position the white tigran found himself thrust into—fleeing captivity not only for himself but for his kit, a pregnant mate, and two other young tigran—she was sure his mind was spinning as rapidly as hers.

The light inside the transport hold was dim, but she tried to distract herself by looking at all the other creatures in there with them. There weren't any stray kits, so either they had all been claimed or they were together in a separate transport. Maybe the Enforcers had only kept young ones at that facility who were specific leverage for an older creature. If that was true, she hoped they'd all been matched up again and were on their way to safety.

Across from her was one of the female cheetah/human creatures, her head leaned against the wall of the vehicle like she was asleep, though Taliya could tell from her breathing that she was not. A distinctive purr vibrated from her, which Taliya found fascinating. Neither tigers nor tigran could purr. Three teenage male liran—tufts of the starts of manes sprouting out around their faces—sat staring at the floor. She couldn't see who was farther down on her side without being obvious about it, so she didn't try. When they'd loaded in, she'd noticed more tigran, so that must be where they were. There were around two dozen uniformed soldiers in with them too, though their guns were holstered and they seemed calm. Maybe they were just catching a ride instead of serving as guards.

"Whatever happens," Kano whispered, "we stay together. Don't let them split us up or take the kits somewhere else."

"Absolutely." She'd thought the same thing. *Stay together.*

"I'm sorry I never told you about Ali."

She sighed. It was definitely flitting around in the back of her mind, why he'd kept that secret from her.

"I understand," she said, "but I still wish you'd told me."

"I know. I almost did, so many times. But I couldn't imagine ever seeing her again. Someone was sure to pay a pretty penny for her." He swallowed a growl. "I tried not to think about it. I guess, if you knew, we'd have to talk about it and worry about it. I just couldn't."

She nodded and looked down at the white kit, sleeping peacefully.

"And part of me . . ." He ran a hand tenderly across Aliania's head. "Part of me worried you wouldn't want to raise another female's kit."

"A motherless kit is a terrible thing," Taliya said. "She's yours, so now she's mine too. We're a family. The rest of it . . . Well, the rest of it we'll just have to figure out as we go."

Panic fluttered in her chest at the thought, but she tamped it down so Kano wouldn't sense her fears. How in the world would she manage all of these kits? She'd never wanted her own mother so much in her whole life. It was a desperate ache in her heart.

After about five hours, during which Taliya finally dozed off, the transport halted. The soldiers stretched and stood up, but there was no urgency about it.

"We'll take a break here," one of them said as he peeked out a small window in the back of the vehicle. "We have the area secured. There will be snacks and water. But don't stray too far from the trucks and the buildings, and make sure you come back to this same transport, number five, so we can keep track of everyone."

The back of the vehicle opened, and cold washed over them. Taliya inhaled deeply, relishing the fresh air—pine trees and dirt mixed with human and natural creature smells. It looked like a rest stop along the highway. There was deep snow in the evergreen forest around them, but a large area of parking lot had been cleared. There were picnic tables scattered around, with soldiers setting up supplies, and a couple of small buildings across the cleared lot. The occupants of the transport struggled to their feet, stretching and working out the kinks after hours of sitting. The twins rubbed sleep from their eyes. Aliania woke and snuffled into her father's stomach, then she looked up at Taliya with her amazing blue eyes.

"We're making a stop for the bathroom and some snacks," Taliya said. "Are you hungry?"

Aliania nodded and wobbled to her feet. Kano helped them all off the transport, but they froze at what they saw around them—a dazzling display of creatures.

There was a small group of youngsters standing with two of their rescuers, so not every kit had been claimed, but that wasn't the shocking part. Taliya knew that many different species were part of the same experiments as tigran, but seeing a sampling of each gathered together was astounding. Tigran were the only genetic creations who lived among humans. *Have these creatures ever spent a day out of the confines of a laboratory?*

There were many orange tigran, the most commonly successful hybrid, two white tigran females, dozens of liran, the cheetah mix, and what must be a leopard/human mix with spots but no face markings like the cheetahs. She spotted a pair of black leopard/human creatures. The female looked pregnant, and Taliya imagined that offspring was quite valuable. But what really held her eye was two massive individuals—a good foot taller and a hundred pounds heavier than even the male tigran, with dark-brown fur from head to toe. Kano noticed her fascination.

"Those must be berman," he said. "They're pretty rare. I've never actually seen one before."

Berman? A bear/human hybrid?

"From what I've heard, male berman are a special treat for wealthy women."

"You're kidding," Taliya said.

Kano pursed his whiskers at her. "Weird fetishes, they swing all different ways."

Taliya glanced over at the berman again, wondering what kind of leverage you'd need on one of those massive males to get him to cooperate with rich human females. Her ears laid back involuntarily at the thought.

"Funny," Kano said, adjusting Aliania on his hip, "all of us were in that same facility and never knew about each other."

He started toward the building, and Taliya took the twins by the hands and followed, trying not to stare at the berman. The soldiers had formed a loose perimeter around the group, weapons held across their bodies, but she didn't sense any fear or agitation from them. Probably just a precaution.

After using the bathrooms, which were primitive at best, Taliya got in line for a snack and some water while Kano waited out of the way with the kits. As she turned to leave with her hands full, Taliya found herself face to chest with a female berman. A rounded belly was not far from her eye level. She looked up, and the female gazed down at her with what could only be sadness or sympathy in her dark eyes. The berman made a grumbling noise, very bear-like, and then placed one massive hand on her tummy and the other on the side of Taliya's face—a hand so large it encompassed the tigran's head and made her feel the size of a newborn kit.

"Our young belong to us now," the berman said in a deep voice. "No one will take them away."

"I hope you're right," Taliya said.

The berman patted her cub-bump and stepped up in line to get her snacks. Kano had been watching, his face wrinkled in concern. Taliya smiled at him and pointed to an empty table nearby. Once their group had settled in and everyone had food, Kano turned to her.

"What was that about, with the berman?"

"She was just telling me that our future offspring will be ours and no one will take them away."

Kano looked over at the berman. "She's pregnant too?"

Taliya laughed. "Obviously. Showing much more than I am."

"I hadn't noticed," he said. "I couldn't quite get past the size of them. It's not often I meet anyone larger than me, not to mention a female."

"They are quite impressive," Taliya agreed.

Kano shifted and frowned. "You know, I'd always heard that berman were sterile, along with the liran and so many others. But clearly that isn't true."

"Or the scientists figured out a way around it," Taliya said, a chill running down her back and making her shudder.

"Either way, that would make them very, very valuable. I hope all the records on her were destroyed, or they'll never stop looking."

Taliya reached across the table and took his hand, suspecting he was worrying about her in the same way. White tigran were also rare and valuable. She glanced at Aliania, chewing on some jerky with two-year-old abandon. *He should be more worried for the daughter the government has already seen and documented.* A pure-white tigran would be worth an astounding amount of money to a private collector. Kano made a growling snort, probably considering the same things, and took a swig from his water jug.

The twins finished eating and started to get restless, so Taliya challenged them to see who could race around the table and a nearby tree the fastest. It made her heart leap with joy to watch them run freely and push and jockey for position, thrashing through the snow when they reached the tree line and basically just being young tigran without a care in the world. Aliania laughed and clapped her hands with delight, but she didn't join them. Probably for the best. They'd have mowed her down.

A car horn sounded, and all of the creatures looked back toward the transports. Soldiers motioned for them to come back and load up.

"Aww," the twins yowled together. "Already?"

"Let's get to our real destination," Kano said, scooping his daughter up. "I'm excited to see where we're headed."

That seemed to pique the boys' interest, and they scooted to Kano's side. As Taliya cleaned up the last of their garbage and collected the water jugs, she noticed that Tuscan had curled his tail around Kano's leg and Tyler was holding on to his free hand on the other side. The four of them walked slowly back to the transport, and she followed, grateful the twins had grown accustomed to Kano and were trusting him. He might well be the father figure in their lives from now on. Even if they found Mother, the likelihood of Father still being alive was slim. He was a tigran, but he was not a warrior or a trained soldier. Deep in her heart, she held out hope that he was still alive, but she tried not to cling to it too tightly. That way, there would be less mourning when she found out the truth.

When one and all were loaded back into the transports and the soldiers had done final checks of the area, the doors were closed.

"We should get to the reservation in about seven hours," a soldier said, storing his gun in a rack above their heads. "It's getting dark, so we'll use that cover to get well into South Dakota. We've heard the pathway is clear, and there are troops working to keep it that way. Everyone try to get some sleep."

Taliya thought it was highly unlikely any of them would rest much. A silly niggle in her soul wished she could have grabbed her books before they escaped, like what she needed at that moment was a suitcase full of novels to tote around. With nothing else to do in the dark truck, they all slept eventually. She woke once to find even Kano had drifted off, his head leaned back against the wall of the vehicle. He didn't even wake when she and Ali used the tiny bathroom in the truck. Seven hours was a long time for a young bladder and a pregnant one. Before that trip was over, Taliya suspected everyone in the transport had used it at least once.

The stop at Standing Rock Reservation was more substantial and allowed some time for a real meal and sleep on makeshift beds on the ground under a large enclosed tent. A fire in the middle vented out an opening in the top and kept the area comfortably warm.

Taliya had never met a Native American, but the group there tended to the needs of the escaped captives like they were caring for family members. Every interaction was filled with grace and quiet voices, careful not to startle or upset any of the species gathered there. While tigran were familiar to the Lakota, it must have been alarming dealing with so many formidable guests. If any of their hosts were scared, they never behaved like it or raised an odor of fear or concern. Taliya had never been more grateful for the patience and kindness of strangers.

While the rescued creatures found spots to sleep, the Lakota gathered around the campfire in the middle of the tent, singing quietly in what Taliya imagined to be prayers. *Whoever you are praying to, keep at it. We need the protection of every power in the universe.*

As Kano settled in next to her on a sleeping roll, he whispered, "From what I can catch here and there, we're heading to Canada. Outside Winnipeg. We may well be there until the war is over, assuming our side wins. There's a national park in the area and a huge refugee camp."

Refugees. It was the first time anyone had used that term to describe them, but it was the most accurate she could think of. They couldn't go home, assuming her home was even still there. The government wanted them dead, or worse. They were running from the powers that be in their own country and had nothing but the clothes on their bodies. She hoped Canada held a safe refuge for all of them.

Chapter 17

After another long day of travel, the transports all arrived safely at the refugee camp outside of Winnipeg. Taliya wasn't even sure when they'd crossed the border into Canada. There must have been a special government agent who knew they were coming and let them go right through. She was just grateful to finally feel safe, free from the threat of the whole group being attacked and recaptured. She didn't know how the army had accomplished it or what special blocking technological equipment had been used, she was just glad they were done with running, at least for the time being.

The transports were unloaded, and Taliya stretched and groaned as she stepped out onto the hard earth of Canada.

"Awesome! Look!" Tyler said, pointing up.

Taliya was ready to shade her eyes, but she quickly realized that wouldn't be necessary. There was no sun, no sky. They were under a habitat dome. An expansively massive habitat dome. The top was high above them, maybe 200 yards. Glancing around, she couldn't see any of the sides of the dome.

"I didn't know it was possible to make them this large," Kano said.

"Neither did I," Taliya agreed in awe.

"The dome is amazing," Carl said, stopping to join their group. "The Canadian government already had this as an agricultural research facility and were generous to let us take over. The outside layer melts snow and ice using thermals from inside. We can keep the temperature in here consistent year round. It even rains on schedule. The winters outside here are ridiculously cold. I'm glad we made it through without facing a blizzard."

Taliya tested the air. She'd thought the changes she sensed were just because of the northern location, but now she could decipher the dome itself and the air that wasn't truly outdoor.

"I imagine it helps with security too," Kano said.

"Yeah, but that's not a concern here," Carl said. "Kerkaw isn't stupid enough to get Canada involved in the war. Now that you're here, you are safe."

The refugees had been unloaded in a wide dirt-ground area. Once they moved away from the trucks, Taliya noticed a wall to the dome behind them and an entrance for trucks, heavily guarded. They were led to an expansive army-green tent with a giant red cross on the front. Carl lifted the flap to reveal an open space filled with dozens of cots and busy humans in white coats pushing around carts of medical equipment. He motioned to several open beds near the back of the room.

"Each of you pick a cot until one of the doctors has checked you in," he said as they moved past him.

The twins clung to Taliya's waist, panting with anxiousness. Carl hesitated and squatted down to be eye level with the boys.

"It's okay," he assured them. "These are *good* doctors. No one is going to hurt you. Well, they may want to take a quick blood sample, but that's all. This is just a checkup and a way to register you in our system so we can keep track of everyone who has been rescued." He stood and met Taliya's eye. "You can trust everyone in this camp."

She nodded, though she knew it would be hard for all of them. The scientist/doctor at the facility had been cold but never cruel, to her at least, but Taliya had never trusted her. The twins had obviously had some bad run-ins with a doctor at the facility. She rubbed their backs gently to help dispel the anxiety and fear radiating from them. Working their way through the swarms of other creatures and humans, Taliya finally got each of them settled on a cot. Kano still held Aliania with him, but she doubted anyone expected a kit as young as her to be separated.

"So, who we have here?"

A tiny human female pushed a wheeled medical cart toward them across the tarp-covered floor. She couldn't have been more than five feet tall, her shoulder-length hair was jet black, and she appeared to be part of the Asian human line. She stopped and took in the small group.

"My name Agnus," she said in broken English. "I get you all check over and out of here. Okay, boys, you lie down. Take nap now. I get you soon."

The twins looked at each other and then at Taliya.

"What problem?" Agnus said with a chuckle. "You not like naps?"

The twins giggled. "We're too old for naps," Tuscan said.

"Oh no," Agnus said. "Older you get, more you like naps. You see. Lie down and be still now. Wait your turn, okay?"

The twins nodded and lay down obediently, but Taliya suspected they wouldn't stay that way long.

"Now you," she said, turning to Kano. "Little one is okay? Just scared?"

"Yes, she's fine. Just a bit overwhelmed."

"Okay, then." She turned to Taliya. "You I start with. Either you eat many too many donuts or you carrying kits. That come first."

Taliya laughed at the bluntness. "It's the second one, though I wouldn't say no to a donut or two."

"We get you lot of donuts soon. Right now, lie down. I get your vitals and check on kits."

218

Agnus continued to chatter and ask health-related questions as she took Taliya's blood pressure, heart rate, and temperature. Then she ran a scanner over Taliya's belly.

"How many you have before?" she asked.

"These are my first," Taliya said. Agnus's eyes shifted around through the group, and Taliya realized some clarification was probably in order. "Those are my brothers. My parents are with the army. Kano and I were put together in the facility. Do you know about all of that?"

Agnus nodded sharply. "Terrible business. *Disgusting* business."

"But the young one with him is not mine," Taliya whispered. "Her mother, his first wife, is dead."

Agnus leaned down close, pretending to adjust a piece of equipment. "So, she yours now, yes? She need a mama now."

Taliya nodded. "Yes. Now she is mine."

Kano carefully observed all of Agnus's fussing and scanning, while Aliania refused to look up from his chest. The twins peeked around the cart. Finally, Agnus seemed satisfied.

"You fine. Kits fine. All good. You in system now. You see me lots. Tigran and tigran kits my . . . How you say? My *specialty*. That why they bring me here when they plan this big rescue. So many tigran." She stopped and put her hands on her hips. "Where I come from, great honor to be tigran doctor. Killing a tigran, we never do this. Never."

She snorted and fussed around with her medical cart,

clearly angry with the dishonorable Americans who were exterminating and imprisoning tigran as fast as they could. Then she paused and turned back to Taliya, her dark eyes flashing.

"They separate you, you know. Male and female. Hard to keep together in camp if not really family. Hmm."

Taliya felt her heart sink, and her eyes met Kano's.

"No," Kano said firmly. "We want to stay together. We are a real family."

"Not *legal* family," Agnus said, frowning. "Taliya and the boys, yes, okay. You and your daughter, yes. All you together? I not know for sure."

Taliya's thoughts raced. Tigran were not allowed to enter into any kind of contracts under Kerkaw's laws. They didn't have any rights or legal standing. What kind of proof or family structure could she come up with to stay with Kano? The unborn kits were his. Didn't that count for something? How in the world would she manage the twins and two newborn kits in what was no doubt not much more than a survival camp?

"What if we are handfast?" Kano asked.

This prospect seemed intriguing to Agnus, but Taliya didn't understand.

"You do this?" Agnus asked her. "You be handfast with this big white tigran?"

Taliya looked over at Kano blankly, and the lines on his face shifted to worry.

"I thought we agreed to stay together," he said, clutching

Aliania tighter. "I know it may have gotten more complicated than you thought but . . ." He moved to her cot, sitting next to her and grabbing her hand. "Please, Taliya. We can't let them separate us."

She squeezed his hand. "I'm not upset. I just don't know what it means to be handfast?"

"It's based on old human traditions," he said, "when the population was scattered and you couldn't count on a minister or someone official to perform wedding ceremonies. The families would oversee the marriage agreement, and an informal ceremony was held making the couple handfast until a full wedding could be performed. Tigran have been using them since legal marriages were forbidden."

His eyes shifted away from her for a moment. *Of course, Kano and his wife must have had a ceremony like that*, she realized.

"But what difference would it make?" Taliya said. "It can't be anything legal that authorities would care about to help keep us together."

"We not living under Kerkaw nonsense 'round here," Agnus said with a snort. "Here, you have rights. Here, you citizens. So I ask again, you willing to be handfast to this tigran? Just because bad scientists make you mates no mean you have to stay mates. Here, you have choice. Female have *choice*," she added with a firm glare at Kano.

"Of course you have a choice," he said huskily.

She sensed nervous tension in his voice. Was he worried

that she'd felt forced into a bond of some kind in order to escape? It certainly wasn't what she'd planned for herself at seventeen. None of it was. But she couldn't imagine her future without Kano. Nothing about what she'd felt for him in their prison cell had changed. The foreverness of marriage was hard to even imagine. She didn't know what the next hour held for them. Now, today, she needed to assure they all stayed together. That was enough.

"Yes, I will be handfast to this amazing tigran," she said to Agnus. Taliya looked back to Kano and the familiar lines of his face, his bright-blue eyes, his pink nose. "Kano is my mate by choice."

Kano relaxed visibly, and Aliania peeked up at Taliya with a small smile. Taliya rubbed the kit's back and smiled in return.

"We are a family," she said.

"Fine," Agnus said, clapping her hands once, as if to seal the deal. "Done. I get you all check in. Then we find tigran who can witness ceremony. I tell housing now, so they get ready place for all five of you. With room for two more soon."

Agnus looked very pleased with herself and started typing messages into her computer. Taliya looked back down at Aliania, and the kit reached out and took her hand. Kano sighed and tried to shift the kit on his lap, but instead she crawled over onto Taliya's lap and settled in, her legs wrapped around Taliya's middle, head on her chest. The kit popped a thumb in her mouth and snuggled down. Taliya wasn't sure how Kano felt about the transfer, but when she met his eyes, she knew all was well.

Aliania giggled. "My sister is wiggly," she said, leaning back and looking at Taliya's tummy.

Taliya was pretty sure it was just some stomach rumbles and not the kits that Aliania felt, but it was still adorable, realizing she understood that she might have a sister inside of that belly.

"What if it's a brother?" Taliya said, glancing at her own brothers.

"Or *two* brothers," Kano added, ruffling the fur on his daughter's head and pulling on one white ear gently over the face she made at the prospect of two bothers.

"Will they be white, like me?" Aliania asked.

"Well," Kano said, "the doctor back at the facility said one is orange and one is white, but I think he meant white like me, not pure white like you. You are very rare."

"Maybe the white one is a girl," Aliania said with a smile, her little fangs poking out.

"You not know?" Agnus said as she wrapped a sensor around Tuscan's arm to take his vitals.

"No," Taliya said. "The scientist just said one orange and one white. They didn't care what sex they were."

"Or about the orange one at all," Kano added with a low growl.

"Bad doctors," Agnus said again. "Bad, bad doctors. You want know?"

Taliya looked at Kano, and he smiled.

"Yes," she said. "Maybe it will help us mentally prepare a bit more. I wasn't exactly planning on being a parent this soon in my life."

"Oh, you gonna be parent," Agnus said. "That for sure. *Big time* parent. Already one." She pointed at Aliania, contentedly sucking her thumb and cuddled into Taliya again. "And these boys. Until you find your mama, they yours too."

Agnus pulled up Taliya's scans and clicked around on the screen a bit.

"There you have it," she said with pride. "One boy. One girl."

Taliya had been ready to ask if she could tell which was which color from the scans, but it suddenly didn't matter. A boy and a girl. Hearing that fact thrust the whole future into clarity. Her heart fluttered. She knew what a handful her brothers had been, and that was when they lived on open acres with plenty of room to run and play like wild animals. In her panic, she looked to Kano, but he appeared about ready to burst at the seams with pride.

"A boy and a girl," he said with a smile.

"Not two sisters," Aliania mumbled around her thumb.

"Not this time," Kano said.

Taliya's heart fluttered and leapt again. *This time?*

"Okay now," Agnus said, reading a message on her screen and interrupting their family planning. "Samson on the way to perform ceremony, so we hurry up now."

In a matter of a few minutes, Agnus had poked and prodded and scanned and gotten them all registered in her system.

"You in unit number two hundred six," she said, passing a piece of paper to Kano. "Food and rest. That what you need. Ah, here he is."

The group followed Agnus's gaze to see a massive creature heading their way. Even Kano's eyes went wide at the sight of him. Taliya estimated him at eight feet tall, at the bare minimum, and over a hundred pounds more than Kano in solid muscle. The creature was only wearing slacks, so his markings were on full display. Black stripes like a tigran—though his were faint and few, with an elaborate spots and stripes combination on his face—but his base coat of fur was tawny instead of orange.

"That Samson," Agnus said. "He a ligran. Mother was tigran, and father was liran. Very rare. Maybe only one."

As Samson languidly strode toward Taliya's group, the soldiers in the medical tent stopped to shake his hand or pat him on the back, and the doctors and nurses acknowledged him with nods and friendly greetings. This majestic creature was obviously someone important and well-known at the camp.

"Try not stare," Agnus said.

Taliya tried, but Samson was hard to not gawk at. The government scientists would certainly go to great lengths to get their hands on him. It made her worry how safe they really were in the refugee camp—millions of dollars of U.S. Government property.

Samson stopped at their cots and looked down at the group of tigran. Taliya felt waves of excitement from her brothers, and the strong aroma of male pheromones wafted from Kano. She worried he might instinctively leap up with his hackles raised, but he remained seated and calm.

"Is this the new family you messaged me about?" Samson asked in a voice deeply resonant and as impressive as his stature.

"Yes," Agnus said, staring up at the creature twice her height. "Kano and Taliya were paired at facility, but they wish to make official. You read details I send you?"

"Yes," he said. "I will take it from here. I am Samson, and I am in charge of day to day events. Mostly because I have been around the longest."

Taliya suspected his imposing size and uniqueness had a bit more to do with it.

"Are you done with them, Doctor Agnus?" Samson asked.

"Yes, sir. Off you go. Make them family now."

"Follow me, then," Samson said, motioning with a sweep of his enormous arm.

The family stood up, and Kano took his daughter back from Taliya. Aliania protested, but Kano whispered something in her ear about Taliya already having enough to carry that made the kit giggle.

"Thank you, Agnus," Taliya said, taking the twins by the hands, sensing fear from them at the next transition.

"I *good* doctor," she said with a wink. "But you not seen last of me. We check on those kits again soon, yes?"

"Absolutely," Taliya said.

Without another word, Agnus pushed the medical cart that was bigger than her over to the next cot. "So, who we have here?" she said to the waiting patient, a female liran, who looked exhausted.

Taliya smiled, and her family followed Samson out the back of the medical tent. She was not prepared for what greeted her. It was dusk now, but the grounds were swarming with tigran and every other species mix, many she'd never seen before. There were large bamboo buildings along the path, but they looked official instead of home-like. Everyone was calm and at ease, how life had felt at tigran settlements before the war. Fear and worry had surrounded her for so long, Taliya wasn't sure how to let it go.

"Come over to the fire," Samson said. "We will have you two handfast before these young ones fall asleep on their feet."

Taliya doubted either of the twins would fall asleep that easily, but it was true they could all use a good rest. Hopefully in a real bed. The firepit sat in a large open area with benches and a few small tables, and some creatures were hanging around with musical instruments. Samson raised his long arms and called out to all around.

"Come! Come witness the handfast ceremony of these two tigran! Come!"

Cheers and howls rose from the crowd, and a mass of furry bodies shifted in their direction. It was a bit overwhelming, and Taliya found herself instinctively moving closer to Kano. He wrapped his free arm around her protectively, and the twins clutched at her hands, though she didn't sense too much fear from them. Aliania looked fascinated by all the different colors and shapes of living beings around her, not afraid at all. Samson motioned them to a well-worn spot in front of the fire, clearly where get-togethers were held.

"Boys, you come stand here to be witnesses for your sister." Samson moved the twins to stand just behind and on either side of Taliya. "And you, darling kit, can you stand next to your father? Papa is going to require both hands free for this ceremony, but he needs you to be right next to him."

Aliania nodded her consent, and Kano set her down. She hovered with one hand clutching his pant leg.

"We cannot make this as fancy as the old Highlanders might like," Samson called out to the crowd, "but we can give this couple a binding agreement to carry with them always." He turned to Taliya and Kano. "Taliya, hold out your hands, palms up. Kano, take her hands so your palms meet."

They did as they were told, and Taliya reveled in the warmth of his touch. It felt like forever since they were wrapped up together in their quiet bed, alone. She was glad no one could see the flush she felt sweep over her skin. He chuffed at her quietly, and she chuffed and slow-blinked in return.

228

"Kano and Taliya," Samson continued, "as your hands are joined together, so may your hearts always be. Taliya, do you agree to be handfast with this tigran? To be his mate for the rest of your life, to care for the kits you may bear, and to support him in all of his endeavors?"

"Yes," she said easily, "I agree."

"And you, Kano. Do you agree to be handfast with this tigran? To be her mate for the rest of your life, to care for the kits she may bear, and to support her in all of her endeavors?"

"Yes," he said, his voice strained, "I agree with all of my heart."

"And do you, the witnesses to this ceremony, agree to support them to the best of your ability?" Samson looked to the twins, who nodded, and then to Aliania, who hid her face in Kano's pants but nodded as well.

"And you, tigran and others too, will you honor this ceremony and treat their union and their family with the respect it is due?"

Cheers and calls of "aye" and "yes" went up from the crowd in a blast of sound.

"This union that began under cruel circumstances will now come out into the world by choice," Samson boomed loudly enough for the whole medical tent to hear. "We are all witnesses to it and will fight to see that this family remains intact, together, and will never be divided by any force on this earth."

The massive ligran pulled a long cord of rope from his

pocket and laid it over their joined hands. Then he wove the cord up and around and through their arms, finally tying the ends together in a large knot. Taliya looked down at Aliania and saw the kit was fascinated with the intricate loops of the rope. She felt her brothers move up closer to her, each lightly touching her side and wrapping their tails around her legs. She swished her tail, tapping each of them gently. Kano smiled down at the boys, and Taliya felt the kits stir inside her.

"Kano and Taliya are now handfast," Samson announced. "The knot joining them is tied."

Kano smiled and leaned in to kiss her.

"I love you, Taliya," he said, resting his forehead against hers so the ends of their whiskers overlapped.

"I love you too." It was the truth, though she realized neither of them had said the words aloud before. She hoped their love would hold firm under what lay ahead.

A cheer went up from the crowd again, and someone started playing rapid notes on a guitar, like something flamenco dancers would click their heels to. The creatures around them went back to their conversations, drinks, and music as Samson set his large hands on Kano and Taliya's shoulders.

"Gently pull free of the knot," he said. "A day will come for more formal and legally binding ceremonies in the future."

Tuscan spoke up. "After the war is over."

"Yes, little one," Samson said. "After the war."

Chapter 18

Samson showed Taliya's family to Unit 206 and then left them to clean up, settle in, and have a nice long rest. The unit was a tidy prefab bamboo house, comfortably furnished. There was a sparsely stocked kitchen and dining area, a small living room with a sofa and some chairs, three bedrooms, and a full bathroom. Towels and several sets of fresh clothing were laid out on the kitchen table, and beds, nightstands, and dressers had been set up—three singles in one room for the young ones and a tigran-sized bed in another bedroom for Taliya and Kano. The third bedroom was empty, for now.

The twins and Aliania rushed around exploring, and something that had been clenched deep inside Taliya finally let go. They were not going to be struggling to get by, and she wouldn't be giving birth on a mat out in the open somewhere. The unit was more comfortable than she'd dreamed. And she was a bit in awe of whoever had been scrambling around since their arrival to prepare it all for them. Even clothes in the right sizes!

"There's no media wall," she heard Tuscan whisper to his brother.

Aliania stopped in the middle of the living room and looked around, as if noticing that fact for the first time. Taliya understood their disappointment. At the facility, technology had been used freely, if not aggressively, to keep them occupied and content. Now they were suddenly left with even less than her conservative father had allowed at home.

"It'll be okay," Tyler said, a guilty gaze slipping over to his big sister. "I'm sure there's other stuff to do."

Taliya smiled and nodded. "I'm sure there will be."

Several platters of food had been left on the kitchen counter —bits of dried meat, rolls, and chopped vegetables—and Taliya's stomach rumbled.

"You and Ali eat first," Kano said, picking up three piles of clothes from the table, "while the men get cleaned up."

Tyler snickered, and Tuscan puffed out his five-year-old chest.

"Come on, *men*," Kano said, ruffling the fur on Tuscan's head as the boys rushed for the bathroom.

Taliya and Aliania sat down at the small table, and Taliya

put together a plate of food for her daughter. *My daughter.* She let that rumble around in her head a bit, and they ate quietly while Kano supervised the showers.

"Soap, boys," she heard him say from the bathroom area. "You need to use some soap."

The twins laughed in response, and Taliya was amazed by how they seemed to be bouncing back from whatever they'd been through at the facility. Time would tell if that resilience was temporary or permanent.

The sound of dryers from the bathroom was followed by both twins bounding out, clean and dressed in pajamas and ready to eat. The shower started again, and Kano moaned happily. It was easy to imagine the joy he felt at letting hot water and soapy bubbles remove any last vestige of his nightmare experience, much worse than hers in many ways. Watching his wife be murdered in cold blood. Being separated from his daughter, with no idea what might be happening to her, knowing how valuable she was with her pure-white coat. All those worries and fears he'd been suffering through for months but never shared. Dealing with Narlin and his threats for a month longer than her. She gave the boys plates of food and hoped Kano didn't rush his relaxing shower too much, though she knew he probably would on her account.

With a full stomach came bone-aching weariness. It was tempting to lay her head on the table and nap, but she would not sleep until she'd showered too. No point in bringing those nasty smells into bed on their first night as a free family.

Kano joined them at the table, fur damp and rumpled, wearing only pajama bottoms. Taliya had set aside a plate for him before the twins ate everything in sight. With a smile, she slid it toward him and rose wearily. Aliania hopped up to join her.

"My fur is *stinky*!" she said.

"We'll take care of that right now," Taliya assured her.

Carrying their new pajamas into the bathroom, they both undressed, and Taliya kicked the dirty clothes into a corner where the boys' clothes were as well. She'd figure out laundry tomorrow. Taliya turned on the shower, adjusted the temperature, and she and Aliania stood together under the rain of warm water. Ali grabbed the soap and reached up to lather Taliya's round belly.

"Brother and sister need a bath too," she said.

Taliya laughed and helped the kit scrub off every smell from the last two days. Aliania hopped out and played with the blower, mostly getting her fur dry, while Taliya quickly finished her own shower.

Once they were dried, brushed, and tucked into fresh pajamas, Taliya helped Aliania brush her teeth and then cleaned her own. By the time they came out of the bathroom, Kano had tucked both boys into bed and they were already asleep. He picked up Ali and carried her over to her bed. She didn't resist being tucked in, too tired to fuss. Kano sat with her for a moment and rubbed her back.

"G'night, Papa," she mumbled, tucking her thumb into her mouth and closing her eyes.

234

Taliya watched from the door and felt her own eyes drooping. Kano looked up at her and smiled.

"You're next," he said, standing up and coming to her, wrapping his arms around her in a gentle hug.

"Okay," she said into his furry chest, enjoying the fresh yet musky smell of her husband.

They both staggered into their bedroom and crawled under the covers. Taliya was sure no bed had ever been more comfortable. Kano pulled her in to spoon against him and wrapped one arm around her bulging stomach. She draped her tail across his legs and closed her eyes.

"Taliya," he whispered in the dark, "can we name the girl after my mother? Amrita?"

"Of course. Amrita is a beautiful name."

"Will it be too confusing, having both daughters' names start with A?"

"You do realize that my name and my brothers' all start with T? My mother managed it just fine."

He chuckled and snuggled into her neck. "Should we name the boy after your father?"

Taliya whoofed sadly but considered this. Did it matter whether her father was alive or dead? Tradition was to never name a kit after someone alive, but what did it really matter?

"Yes, we should," she said. "If we ever find him again, he would be thrilled."

Kano chuffed and rubbed the roundness of her belly. It

brought her a great sense of peace to pick names and claim the unborn kits as part of their lineage. Generation 12 of her family.

She felt a shifting on the bed as Aliania slipped in with them. She curled up in Taliya's arms with a happy sigh, and Kano reached over to pat his daughter. It was not remotely the wedding night Taliya had imagined in her youth, but nothing about her life now was like she'd expected.

In the quiet of the night, a strange sound echoed through the camp. Taliya felt Kano tense next to her as they both listened.

"Wrooor, wrooor, wrooor," the call came from one side. Then "wrooor, wrooor, wrooor" reverberated from another part of the camp. For several minutes, the deep rumbling roars enveloped everything else as the conversation spread to include dozens of voices.

"What is that?" Aliania whispered.

"I think it's the liran," Kano said. "They're caroling, just like wild lions."

The three tigran relaxed into the comforting "all's-well" of the liran refugees and drifted off to sleep.

The next morning, not long after they were up and dressed, a young tigran arrived at the door with a note calling them to a meeting of all the creatures from their facility. They followed along to the large assembly area at the front of the camp, where they found tables covered with clothing, toys, books, and other personal items.

"We were able to grab some things while doing a final check of the building," a soldier announced. "Please see if any of these items belong to you."

Taliya wandered along the tables, fascinated by what others had managed to keep with them in captivity. Then she gasped. There on the table, a bit worse for wear but still in one piece, was her copy of Anne Frank's diary. She picked it up and thumbed through, seeing underlining and notes on the pages. Her time in that attic room with Anne's story felt like a different life, a different Taliya. She searched the rest of the tables, but none of her other books were there. Anne's diary had been by the sofa in the living room. Kano had been reading it. A guard must have swept the room and just grabbed what he could see. Her deck of cards was there too, and she smiled at the memory of teaching Kano to play solitaire without a tablet, like Marla had taught her. Then sadness washed in as she realized that all of her letters and journals and photos had not been recovered and were now buried in the rubble of the facility. A small price to pay. No one else in her family found anything to claim, and she watched the sad eyes of other refugees as they picked up treasured items or left empty-handed.

Then the whole group from their facility gathered together,

maybe two hundred creatures, though she didn't see the berman, so not everyone was there. Samson led an orientation with information about what would be provided for them and expected of them in their new home.

Life in the camp was filled with routine, and their family quickly fell in line.

The habitat dome covered ten square miles, one of the largest individual domes in existence, and contained over three hundred of the prefab bamboo houses, a hospital, a library, and several acres of vertically farmed space to provide fresh produce year-round—extensive rows of what looked like double-stacked grocery store shelves covered in plants. In a separate dome nearby, chickens and goats were raised for eggs, milk, cheese, and meat. The camp's goal was to be as self-reliant as possible. Other necessary items were donated by strangers in Canada and shipped in courtesy of the government. The entire camp was governed by a council of ten members, all human, who coordinated with the American rebellion and the Canadian government.

Five days a week—the traditional Monday through Friday—the twins attended classes in a simple school building. Changa, a male liran with a glorious dark mane, was in charge of all the students as superintendent of studies. Two female tigran and an enormous male black panthran served as teachers. Every species mixed in there together—including a few human children whose parents worked at the camp—and Taliya marveled at how the young ones didn't fuss about being different and just got on with the business of learning and playing. There was also a nursery and preschool to care for the younger refugees as needed.

Kano was able to use his skills as a mason and builder, his trade before he was captured, to help with maintenance around the camp. Between the hundreds of houses and other facilities on site, there was always a need for repairs, and work was beginning on a massive new structure at the far end of the dome. A truck picked Kano up each morning and drove him wherever he was needed, bringing him back home at the end of the day.

Taliya was still a student before the war began, without a profession to claim, and she was now well into her pregnancy, besides needing to supervise Aliania and the twins. Finding herself thrust into the world of mates and mommies was disorienting. A few months ago, she'd been a carefree teenager. Now she was helping with the farming—fortunately, something she did know about—and in charge of a two-year-old kit while two more kits tossed around inside of her, a constant reminder of their impending arrival. And then there were her brothers, who were only five—and very good at it. There had been no word yet on the location or status of her parents, so the twins were her responsibility.

She was exhausted much of the time and was grateful for the days when schooling occupied the twins. Mothers with young ones their age often invited the boys by in the afternoon so Taliya could have some peace. The atmosphere of the camp provided space for running and playing, something all of the kits had been missing. Between helping in the gardens, sorting donations, coming up with meals she could actually cook from their rations, caring for the kits, and keeping laundry done and the small house somewhat tidy, Taliya finished most days in silent shock at her housewife life. In the flick of a whisker, she'd become her mother.

The one blessing in it all, beside their obvious safety and freedom of a sort, was that Aliania was a delightful kit. She did as she was told to help weed gardens and harvest what was ready, and if she woke up from their afternoon nap before Taliya did, she would wait quietly in bed or slip off to play with the stuffed tigran doll some generous Canadian had donated.

Aliania had immediately taken to calling Taliya "mama," which worried Taliya at first. Would Kano feel it was disrespectful? Should they come up with some made-up word, or should the kit simply call her Taliya, like her brothers did? When she noticed that he also started referring to her as "mama" when talking to Ali, her worries abated. As Agnus had said, they were a family now, and Taliya was the mother. A seventeen-year-old mother.

Two months of spring slipped by in a swirl of family life and responsibilities.

The medical tent served for checking in new arrivals, minor

daily injuries and medical needs, but the hospital was a solid building with four bamboo walls and a fabricated floor. As Taliya's belly grew, she visited Agnus weekly at the hospital for scans, blood work, and checks on both her and the kits. Aliania was always excited for those visits because it involved a chance to see what her unborn siblings were up to inside of Taliya.

"He's sucking his thumb," Aliania noticed during a visit, pointing at one of the fetuses on the monitor.

"Sure look like it," Agnus agreed. "Bad habit before he even born."

Aliania looked crushed by that statement, but Agnus was busy and didn't notice. Taliya smiled at her daughter and pulled her up next to her on the exam table.

"It's okay," she whispered. "You'll stop when you're ready. Everybody deserves to have a little bad habit or two."

Aliania sighed, curled up next to Taliya, and started to slip her thumb into her mouth. Then she tucked it under her arm instead.

"All look good," Agnus declared. "You maybe got four more week till kits come."

Taliya nodded. That's what she'd expected too.

"We have find cribs and clothes," Agnus said. "Cloth diapers only here. None of that fancy modern stuff. Too much waste when we no have place for garbage as is."

"That's fine," Taliya said. "I know how to use them. That's what my mother had for the twins. My parents loved the old ways."

"Good, good," Agnus said. "Lot of laundry, but others can help make trips to machines in early days when you tired. Husband will no have to work so much for a while. He help too."

Taliya certainly hoped so.

"I'll help," Ali said determinedly. "I'll be the best help ever."

Agnus looked skeptical, but Taliya just hugged Ali tight. "I know you will."

On the way back from the appointment, they stopped at the school to pick up the twins. Changa, the liran in charge, met her at the door. He wasn't much taller than her, but his black mane presented quite an imposing picture.

"Tuscan and Tyler, you be good to your sister tonight," he said, one hand on each of the boys' shoulders. "She has much else to worry about instead of fussing with the two of you."

"I hope they were well-behaved today," Taliya said.

Tuscan and Tyler exchanged a look that made her doubt that was true, but Changa simply shrugged one shoulder.

"See you tomorrow, gentlemen," he said and gently pushed them out the door.

Taliya nodded politely as the boys ran full-tilt toward their unit. She and Aliania followed behind. She knew it was hard on them, not having even the basics of a media wall to enjoy in the house. Limited technology, in the way they'd grown up, was one thing. But none at all? She understood why her parents had never gone without the wall. It was a highly effective distraction for rambunctious young tigran.

Even Aliania missed having a media wall and movies and games. There was one at the nursery in the camp, where she and others her age were supervised sometimes to give the mothers a chance to work or have a break. That technology was on all day, according to Aliania. Taliya didn't blame the teachers one bit.

There was a media wall at the school too, used for educational purposes, but at night there was a free time for the whole camp. Refugees took turns in rotation, watching the news and a movie or two. Their family's night was Monday, which was still two school-free days away. The thought of keeping the boys occupied and out of trouble until then made her tail thrash.

Those media nights had revealed some interesting things about life at the camp and given Taliya a chance to interact with other creatures—casual conversations she rarely had time for during the day. What had been most intriguing to Taliya was discovering romantic connections between the guards Dan and Carl and two of the refugees.

She'd noticed some curious exchanges between Dan and Kallie the liran the day of their escape, but since then she'd seen them together around camp many times, including media night. Canadian law had no restrictions about inter-species relationships, and Dan and Kallie were most certainly in a relationship. Taliya didn't know if it had started before the rescue or if they had met that day, but there was no doubting the gooey looks and close conversations between the liran and her rescuer.

Even more fascinating, Carl had a mate among the refugees. From what Taliya could determine, it was new since their arrival. Many Monday evenings during the media time she had spotted Carl and Reynaldo—the male black panthran who taught at the refugee school—sitting together in cozy contact. During the occasional musical get-together around the firepit, the pair often played and sang together. In the United States, their pairing was doubly illegal. Shot on sight, no questions asked illegal. But in the camp, no one batted an eye. Neither interspecies nor same-sex relationships were against the law in Canada. Reynaldo had been living there for many months already and was well-respected, and Carl had been a valiant rescuer to a huge percentage of the current population. As a pair, they could live however they chose. Taliya appreciated the charms of the articulate, well-built Reynaldo and his unique black fur and could understand the allure that Carl felt, despite the problems it might cause him, but she still preferred her Kano.

She wasn't the only one. While Taliya's group lived in the more family friendly part of the camp—with neighbors who were tigran families secreted out of the U.S. in the early stages of the Gathering—in another section were the "dorms" of unattached teenage females and males. Kano wasn't the only white tigran male in camp, but he still caught the attention of many of the stray teen tigran ladies. When Taliya had commented on the subtle and not-so-subtle flirting he attracted, he'd laughed.

"What would I want with one of those silly teenage girls?"

"I'm a teenage girl," Taliya had said with frustration.

Kano had wrapped his arms around her and nuzzled into her neck. "You, my love, are not silly. There's a big difference. Were you *ever* silly?"

"No, never," she said with a smile, hoping he never asked her brothers that same question about her younger years. They would surely disagree.

Despite his protested lack of interest, Taliya was grateful they'd done the handfasting ceremony when they arrived. Honoring bonds like that was considered sacred around camp. So while she didn't love the tittering and giggling of the teenagers, so knew they wouldn't risk the wrath of the council and other tigran by actually attempting to steal Kano away. At least she hoped they wouldn't.

While most tigran were grateful to be safe and away from the battles, many of the younger males often congregated and discussed joining the war to fight back. They were angry, frustrated, and they wanted to take action. The council had made it clear that no one from the camp would be allowed to leave for the time being, but the territorial instinct and testosterone of teenage male tigran was difficult to contain. Many of them were put to work helping with building, to keep them busy and out of trouble. A gaggle of basically unsupervised teenagers was a litany of problems waiting to happen. Taliya was glad it wasn't her responsibility.

The council was more concerned with the handful of unclaimed tigran kits and young liran, who were created at the facility and never had a true parent. Some liran females were willing to foster and help care for them, and others stayed at the nursery 24/7. Taliya felt bad for those kits, but she already had her hands full, as did most of the other mothers at the camp.

Taliya watched as Tuscan and Tyler sprinted the final yards to their unit and then battled for who made it through the door first—shouldering and growling playfully until they tumbled inside. She definitely had her hands full. She'd have to take them out for a run once they had a snack or they'd tear the small unit apart with their roughhousing. How in the world would she deal with them after the new kits arrived? Best not to worry that far ahead, she decided. Take each day as it comes and do the best she could. So Taliya kept everyone clean, fed, and happy—media wall or no media wall—and they settled into a temporary new normal.

But if she'd learned nothing else in the last few months, their lives could change completely in seconds.

Chapter 19

Taliya had been attempting to nap, but the kits were not cooperating at all. Every time she found a comfortable position, they would begin to roll and shift, like a wrestling match going on inside of her. Sometimes she could calm them by rubbing her middle and singing, but not that afternoon. They were due in a week, and it must be getting crowded and uncomfortable in there.

A knock at the door ended her attempts to rest. Grumbling, she rolled from the bed carefully and answered it. On the other side was a young liran, barely old enough to be used for errands around camp, with a message for her. He eyed her blooming belly under her tunic at eye level with him and giggled.

"Message for Taliya from the medical tent," he said.

"That's me," she assured him.

He rushed off the moment she took the note, hurrying to other deliveries. She frowned. *What could they want with me in medical?* She'd just had an appointment with Agnus. Was something wrong? All the note said was that she should report to Samson there immediately. If he was involved, it was important. He had a whole camp of creatures to worry about.

She tidied up quickly and used the bathroom—for the seventh time since breakfast. Taliya was grateful going barefoot around camp was acceptable. Her shoes wouldn't fit on her swollen feet if her life depended on it. She left the note on the table in case the family came home before she did. Aliania was napping in the nursery that day, and Kano had agreed to pick her up, along with the boys, after school. He was already cutting back his work hours with the possibility that the kits could arrive early.

Hurrying as best she could, supporting under her belly with one hand, Taliya made her way through the crowded streets. Other female tigran smiled at her in sympathy, and one gave her a small chuff as they passed. Before Taliya made it to the tent, she spotted indications that a new group had arrived. Medical was often busy, but there were more soldiers than usual and two dozen confused-looking tigran.

She let a tiger moan escape. All she wanted to do was rest, not help process new arrivals. There had to be someone else they could call on. Samson, the massive ligran, stepped out of the medical tent and spotted her hovering nearby.

"Taliya, thank goodness," he said.

She headed grudgingly in his direction. "I got your message."

"Thank you for coming so quickly. I know it is a bit trickier than normal." He smiled and looked appreciatively at her belly. "Almost time now?"

"Almost," she said with a sigh.

"Good. I'm glad we can tuck this in before then. Come."

She had no idea what needed tucking, but she trundled after him into the medical tent. Inside was a full-on hubbub of doctors and nurses, with new arrivals filling every cot and hanging out at the entrance, waiting their turn. There were even humans among them, and she shuddered at the bandages, the tang of blood, and the aroma of sour bodies that circulated in the air. Were they from a facility or somewhere worse?

"The last cot on the right," Samson said with a huge grin, showing off his fangs.

Taliya nodded numbly and started working her way in that direction, but she wasn't halfway there before she halted in shock. A nurse was taking the vital signs of a tigran. Taliya scanned the stripe pattern again. She could only see the back of the tigran's head, and she couldn't smell clearly through all the chemicals and bodies in the tent. Only the markings on the face would tell her for sure. Pushing through the crowd, she burst around the far side of the cot. The new arrival sitting there looked up wearily. Then she smiled.

249

"Oh, Taliya. You're really here."

Taliya burst into tears and heaved several gasping sobs. Her mother reached out, her hands wrapped in medical bandages. Taliya sat down awkwardly on the cot next to her mother and watched the tigran's eyes shift from her face to her belly. Tears sprung to her mother's eyes as well.

"It's fine," Taliya assured her, wiping her eyes on her sleeve. "I'm fine."

Mother and daughter embraced as best they could and rubbed foreheads, taking in the smell of the loved-one who'd been separate for so many months.

"I should have warned you," her mother said, "but how could I explain something as horrific as forced breeding to my innocent daughter? I prayed you'd never be found. Never have to know about any of it."

"Shreya, you need to lie down now," the nurse said.

Shreya nodded, and Taliya shifted so her mother could stretch out on the cot. Moving past the initial shock, Taliya realized her mother had extensive bandages not only on her hands but on her feet as well. She smelled stale blood and hints of infection. Taliya whoofed sadly at her mother, and Shreya slow-blinked in return.

"I'll be all right, Taliya. I just need to rest. They said the boys are here too."

"Yes, they are perfectly fine. A bit too fine some days."

Shreya sighed and chuffed quietly. Her eyes blinked slowly again and then closed.

"I've given her a light sedative," the nurse explained. "We hoped you'd get here before she fell asleep, but I didn't want to wait. She must be in terrible pain."

Taliya rested her hand on her mother's chest and was comforted by the regular heartbeat. Before she could ask any questions, she smelled Samson behind her. He stretched out his massive hand and helped her up.

"She will rest better now that she has seen you," he said. "We assured her you and the boys were here and safe, but she had to see for herself. I considered sending a message to the school, but I was not sure if the young ones should see her like this."

Taliya looked back at her mother, resting peacefully but clearly not well. Probably best not to let the boys see her just yet.

"Everyone here was rescued from a prisoner of war camp," Samson said.

But those weren't battle wounds on her mother's hands and feet. Taliya's heart raced.

"Your mother will be healthy again," Samson said, taking her firmly by the shoulders.

A sob caught in her throat, and she collapsed onto his solid chest, his tunic absorbing her tears. She had imagined her mother off fighting in the war, facing terrible dangers. She was prepared for her mother to be dead, but somehow it was infinitely worse to discover that she had been captured and tortured. Taliya looked up into Samson's golden eyes.

251

"What did they do to her?"

"We do not know the full extent of what happened," he said quietly, "but the bandages you see are from one of the most common punishments for tigran. She was declawed."

Taliya had heard of the ancient practice. Felines had often had their claws removed to make them more compatible with a civilized human environment. The process involved removing the claw and top knuckle from each paw. What would that even look like on a tigran with human-like hands? She studied the bandages on her mother and involuntarily flexed her own claws in and out, grateful that was one horror she had been spared at the facility.

"I smell infection," she said.

"Yes. That's the bigger concern at the moment. Once we get that under control, the doctors here can do some corrective surgery."

"But they can't restore her claws, can they."

"No. The Enforcers usually just chop off the tips of the fingers with little regard for what is left behind. Your mother's wounds look new, just within the week."

She flinched at his bluntness, but there was a tent full of victims of the Enforcers. He had more to worry about than her family. She looked around at all of the creatures. *So many.* At least forty already in the tent, with more waiting to come in. A spark flickered in her mind.

"My father?"

"We do not believe he is with this group. We asked your mother, but she did not want to talk about it. I have to assume he is not here."

Taliya nodded. That could mean he was still alive and fighting somewhere.

"We will transfer Shreya to your unit as soon as the medical staff feels she is ready. I have already ordered supplies for her, and they should be on the way shortly."

"Thank you," she said, her voice cracking at the thought of them all under one roof again.

"You are welcome, but there is one more thing. It will be more difficult. Are you feeling okay?" His eyes travelled down to her belly.

The kits were being remarkably calm in the middle of what was swarming around them. She nodded, though she couldn't imagine what would be harder than seeing her mother like that.

"Then follow me," he said, heading to another section of the tent.

Weaving their way through the patients and medics, he led her to a cot where a human female was sleeping. Her face was swollen and covered in bruises of varying shades from on-going abuse. Medical leads and wires ran out from under her dirty tunic and were hooked up to monitors. One arm was in a cast, and the bulkiness under the blanket over her legs suggested they were bandaged as well. Taliya couldn't imagine why Samson thought she needed to see this woman. Maybe to understand that her mother could be in worse shape?

"Your mother says you know this tigran."

"Tigran? This can't be a tigran."

Deep within the odors of sickness and injury, Taliya caught a familiar scent. Her chest clenched, and she couldn't draw breath. It was impossible to be sure based on appearance. The battered face was unrecognizable, and the patient's brown hair had been shaved close to her head. Taliya clamped a hand over her mouth, feeling her gorge rise, and her hackles spiked from her tail all the way up the back of her head. She swallowed and moaned.

"Is that Marla?" she whispered.

Samson picked up the medical chart. "Marla Jones," he read. "Tests show she is definitely part tigran. A highly illegal tigran, I would guess."

"Her father was human, and her mother was a white tigran."

"So you do know her?"

"She hid me. She took care of me and tried to keep me safe. I never knew what happened to her after I was captured." She swallowed roughly again, willing herself not to vomit. *Gods, Marla, what did they do to you?*

"They must have figured out what she was," Samson said. "Any blood test would have revealed it, no matter how hard she had tried to cover it up physically. I imagine . . . Well, I imagine they were cruel. Ruthless, even. I am shocked they let her live."

Taliya stared at her friend, trying to piece together features

254

under all of the swelling. A wave of depression washed over her, sheer exhaustion in her soul at the reckless destruction of two tigran she loved—and many others she'd never met being cared for in the tent around her.

"Will she survive?"

"Her injuries are mostly breaks and bruises," Samson said. "Nothing life-threatening. She should heal with time. At least physically."

Taliya checked Marla's hands and growled. They had been declawed—both hands missing the end of each finger at the first knuckle—even though Marla never had actual claws at all. Her amputations were already healed over and gave a picture of what Shreya's would look like eventually. Marla must have been in the POW camp a while. Maybe since the day Taliya was captured.

Was she tortured to give away my hiding place?

The Taliya who had first gone into hiding would have judged her for that. The Taliya who stood by her cot in that moment forgave her immediately.

"She will be sedated for a couple of days," Samson said. "They will be transferring her to the hospital any moment. She will need a friend."

"I understand. My family will certainly stand with her after all she sacrificed for me. And endured *because* of me." She sniffled and wiped her eyes. "Thank you. Again."

The ligran placed his massive tawny hand on her shoulder

for a moment and then, with a small nod, moved on to other business. Taliya stood alone, watching Marla sleep.

"Taliya?"

She looked toward the call and found Kano at the back of the tent. He must have stopped by the house and seen her note. She waved to him. There was no way he'd be able to single out her smell quickly in that mass of stench. He rushed to her side.

"This is what they called you for?" he said, looking at the victim on the cot.

"Yes, well, not entirely. I'll explain it all on the way home."

He wrapped his arm around her and guided her through the crowd of weary and injured strangers, out the back of the tent. On the walk to their unit, she shared everything she'd learned.

"At least they're free now," he said, stopping on the side of the road and pulling her in as close as possible. "We have the extra bedroom for the new kits. Why don't we bring them both to live with us?"

"Are you sure?" she said, unable to keep more tears from coming. "My mother is one thing, but Marla too?"

"Didn't Marla risk her life to save you?"

"Yes, you know she did."

"Then that's all I need. We should support and help her now. It sounds like she won't be able to live alone for ages and will have a long full recovery. Housing is going to be in short supply. We can't have her crammed in with strangers."

Taliya wiped her eyes with the sleeve of her tunic and nodded.

"And being with your mother is sure to be helpful for Marla," he added. "They'll know what the other one went through and be able to offer support."

"Thank you, Kano."

"You're welcome, but how could we do anything less?"

She buried her face into his chest and took a moment to absorb his warmth and smell. Then she stepped back and got control of herself.

"We should go to the school and tell the boys," she said. "I don't want to take them into the medical tent or have them see her just yet, but at least we can let them know that Mother is here and safe."

"And moving in," Kano said with a smile.

"And moving in, yes. We should let Samson and the doctors know about Marla so they can plan to transfer her to us when she's ready."

Kano nodded, and they headed for the schoolhouse, hand in hand. As she lumbered along slowly next to him, Taliya sighed and rubbed her belly.

Every time I think my world's getting a bit more settled, it just flips right over again. In a week, we will have two infant kits and two injured tigran to care for.

How she was going to manage all of that in a refugee camp, she had no idea. At least they were all safe and free. Well, free enough.

Shreya was able to move in after only two days. Her infection was healed, and the doctors made some repairs to the crude declawing of her hands and feet. Tuscan and Tyler had been able to visit her after she was transferred to the hospital and were hesitant to leave her side. They took a few days away from school once Shreya moved in, and Taliya often found them curled up in their mother's bed or on the floor next to it. They were proud to show their mother how much they had learned and kept all three of them entertained by reading aloud and playing board games they borrowed from the camp library. The boys had to move the game pieces for Shreya because her hands were still bandaged, but that was temporary.

Aliania had already started to call her Grandma, but she didn't join in on the cuddling sessions, as if she understood the twins needed that time alone with their mother. Taliya noticed a look in the young kit's eyes now and then and was sure something deep in Ali's soul was missing her own mother—who would never be rescued and turn up at the medical tent, who had been murdered in front of her. Even though she didn't have much of a lap left, Taliya made sure Ali got extra attention.

With all the activity in the house, Taliya stayed quiet about the mild contractions she felt at least once an hour. Agnus assured her this was normal and quite helpful, just her body getting ready, but each twinge set the tigran's heart racing. In the rare moments she was alone, she explained to the kits in her belly that she needed them to hang in there just a bit longer.

"Wait until Marla is settled," she begged, patting the bulge gently.

The third bedroom had been supplied with two large beds and dressers, and a crib in Taliya and Kano's room would serve the newborn kits temporarily. The small unit was definitely going to be crowded, but Taliya was glad they would all be tucked in together. Everyone needed to be in one place before the kits came, if she could possibly arrange it.

It was closer to the end of the week before Marla was ready to leave the hospital. The swelling of her face was down, and the doctors had reset her broken nose. The wounds on her legs and the bottoms of her feet from being beaten with a cane were improving, and her broken arm would heal with time. The declawing had been done months earlier, so improving that, if it was even possible, could happen later. Taliya had visited her several times, but Marla was always sleeping or sedated. The medical team had told Marla she would move in with the family when she was ready, but the two tigran had not spoken yet.

Now that her mother was settled in, Taliya headed back to the hospital. She hoped the doctors would release Marla to her care soon. Agnus encouraged the pregnant tigran to get some walking in every day, but Taliya felt like her belly might explode. If the false labor pains—now coming more like every twenty minutes—and the heaviness of the kits were signs, they didn't have much runway left. She panted her way through a contraction as she entered the hospital. *Not yet. Not yet.*

Taliya smiled at the tigran nurse sitting at the entrance of the recovery wing, and the nurse grinned broadly, revealing lovely fangs.

"She's awake," she said. "At least she was a few minutes ago. I was so worried you'd miss each other again."

"Wonderful." Taliya sighed. "We have my mother moved into the house, and I'm hoping we can transfer Marla today. What did the doctor say?"

"He says you can take her whenever you're ready. Besides monitoring her, there's no reason to keep her in the hospital at this point. We'll want to move her by wheelchair. I wish we had some hover beds, but a wheelchair will do."

"Perfect."

Taliya gave the nurse a thumbs-up and hurried to Marla's bed. She was awake and smiled when she saw Taliya coming. Then her eyes shifted to the massive belly and tears formed. Taliya eased down in a chair next to the bed and took Marla's hand as she reached for her.

"Oh, Taliya. I'm so sorry."

"Great gods, what for?"

"I never told them where you were. Never. I swear."

Taliya squeezed her friend's hand gently before letting it go, not sure how much it might still hurt, and shook her head.

"I wouldn't blame you if you had. I'm not a kit who thinks it's possible to resist."

"But I still didn't tell them. They never asked. They already knew. I don't know how, but they did. They knew about me. What I was hiding from the world about my tigran mother. And they knew where you were. Enforcers were waiting for me that morning when I got back from the market. They arrested me and shut down the facility for the day. Probably so no one saw them capture you."

"I worried when you didn't come that morning, but I hoped it was something else. Like you were sick or just unable to sneak up without being seen. I hate that you had to suffer so much. If you'd stayed out of my life, you could have kept on hiding and the Enforcers wouldn't have found you."

"Maybe," Marla said. "But I'm not sure it was related. From little things they said, I think I led them to you, not the other way around."

"But then what did they want to know? Why were they beating you?"

"Besides just hating me? When they'd show up at my cell with the cane . . ." She adjusted herself in the bed. "They never asked me anything. I think they just enjoyed seeing me suffer. They . . . They enjoyed a lot of terrible things."

Marla's eyes lowered to Taliya's belly. Flashes of Narlin, cattle prod in hand and smirk on his face, slipped through Taliya's mind. What she had escaped, she suspected Marla had not. Taliya's skin prickled.

Are all human men so violent and disgusting? She closed her eyes for a moment and thought of Carl and Dan and the doctors there. *No, not all of them.*

"I met Agnus," Marla said, changing the subject, "and she told me about what you'd been through, your situation. You have a husband now?"

"Yes. Kano. He's very kind. You'll meet him soon. Hopefully very, very soon."

"Good. That's a blessing in all of this horror."

An image of Narlin, blood spurting from his neck, flashed through Taliya's mind.

"A lot more went on at that facility than just breeding," she said. "They had a whole stock of females. I didn't know about any of that until the last minute, when we were escaping and everything was crazy, but the man in charge had plans for me." A growl rumbled up from her chest, and she glowered. "I would have done what was necessary to save the kits and my brothers, but rescue came in time."

Marla smiled but looked confused. "That's good, right?"

"I killed him. I slit his throat with my claws and didn't feel the least bit sorry."

"Why would you? I can think of a few human males I'd gladly rip apart if I could. Going right for the throat would be far too quick."

"I killed two Enforcers too," Taliya admitted. "When they came to capture me in the attic." A memory of the metallic taste of their blood and the warmth of it running out of her mouth as she held her jaws on their necks, fangs deep in their jugulars, made her swallow uncomfortably.

"Well done, again," Marla said. "Taliya, you aren't going to get any guilt trips from me. This is, quite literally, war. If the Enforcers had left you in peace, you'd still be at your family's compound, wandering happily through the woods in Arkansas and never killing anything, ever."

"True. It's hard to even stir up what that life felt like."

"But you have a home here, for now, and family surrounding you."

Taliya laughed. "So much family!"

"Are you sure there's room for me? They can find me other housing."

"Not a chance. You're coming to live with us. Unless you have some relatives or other friends here?"

"Not that I know of. I'm sure the council would have found connections by now, if they could."

"Then you're a part of *our* family. You'll be sharing a room with my mother, until the new kits are old enough to require their own space. Then maybe they'll move us into a larger unit. Or Mother and the boys will get their own place. Otherwise, we will just be cozy."

Taliya's stomach visibly tightened and peaked in a contraction, like the kits knew she was talking about them. Marla's eyes widened, and she sat up more on the bed.

"Are you in labor? I could see that right through your tunic."

"It's nothing," Taliya said, panting as the pain eased off. "Well, maybe not nothing, but not the real thing. Not yet. But it won't be long now."

Marla giggled, a sound that caught Taliya off guard. Then she placed her maimed hand on Taliya's belly. One of the kits gave it a solid kick in response, and Marla giggled again.

"It will be delightful beyond words to be in a house filled with kits," she said. "That sounds like the perfect place to recover and remember what life is really about."

"Then let's get you moved," Taliya said as she struggled out of the chair.

After a few phone calls to locate her husband and much paperwork, Kano met them at the hospital and wheeled Marla to her new home. Shreya was resting on the sofa when they arrived—her hands and feet still too tender to do much else—but she smiled softly at Marla and gave her a small wave as Kano pushed the chair past and into the bedroom.

"Welcome home," Kano said once Marla was settled into her new bed. "I put a bell here on the bedside table, in case you need anything. That's what my mom would always do when I was sick so I wouldn't holler for her all the time. They use them at the school now."

Marla laughed and touched the old-fashioned, long-handled bell. "I can't imagine I'll need this. I can walk, you know."

"Of course," he said. "But just in case."

Then he rolled the wheelchair back out to return it to the hospital. Taliya sat down on the other bed and watched Marla settle in and adjust. She was quite pale, and Taliya hoped they hadn't rushed things.

"Get some rest now," she said. "You look exhausted."

"I am, and maybe I can actually sleep some here. At the hospital, they're forever waking you up to take vital signs or ask questions. They even wanted to measure my pee every time I went."

"I promise not to measure your pee," Taliya said with a smile.

"Excellent," Marla said, returning the smile. "That Kano is something else. You won the lottery, no doubt about it."

Taliya knew it was true. In the middle of madness, she'd gotten quite lucky.

"He's wonderful, yes."

"Wonderful? He's a freakin' white tigran demi-god! And those eyes. Oh dear! There aren't many creatures like him in the world. You two are going to have some amazing-looking kits."

Taliya agreed and hoped Marla was right. From the increasing strength and frequency of her contractions, they'd know the answer quite soon.

"Once you're better," Taliya said, "you'll see there are some outstanding candidates here in the camp."

A shadow crossed Marla's face, but she forced a smile as she adjusted her pillow one last time. Taliya realized it would require a different kind of recovery—help repairing more than her body—before Marla would be willing to consider a male of any species. There were counselors she could see. Taliya would have to arrange that right away. She helped adjust the covers as her friend sighed and closed her eyes.

It was Taliya's turn to care for Marla now.

Chapter 20

It was one o'clock in the morning when a searing pain across her abdomen woke her. Taliya breathed through it, like Agnus had taught her, but the contraction lasted longer and was definitely stronger than those over the last few days. Kano was sleeping soundly next to her, his tail draped across her legs, but she could hear someone else awake, in the living room. She slipped from the bed to investigate. Her mother was stretched out on the sofa, reading a book. She'd heard Taliya coming and was already looking in her direction.

"I couldn't sleep and didn't want to disturb Marla," Shreya said, "though the pills they sent for her should have her out for a while."

Taliya joined her on the sofa, plopping down near her

mother's feet. There were only minor bandages remaining, but she avoided touching them.

"Are you hurting?" Taliya asked. "You avoid taking the pain pills, but you really should if you need to."

"They make me loopy," Shreya said. "You have enough to worry about without having to fuss more over me."

Taliya chuffed, and Shreya returned it. They sat quietly for a minute before another sharp pain and muscle spasm gripped Taliya.

"Wow!" she gasped, curling around her belly, grabbing her mother's leg and panting until she felt the last of the pain subside.

"That was a strong one," Shreya said. "How close together are they now?"

"One like that woke me up right before I came out here."

Shreya sat up and swung her legs off the sofa. "That's close enough to take seriously. I'll go wake Kano."

Taliya wanted to delay, to tell her mother not to walk on her sore feet, but the kits shifted and made her catch her breath. Maybe it really was time. She heard Shreya and Kano mumbling to each other, then Kano burst from the bedroom— eyes wide, white fur standing on end. He rushed over and sat down beside her.

"Are you okay? Why didn't you wake me?"

"I'm fine. And I didn't think it was time to wake everyone up. Mother disagrees."

He raked his fingers through his ruff and then headed back into the bedroom.

"I'm going to get dressed and find Agnus," he called over his shoulder.

He was back in a few seconds. Shreya was busy opening kitchen cupboards and getting out the supplies already stored there. The birthing chair had been waiting in the corner for over a week. Agnus had decided they could have the kits at home, unless there was some complication. It would be more peaceful than the clinical setting of the hospital. All Taliya's tests showed that the birth should be routine. Agnus would come and assist.

Observing the preparations, Taliya's heart raced. She was excited and terrified and elated all at the same time. She wanted to help so her mother didn't hurt her hands, but another pain gripped her. Kano and Shreya both paused, watching her breathe through it.

"Four minutes apart," Shreya said with authority. "Get Doctor Agnus now, but we may not be able to wait for you."

Kano hesitated, staring at Taliya in panic. "But what if I miss it?"

"I can go," Tuscan said from his bedroom doorway.

Kano slow-blinked at his brother-in-law, and Tuscan ran out the door, not worrying about wearing his PJs or being barefoot. Tyler staggered out of the bedroom next, and Aliania peeked around the corner behind him. Kano motioned for her

269

to join them, and Ali hesitantly moved to the sofa and curled up next to Taliya.

"Are they ready to come out now?" Ali asked.

"I think so," Taliya said. "I know I'm ready for them to come out. How about you?"

Ali nodded and smiled. Shreya sat down on the other side of Aliania and scooped the little one onto her lap.

"Remember how we talked about being a helper to Mama when the new kits arrive?"

"I remember. I will be the biggest helper ever."

Kano chuckled and sat down next to Taliya. He reached across her and patted his daughter's leg. Then he let his hand rest on Taliya's massive belly. One of the kits pressed against it with a tiny foot.

"I want to help them be born," Ali said, rubbing sleep from her eyes.

"As long as things are going well," Kano said, "you can stay, like we planned. But remember, if an adult tells you to go to your room, you are to go immediately, without a fuss. Can you do that?"

"Yes, Papa."

"Good."

Taliya's middle clenched under Kano's hand. He caught her eye, and she smiled. With her hands on either side of her visibly peaked belly, she took deep breaths in and out.

"That seems like less than four minutes," he said.

She nodded her agreement, panting through the last of the contraction.

"I think a change of clothes is in order," Shreya said. "Let's get you into the gown."

Tyler had slipped back into his room, but Taliya could sense him near the doorway. He'd been excited to be part of the birth, but maybe it was too much for him now. She'd let him decide.

"It's odd," she said to Shreya as her mother helped her change. "There's so much technology in the world, but having kits is still having kits. Mammal infants come like they have for thousands of years."

"More like millions," Shreya said, adjusting the gown over Taliya's shoulders so it fell evenly. "There's medical help if you need it, but nature usually takes care of things. Twins are a bit more complicated, but your brothers were born in our home without incident. We can expect the same. Twins, even triplets, are very normal for tigran."

Taliya hugged her close—as close as her belly would allow —and sighed, silently grateful it wasn't triplets.

"It will all be fine," Shreya assured her. "And it will be over before you know it. Then the real work begins."

Taliya laughed, nuzzling her nose into her mother's neck like a toddler. "Great."

Shreya pulled away and took Taliya by the shoulders, looking into her golden eyes.

"I know this wasn't the plan for your life. Being a mother at seventeen. Being married. Caring for Ali and all of us now. Life rarely goes along just how we planned. But you can do this. And be good at it. *Enjoy* it."

Taliya nodded and started to respond, but another pain seized her.

"Let's get you to the chair," Shreya said as soon as it passed.

Taliya settled in on the bamboo birthing chair. There was a large cut-out in the seat, ready for the delivery of newborns of every species, and ceramic bowls and absorbent pads were arranged underneath. Kano pulled up a chair on one side of her, and Shreya did the same on the other side. Aliania stood in front of her and put her hands on Taliya's furry knees.

"It will be okay, Mama," she said, copying what she'd seen from the adults. "You can do this."

Such serious words from the little mouth made Taliya smile. "Thank you, Ali."

After a quick knock at the door, Tuscan came in followed by Agnus, who stepped inside with authority, a medical bag at her side, rapidly donning a cap and gown.

"Okay, okay, I here now," she said, filling the room with her presence.

The tiny woman gently moved Ali to the side and immediately began some checks on her patient's heart and blood pressure. Tuscan carried a cylindrical tank with a breathing mask. He set it down next to Taliya and then stepped back, looking overwhelmed by the whole scene.

272

"Thank you for getting Agnus," Kano said. "You can stay here, or you can wait in your room. Or the sofa. It's up to you. It could still be a while."

"I'll wait in our room," he said, glancing at Tyler peeking from the door. "But I wanna meet our niece and nephew as soon as they're out."

Another contraction started, and attention turned to Taliya. Tuscan slipped away, and Ali tucked herself between Kano and the chair.

"Good, good," Agnus said. "Keep breathing." She used her scanner to check the kits' heartbeats and looked pleased. "Solid, strong contractions. Good, good. Kits nice and low. Ready to come." She moved over to the tank and hooked up the mask. Bringing it right in front of the chair, she offered it to Taliya. "Breathe in little bit gas. It help relax you but no put you to sleep. Help things open up. Less pain. Not fancy, like in big-city hospital, but it do the trick."

Taliya leaned into the mask, breathing in the gas. She could only detect the slightest of odors. Nothing unpleasant. After three breaths, Agnus moved the mask away. Sitting back in the chair, Taliya felt a delightful relaxation flow through her body, but her mind stayed alert. The world just felt suddenly much more calm and peaceful.

"Happy stuff, huh?" Agnus said.

"Oh yeah," Taliya agreed with a smile.

Her stomach peaked again, and she was vaguely aware

273

of pain and pressure, but it was less aggressive. She heard a splash and realized the water had broken for one of the kits. Ali looked alarmed, but Agnus just clapped her hands twice in delight.

"Here we go," she said. "Kit number one not be long now."

Kano whispered something in Ali's ear about what the water meant, and she smiled. Taliya felt an odd sensation, pressing down like she might burst.

"Oh," she said in confusion. "I think something's wrong. It burns."

"No, no, no," Agnus said, waving a hand to whish away the fear, "burning means kit is coming. Coming *now*." She reached under the chair and between Taliya's legs. "Yes, I can feel top of furry little head. Next time you feel contraction start, you push little bit. Not too much yet. Need kit to crown."

Taliya nodded, but she didn't have to wait long. Her muscles tightened, and she tried her first push. The kit slipped more into place, and she whoofed in shock.

"Breathe!" Agnus yelled.

Taliya hadn't realized she was seizing up, but she started to pant and did her best to relax. She looked over at Kano, and tears were pooled up in his eyes. When that contraction was done, Agnus leaned back and looked intently at Taliya.

"Okay, Mama, next contraction, you push hard. This kit ready."

Taliya nodded and took a deep breath. The gas must have

been wearing off because there was no doubt about the next contraction. It gripped her whole body. She grabbed the chair arms on either side of her and pushed. With a whush, the kit slid out and into Agnus's waiting hands. She clipped the cord with a practiced move and wrapped the newborn in a blanket while everyone waited expectantly. Agnus pulled the bundle up where the family could see him.

"Say hello to little boy."

The orange and black kit opened his mouth in a startled squeak, and everyone sighed in awe. Agnus handed him to Taliya, and her heart leapt. After all those months, it still hadn't seemed quite real. Now here he was, writhing and squealing and making a yelpy fuss about his rude introduction to the world.

"Hello, Jai," Taliya said, wiping his face with the blanket.

Kano leaned in close, and Ali giggled.

"He's so tiny," she said.

"Give kit to Daddy now," Agnus said. "He can do cleanup while we get you ready for number two."

Taliya reluctantly handed Jai to Kano, and he tucked the newborn kit into his arms.

"Come on, buddy," Kano said. "Let's get you ready for the world."

He had already prepared the kitchen table with towels and blankets and some warm water. Ali helped Kano wash the kit, fasten him into a diaper, and swaddle him in a fresh blanket

275

while Agnus tended to the afterbirth and preparing Taliya for the next delivery.

"Good, good," Agnus said. "Everything perfect. Perfect kit. Good."

Shreya handed Taliya a glass of water, and she took a few sips. Then her mother patted her hand and sat back down. Kano took Jai to the boys' room so they could see him, then he handed the newborn kit back to Taliya for a few minutes. They all sat in wonder and stared at the new member of the family until Taliya felt another contraction coming on. Kano took the newborn back and snuggled him close with one arm while holding her hand with the other. Agnus got the gas again and gave Taliya a few whiffs. It helped to ease her pains, but the waters on the second kit had not come yet.

"Sometime number two take own sweet time," Agnus said. "No problem. No worry. Just try relax and breathe."

After thirty minutes of no more progress, Jai started to fuss louder, and Kano was unable to comfort his son.

"Try nurse him," Agnus suggested. "Definitely help him. Maybe help kit number two also. Make body get going."

Agnus helped Taliya lift the gown over her head. It seemed kind of silly to be worrying about modesty at that point anyhow. Then Kano handed her the kit, and Agnus helped her adjust and direct him. Jai latched on immediately, like he wasn't sure why they had all been denying him this luxury. Taliya was only mildly aware of the tugging of her son nursing and wished she hadn't taken more of the gas. Agnus seemed to sense her thoughts.

"You have plenty time to feel over next few months," she said with a smile. "Plenty time. And two of them."

Taliya laughed and looked down at Jai. She was sure there wasn't a more perfect kit in the whole universe. How could any human, ever, have considered him worthless?

"Oh my!" Marla exclaimed.

Everyone turned toward where she held onto the door frame in surprise.

"Big party here," Agnus said. "Get chair. Come on."

Shreya pulled over a chair from the kitchen table and sat Marla down next to her. Jai had already stopped nursing and fallen asleep, his energy spent. Taliya handed him to Marla—adjusting him carefully to avoid her broken arm—and she and Shreya marveled at how beautiful he was.

"What lovely markings he has," Marla said, gently touching the pattern of dots and stripes on Jai's little face.

Taliya smiled. She had already memorized every mark and agreed they were magnificent. Agnus handed her the gas mask, and she inhaled as another contraction started. Agnus checked on the kit's progress and seemed concerned.

"Water not coming, but I think kit ready. Time help out." She dug in her bag and found what looked like a crochet hook. After wiping it with one of the alcohol pads, she reached under the chair again. "This not hurt, but hold still."

With a gentle poke and pull, the waters broke for kit number two. She slipped more into place, and Taliya gasped, grabbing the arms of the chair.

"There we go," Agnus said. "Better."

Better wasn't the first word Taliya would have gone for, but she knew it meant they were nearly there.

"Same as last time," Agnus said, "when next pain come, push only little bit."

Kano took Taliya's hand and squeezed. "Almost over now."

She nodded and felt the next contraction begin. *Little push. Little push.* Knowing now what the burning sensation meant, instinct tempted her to just push the kit out. Now. But she could feel Agnus checking that all was well. She needed to wait.

"Okay," Agnus said. "Everything in place. Next time, push big. Okay?"

Taliya nodded, relieved and definitely ready to push big.

"Push out my *sister*," Aliania whispered.

Taliya looked over at her and smiled. She knew the little one was very excited to have two new siblings, but a sister was what really interested her. Her uncles were a bit much. A sister would be all hers to play with. Kano adjusted Ali on his lap and gave her a hug. He caught Taliya's eyes as the next contraction started. She panted, and he grinned.

"Here we go," Agnus said. "Push."

Taliya wanted to laugh. Like she had any choice. Her body had all but taken over now and knew it was time for that kit to come out. She was barely even conscious of pushing as her daughter slid into the world.

Agnus caught the kit and started her quick checks, but the family could hear the offended squeals already. Ali tried peeking under the chair to see her sister, but Kano held her back out of the way. Taliya just panted and tried to relax. It was done. The kits were here. But as seconds ticked on and Agnus didn't pull the newborn up where they could see, concern rushed through her. Was something wrong?

"What is it?" Shreya said.

Agnus was silent, which was even more terrifying than not seeing the kit.

"Agnus, what's wrong?" Taliya said firmly.

"Oh, no. Nothing wrong," Agnus said. "I just being sure. Never seen anything like it."

Kano's eyes looked panicked. "Like what?" he said, craning his neck to look under the chair at the kit.

"We get her clean up and know for sure," Agnus said, finally lifting the bundle into view and handing her to Taliya.

Kano caught his breath, and Shreya clasped both bandaged hands over her mouth.

"What in the world?" Marla said.

Taliya gazed into the face of her daughter, and loved washed over her. She realized what all the fuss was about. The kit was a white tigran, as expected, but her stripes were not black. Nor were they missing, like Aliania's. The kit was white and lightly covered in an amazing pattern of pale-orange stripes, with a few peach-colored dots on her face and between her ears.

"She what they call golden tabby tigran," Agnus said. "I only ever hear about it. Never see it."

"A strawberry tigran," Marla added. "I've read about them. It's like the white gene mutation taken to another level. They are very rare. I mean, like, I'm not sure there are any others in the world."

Taliya set her daughter to nursing, but her heart clenched. Rare was not good. Rare brought too much attention. She looked up at Agnus and could tell the doctor was pondering something.

"I not recording this," Agnus said. "Not going in computer. Just say 'white' and no more."

"That's probably best," Kano said. "We feel safe now, but you never know what the future will bring."

"The scientists would want her very badly, wouldn't they," Taliya said.

"Super badly," Agnus agreed. "Thing like this make lot of money. Always about *money*."

The kit had stopped nursing, and Taliya cradled her gently.

"No one will take you from us, Amrita," she cooed. "You are our little strawberry miracle."

Kano reached for Amrita, and Taliya handed her over. He chuffed at his new daughter, and he and Ali took her over to the table for a bit of cleanup and a diaper. Watching, Taliya could see what had captivated Agnus for so long. Nothing but white fur and peach stripes. *Dangerously unique.*

While Shreya and Kano tended to the newborns, Agnus helped Taliya tidy up, wrap up in what felt like a diaper, slip back into her pajamas, and get settled onto the sofa. The doctor dealt with the mess in the corner and bagged everything up for removal. Then Agnus checked over the newborns one more time, weighing and poking them and making notes in the portable tech tablet from her bag. Kano opened the kitchen window, and Taliya was grateful. The house had a definite funk to it. It was still dark outside, but any creature walking past would certainly know the kits had arrived.

"You got two healthy, beautiful newborns," Agnus finally pronounced. "I hope council has bigger place ready soon. This lot of tigran in one house."

Everyone chuckled. Yes, lots of tigran. Kano sat down with the twins and handed Jai to his mother. Ali curled up on the sofa next to Kano. The new uncles slipped out of their room to meet their niece, then staggered back to bed. Marla and Shreya sat at the kitchen table, both looking sleepy but happy.

"My father would have loved this," Taliya said. "All of us under one roof, like in the old days. He hated how spread out society had become. 'Family is the most important thing, and family should stay together.' He loved to say that."

Taliya looked at her mother. There were tears in her eyes but a smile on her face. They could remember him with love every time they saw the furry face of his namesake, Jai.

"I go for now," Agnus said, "but I come back 'round dinnertime when clinic close. Just do quick check in with all the females here." Her eyes scanned Shreya quickly but came to rest on Marla, probably checking her over with a medical eye. "Someone come soon and get all those supplies and mess out of way. Nature take over now. Nurse them. Keep diapers clean. Sleep. Everybody try to *sleep*." She looked around at the group, and they all nodded obediently. "You have big support here," she said to Taliya. "Take help."

"I will," Taliya promised, though she doubted she would have a choice. There were many hands, regardless of damage or bandages, waiting for their chance with the kits.

Amrita had roused and was nuzzling around fruitlessly on Kano's chest. He switched kits with Taliya so she could let their daughter nurse some more. Jai was sound asleep, so Kano just held his son and admired him. Aliania had already drifted off to sleep on the sofa next to him.

After goodbyes to Agnus, Shreya helped Marla back to bed and then climbed into her own bed. They could help more later in the day if they rested now. Kano settled Jai into the waiting crib in their bedroom and carried Aliania to her own bed. Taliya realized she was nodding off when Kano took Amrita from her.

"Let's all try to get some sleep," he said. "I think we've earned it."

"And I suspect we're going to need it," Taliya said with a contented smile.

Chapter 21

Chaos. Taliya's life was simply chaos. The first two days with the new kits had been magical. Everyone took turns making a fuss over them, and they slept for hours at a time. But as the days progressed, Kano went back to work, the twins went back to school, and Taliya was left all day with her newborns, Aliania, and two adults who could help but still also needed care.

The magic had worn off quickly.

Marla was kept well medicated and slept for great lengths of time. She was not supposed to be up and active any more than necessary, though when she was awake she did try to rock and comfort whichever twin Taliya was not nursing or getting a fresh diaper. Shreya tried to occupy Aliania, but her hands and feet were still healing. Aliania was a good big sister, but she was too little to be of much assistance—and Taliya suspected Ali was feeling less appreciative of the newcomers as they drained the energy and attention of every adult in the house.

Nurse. Change the diaper. Nurse the other twin. Change that diaper. Try to bathe each kit once a day. Nurse again. Maybe sleep for an hour. Eat anything not nailed down because she was hungry incessantly. It felt like the twins were sucking every ounce of nutrition out of her. And tigran needed sleep. Taliya seriously worried she'd lose her mind if she didn't get more sleep.

"This will pass," Shreya assured her. "They will stop nursing so much, and everyone will sleep better. These first few weeks can feel overwhelming, but it will pass."

Taliya nodded, but it was hard to see any future beyond serving cow duty to ravenous kits. She wanted to shower without a crying kit in the background. She wanted to sleep for three hours at once.

She wanted to be a feckless teenager again. Just for a day or two.

"Do you want me to stay home from work tomorrow?" Kano asked, swaying back and forth to keep Jai asleep while she nursed Amrita. "I can, you know."

"No," Taliya said, resting her head on the back of the sofa. "You've told me how anxious the crew is to get that new building done. It must be for something important. You're the only trained mason here. They need you. We'll be fine."

Kano looked doubtful, but he didn't argue. Taliya wished he'd stay home anyhow, regardless of what she said, but she felt she should be able to handle things. It wasn't that big a deal, was it? Mothers of all species managed to survive. She would too. It would all get better.

"We could use bottles sometimes," he suggested, "so you don't always have to do the feedings."

"No," she insisted. "Nursing is better. I should be nursing them. No one wants to fuss with prepping and cleaning bottles, and we'd have to get special permission for supplies like that anyhow."

As they staggered their way into the third week since the kits arrived, Shreya was able to walk Aliania to the nursery for several hours of the day. She was mostly healed, and now she could help with laundry duty. So many diapers to wash. So many loads of clothes and sheets just to keep up with the nine of them. The kitchen table was in perpetual use as either a diaper changing or laundry folding station—or both at the same time. Meals were eaten in fits and starts. Tuscan and Tyler said it was fun, taking their plates to a corner of the sofa or into their room, which hadn't been allowed before. Aliania seemed less impressed. She'd grown quiet and clingy, especially of Kano in the evenings.

As Taliya shuffled to the kitchen in the wee hours of one morning—Jai held to her breast, nursing contentedly—she stopped in front of the calendar. Someone had been marking out the days, keeping track of their agendas. Probably Kano. It mattered to him what day it was. She stared at it blankly, then the dates came into focus.

June. It's June. June 25th.

A sadness she had never known washed over her.

It was almost her birthday. On June 27th, she would be eighteen.

Someone had circled the date and added a smiley face. Shreya, most likely. Taliya and Kano had surely discussed birthdates at some point, but she couldn't remember when his was.

She sat down at the kitchen table and rested her head on a tall stack of clean cloth diapers. Jai clamped down roughly and made her yelp. This was not how she'd expected her life to be when she turned eighteen. Not in her wildest dreams—or would that be nightmares?

Taliya closed her eyes and let her thoughts wander back to her real home. Their lovely lair deep in the Arkansas woods. No humans. No one but their family and a few tigran friends who also had homesteads nearby and stopped over now and then. Her friend Anya, the two of them giggling at something silly on the media wall, not a care in the world. The smell of pine trees replaced whatever fake-pine-scented cleaner had been used on the diapers under her head.

Home. I just want to go home.

A sob caught in her throat, and she couldn't hold it back

any longer. She buried her face in the pile of diapers and screamed—a muffled long, exhausted, bitter scream. Then she let herself cry until she had nothing left. No tears. No energy.

Jai clutching at her brought her back to the moment. He had finished nursing and was staring up at her with adoring golden eyes, tiny orange fists full of white fur. He mewed and gurgled and then yawned so widely it made him squeak. Taliya used the damp diaper on the top of the pile to wipe her face, then she shifted her son onto her lap, resting along her legs so he faced her.

"Don't tell your papa about that, okay?" she said. "Let's just keep it between us."

Jai wiggled and then burped, a bit of milk running out the side of his mouth. Taliya wiped it with the diaper and sighed.

"I'll take that as a yes."

She grabbed a clean diaper and changed him right there on her lap. It was easier than making a clear spot on the table. Staggering over to the diaper pail, she tossed both of the used diapers in, shut the lid, and carried him over to the sofa. She sat there for a moment, Jai up on her shoulder to make sure all the gas was clear before she took him back to bed. Amrita was sure to wake up soon, ready for her own meal.

"This will pass. This will pass," she repeated.

In that moment, it felt impossible that her life would ever be anything but diapers, nursing, sleep deprivation, and newborn kits.

June 27th arrived, and the family appeared determined to make it as special as any birthday could be in a refugee camp for a mother of twins only a few weeks old. Her brothers chipped in and cleaned the house from top to bottom, with Aliania helping where she could. Marla and Shreya baked a frosted white cake with loans of sugar rations from the neighbors, even though there was nothing to decorate it with. Kano took the day off and insisted on changing every diaper and giving the kits their baths.

But the biggest gift—whether it was meant that way or not—was when everyone went for a walk and left Taliya alone for two full hours. Shreya suggested she take a nap, but Taliya ran a bath instead. She slipped down into the warm water and lathered herself from furry head to furry toe. Then she soaked until the water turned chilly. She dried her fur and stretched out on the sofa in her favorite pajamas. The house was so quiet, it was unnerving, but she forced herself to lie still and relax.

Silence. Maybe not total silence, like when she was in hiding in the attic room. She could hear snatches of conversations from guards or other refugees wandering by the house, the constant murmur of the camp when the daylight was up. Still, it was peaceful. She was going to need to find a way to get more moments of peace like this—moments away from being Mama. It was the first time in weeks she'd seen a light at the end of the tunnel and thought she'd make it out with her sanity intact. But out to where? *What will my life end up being? Are we Canadians now? Refugees forever?*

She sighed and pushed all of that from her thought. Today was her birthday. She consciously relaxed again, working on releasing the tension in every muscle of her body. Her nipples were sore. *That will pass.* She was exhausted. *That will pass. It all will pass.* She drifted off to sleep until her clan returned. Then the clamor of making dinner surrounded her, though Kano insisted she stay on the sofa.

"No way you are helping with your birthday dinner," he insisted.

The kits were sleeping in their crib, and Shreya cleared off the kitchen table—possibly the first time in weeks that all the laundry was put away at once—so the family could sit down together. Shreya and Kano served up chicken and vegetables from the camp gardens. Aliania crawled into Taliya's lap and nibbled bits off her plate. They were able to finish the whole meal and have cake before the twins woke up.

"You can still make a birthday wish, even without candles," Tuscan insisted.

"I'm not sure what I'd wish for," Taliya admitted. *A full night's sleep? To be free of all of this? No. Not all of it.* She glanced over at Kano, who was serving cake to her mother. *I could've been dead before I turned eighteen. Part of Narlin's harem, still stuck in that breeding facility. Never getting to be part of Jai and Amrita's lives, not being able to save Jai at all.* Going home was top on her wish list, but saying it out loud would just depress everyone.

"I have everything I need right here," she said instead. "No one knows what our future will be, but here, today, we have everything we need."

"Hear, hear," Marla said, raising her cup in a toast. "Here's to having everything we need."

The others raised their glasses in response, and everyone took a sip of the weak ale that Carl had sent over as a special treat for that night. Aliania made a face at the taste, but Tuscan and Tyler looked proud of themselves for enjoying the adult beverage. Taliya smiled and then twisted an ear at sound from the bedroom. One of the twins was waking. The other wouldn't be far behind.

"At least we got to enjoy a family dinner," she said, shifting Ali to stand next to her, kissing her on the top of her head, and starting to get up.

"Wait," Kano said. "You go to the sofa, and I'll bring them to you. Your mother has an idea, now that the twins are bigger."

Taliya headed for the couch, and her mother followed.

"When they were so little," Shreya said, "it's safest to nurse them individually, so you can support their heads. But now that they're older, we can improvise a bit."

The others cleaned the kitchen while Kano brought both kits out to Taliya.

"Here," Shreya said. "One on each side."

She showed her daughter how to tuck a kit under each arm so they could nurse at the same time. It took Taliya a moment to settle into it, but then she looked up and smiled.

"It's working! This will cut feeding times in half."

"You forget," Shreya said. "I raised twins myself."

"And once they're done, it's off to bed with you," Kano said. "And not just because it's your birthday. You have three other adults who can help you. Let us."

Taliya rested her head on the back of the sofa and smiled.

"Okay," she agreed.

Going to bed early sounded like the oddest 18th birthday present ever, but she was grateful beyond words to receive it.

As Shreya had promised, the nursing and diapers and drama all passed. Tigran kits mature faster than human babies, and the twins were eating solid food by two months. They both weaned themselves completely by three months. Losing the diapers took a bit longer, but by October the household was diaper-free. The chaos shifted from nursing and diapers to chasing toddling kits. Now that they were older, Taliya felt freer to hand Amrita and Jai over to the nursery staff two mornings a week. Aliania joined them, though she was almost ready to start school. There was a class for little ones. Those mornings of quiet were a little bit of peace, though it mostly included piles of laundry.

Marla had healed enough to join the ranks of single females around the camp. She volunteered at the medical tent, putting her organizational skills and computer knowledge to use. In September, she'd moved into a house with a group of other adult female tigran with no family in the camp. Not that she wasn't over visiting at Taliya's on a daily basis. "Aunty Marla" was often on hand to help watch the kits, but she was also happy to have her own space away from the big, bustling family. Taliya hoped Marla's nightmares were easing some, but she trusted the other tigran to support her friend, even though she looked so human. No one at the camp was free of trauma of one kind or another.

After a makeshift Halloween—with parties but no costumes and only a bit of candy—and a simple Diwali celebration, the council suggested Taliya's group shift into a different living arrangement. There was a large family of tigran with seven young ones who were not housed together. They would be relocated into Taliya's house, and her family would be placed in two smaller units across the road from each other. Shreya and the boys would have a two-bedroom place, and Taliya and her family would have another two-bedroom, Aliania sharing with Amrita and Jai. Sensing it really wasn't a choice, more like a directive, they packed what little they had and moved units.

The first night in their new house, Taliya leaned against the kitchen counter and breathed deeply. It was so quiet. Ridiculously quiet. She was used to her brothers and their constant movement and noise, but now they were across the road with their mother. Kano was stretched out on the sofa with Aliania, reading a picture book from the camp library, and the kits were bathed, full of dinner, and sleeping soundly. Most likely, they wouldn't wake until morning.

It suddenly struck her what a lucky creature she was. All of them were healthy. They had a roof over their heads, more than enough food, and comfortable beds at night. And there was Kano. *Ah, Kano.* She'd thought her attraction to him would ease out over time, but struggling through those last few crazy months with him had only deepened it. He was an amazing father and a supportive husband. She realized she needed to lean into that a bit more.

A few weeks after the kits were born, Agnus had given Taliya the prophylactic shot that should last six months. It was required of all females at the camp. Taliya hadn't hesitated. She wasn't sure she'd ever want more kits. Certainly not in that camp. So the path was clear for Taliya and Kano to get back to being Taliya and Kano more often without having to worry about breeding of any sort. Not like they'd been abstaining for five months, but a crowded, bustling house did not lend itself to romance.

Definitely need to lean into that more.

Kano carried the now sleeping Aliania into her bed and

tucked her in. With all the late-night feeding of the twins in her parents' bedroom, she'd quickly gotten over trying to sleep with them. She still had nightmares now and then, but being so young, her time in the facility had been mostly in a nursery with other kits her age. She'd missed her father and mother, but even memories of that were quickly fading. Taliya was grateful for the resiliency of youth.

With all three little ones happily slumbering, Kano came to her in the kitchen and pulled her into a gentle embrace.

"It's so quiet," he whispered into her neck.

"I was thinking the same thing."

With a rumble in his throat, Kano shifted his hand lower on her back and pulled her in tighter.

"There's a lock on our bedroom door in this unit," he said in a husky voice.

"There is, is there?" she said, pulling her head back to meet his beautiful blue eyes.

"We should test it out."

"Definitely. Wouldn't want a perfectly good lock to go to waste."

Chapter 22

Marla burst through the door while they were still eating breakfast. The family stopped and stared. She was supposed to be at work in the medical tent. Something must be wrong, but Marla's eyes glittered with gold and her smile was wide, which confused matters even more.

"Marla, what on earth's going on?" Taliya said, shifting Amrita on her hip.

"They're here!" Marla gasped. "It's all true!"

"Who's here?" Kano said, setting down the spoon he was using to feed Jai.

"Come see! You have to come see!"

Aliania giggled at her silly aunty as Taliya looked around the table and wondered how Marla felt they could just pick up and follow her. Kano smiled and rose to take Amrita.

"Go, Taliya. Have an adventure. Shreya will be over shortly once the boys head out for school. She can handle things if I have to leave before you get back."

Marla didn't wait for any more response than that. She grabbed Taliya by the arm and dragged her out the door like a frantic teenager. Whatever Marla was so excited about, it had spread to the entire camp. All around them creatures were rushing in the same direction with wide smiles and animated chatter.

"Marla, wait!" Taliya resisted. "Stop pulling. I'm coming. But what's this all about? What's happening?"

"They raided a facility last night and freed everything there."

Marla continued to hurry her along, but Taliya still didn't understand the rush. Refugees of one sort or another arrived all the time. However, the use of the word *everything* instead of *everyone* was odd. When she wasn't hustling like Marla wanted, her friend finally turned and explained herself.

"There've always been rumors about what went on at other labs," Marla said. "Genetic experiments and monsters being created. Now we have proof it's all true."

"Monsters?" An image of Godzilla flashed through Taliya's head.

"Well, not *monsters*, really, but . . . you just have to see for yourself."

Taliya was inspired now, and the pair joined the stream of creatures heading toward the front of the camp where new arrivals were processed. As they got closer, the mob started to crowd together and slow down. Something up ahead was holding them back. Taliya squinched her nose at the vivid aroma of excitement wafting from the group. Marla grabbed her hand and pulled her along to the edge of the sea of bodies, where they could slip sideways and get to the front easier.

"Kaah! Kaah! Kaah!"

A screeching call filled the air, and everyone froze. *What in the world made that sound?* Marla giggled at their shock, already knowing the answer and seeming quite pleased with herself. While others stood still, Marla shoved their way closer.

"Here," she said, directing them around the back of the medical tent and up the side in a shortcut around the crowd.

Taliya followed at a run, but she stopped dead when she spotted the new arrivals. Standing in the middle of the receiving ground were four massive white beasts. Taliya could think of only one word to describe them: dragons.

Each was as large as the medical tent, and an image of her riding on the back of one flitted through her mind. The body was stocky—fairy-tale dragon in appearance—but the wings were bat-like, with clawed hands halfway along the span, and were covered in a beautiful layer of white feathers. A whole array of new odors Taliya didn't even have a category for assaulted her. *Musty, maybe?* There was more to it, though. *Maybe just an abundance of feathers.* The creatures' heads were an odd shape, with a large horn sort of protrusion sticking up in back, but their mouths resembled eagle beaks. Massive three-toed feet with scary-looking claws and plumes of white feathers up the squatty legs—legs that stomped in agitation as whispers from the crowd grew louder—completed the "monster."

"But how?" Taliya said.

"From what I've overheard at check-in, scientists found a way to extract DNA from dinosaur teeth. It's not enough to recreate the animal, but if you mix it with other DNA you can create, well, you can get *that*."

They both stared in wonder as one of the creatures spread its wings and lifted its head to make that strange cawing noise again.

"Kaah! Kaah! Kaah!"

Murmurs rose up from the crowd.

"So that thing is part pterodactyl?"

"That would be my guess too, from the look of its head," Marla said. "But it has feathers."

"Other half cockatiel," Agnus said, walking up from the arrival field. "Very smart bird. Make for smart animal, I hope. Other stuff in there too, but mostly those two."

"Where're they going to put them?" Taliya asked. Life within the camp was already constricted.

"Not my problem," Agnus said matter-of-factly. "They healthy. My work done." She nodded and headed inside the medical tent.

How can she not be fascinated by this? Taliya wondered, sure she could stare at the animals all day.

"I heard they're making room at the far end of camp," Marla said, "where the things can have space."

The huge building Kano has been working on. They knew these animals were out there and got ready for them.

"Do those things understand where they are and what they are?" Taliya wondered. "I mean, most everything here is partly human and has reasoning. They just look like animals."

"No clue," Marla admitted.

One of the dinosaur/birds flapped its wings, attempting to fly, but then settled back down with a sad-sounding cry. Taliya noticed that each one had heavy weights attached to their legs. Grief that they were shackled eased quickly when she imagined one loose in the camp. What was to be done with a beast like that in the long run? Was it always destined to be trapped in some kind of lab? Could it be trained? She noticed that guards were starting to encourage the crowd to move along, which most were reluctantly doing. She gawked at the dragon-things as long as she could until she saw Carl heading their way.

"Amazing, isn't it?" he said.

"Stunning," Taliya said.

"More like terrifyingly magnificent," Marla added.

"What're they called?" Taliya asked. Her brain spun with options of how the government scientists normally combined species names to create a new one. "Cockadactyl?" she guessed with a chuckle.

"Cocka*dick*tyl?" Marla added with a snort.

"They are pterodragons," Carl said, "though your names are more fun. And they are only some of the crazy beasties we rescued."

"There's more like this?" Taliya said with wide eyes, her tail thrashing.

"Oh yes," Carl said. "Nothing else this big, but some really weird shit."

The three of them watched the pterodragons preen and nuzzle at each other.

"We're gonna need help caring for them," Carl said. "Figuring out if they can be tamed and trained and how smart they are. You interested?"

Taliya realized he was looking at her. "Me?"

"Sure, why not?"

"I have three little kits. How am I supposed to be a Pterodragon Wrangler on top of all of that?"

"Your mom's here, right? The oldest can start school, so only the twins are home all day. And they're old enough to spend some hours in the camp nursery. You could swing it."

Taliya suspected Carl had no idea what was involved in caring for a home and young ones.

"I could help too," Marla said. "Like an old-school nanny. I'm already at your place most days anyhow."

That was true. Aunty Marla was a huge part of their family life. A spark of freedom tickled its way up Taliya's spine, and she flexed all four sets of claws. If Marla was serious, and the look in her eyes suggested she was, could they manage it? Taliya wanted to take Carl up on his offer more than she'd wanted anything for a very long time. Maybe ever. Her breath came out in a whoof, and Carl laughed.

"You know you want to," he said with a smile.

Need to was more how it felt. Needed to feel young and free and independent, if only for part of each day. Nothing about her life for the last year had been a genuine freewill choice. Nothing. It had all been based on fear and manipulation and the will to survive. Except marrying Kano, but even that was still a union based on all of the other forced decisions. Otherwise, she would never be married, to him or anyone. A simple, selfish desire for something outside of all of that was staring her right in her black-striped face.

"Taliya, the Pterodragon Master," Marla whispered with delight.

Taliya looked at each of them. Marla's eyes sparkled with anticipation, and Carl nodded with encouragement.

"Reynaldo is leaving the school to take charge of all the animals from this rescue," Carl said. "He worked as a military horse trainer for the government before the war. Hopefully, that experience will come in handy. We haven't even asked for helpers yet. Get in before everyone and their brother finds out."

Taliya considered the pterodragons. One on the end stared back at her—green eyes meeting golden. Just like the moment she had first looked into the eyes of her kits, Taliya knew her fate was sealed.

"Go find Kano, quickly," she said to Marla as she stepped forward into the field.

The same pterodragon that had eyed her lowered its head as she drew closer. Carl was right behind her, so none of the guards tried to stop them. A few yards away from the massive animal, Taliya hesitated. *Is it even reasonably tame?* The dragon raised its head and stretched its neck up toward the roof of the habitat dome far overhead.

"Kaah! Kaah! Kaah!"

The same call as before, but this time Taliya felt it as a greeting. A welcome.

"Hello, yourself," she said, taking a few steps closer. The dragon lowered its head and watched her. "Is it safe? Do they bite?" she asked Carl. That beak looked like it could take off a leg.

"They gave the rescuers a hard time, but it was chaotic and scary for them, I'm sure, having us show up and clear out their building."

Carl waved over a guard who looked disheveled, like he'd just come from battle. He military jogged to them with a smile.

"You found a volunteer already?" he said.

"Did you think it was going to be hard to find creatures who wanted to get involved with these amazing beasts?" Carl asked.

"Yeah," he admitted, "but it's not going to be for the faint of heart. Are you sure about this?" he asked, looking at Taliya.

She nodded and grinned.

"No one in their right mind would call Taliya fainthearted." Carl laughed. "This pterodragon here seems to have taken a liking to her."

They all turned to face the animal in question. It cocked its head and flared out the ruff of feathers around its neck, very bird-like. The guard pulled out a notepad and scanned through it, checking the numbers on the dragon's ankle band.

"It's a female."

"Do they have names?" Taliya asked.

"Nope, just lengthy numbers, like there had been a few thousand versions of the experiment before they were successful with these four."

"Should we set you up with this one?" Carl asked. "Or do you want to check them all out?"

Taliya glanced over at the other dragons, but none of them were paying any attention to her. The female in front of them stomped her feet back and forth several times. Taliya felt agitation coming from her.

"So you don't like it when I pay the others some mind," Taliya said. "Interesting."

"Looks like she's picked you already," the guard said. He made a note in his little book, smiled, and headed back to his group. "Might want to keep your distance for now," he advised over his shoulder.

Taliya heard his warning, but she didn't feel the least bit

threatened by her dragon. *My dragon.* She took a few more steps forward, and the animal lowered her head to be eye level with the tigran.

"Good morning," she said. "I'm Taliya. We're going to be spending a lot of time together figuring out exactly what you are."

She scanned the beast's face closely. Both eyes were facing her, like a hunter, instead of on the sides of the head like a bird. The beak was sharp and the feet were taloned, like a hawk. *Was it designed to be a predator, or is that just how this version of the experiment came out?*

She caught movement out of the corner of her eye and turned to see Kano staring up at her dragon. He looked gob-smacked, mouth open and eyes wide. She laughed, and he started walking toward her, eyes still on the dragon.

"What do you think of my new pet?" she said.

"I think he won't fit in the house."

"She."

"She?"

"It's a female."

"Okay. *She* won't fit in the house."

"Obviously. You already built her house."

"The huge building we've been working on? That's for these things?"

"I'm assuming, but it makes sense. Carl enlisted me to help train and care for one."

Kano shifted his gaze to her. "Marla was rattling on about something like that. Are you serious? You're considering this?"

"I sort of already agreed."

Kano did not appear pleased with that plan. He looked like he was going to object, but then he just shifted his feet instead.

"You told me to go have an adventure," she said with a smile.

"I didn't mean quite this big or quite this long of an adventure."

He stepped closer to her, and the pterodragon stomped her feet in agitation. "Kaah!"

Both tigran looked back at her, and she glared at Kano with her bright-green eyes.

"Is it possible she's jealous or protective of me already?" Taliya said.

"That's not scary at all," Kano said with a half laugh.

As if to test the theory, he wrapped an arm around Taliya.

"Kaah! Kaah! Kaah!" the dragon squawked and took a hop closer to them, feathery wings spread.

They stumbled back a few steps, and Taliya burst out laughing.

"She's as bad as you. Now I have two creatures who think I belong to them."

"And a few more back at home too," Kano said with a frown.

"I know, I know, but look at her. How can I not take this opportunity? This is, like, historic! It's the chance of a lifetime."

They both turned at the sounds of others approaching the remaining three pterodragons. More potential trainers.

"You'd better grab one now," she said.

"No way. Not a chance."

Taliya was surprised by his reaction. "What? You're going to let someone else get a shot?"

"This is as close as I ever want to get to that beak," he said. "Birds freak me out. She seems to like you, but that's not the feeling *I'm* getting from her."

"Well, sure. But you can go bond with another of them."

"No. If you're going to do this, I'm going to have to cover for things at the house."

"Marla says she'll help, and Mother will too. And there's the nursery for the kits and school for Ali."

Kano shifted his shoulders but didn't respond.

"Kano, you're my mate, and I don't want to upset you, but I'm doing this. I *need* to do this."

He nodded, but she could feel his frustration and anxiety. *Is he upset to have me step away from the bubble of our home life, or is he just scared of the dragon?*

"I guess it's decided then," he said with a grumble.

"Yes, it is."

Carl jogged back over and smiled at Kano.

"Isn't it amazing?" he said.

Kano looked the dragon over again and shrugged. "We should've known government scientists were busy making monsters like this."

Taliya felt her fur rankle at her dragon being called a

monster. Kano was definitely not responding with the enthusiasm she'd expected. She looked back up at her dragon and realized she didn't give a damn what Kano thought about it. *That's my dragon, and he's just going to have to figure out how to deal with it.*

"We're getting ready to move them to the training building, Taliya," Carl said. "The easiest plan is to walk them around the outskirts of the dome. We're taking off one ankle weight. It should still be enough to keep them from flying but make the walk easier."

Taliya noticed three other creatures now stood in front of the three other dragons, each looking attentive: one liran and two other orange tigran. Selections had been made.

"Let Mother know what's happening," Taliya said to Kano, "and ask her to help out today if Marla can't. I'll set things up with the nursery and school shortly. You can go on and do whatever your plan was for the day. I'm going to walk with my dragon."

Kano frowned again, but he nodded. "I'll see you at the house later."

The dragon at the far end turned to leave, and the other three started to follow along.

"Kaah! Kaah!" Taliya's dragon called to her.

"Yes, yes. I'm coming."

Taliya fell into line next to her, the animal's head bopping along with each step, and they started the journey. When she turned back to wave to Kano, a glower was securely etched in the black lines on his face.

Chapter 23

The walk to the pterodragon building took three hours. The animals themselves seemed nonplussed by the journey, simply scanning and assessing their surroundings and plodding along next to their selected trainer. Crowds of creatures from the refugee camp were scattered along the path, excited for a chance to see the new arrivals. Changa, the school supervisor, showed up halfway through with all of his charges. From a safe distance, Tuscan and Tyler waved frantically to Taliya. She imagined they would be eager for a chance to get closer to the dragons but wondered if the animal would react to them like she had to Kano.

Taliya used the journey time to come up with a name for her dragon. The animal needed a name, not just some government number. *Ivory? Hmmm. But all four of them are white.* Watching the animal hop/walk along, "Bunny" came to mind. *Is that too cutesy?*

By the time they made it to the far end of the dome, everyone was dragging a bit, including the four pterodragons. Taliya hadn't seen the building before, just heard from Kano about how enormous it was. He was certainly right about that. It looked like someone had taken an old-school red barn and put it in a super-sizing machine. The dragons were able to walk right in the wide main doors without ducking, and once they were inside, Taliya realized it was large enough for the dragons to fly around. There were giant stalls along one wall, like in a horse barn, and the floor of the building was some kind of dirt/sand/wood-shaving mix. It was basically an immense training arena for massive animals. Animals who could fly.

Reynaldo was there waiting for them, ready to assume the supervision of the new rescues. Carl jogged over to him, and they spoke quietly for several minutes while the dragons and their trainers waited. At one point, Reynaldo gently held onto Carl's arm as they talked, seeming to confirm Taliya's earlier suspicions about their relationship. Finally, Carl turned and waved them in his direction.

"There are stalls for each dragon this way," he said.

The group headed toward him, though Taliya noticed the dragons were hesitant about the soft flooring. Hers picked her feet up higher than necessary and glared at the ground with each step.

310

"It's okay," Taliya assured her. "It's just soft stuff."

She kicked up a bit of the dusty ground, and her dragon sneezed and shook her head. Each dragon was settled into a straw-lined stall. Then each trainer was handed a bucket of food.

"You need to be the one to handle the feedings directly," Reynaldo said to each trainer. "It will help cement the bond it looks like these dragons have quickly formed with each of you. Cockatiels do that with their owners, and we were hoping it would carry over to the pterodragons."

Taliya emptied her bucket of seeds, nuts, and berries into a long trough in the stall.

"Kaaah!" her dragon said and waddled over to eat.

There was another trough with a hose attached, and Taliya filled that one with water. Then she sat down on the ground next to the stall door and watched her dragon eat. She marveled at how, once again, her whole life had changed direction. She loved Amrita, Jai, and Aliania, but this was something different. Something more. Something that was 100% her own choice. There was not the slightest chance she was giving it up.

"Have you named yours yet?" The liran trainer leaned out of her dragon's stall, looking at Taliya.

"I'm trying, but I haven't settled on anything."

"I'm going with Pegasus for my boy," the tigran on the other side of Taliya said, stepping out into the arena. "And I'm going to fly him around this place, riding on his back, if it's the last thing I do."

That possibility had certainly occurred to Taliya when she saw the size of the building. The dragons would easily be able to fly around, but were the trainers expected to actually ride them?

"I'm calling mine Polly," the other tigran said, joining them outside the stalls. "You know, like 'Polly want a cracker?' They are part bird, after all."

All four chuckled at that image. It would have to be a mighty big cracker.

"Should they all get P names?" the liran asked. "That could get confusing."

"I keep feeling like I should name mine Bunny," Taliya admitted, "but that just seems wrong. A huge creature like this."

"Bunny. I like it," the liran said.

Maybe I should just go with my gut.

"I'm Nimmy, by the way," the tigran with Pegasus said.

"I'm Taliya," she said, waving a hand in greeting.

"I'm Karma," the tigran with Polly said.

"And I'm Faria," the liran said. "I think we're going to be spending lots of time together."

"Is it weird that we're all female?" Karma said. "You'd think the males would want in on this."

"My mate wanted nothing to do with it," Taliya said. "He wasn't interested. At all." *And doesn't seem thrilled that I'm involved either.* She kept that part to herself. He'd come around. No reason to make the other trainers think less of him.

312

"There were males with me, several of them, but Pegasus picked me," Nimmy said. "He was very clear about it."

The four of them pondered this for a second until Reynaldo joined them.

"That's probably enough for today," he said. "They've been through a lot. Best to let them rest. We're going to provide each of you with a shuttle so you can come and go as needed for the next few weeks. Please be sure to come by at least twice a day to feed and water your pterodragon, and we'll want to get them used to the building here. Let them out of their stalls to wander around and stretch their wings. They didn't have space for that back at the lab we rescued them from. We're not sure if they've ever been allowed to fly."

The four new trainers nodded and stood up.

"Before you go," Reynaldo said, "do you want a peek at a couple of the other animals we rescued?"

Carl had mentioned other beasts, but she'd forgotten all about it in the flush of her new dragon. Reynaldo motioned with his head to stalls farther down the wall, and the four followed him.

"As best we can tell, this one is some mix between a dog and a chameleon," he said as they came to a stop in front of the first stall.

Taliya could see why he assumed that, but it was clearly not a successful mix. The animal had patches of fur on what looked like partially scaly skin. It was a beige color when they first peeked in, but she watched it shift to red and then brown as it wandered around the stall and encountered different colors on the walls. The eyes were like a chameleon, all bugged and creepy weird, but they were both in front, like a dog. The long curled tail wagged to greet them.

"Damn," Faria said, "that's an experiment that never should have happened."

"Why don't they ever make dog/human creatures?" Nimmy wondered.

"I'm sure they've tried," Carl said, joining them. "The canine/human mix, I mean, but I've never seen one. Something about the combination must not come out right."

They moved to the next stall and found a huge tank of what smelled like salt water. Inside was some kind of jellyfish thing. It looked like a fish but had strands hanging down from a domed abdomen. Again, weird and unnecessary.

"What's the point of this one?" Nimmy asked.

Reynaldo just shook his head and moved them along to the next few stalls. All of them held bizarre creatures, but at least none of them were a human/animal mix. Taliya knew she would keep the family well-entertained at dinner that night with tales of these beasties.

Carl showed the trainers where the shuttles were stored and gave a quick lesson on how to use them. It was like a golf cart and ran on an electrical charge. Taliya had never really learned how to drive beyond the solar-powered truck on their land at home, but she figured it out quickly. Then they were dismissed for the day.

"I'm going to check on Pegasus before I go home," Nimmy said.

The other three nodded and followed her back to the dragon stalls. All four animals were sound asleep, heads hanging low. Taliya peeked in Bunny's stall and saw there was still food and water for her.

"Coconut," Faria whispered.

The other three turned to stare at her questioningly.

"His name is Coconut," she said. "I just can't get it out of my head."

Taliya smiled, knowing what she meant. Bunny was a strange name for a giant white-feathered dragon, but she couldn't get past it. *Can the dragons tell us their names?* She shook off that thought as even weirder than calling a dragon Bunny or Coconut.

A guard started shutting off the overhead lights in the building, and the four trainers took that as a signal to leave. Hopping in their individual carts, they each headed home. It took Taliya a few minutes to figure out a route, but once she found the gardens, she knew where she was. After parking the shuttle next to their unit and plugging it into a power outlet, she clomped her way inside, suddenly exhausted.

"Mama!" Aliania yelled as Taliya came through the door.

Marla was in the kitchen, stirring a pot of stew with Jai on her hip, and Amrita was playing with blocks on the living room floor. She looked up and smiled, the start of her tiny fangs poking out.

"So," Marla said, "tell us everything."

"Is Kano here?" Taliya asked.

"No, he went on to work when I said I could stay with the kits today."

Taliya frowned. He'd seemed annoyed by the whole dragon training thing, but maybe she was making too much of it. He was expected at work, so he went. That might well be all there was to it. Taliya hoped so.

"Is it really happening, you as a dragon wrangler?" Marla said.

"Oh, yes. It's real."

Taliya plopped down in a chair at the kitchen table, and Aliania climbed up in her lap, wrapping her legs around Taliya's waist so she could face her.

"Mama, are the dragons scary?"

"No, not to me, at least. I think they pick a human to bond with. I'm glad Bunny picked me."

"Bunny?" Marla said with a chuckle.

"Yep. And the others are Polly, Pegasus, and Coconut. Two males and two females. They were probably planning on breeding more."

A chill ran down Taliya's spine at the thought of that, though maybe animals like the pterodragons didn't fuss about forced breeding as much as creatures who were half human.

"Can I meet Bunny?" Aliania asked.

"Eventually," Taliya said. "Let me get to know her first and be sure she's safe. We really don't know much about them."

Aliania rested her head on Taliya's chest and slipped her thumb into her mouth. She did that less and less now, but it still comforted her.

"I missed you today, Mama."

"Did you? Aunty Marla was here."

"Not the same," Aliania mumbled.

Marla and Taliya locked eyes over the kit's head, and Marla smiled weakly. Taliya felt Aliania's words tug at her heart. Was it fair to leave the little ones all day? What if the training program required more than that?

"Taliya, stop it," Marla said. "You're not the only creature who can make these kits happy. It's good for them to have relationships with our whole community—aunties and grandmas and nursery workers. You are Mama, but even mamas deserve to have more in their lives than cooking and cleaning if they want to."

"I hope Kano agrees with you," Taliya said. "He wasn't thrilled with the idea earlier today."

"I noticed. He was grumpy when he came back. But he'll survive too. He has the chance to go out into the camp every day and come back whenever he pleases. You should have those same options. Frankly, I'm content to spend some quiet time with your kits. The camp is overwhelming to me, especially the medical tent. I'm glad to get free of that for a while."

"I need to work out some kind of schedule with the nursery. And you, Miss Aliania," she kissed the top of her daughter's head, "you get to start school three days a week."

That got the white kit's attention. She leaned back, looked at Taliya, and removed her thumb from her mouth.

"Like with my uncles? At school?"

"Yes. Though you'll spend more time with the younger students. Tuscan and Tyler are big boys, but you'll be in the same building. Maybe you can even walk to school with them. Would you like that?"

The light in Aliania's eyes told her the kit would love that. Taliya figured she'd have to give her brothers some special dragon visits to get them to agree to shepherding their niece around, but she knew they would watch out for Ali.

"Here," Marla said, slipping a plate of snacks in front of Taliya. "Have a late lunch and something to drink, then you can head over to the nursery and the school and get things set up there. Three days a week is perfect. I'll cover the others. Shreya can help. Kano . . . well, Kano can do as he pleases. Males always do."

Taliya wasn't sure that was fair, but she'd have to deal with him later. Snack. Childcare arrangements. Then a nap. Definitely a nap.

"Do you want to come with me," Taliya said to Ali, "to check out the school? I have a shuttle we can ride in."

"Yay!" the kit squealed and crawled off her lap, drama about missing Mama forgotten.

Taliya smiled and looked for the kit's shoes, but her mind whirled with images of the curved head, feathered wings, and the distinctive musty smells of her dragon. Her Bunny.

Schedules were set for the kits, and the plans for Taliya to work with the pterodragons charged full-steam ahead. Taliya had done some research at the camp library and learned what she could about the species involved in the creation of her dragon. Obviously, not much was known about the dinosaur part, but cockatiels had been thoroughly studied and kept as pets by humans for hundreds of years. They were quite smart, could learn some simple words and sounds, and frequently attached themselves to one human owner—and were often possessive of that owner, sometimes to the point of aggression. That certainly described Bunny's behavior toward Kano the day the dragons arrived.

As the training sessions progressed, Kano remained quiet on the matter. He didn't say anything to stop her. However, he also didn't express the excitement and enthusiasm about the venture that the rest of the camp shared. Crowds gathered daily to watch the four keepers work with their dragons, even if it was just walking them in a circle around the ring to get some exercise and help them adjust to the new living arrangements. Guards at the large doors of the training building kept spectators back, but they still gathered to spy through the openings.

The school had brought all of the little ones by early the first week, once it became clear the pterodragons weren't aggressive. Tuscan and Tyler had all but strutted, so proud of their sister out in the ring with her dragon. Aliania was more humble about it, but Taliya could tell the kit thought Bunny was amazing by her giggles and grins. Taliya had brought home one of Bunny's feathers for the kit, and Aliania kept it tucked away safely.

Marla had come to visit on her own while the twins were in the camp nursery, and she gushed and fawned over all of the dragons.

"Maybe you should have claimed one of the dragons too," Taliya said, worried Marla had regrets about how the arrangements had worked out.

"No way! That's all too much for me. Too many people staring. Too much attention. I'm perfectly happy tending to your kits and being Aunty Marla. Maybe I can help out on occasion, but that's enough for me."

Taliya was sure she'd take her friend up on the offer of assistance because caring for the dragons was a huge amount of work. The straw in the stalls had to be changed daily. There was feeding and exercise and watery showers with a large hose and training tests to see what the dragons were capable of. Every day, it was something.

After two weeks, Reynaldo decided it was time to let the dragons try to fly.

The building was locked down so there was no chance of a curious observer being injured or a dragon getting loose. It seemed safest to go one at a time since no one was sure what the pterodragons might do once they were given the freedom to take to the air. The four trainers had drawn straws, and Taliya had won. Bunny would be allowed to fly first.

The other three trainers were shut in the stalls with their dragons, and Reynaldo waited in the middle of the arena while Taliya led Bunny out to him. The dragon didn't know what was ahead, so she just did her normal hop/walk and followed her trainer. When they reached the black panthran, he approached Bunny slowly, resting his hand on her chest for a moment before leaning down and removing the weight on her ankle. Then he and Taliya stepped back quickly.

Bunny tipped her head, eyeing them, then stomped her feet several times, testing the freedom.

"Kaah! Kaah!" she crooned and then spread her massive wings.

"Go on," Taliya encouraged her. "Fly!"

Taliya spread her arms out and flapped them, then pretended to fly around in a circle. Bunny flapped, and she lifted a few feet off the ground before settling back down.

Reynaldo frowned. "Do you suppose they're weak from being grounded for too long or haven't ever been given the chance to fly?"

"Maybe," Taliya said. "Let's give her a minute."

Bunny flapped around a bit, stirring up dust, then she rose from the ground again and flapped in place.

"Go!" Taliya yelled encouragingly, pointing to the roof. "Go!"

Bunny gave a funny squawk, almost like she was repeating the word, then her wings stretched wide and she took to the air. Taliya jumped and cheered, and she heard the other trainers laughing and cheering too. Polly, Pegasus, and Coconut hopped around in their stalls, watching their comrade fly. Bunny made several circles around the arena, and Taliya wondered if she was enjoying herself or looking for a way out. Finally, Bunny returned to her spot and came to rest. Taliya rushed over and patted her chest.

"Good girl, Bunny. Good job!"

Taliya thought her dragon looked quite pleased with herself—standing up taller than before and strutting around the arena.

"That's enough for now," Reynaldo said. "See if you can lure her back into her stall with some food."

Taliya grabbed a waiting pail of dragon chow and swished it into the trough in Bunny's stall. The dragon cawed and hop/walked in, bouncing higher now without the ankle weight and looking even more like a rabbit. Taliya shut the stall door and then watched as the other three dragons got their chance.

It didn't take Polly long to figure out what to do. She had clearly observed Bunny and was ready. The moment her weight was taken off, she hopped twice and then spread her wings and flew.

"Go! Go! Go!" Karma called to her, laughing and running around the arena below her dragon.

By the time Pegasus got his chance, Taliya noticed something odd. The dragons were not cawing to each other in the same way. Their cries sounded more like an actual word.

As Pegasus took to the air, Bunny hopped in a circle, lifted her head, and cried, "Go! Go!" Polly and Coconut took up the chant as well. "Go! Go!" they called to him.

Taliya looked at Reynaldo through the bars of the stall, and his fang-filled smile assured her that she wasn't just imagining it. The dragons had learned a word and were using it in context. *Amazing!*

Taliya's life once again felt like chaos, but more of a well-organized chaos. She woke up early to spend some time with the kits before she left for training sessions. Animals don't understand days off or weekends. She needed to be there every day. Once Aliania was off to school, the kits delivered to the nursery, or Marla arrived to watch them, Taliya would jump in her shuttle and head to the arena. Kano covered weekend days with some support from Shreya, and he'd started cutting his work hours shorter so he could be home to make dinner. Taliya knew the council understood and didn't feel like Kano was slacking off, but her mate's annoyance at her choice to work with the dragons still hovered ominously in the air. She knew it wasn't just about cooking. She'd never been able to create more than the most basic of meals. He was the chef in their relationship. But if she tried to talk to him about his frustrations, he said she was imagining it, everything was fine.

"I'd say just give him time," Marla said one morning as Taliya shared her frustrations, "but it's more than that. Males are very territorial. You know that, Taliya. And you now have this interest, this job, that has nothing to do with him and takes you away from him."

"He thinks I'm not being a good wife and mother."

"He said that?" Marla said with a gasp.

"No, of course not. Not in so many words. But he huffs and puffs when I want him to help with the laundry or do some of the chores that I used to handle on my own. I don't know. It's just little things. If Kano could get as excited about my dragon as I am, maybe he'd understand why it's all worth it."

Or maybe he wouldn't. Ever. And the young, single female tigran around camp would finally get their chance at him. Taliya didn't dare voice that fear to Marla or anyone else.

Chapter 24

After working with their dragons for a month and teaching them a few command words—like Go, Down, and Stop—Reynaldo suggested they try riding the animals. The trainers exchanged excited looks because they'd all been waiting for that chance.

"The dragons are clearly strong enough now to handle your weight," Reynaldo said. "It's time to at least try. Who wants to go first?" All four of them raised their hands immediately, and Reynaldo laughed. "We know they learn from watching each other, and they're used to being in the air at the same time, so maybe you should all try together and learn from each other."

He'd designed a rigging that looped around the dragon's neck, over its back between the wings, and then around again over the tail end. In the middle was a spot for a rider and long leather reins to hold on to.

"I think a saddle situation would get in the way and bother the dragons," Reynaldo said, "but this system of leads should allow you to ride safely."

Ladders were brought in to reach the dragons' backs, and each trainer followed Reynaldo's directions for hooking the rigging up. Despite some squawks of "Stop" from the dragons, the straps were secured in place. Carl had come to assist Reynaldo with the trials that day, and he helped check over each dragon. Bunny had pranced restlessly at first, but now she was calm.

"If you fall in here," Reynaldo said, "the soft ground should keep injuries minimal, but let's not test that theory. Secure yourself well every time."

Taliya glanced over at Faria, and the liran smiled back at her. Yes, they were really going to do this.

"Don't worry about directing them today," Reynaldo said. "Let them get used to you on their backs. Just let them fly and use the basic commands we've taught them."

Taliya motioned for Bunny to lower her head, and the dragon complied, though her green eyes looked agitated. As she scratched between Bunny's eyes, the tigran struggled to keep her heart rate calm so she wouldn't aggravate the dragon more. It wasn't easy with the excitement and anxiety flowing around the room.

"It's okay, Bun-Bun," she said. "It won't be that different from flying on your own. I just get to join you now."

Carl held the ladder for her, and Taliya hesitantly climbed, keeping one hand on Bunny at all times since the dragon couldn't see her well. Startling the animal could take the whole process south quickly. Once she was level with Bunny's back, she gently rested her upper body across it, like Reynaldo had told them to. She could feel the dragon breathing. It was calm and controlled, not raspy or choppy. Carefully, she swung her right leg over Bunny's back and sat astride her, grabbing hold of the leather straps.

Bunny hop/walked a few steps, seeming unsure about having her trainer on her back. Taliya forced her body to relax and stroked Bunny's neck. She noticed the other three trainers were on their dragons as well. None were throwing a fit. *So far, so good.*

Carl pulled the ladders out of the way, and Reynaldo walked around his charges, checking that none of the riggings had come loose.

"Okay," Reynaldo finally said, "you know the command. Give it when you're ready."

"Go!" Nimmy shouted without hesitation.

Her dragon chirped a "go" of his own and then leapt into the air with a flap of his massive wings. The other dragons didn't wait for personal invitations. Following Pegasus's lead, the other three launched themselves up. Taliya yelped and held on tight. Getting airborne was rough and jerky, but once Bunny achieved the height she wanted, it was like sliding on ice. Taliya had done that once on a frozen lake, just shushed along on her furry bare feet. This was even better. It was like floating. Giving Bunny a pat on the shoulder, Taliya relished the wind in her fur.

Below them in the center of the arena, Reynaldo clapped and cheered at the spectacle of all four dragons and their trainers whirling around. Carl ran out to him, and they embraced and smacked each other on the back while jumping up and down in a circle like kits. Taliya laughed at the celebration and was tempted to let go of the straps and spread her arms wide—feel the wind with every inch of her body—but she thought better of it. For now, at least.

It was a wise decision because the dragons picked up the excited energy and began to swoop and chase and play with each other, regardless of the riders on their backs. One close pass with Karma revealed a rather terrified look on the tigran's face. Taliya just leaned close to her dragon and held on. Diving and rising and plunging on the back of Bunny was exhilarating beyond words.

After several minutes of watching them in awe, Reynaldo gave the command "down," and the dragons were obedient. Bunny landed with a hop, slow ran, and came to a stop. Carl brought the ladder back to her, and Taliya reluctantly climbed down.

"Was that as amazing as it looked?" Carl asked, his eyes wide.

"Oh yes," Taliya said. "It was breathtaking!"

"We need to make some kind of climbing rope as part of the rigging," Faria suggested, waiting for Reynaldo to set up a ladder for her. "So we don't need help every time."

"But then I won't have an excuse to be here for the flights," Carl said.

The adoring look in Reynaldo's dark-golden eyes told Taliya that Carl never needed an excuse to come see the panthran at work.

After a rest, Reynaldo let them take the dragons up twice more, and each time they got a bit better at directing them and being in control of where the flight was headed. For Taliya, the third flight was as glorious as the first.

When she arrived home that evening, Kano was alone with the three kits. He'd already gotten dinner ready, and they were eating at the table.

"Mama!" all three kits yelled when she came in the door, as they'd started doing every evening.

"My kittens!" she yelled in return, as they were expecting her to.

Taliya really wanted to shower first, but she knew she'd miss the whole thing if she didn't just sit down and join them. So she did.

"How'd training go today?" Kano asked, his standard end-of-day question.

She found herself hesitant to tell him about flying with Bunny. If he was sour about it—which she suspected he would be—the whole experience would be ruined. So she didn't.

"Fine. All good," she said instead.

"I don't have your dinner ready yet," Kano said.

"No problem. I can eat after I get cleaned up." She served Aliania diced meat from a tray on the table and then helped Jai stab some food on his plate with a fork. "I'd rather get time in with my kittens before they head to bed."

"You could shower with me, Mama," Aliania offered with a toothy grin.

"No. Bath with me!" Amrita said, pounding a little fist on the table.

Kano smiled, a rare event now. Jai just stared with wide eyes and chewed his dinner.

"Since it's bath night, how about I help with all of it," Taliya said.

"You smell dusty," Aliania said, wrinkling her nose. "Don't get in Amrita's bath with all that dust."

"I won't," Taliya assured her.

"But you need to shower before you sit on my bed for story time," Aliania said, flaring her tiny white whiskers at her stinky mama.

330

"It's a deal," Taliya said with a laugh.

Once dinners and baths, including her own, were over and the kits were cuddled, read stories, and tucked in bed, Taliya found herself alone with Kano and was tempted to tell him the truth about her day. She finished cleaning up in the kitchen while he put away three loads of laundry Marla had done. Their lives had become all about efficiency, and she knew part of that was due to her absence during the day. But Kano was just as capable of putting away laundry as she was. She tamped down the grumble she felt building in her throat.

After dealing with the last of the plates and wiping the counters, she sat down at the kitchen table to rest. Her legs ached from squeezing to hang onto Bunny's back as they flew around the arena. Closing her eyes, she let that fabulous feeling wash over her again. Flying. She smelled Kano's presence before she opened her eyes. He was leaning against the archway to the living room, watching her. His forehead was crinkled, making his stripes aim down at his pink nose, and his blue eyes looked worried.

"We've lost you to those dragons, haven't we."

"Lost me? What are you talking about?"

"Even when you're here, you're thinking about them. About Bunny and what you hope to teach her tomorrow."

Taliya opened her mouth to correct him, but she knew it was partly true. *What was I just doing ten seconds ago?*

"I understand," he said. "I knew it would happen that first day in the field when we learned the dragons existed. How could you not get lost in something that incredible?"

"You haven't lost me, Kano," she said, standing and moving over to him, wrapping her arms around his waist. "It's just all new and, yes, incredible. But I'm sure eventually it will be a job, just like any other job around here."

He looked down at her with a frown of doubt.

"Okay," she admitted, "maybe not like just *any* job, but there's a lot to it that isn't glamourous or exciting. Like cleaning up hay covered in massive dino-dragon poo."

"Dino poo does sound pretty nasty." He kissed her on the top of the head, pausing and inhaling her scent. "I wish you could step away from it all for a few days, but I know that's not possible."

"It's rather like having a really big dog. You have to walk it and feed it regularly."

"A *stupendously* big dog. That can fly," he said with a laugh. "Are you going to have the day off for Christmas at least?"

"I'll go in early to get Bunny fed and a bit of exercise, but we won't be doing any training. It will be quick, and then I'll be home."

"Good."

"It'll be a weird Christmas without any gifts."

"True, but we are all here. We're all safe. That's a better gift than last Christmas, for sure."

"I was in the attic last Christmas. Marla and I had a bit of a party."

"I was already with Narlin. We did not."

"That's good. I don't think you would have enjoyed any party with him."

Kano exaggerated a shudder. "No."

Taliya snuggled in close to his chest, and then she had a brilliant idea. A way they could all enjoy a special treat that holiday.

"Kano," she whispered into his chest, "have you ever dreamed of flying?"

Taliya was grateful the secret only needed to hold for a few days. Camp life was full of gossip, and she knew the word would eventually spread about the trainers riding the dragons. Preparations to create a festive holiday atmosphere had everyone distracted just enough. Many tigran celebrated the holiday, Christian or not, and the creatures who'd lived in a lab setting were used to some kind of holiday activity through the humans they interacted with. Evergreen wreaths appeared here and there, and donations of extra toys and books for the young ones had come from outside the camp.

On Christmas morning, Taliya woke long before the family and rushed to the training building. She cleaned up Bunny's stall, fed her, and then let her fly free for a while, releasing the overnight pent-up energy. Then she secured Bunny in her stall again and drove back to the house through the dark streets.

Kano was up when she got home, and his eyes were filled with nervousness.

"Are you sure about this?" he said.

"Absolutely. It will be perfectly fine."

They both worked on putting together a holiday breakfast from their family rations—eggs and ham, cinnamon rolls Marla had prepped the day before, and spiced apple juice. The aroma of the rolls baking roused all three kits from their beds.

"Merry Christmas!" Taliya said, watching them stagger out of the bedroom, noses in the air.

She helped them get dressed while Kano served the food. Shreya brought Tuscan and Tyler over—along with a pile of fried bacon—and they all stuffed their faces with the delicious breakfast and gooey rolls. Taliya could only assume that Marla had kicked in some of her sugar ration to make the treats possible—and who knows where she got the cinnamon—so three rolls were set aside for her. Once breakfast was cleaned up, it was time. Taliya clinked a claw on her glass to get everyone's attention.

"Family," she said, "I have a special gift for you today. I know I've been gone a lot over the last few weeks, but it's been important for me to help out with the rescued dragons."

Shreya winked at her and smiled. "It was an honor to be selected for such an important job. We're all so proud of you, aren't we?"

The family nodded, though Taliya thought Aliania was not as enthusiastic as the rest. She wiggled on Kano's lap and stuck her thumb in her mouth.

"I appreciate that," Taliya said, "and I found out a way to thank you. It's a surprise."

That got Ali's attention. She adored surprises.

"I borrowed a larger shuttle from the training building," Taliya said, "and we're all going to drive there together."

"Do we get to pet the dragons?" Tuscan asked excitedly.

"Can we feed them?" Tyler added.

"Something like that," Taliya said. "Everyone grab your shoes and let's go. We'll pick up Marla on the way."

Taliya drove the group to Marla's, where she was pacing in excitement. Once she was tucked in with Amrita on her lap, they headed for the dragon building. Taliya pulled up to a side entrance and used her code to let everyone in.

"Remember to move slowly and calmly," she said. "No running or screaming. It scares them."

The kits all nodded, and Marla winked at her. Kano followed behind the group, hands stuffed in his pants pockets. Taliya suspected this wasn't a welcome trip for him, but maybe if she could get Bunny to accept him, he would be more interested in her work. First, she needed to get the surprise rolling. They all walked over to Bunny's stall, and the dragon eyed them through the slats. Taliya felt waves of energy coming from the kits. She'd better let them get it all out now.

"So, there's something I haven't told you yet," she said. "We've learned how to ride them."

Everyone turned to stare at her.

"You ride them, like, in the air?" Marla said.

"Awesome!" Tuscan and Tyler shout-whispered.

"Can I ride one, Mama?" Aliania said.

"Well, that's why we're here, of course. Merry Christmas."

There were excited smiles from all as they tried to stay calm.

"You can't expect the kits to control that thing," Kano said, eyes narrow.

"No, but they can ride with me, like we talked about."

Kano looked up at the roof, like he was mentally measuring how high this flying would be, and he frowned before staring daggers at the ground. He did not look like he was on board, even though he'd agreed to the plan at home. At least he was keeping his fears to himself for the moment.

"I'm going to let Bunny out," Taliya said, "so she can fly around a bit and stretch her wings. Then I'll get her in the riggings and take you each up for a flight. Marla and Mother, you two can go on your own. Kano, you don't have to ride her if you don't want to, but she can't hold two adults. You'll have to go on your own."

He didn't respond, just stared at Bunny in her stall.

"You can't have been riding these things around camp," Shreya said. "We'd have heard about that."

"No, not yet," Taliya said. "But imagine how useful they could be, moving things and creatures around. Okay, everyone come over here to the side so she can walk out."

Taliya slid the stall door open, and Bunny hop/walked out, keeping a wary eye on the visitors. Once Bunny was clear of the stall, Taliya gave the command. "Go!"

"Go! Go!" Bunny squawked and flapped her wings into the air, swishing dust over the tigran.

"Did she just talk?" Tyler asked, watching Bunny fly slow circles around the area.

"It's more like mimicking, like a bird does, but she knows what the word means and uses it often."

"Wow," Tuscan whispered, hackles raised and tail lashing in anticipation.

Once Bunny had settled back on the ground, Taliya had Marla and Shreya help her hook up the flying harness while the kits watched. Kano held the ladder, and Taliya could feel how nervous he was near the dragon. Bunny was surely feeling it too. He would definitely need to go last, if he wanted to ride at all.

When they were set, Taliya climbed up the new ladder portion of the rigging, and Shreya helped Aliania up to her. The group had decided she would take the first ride so neither Tuscan nor Tyler got to be first and argued about it. Bunny seemed to notice that the kit was on her back, but Taliya didn't sense any concern from the big white dragon. Kano's tension hung in the air, but he stayed quiet. Motherly instinct tried to kick in and make Taliya nervous too, but she kept it in check. If she really thought there was any danger, so wouldn't allow Ali anywhere near the dragons.

"Hold on to this strap here," Taliya directed the kit. "I'll be holding on to you too. We're only going to do slow circles, like you saw Bunny doing on her own."

"Okay."

Taliya didn't sense any tension from her daughter, so she gave the command. "Go!" Bunny flapped her wings and rose into the air. Now Taliya could sense all kinds of emotions radiating from the kit, but none of it was fear. They swooped around and even dove gently a few times. Then Taliya directed Bunny to land so they could change riders. Aliania stood up on the dragon's back and turned around to face Taliya.

"I flew, Mama," she said, her bright-blue eyes sparkling.

"You sure did."

Kano was waiting as Taliya dropped the ladder down. He collected Aliania, and Taliya felt relief from him. At least he'd trusted his mate enough to keep his fears to himself and let the kit ride. Tuscan was hopping on one foot, waiting for his turn.

"Calm down," Shreya said, placing a hand on his head.

He nodded and stopped hopping, but his tail still lashed back and forth. Shreya helped him up the ladder, and off they went. Then Tyler, Jai, and Amrita all took turns. Finally, after a few quick directions, Shreya and then Marla took Bunny for a flight all on their own. Taliya had been worried Bunny might not like strangers on her back, but she just flapped into the air obediently. Of course, everyone thought flying was the most fabulous thing ever.

Then it was Kano's turn. He hadn't said anything about riding or not, so Taliya just moved ahead.

"Okay, Kano. You're up," she said.

The massive white tigran chuffed at her but didn't move.

"Bunny hates me."

He'd never admitted his feelings outright like that. Taliya chuffed back and walked over to him.

"I don't think she *hates* you. She was just jealous and protective of me, right from the start. Move around front where she can see you and give her a pat on the chest. She likes that. But watch your emotions. She's as good as any tigran at reading body language and feelings."

"Go on, Papa," Aliania said. "You don't want to be the only one of us who hasn't ridden a dragon."

Kano whoofed in agreement at that. Then he stepped hesitantly over to Bunny and stood in front of her. They examined each other. As instructed, Kano moved closer and put his hand on Bunny's chest. The dragon bent her head down and gave him a few sniffs, then she raised her head again.

"Drag your hand along her so she can feel where you're going," Taliya said. "Then climb the ladder. The ground is super soft. If she doesn't like you up there, you can just jump down."

Kano grimaced at that idea, but he followed her directions. Bunny didn't flinch, and soon Kano was sitting astride the dragon with the ladder pulled up and secured. He wrapped the straps around his hands, like he'd seen the others do. Looking down at Taliya, he smiled.

"So far, so good."

"Excellent," Taliya said. "You know the command, whenever

you're ready. Don't forget to hold on with your legs too. It keeps you from slipping off."

Kano looked down at the rigging again, then he told Bunny to go. She stomped a few times first, but she obeyed and lifted off. Taliya's heart felt like it jumped into her throat, and she desperately hoped Bunny didn't get testy up in the air. The family watched as Kano circled a few times, but then Bunny started to dip and dive around the arena. Taliya couldn't see Kano's face, but she worried he might fall. Bunny had been so calm with the other adults, and now she was whipping around the building, faster than Taliya had ever flown her, sailing up and then down again, tipping one wing and then the other. Kano knew the command to make her stop, but he wasn't saying it. *Maybe he's too scared.* After several minutes of that, Taliya couldn't take it anymore.

"Bunny, down!"

The dragon completed a few more circles to slow her momentum before coming to land in the middle of the arena. Taliya strode toward them as fast as she could without running, but Kano was already down by the time she got there. He was panting and bent over to put his hands on his knees.

"I'm sorry, Kano. I thought she'd behave better."

"What? Oh, no. She was great. I was steering her."

"Steering? You mean she flew like that because you told her to?"

Kano's eyes met hers, and there was no mistaking the

devious delight there. He hadn't just sat on Bunny and gone where the dragon wanted, he'd directed her and made it quite a freewheeling show.

"No wonder you come home so late," he said, standing upright. "If I got to do that every day, I might never go home."

Taliya felt a huge weight lift from her shoulders. He understood. He finally understood.

"I wish you'd joined me in being a trainer," she said.

"No, it's better this way. But I hope you'll let me ride her again every once in a while."

Taliya wrapped her arms around his waist and snuggled her face into his chest. He hugged her close and then leaned back to give her a kiss long enough to make the kits squeal and beg them to stop.

"Merry Christmas, husband," Taliya said with a grin.

"Merry Christmas, wife."

Chapter 25

New Year's Eve was celebrated with a party around the firepit at the front of camp, where Kano and Taliya had been handfast. Then life went back to its routine, though the family did come by more often to enjoy a flight on Bunny, and Kano was more supportive of Taliya's work. The other trainers had brought friends by too—and Samson and Carl had flown on Pegasus, the largest dragon—so word had definitely spread about the dragons and their capabilities.

Taliya did find it hard to go home some nights. In one place, she flew around on the back of a dragon. In the other place, she had laundry waiting, dishes to wash, and kits who were clingy and demanding. Many nights she dreamed about flying away on Bunny, swooping over her forest home in Arkansas and never coming back. She was the only one of the trainers with kits, and it sometimes felt like a great injustice in her life. Then she'd have a bad day with Bunny—where the dragon refused to cooperate or was in a sour mood, making Taliya want to give up the whole thing—and a great day at home, with kits so loving it made her heart sing, and she'd wonder if she was losing her mind a bit. As much as she loved working with Bunny, in the end nothing was quite as satisfying as cuddling on the sofa with her three kits, hearing about their days, and reading them a book before bed. They would be too grown up for that before she knew it, so Taliya tried to drink in as much of that special family time as she could.

It was mid-January when Samson came to find Taliya at the training building. She was just taking the riggings off Bunny after a session of trying some new commands.

"Taliya, I am glad I found you here," he said, approaching in his languid gate and giving Bunny a pat.

"Would you like a ride?" she offered, though not sure Bunny could handle the massive ligran.

"No, but thank you. I am here about something else. Canadian reporters are terribly interested in what goes on in here. Our dome keeps them from being able to observe anything. The council has decided it would be wise to allow a few of them inside to do some interviews. Then they can share with the country why this camp is necessary and that the refugees are doing more than just sitting around all day waiting to be fed and clothed."

"I can understand that. Sometimes I forget where we are, country-wise. We really owe our lives to the Canadian government. There's nowhere in the U.S. we could remain hidden like this."

"Definitely not. So are you willing to be interviewed and speak with the reporters?"

"About the dragons?"

"Yes, and about your personal story. I am sure they will want footage of these magnificent animals, but they will also want to stress why *you* are here and why you must hide. I think it is hard for other countries to grasp how bad life in America has become if you disagree with Kerkaw's policies. Or are a genetically created species. If you are willing to share, it could help raise more support and funds for the war effort."

Taliya hesitated. She didn't mind talking about the dragons, but sharing the details of her own story was another thing. *Would I have to admit to killing three humans? Details about Narlin?* Her hackles rose at the thought.

"You can decide what you are willing to share," Samson said, "but the crew is coming tomorrow. There is a break in the weather for the next three days, and they want to get in and out before then."

"I forget it's winter outside the dome. It's always the same temperature in here."

"On the other side of that wall is sixteen feet of snow. Winter in Winnipeg takes no prisoners."

"Sixteen feet? How will the reporters get through that?"

"The roads are always cleared and usually thermally heated to keep them clear. The crews just have to worry about getting hit by a blizzard en route."

"Okay. So I should be ready to speak with them tomorrow?"

"Yes. And thank you, Taliya. I knew I could count on you. The other three trainers will hopefully be interviewed as well. I cannot control what ends up in the documentary report when they broadcast it. We will just have to put on our best faces and hope they are fair and honest."

The next day, Taliya got up early and went in to take care of Bunny and her stall, then she drove home and got cleaned up for the interview. She and Kano had discussed it late into the night. They were both hesitant to share too much but worried if they didn't share enough, the interviewers wouldn't be recording the depth of the problem. They desperately needed the support of the Canadians and probably would for years to come.

She slipped into her favorite outfit—tunic and pants in a blue that matched Kano's eyes, like the ones she'd brought with her into hiding, now buried in the rubble of the breeding facility—and met the family in the kitchen. Kano was subdued and merely going through the motions of making sure everyone got breakfast.

"Are you positive you don't want me to come?" he asked for the fifth time.

"No, it's fine. It's probably better if they don't see you. You're awfully magnificent."

Kano chuffed and helped Amrita down from the table.

"I'm sure Canadians know about white tigran."

"Yes, but it's one thing to know about it and another thing altogether to see your gloriousness. It could give them ideas about wanting you for themselves."

He chuckled and started clearing the breakfast dishes.

"I don't think I'll ever have the appeal of the berman. Those are the guys who should stay off camera today."

"Oh my, yes," she said with a wink, wiping Jai's face and sending all three kits to finish getting ready for the day. Kano wrapped his arms around her, and Taliya rested her head on his chest. "Though I'd rather have you any day."

He held her close for a moment. "Are we still agreed you won't tell them about Amrita?"

"One hundred percent. I trust this crew to share our stories, but I don't trust humans in general. Probably never will. All it takes is one who knows how valuable she is, and who knows what he would do to get his hands on her."

"Good. I'm glad they're letting Aliania and me stay off camera and not talk about what we went through. It's an important story, but I just can't."

"I'm sure the council understands," Taliya said. "They have

enough terrible stories without showing Ali to the world. I'll tell them what they need to know."

With an interview plan in place, Kano left for work, Aliania headed to school with her uncles, and Taliya walked the twins to the nursery. Marla was also going to be interviewed, to talk about her experience in the POW camp. She'd fussed about her hair, though it was growing back in nicely. Shreya had agreed to watch all of the kits if the interviews ran late.

By the time Taliya arrived at the dragon training building, there were already several shuttles parked out front. She straightened her tunic, pursed her whiskers, and marched inside. What greeted her was more than she'd expected. It wasn't just cameras and dozens of humans but there were giant, bright hanging lights and white screens for background. One of the men looked up when she entered.

"Which one are you?" he said bluntly.

"I'm Taliya."

"Joe!" he shouted. "Your tigran's here."

Taliya swished her tail at such an informal and borderline rude greeting, and she began to reconsider how much she would share. Were they going to treat the stories respectfully or make it all sensationalized nonsense like the news often did? A man walked toward her, and she assumed this was Joe. He was a full head shorter than her, and he was dressed in a red snakeskin-print jacket and pants, like someone from a fashion magazine. *Very trendy.* The darkness of his hair and eyes gave him a bit of an evil villain look. She struggled to keep her ears from twisting flat in an instinctive reaction.

"Taliya, it's nice to meet you." He extended his hand in greeting, and she shook it politely. "We definitely want to sit down with you and have a chat, but we also want footage of you and your pterodragon. Do you really ride on them and fly?"

"Yes, we really do," she said. "Would it be possible to do the interview first? Riding and flying stirs up a lot of dust."

"Of course."

They settled into two wooden chairs in front of one of the screens, and three cameramen joined them, along with someone who looked like he was an expert in technical equipment. Bright lights shone down on them. Taliya found the heat uncomfortable, but she appreciated how well the two of them would stand out against the white background.

"We have this section set up with microphones," Joe said, "so you can just speak to me directly and be recorded with no problem. We will both be on camera the whole time, along with a wide shot of both of us, that's why there's three guys, and then later we'll cut and edit things together. Okay?"

She nodded and straightened her tunic again. It was hard not to feel nervous, but she did her best to avoid thinking about how many people might see the interview. On the other hand, she might not even make the final cut. Bunny certainly would, but Taliya's story was probably like many, many others in the camp. Joe gave her a nod, and she smiled weakly in return.

"Okay, here we go." He cleared his throat, and someone Taliya couldn't see told the cameramen to start recording. "I'm at the Winnipeg refugee camp with a tigran named Taliya. She has survived a harrowing year of terror and abuse but has found a home here for herself and her family. Taliya, walk us through what your life has been like since you fled the Gathering in the United States."

Taliya detailed her story, going back even more, to when tigran lived happily with humans, before her father was fired and the school closed. She talked about going into hiding and being captured. She and Kano had agreed to leave out the part about killing the guards, so she just talked about fighting and being drugged. She was explicit, however, about her time in the breeding facility, the details of how Kano ended up there and his wife's murder, and her own personal experiences with Colonel Narlin—but she only said she was rescued in time, not that she killed him. Joe uttered appropriate small noises of sadness and made all the right reactionary faces during her sad tale.

"Tigran have been living and working alongside humans for over a hundred years," she said. "We always had very few rights, even though roughly half of our genetic makeup is human, but we never fought about that. Tigran worked as builders, teachers, even served as warriors in the army. It's only since President Kerkaw stirred up hatred toward our race that humans have become afraid."

She turned to the camera. "Remember how things were before, not so long ago. Tigran are workers. Tigran are rescuers. Tigran are intelligent creatures who want nothing more than to live their lives and love their families in peace. We did not start this war, and we would love nothing more than to see it end and go back to quiet, productive lives. But when our homes are attacked, our friends murdered in the streets, we will fight back, just like any of you would."

Looking back at Joe, she set her face to show sadness, like she'd practiced in the mirror, avoiding any trace of aggression or anger. "I hope your viewers understand that facilities like the one I was captured for, those places prove that the government doesn't really think tigran are abominations. It's all a big cover-up. Government-sanctioned scientists are breeding tigran for profit. It's only the creatures of no financial value who are being exterminated or imprisoned."

"That's an amazing story, Taliya," Joe said. "Thank you for sharing it with us. I understand that you have been reunited with your mother here."

"Yes. She was rescued from a prisoner of war camp."

"And the kits you conceived in the breeding facility, they have been born and are here with you as well?"

Taliya took a deep breath and let it out slowly. This subject she was going to tiptoe through like a field of scorpions.

"Yes, they were born here with the help of a wonderful doctor and are both healthy."

"And one of them was white?"

"Yes." He wasn't getting any more than that.

"And your husband, Kano, he already had a white tigran daughter. Is she here as well?"

"Yes. She was in another part of the breeding facility, as I said, as leverage to make Kano cooperate, but she's safe with us now."

"So, Taliya, tell me about these dragons we're going to see."

Taliya felt like a corset around her middle had been released. He was done talking about the personal stuff and hadn't insisted on revealing information that wasn't already part of the government files. She babbled on about the pterodragons and their daily schedule for a minute or two. Then they recorded her putting on the harness and riding Bunny in flight. Other groups were recording Pegasus, Polly, and Coconut with their trainers. The crew was fascinated by the animals, as they should be, but they kept their distance. All four trainers insisted their dragons didn't like strangers, and the reporters seemed reluctant to push it. Reynaldo did not put in an appearance, and Taliya thought that was a good call. Just like with Kano, it was better to keep the more magnificent and rare creatures out of sight.

When the cameras were put away, Taliya was pleased with how well it had gone. As she left, she noticed a cameraman outside, filming the area around the building and the back wall of the habitat dome. That seemed strange, but maybe they just wanted outside shots of how large the arena was. She hoped they made it clear that the whole thing had been built by the refugees.

She decided to pick up the kits before afternoon nap, but her heart nearly stopped when she saw a camera crew leaving the nursery. No one had warned her of that. Taliya raced inside and had her answer on the faces of the two liran at the check-in desk.

"Oh, Taliya," one gasped. "The council said we had to let them in. They wanted to report on how many kits were here, how sad that was. But I don't believe that's what they were doing. It felt wrong, so wrong." She burst into tears and sat down, face in her hands.

"Did they get images of Amrita?"

The other liran nodded, tears running down her tawny cheeks. "I can't see how they'd have missed her. Amrita and so many others. The little berman cubs. It's so horrible."

The corseted feeling around Taliya's middle was back, but she couldn't blame the liran. How could they have stopped it short of physically fighting and undoing all the good they hoped the recordings would accomplish? Taliya collected Amrita and Jai and got them home quickly. Shreya was at their unit, folding sheets on the kitchen table. Once the kits were down for their naps, Taliya told her everything.

"Are you sure the reporters got video of her?" Shreya asked.

"Yes, the staff seemed certain of it." Taliya hesitated. "Mother, don't tell Kano."

"Are you sure?"

"He will flip out and go to the council or ambush the reporters, if he can catch them, and insist they edit the recordings. I've seen him go into a rage, and we definitely don't want that recorded. It will only call more attention to her. And him and Aliania. Just because they filmed Amrita doesn't mean they will broadcast it. I'm sure they saw all kinds of things here and heard all kinds of stories. It's not like U.S. government troops are going to risk raiding this camp for one little strawberry tigran."

Shreya reluctantly agreed to keep it between them, at least for now.

Marla joined them after her interview. She seemed content with how they'd handled her story. It was risky for her to be on camera too, admitting to her illegal existence, but the promise of the stories helping their cause justified the risk.

A week had gone by, and no one in camp had heard anything more about the documentary. The council said it might be months before it was actually broadcast, so the refugees had just gotten on with their lives.

Reynaldo was hoping they could start using the dragons around camp more, helping to transport supplies or possibly even creatures, and that was the focus of the day. Taliya had just finished doing a training flight with Bunny, having the animal pick up boxes in her claws and move them from one spot to another. Bunny was hunkered down for a nap in her stall, and Taliya plopped in the clean hay and leaned on her dragon's chest. The other trainers had left for lunch, so it was quiet and peaceful.

She'd had Agnus check the records and discovered Kano's birthday was January 30th. They'd need to start planning if they were going to come up with anything special for him next week. As she pondered party ideas, the gentle rise and fall of Bunny's breathing and the familiar musty smell of the dragon's feathers lulled her into a nap.

Taliya woke to a chilly breeze. It took her mind a moment to register it. Breezes were rare in the camp. Bunny was asleep, so it wasn't the dragon's wings, and the other three were resting quietly too. The chilly part was even stranger. The regulated temperature inside the dome only varied by a few degrees. Had they pumped up the air-conditioning unit for some reason? She rubbed her eyes as another waft of cold air—really freezing-cold air—hit her. Bunny squawked and raised her head.

After stepping out of the stall and latching it behind her, Taliya spotted the massive black panthran standing in the middle of the arena, slowly turning in a circle with his arms spread, maybe testing where the cold air was coming from.

"Reynaldo," she called, "what's going on?"

"I don't know," he admitted, "but something's not right."

She walked out to join him, and they both moved around the building, trying to determine the source of the chill. Taliya followed it to the main entrance and stepped outside the building. It was freezing out there, like it probably felt outside the dome. Her tail puffed. *It should not be that cold in here.*

The repeated blast of the camp-wide alarm system rang out, and Taliya froze. A popping of laser gunfire sounded nearby. Over the smell of what could only be outside air, she detected a stronger odor of anxious human males. A large group of them.

"Taliya!" Reynaldo shouted.

She turned in time to see Reynaldo collapse in the dirt of the arena floor and heard "Target number one down" from someone inside the building. All four dragons cawed with rage and banged against the bars of their stalls. A sharp pain jabbed in the middle of Taliya's back. Spinning back around, she faced three masked men with guns held at the ready. The ground around her wobbled and waved, and an eerily familiar feeling washed over her as the camp alarm system continued to blare.

"Target number two acquired," one of the men said.

Then the world went black.

Chapter 26

Taliya woke to darkness and a horrifyingly familiar smell. Dankness. Concrete. *Shit. Shit. Shit!* Her head ached, and she was pretty sure she'd puke if she sat up. Trying to move even her hand required more energy than she could muster.

She focused on what she could remember. The alarm blasting. Men had broken into the refugee camp. They must have hacked their way through the snow outside and busted open the dome at the far end, away from watching eyes, near the dragon building. That's where the cold air had been coming from. She'd seen three men, but someone else had shot Reynaldo from inside the arena. She hoped he'd only been drugged too. *He's valuable. They'd want him alive.* Her stomach churned at the thought of it. Maybe it was the dragons they'd wanted.

As far as anyone knew, those were the only four in the whole world. *Even more valuable.* She felt a flicker of worry for Bunny, but the dragons were incredibly valuable. Whoever the captors were, she couldn't imagine they'd hurt the animals.

But why had they taken her? She was totally expendable. *If they wanted the dragons, why didn't they just kill me or leave me behind?* The answer couldn't be anything good. If she was alive, it was for a reason.

She used her heightened tigran senses to attempt to piece her situation together. There was no one else in with her. She couldn't smell anyone or hear any breathing. It was dark, but as her eyes adjusted there was some faint light coming through the cracks of a doorway across from her. The room was small, with concrete walls. There was a toilet and a sink. Definitely a prison cell of some kind. She was stretched out on a cot and wearing the same clothes she'd had on when they'd captured her. No smell of blood. She closed her eyes and listened to the sounds outside the door. Footsteps now and then. A door opening and closing. The residual drugs pulled her back into sleep.

Taliya woke again to the sound of the door opening. An overhead light turned on. Lurching upright, she immediately regretted the action as her head swam and her stomach roiled.

She gripped the edge of the cot and squinted against the brightness to see who'd entered. A man. No uniform, just black clothes, a cattle prod clutched in his hand—like the one Narlin had nastily flourished in his last moments.

"Good morning," he said.

Taliya didn't answer. He reeked of sour sweat, and his body language expressed nothing but confidence. Determination.

"How's your head feeling?"

"Like you drugged me and stuck me in a prison cell."

"You're lucky to be alive," he said, sitting down on a metal chair across from her cot.

She glared at him, ears back. "That remains to be seen."

He chuckled but didn't release his grip on the cattle prod.

"I suppose it does. How long you're here is totally up to you."

Maybe they need me to control the dragons. Are Karma, Nimmy, and Faria here too?

"We need you to make a recording," he said. "A video."

"A video of what?"

He leaned in close, appearing unconcerned about her teeth or claws. "You're going to record a message to the refugee camp and to your mate. You're going to instruct them to deliver your golden tabby tigran and the pure-white tigran to us in exchange for your life."

Every hair on her body rose, and she growled deep in her throat. Of all the things she'd worried about, danger to the kits had not occurred to her. Taliya hissed and dug her claws into

358

the cot. *That damn documentary crew. They leaked something.* That's the only way anyone would know about Amrita. At least it meant her captors didn't already have them. Or Kano.

"What does the government want with them?" she said.

"Government? Who said anything about the government? When my boss saw footage of all the beasties holed up in that camp, it was like a lottery ticket to billions of dollars. And having the training facility at the far end? We were in and out before the guards knew what happened. We've already sold the dragon things. And there's a highly motivated buyer for the kits. Do you know what they're worth?"

Taliya could hardly breathe, much less answer. She bared her fangs, letting lose a growl/hiss. The man shifted away from her a bit.

"Hey, no point in killin' me. I'm just the messenger. They'll only send someone else in."

She didn't stop her growling, though she realized he was right. Killing him would be pointless. And piss off whoever was holding her captive.

"Those weird kits of yours are worth fifty million dollars," he said. "Isn't that crazy? Fifty million! Just make the video, and we'll turn you loose. We don't have any use for you. Tell them to release the kits to us, and then we'll let you go back home, or whatever you call it there. Simple as that."

She couldn't believe the callousness of his attitude. He honestly seemed to believe it was no big deal.

"How can you possibly think I'll agree to this?" she growled.

"I've heard your story. You didn't want those kits in the first place."

"Just because I didn't plan on having kits doesn't mean I won't defend them. Which part of me do you think will just hand over her own young—the tiger or the human?"

He seemed surprised by her response. "You're serious?"

She sat up tall on her cot. "I will not be making any video."

Without warning, he jabbed the cattle prod into her middle. Her vision went white as pain lashed her entire body. She crumpled on the cot, her muscles like water. Then her whole body cramped in spasms, a Charley horse over every inch of her. She gasped, but it racked her with pain. It was several minutes before the cramping eased. She opened her eyes to see him still sitting there, watching her.

"That was just a quick sample of what you can expect if our demands are not met," he said as he stood and headed for the door. "I'll give you some time to reconsider." He stalked out, locking the cell door behind him.

Taliya rolled to her back and tried to stretch out on the cot. Everything hurt. All the times she'd worn a hotwire, she'd never really understood what it felt like to be hit by an electric current. How many of those zaps could she survive? Was there any hope of rescue if she tried to hold out?

Kano would never surrender our daughters. But what if he saw Taliya on a video telling him to make the trade? *He'd know what it took to get me to do that. He'd know I was being tortured. Would he hand them over to save me?* It would place him in an impossible situation. *I can't do it. Can't do that to him. I have to be strong.*

After not very long, the man came back to see if she'd changed her mind.

Three times he asked.

Three times she said no.

Three times he used the cattle prod on her, holding it in place longer with each stab.

By the time he left, Taliya couldn't move. She could smell that she'd soiled herself. Every muscle was in spasm.

As her body finally relaxed, shifting into a dull ache, she knew one thing for sure: this was only the beginning. It was still Day One. Her captors were determined and probably in a hurry. If she didn't cooperate, their strategies were going to be more aggressive. Soon. He'd give her a few hours to suffer and reconsider. Then he'd be back.

Something else was becoming clear: for Amrita and Aliania, this would never end. Ever. The cell she was in at that moment had nothing to do with the government or President Kerkaw. These men were mercenaries, hired to do a job. Profit was their only agenda. Even if the war was won and Kerkaw fell, the girls would still be valuable prizes. Her darling kits. *How can we ever keep those two truly safe? Truly free? Greedy bastards will always hunt them.*

She curled up in a ball with all the energy she had left and tried to sleep before the next round began.

When the door opened again, two different men came in, and fear flooded her body. One held a fresh pair of pants for her, and the other held what looked like a medical bag. *What are the chances he's a doctor come to help me? Slim. Very slim.* The first man draped the pants across the back of the chair, and the other man set the bag on the chair, opening it and beginning to fuss around inside.

"I suppose we should give you a chance to say you've changed your mind before we get started," Man One said. "Have you?"

Taliya pulled together the strength to shake her head slightly. The aggressive strategies were about to begin. A tear slid down her face.

"No point in changing your pants just yet then, is there?" Man One said, not really a question.

Taliya swallowed but couldn't find the energy for even a hiss.

Man Two pulled a slender metal instrument with a tiny hook at one end from the bag.

"It's always interesting how the smallest acts can have the biggest results," he said with a smile. "All this electrocution. You're never going to yield to that. They'll kill you first. Little things can be so much more persuasive."

Man One rolled her onto her back and wrapped a leather strap around her torso, securing her arms to her body and against the cot. Whatever they had planned, it was going to be terrible. Maybe more than she could resist. Tears ran down the sides of her face and soaked the black-striped fur. Man Two took a strange plastic object out of the bag and leaned over her. She tried to fight him, but her jaw muscles wouldn't respond. He jammed the object into her mouth so it was propped open. And so she couldn't bite.

"Now, we will start simply," Man Two said. "Nothing that will leave a permanent mark. Then I'll ask you again for your cooperation. I hope that's where all of this ends. You still have your claws. You still have your teeth. I'm sure you'll agree to things before we have to go that far."

An image of her mother's butchered hands flashed through her mind. That's where this was headed before long. Man One smirked, and Taliya suspected he hoped she held out. What fun would it be if she gave in right away?

Man Two's method of persuasion was quite simple—and painful beyond anything Taliya had ever experienced. He wedged the hook of the metal stick under the gums around one of her fangs and pressed into the ultra-sensitive nerves there. Those teeth were biologically wired to sense everything from changes in temperature to the heartbeat and pulse point of a victim yards away. Her torturer knew exactly what he was doing.

At the first touch, she screamed, human and tiger rage and pain blended together. Her body arched in reflex, trying to escape, but she was fastened down tightly. Man One smiled and crossed his arms, looking quite pleased with himself. Man Two was more focused, watching her reactions. He shifted the instrument and pressed again, and she screamed for what felt like forever. Then he stopped and sat back, giving her a moment to recover.

Tears soaked the cot on either side of her head, and they had been right about waiting to give her a change of clothes. The pain didn't stop when he removed the instrument but continued to radiate through her jaw and down her neck. She whoofed past the bite guard, and Man Two smiled.

"So, are we done?"

A sob escaped her throat.

"I need a nod yes or no from you, Taliya. Will you make the video and tell your mate to trade your life for the kits?"

Pain still raced through every inch of her, but she slowly shook her head no. Man One grinned. Man Two frowned.

"We continue, then. I didn't bring the dental drill with me. Really didn't think we'd need it. Such a fuss over a couple of kits. Let's try once more before we leave you to reconsider."

Before she could respond, he strategically worked the instrument under the gum of the other fang, starting a fresh round of suffering. Her screaming grew hoarse, and spots flashed before her eyes. With one final jab, she passed out.

When Taliya woke with a gasp, the men were gone. The bite guard and strap across her body had been removed, but anguish flowed through her muscles and nerves. It seemed impossible there was worse torment they could inflict on her, but Man Two had made loaded comments about *permanent damage*. He'd mentioned declawing. A dental drill.

It seemed darker in the cell now, like maybe it was night. Still only Day One, as far as she knew. Maybe Day Two, if it took her as long as the first time to recover from the tranquilizer drugs. How long had she been out just now? Her teeth didn't hurt so dramatically anymore, so it had been a while since the men left, but her body still ached from the tip of her ears to the tip of her tail. Her stomach rumbled and clenched. It had been long enough for severe hunger to set in. And thirst. Glancing around the room, she didn't see any food, but there was a sink. Water was necessary. No living being can survive too long without it.

Carefully rolling off the cot, she wobbled her way to the sink and ran water into her cupped hands, drinking it from there. Then she splashed some on her face. She used the toilet and cleaned up as best she could, changing into the fresh pair of pants, wishing she could do something about the smell. Then she curled back up on the cot. How long till those men came back, or would they send different men with new tools of torture?

If she didn't agree to recording the video, they would kill

365

her. She could see that now. Painfully. Probably in the next day or so. If Amrita and Aliania were really worth fifty million dollars, her captors would only waste so much time on this plan. And she'd seen all of the men's faces, could identify them. Would they really let her live if she made the video? Tears came again and finally great, painful, heaving sobs.

When she finally ran out of energy, she tried to plot her way through the next few hours. Honest logic said she was going to die in that cell in the not-very-distant future. Maybe a day or so. Then those horrible men would go after her daughters again.

If I agree to making the video, is it a way to stall, buy some time? They'd have to keep me alive for the trade. Is anyone looking for me? How long was it before they noticed I was gone along with the dragons? There had been an alarm at the camp. It couldn't have taken too long to figure it out.

If Reynaldo had been taken—or sold, like the dragons— Carl would never stop searching for him. She was sure of that. And Kano? How would he search for *her?* He couldn't wander around free in the world. How would he even know where to start? Why couldn't the humans just leave them alone? She closed her eyes and pictured her family at the table together. Playing in the living room. Cuddled on the sofa.

Take care of them, Kano. Tell them about me now and then. Help them remember.

Feeling more hopeless and helpless than she had since the

moment she'd gotten on a truck in the dark of night and run from her beloved home in the forest, Taliya cried herself to sleep.

Chapter 27

A loud crash vibrated outside the door, and Taliya sat bolt upright. Her body protested, but the instinctive reaction won out. She listened carefully, swiveling her ears. Another crash, closer this time. The distinctive popping sound of laser gunfire. Human voices yelling. More gunfire. Adrenaline rushed through her, and she leapt from the cot, staggering on weak legs.

"Taliya?!"

It sounded like Kano. She rushed to the door.

"Taliya?!"

"Here! I'm here!" she yelled raspingly, banging on the metal door with both fists. She could smell Kano. Right outside the door. No amount of concrete could block that from her. It snuck through the cracks with its message of hope. "Kano!"

"Over here!" he called out.

The floor vibrated with clomping boots. There was a smattering of conversation and rustling sounds. She put her ear to the door, trying to figure out what was happening.

"Taliya, get back. We're gonna blow it." It was Carl's voice this time, not Kano's. "Hide behind something if you can."

Spinning around—and making her head swim—she grabbed the cot and dragged it into a far corner, then crouched down and held it in front of her, her whole body shaking with the effort. There was a hissing sound and then silence. She held her breath.

Boom! Boom! Boom!

Explosions rocked her prison cell, and the acrid odor of tar and the oil used in old trucks filled the room. With a reverberating thud, the door fell inward.

"Taliya?"

She couldn't answer, just sob. Kano rushed to her and scooped her up in his arms. She clung to him as he carried her from the room. Outside the door, Taliya was met by Carl, along with three men and a female guard she recognized from around camp. They smiled at her but then immediately returned to serious expressions.

"We're glad you're still alive," Carl said. "But we aren't out of here yet."

"Reynaldo?" she asked, slipping out of Kano's arms to stand on her own two feet.

"We think he was alive when they captured him," Kano said quietly as Carl frowned and turned away. "But we haven't found him here. Have you seen him?"

"No," she said. "The last time I saw him, he was lying in the middle of the arena."

"We need to get you out of here. Can you walk?"

"Yes, but stay close. It feels like I've been trampled by a hundred berman."

Kano growled deep in his chest, nodded, and picked up a huge laser gun from a table nearby. With Carl and the female guard in the lead, Kano and Taliya jogged down the hallway, the other three guards watching the rear. She'd thought she was in some kind of prison, but it was really just a large house. A demented house with a concrete-block cell in it. They rounded a corner, and Taliya nearly tripped on two men dead on the ground. Their faces were unrecognizable, blown off, but their scents were clear: Man One and Man Two. A deep satisfaction washed over her.

"There's at least one more," she said, and Carl nodded sharply to acknowledge it.

Pausing at the main door, he motioned with his hand, and all the guards came to the front. Kano turned and watched behind them down the hall. In one fluid move, Carl opened the door, daylight poured in, and all the guards spilled out, guns lowered and ready. When there was no attack, they led Taliya out with Kano keeping an eye on their six. A strange whooping sound came from their right, and she realized they were rushing toward it—a military helicopter with a giant red maple leaf on the side.

The smell hit her before she saw him. The man with the cattle prod. He was there, somewhere. Scanning the open field around the house, she spotted him, stepping from behind an outbuilding and taking aim at the group. The next seconds were a blur. She sensed that no one else noticed him, realized they were all focused elsewhere. Kano had a smaller gun, a spare, tucked into the belt around his waist. Taliya wrenched it out, took aim, and fired repeatedly, forcing her arms to cooperate. The guards froze at the sound of shots but quickly spotted her target as he clutched his middle and fell to his knees.

I wish I could see his eyes. Wish I could watch the life drain out of him, like Narlin.

Kano chuffed and went back to scanning behind them. Taliya glanced over at Carl, who was watching her, a puzzled look on his face.

"Not my first gun," she said with a grim smile.

He gave her a quick nod and went back to his task, getting the group safely to the chopper. When they were almost there, a flash of laser fire zipped past her. The noise of the rotors hid the sound, but more gunfire came from their left. Carl lurched, and Kano grabbed him before he fell.

"Thompson!" the female guard yelled, stopping to help Kano support Carl.

"Move! Move!" Carl shouted, staggering toward the helicopter.

The other guards had already turned and were firing in response. Taliya couldn't see if they were successful. They all ducked to avoid the blades, climbed inside the helicopter, and hung on to whatever was closest as it immediately lifted off. A guard slid the door shut, and everyone collapsed back on the benches of seats facing each other. Two of the guards ripped open a first aid kit and tended to the nasty wound on Carl's chest. His skin had turned a scary color of pale gray.

"All cleared and accounted for," the pilot said. "We're headed out."

Taliya realized the pilot was speaking into her headset, not to them, but appreciated the message just the same. All clear. The female guard barked orders to the pilot to call ahead so medics would be waiting to help Major Thompson. Taliya would have laughed at hearing Carl referred to so formally except she was terrified he was going to die before they got to wherever they were headed. This was twice now he'd rescued her. She sent up a prayer to the gods that he had not given his life in return for hers.

Kano took the gun she still had gripped in her hand and set it on the floor with his, then he pulled her close.

"I thought you were gone forever," he said, nuzzling the top of her head.

"I would have been before long. If I hadn't cooperated, they would have killed me."

"Cooperated with what?" he said, pulling back to look at her.

"They wanted our daughters. They wanted Amrita and Aliania."

His whole body stiffened, and his chest rumbled a growl.

"They're safe," he finally said. "They're back at the camp, and they're safe."

Taliya nodded. She'd explain it all later. Right then all that mattered was getting away. Getting help for Carl. The scent of his blood filled the cabin.

"Did you find the dragons?" she asked. "The men said they were sold."

"No. We haven't found a trace of them."

Her heart sank. *Poor Bunny. Poor all of them.* It wasn't the same as losing a kit, but she did love Bunny. It was more like what she imagined humans felt for pet dogs and cats.

"The Canadian government will go looking for them," Kano said. "They won't want to lose them any more than we do. How long can you keep an animal like that hidden?"

Taliya hoped he was right. Even if Bunny never made it back to her, she hoped the dragon was safe and cared for. In the hands of a private citizen might actually be better than a government lab. She let that truth sink in.

A guard handed her an energy bar and a jug of water, and she smiled gratefully. Getting something to eat restored a bit of her energy. They flew on in silence for a while, the guards watching out the windows or resting their heads against the seats and closing their eyes. Carl was stretched out on the floor of the helicopter, blood seeping through his bandages. His breathing suggested he was unconscious. Maybe that was for the best. Kano was surreptitiously checking her over for injuries, surely smelling the trauma in her fur.

"I'll be okay," she said. "Nothing permanent. How did you find me?"

"There are cameras all over the camp. Nobody talks about it because they don't want us to feel watched, but it came in handy when you were captured. Facial recognition brought up several of the attackers. It only took a couple of days to trace where they'd gone."

A couple of days? She thought about the grassy field they'd just crossed and knew they must be far from the camp. It was cold, but there hadn't been a sign of snow anywhere. *I must have been drugged or unconscious for longer than I thought.*

"We think Reynaldo's alive," Kano said. "After they were done with the dragons, they carried him out. If he was dead, they would've left him."

Taliya hoped Kano was right.

"I'm surprised Carl let you come," she said, "but I'm glad you did. So glad."

"He gave me a hard time, but in the end, he knew that I could scent you out if you were unconscious . . . or worse. Dead or alive, I never would have stopped until I found you. He knew that."

She snuggled in closer to Kano, desperately grateful for the dark fates that had brought them together.

"Rest now," he said. "It will take us a couple of hours to get home."

"Is it safe there?"

"Yes. Attack from such a small group had never occurred to them. The council and Canadian government were alert for war, not profiteers. Security has been amped up. It's fortified now."

That was good to hear, but would it be enough? *Will life ever be really safe for us? There or anywhere?*

Getting back to camp was complicated because a winter storm had come through. The helicopter could only take them so far with nowhere to land outside the habitat dome. They stopped at the Winnipeg Airport to change to a military transport. Carl was whisked away by a medical team, and the rest of the group watched helplessly as they loaded him into an ambulance and raced away. He had not regained consciousness, and Taliya was alarmed by how weak his heart had sounded. Kano supported her as they walked across the tarmac, but he stopped before getting in the truck.

"Taliya, look over there."

She turned to where he was pointing and saw a huge mass

of humans—more than a thousand of them, many with signs and banners, held back by temporary waist-high metal fencing. When the crowd realized she could see them, they spontaneously burst into cheers and hoots.

"Kano, what's happening?"

"Canadian news outlets report everything," the transport driver said. "Kerkaw can't control them. The break-in at the refugee camp has been the top story. Footage from the documentary is everywhere now. Your story especially. I'm sure details about your rescue have already been broadcast, including the fact you had to stop here. It looks like you have a fan club."

A fan club? She stood up as straight as she could and took in the scene more carefully. It was her name they were chanting. Over and over and over. Banners had messages like "Tigran Are Terrific" and "Save The Tigran" and flat-out "We Love You, Taliya!" It was so bizarre, she had no words.

"Can you give them a wave at least?" the female guard said, standing beside them with her gun across her, just in case.

Taliya raised her arm and gave a huge wave, and the crowd lost their collective minds, jumping and screaming. She could only laugh. After so many months of feeling like the world wanted her dead, she had cheering fans. Gathering all her energy, she blew them a massive kiss, throwing it to the crowd. She noticed a news crew off to the side and gave them a wave and a big smile as well.

Kano seemed to sense she was at the end of her strength

because he wrapped an arm around her waist and turned her toward the transport. Even once they were inside, Taliya could hear the crowd chanting her name in support.

"Did you see the news camera?" the female guard asked. "It was probably going out live. I'm betting you're all over international news today. People in America will be able to find it on the dark web."

"Will that help the rebellion in the U.S., do you think?" Taliya asked.

"Maybe. Just maybe," Kano said. "The court of public opinion has always been a huge influence. If enough other countries really, really get behind the rebels, that might force Kerkaw's hand. Even if it's just for an open election. Americans haven't been given a chance to replace their leadership for decades."

Kano smiled and pulled her close as the transport lifted and sped away, back to the refugee camp. Taliya knew she wouldn't rest easy until they were there and she could snuggle her kits in her arms.

Once they arrived, however, she had to tell her story to the council and be debriefed for over an hour while she got something more to eat. They had found her, but Reynaldo and the dragons were still missing. Everyone assumed they had been sold, all five of them. Any information Taliya could give the council and Canadian military about the men she had seen could help with a rescue. As much as she just wanted to get home, she answered questions and told them about what she'd witnessed when she was captured, which wasn't much. Every muscle in her body ached, and it was hard to even sit upright, but she knew time was of the essence. Reynaldo would have done the same for her.

It was the middle of the night before she and Kano made it back to their cozy house. Marla was there with the kits, who were sleeping. The moment she saw Taliya, she burst into tears and rushed to hug her, shaking from head to toe. If anyone could have been vividly imagining the terror of Taliya's last few days, Marla was that tigran.

"I'm okay. It's over now. I'm okay," she assured her friend, hugging her tight until the shaking ceased.

"Samson brought over a lap tablet so we could watch the reporting on the news," Marla said, wiping her face. "Stories about you are just *everywhere*. The kits loved seeing you at the airport and hearing people cheer for you. Once we knew you were safe, I put them to bed and your mom and the twins went home."

"Thank you," Taliya said. "Thank you for being here for my family."

She staggered over to the bedroom to peek in at her sleeping kits. They looked too peaceful to disturb. *It's probably better if I clean up first anyhow. I smell disgusting.*

Marla headed back to her own house for some sleep, and Kano helped Taliya shower as exhaustion threatened to take over. Once she was clean and dry and in her favorite PJs, he helped her to bed, but when she closed her eyes, images of the man with the cattle prod and the man with the dental instrument flashed through her mind. A sharp pain radiated through her jaw, even though she knew no one had actually touched her, and she gasped, opening her eyes again. Kano set his hand on her hip.

"If it's too hard to sleep, I can get Agnus," he said. "She dropped me a note that we should call for her at any hour if you needed help."

"I'll be okay, if I can just get the images and smells of that place out of my head. I swear, I may never be able to sit still for a dentist again."

Kano rumbled deep in his chest. He stretched out along her back, pulling her into his warm body like he had done hundreds of times before. Taliya matched her breathing to his, letting that gentle rhythm calm her, and relaxed into sleep.

It felt like she'd just closed her eyes when quiet noises from the kitchen stirred her awake. She still ached in every bone and muscle, so she lay there quietly, anticipating how much it would hurt to move.

"She's awake," Aliania whispered from the kitchen.

Taliya chuckled. There was no faking sleep with tigran around, even little ones. Kano poked his head in the door, and she gave him a weak smile, glad she was already facing that direction. Rolling over felt impossible.

"Please, send them in. Let me see them," she said.

Aliania peeked out from behind Kano with serious eyes.

"Papa said you're going to be ouchy and tired and we need to be extra careful with you."

"Papa is right, but I know a hug would make me feel better."

She reached her hand toward her daughter, and the white kit scrambled up onto the bed and snuggled herself into Taliya's chest.

"You smell funny, Mama," Ali mumbled. "Is that because of the ouchy parts?"

"Probably," Taliya admitted. "It may take a while to get that stink out of my fur."

Aliania nodded and moved aside slightly as Amrita and Jai joined them with little cries of "Mama." Taliya couldn't help hugging Amrita a little tighter than necessary, making the kit squeak.

The front door opened and closed, and Shreya came into the room, her eyes full of tears. "Oh gods, my kitten." She came around the other side of the bed and sat down, wrapping her daughter up in her arms. Taliya leaned into the embrace and assured her mother she was fine. Once again, she hadn't considered how the things happening to her would affect her mother. If she had been willing to be tortured to death for her kits, what must Shreya have been going through, stuck at camp helplessly while they searched for her only daughter?

Tuscan and Tyler came in last, subdued but happy to see

her. Kano sat on the end of the bed, and Aliania crawled into his lap. For several minutes they were just a bed full of teary tigran.

"We should let you get something to eat," Shreya finally said, motioning for the boys to get off the bed.

"Papa already made breakfast," Aliania said. "I'll bring it to you."

Kano helped Taliya to sit up as the rest of the family left her alone. Ali carried the breakfast in like she was serving a queen. Taliya ate what she could, Kano helped her to the bathroom, then she collapsed back into bed.

"Agnus stopped by earlier," Kano said, "and ordered you to nap 'like house cat in ray of sunshine.' She said she'd come check on you later."

Taliya smiled and snuggled down into the soft blankets, taking Agnus's advice.

Chapter 28

The events of the next few weeks were astounding. After giving Taliya a few days of peace, the council called for her. Reports of her capture by the mercenaries, including details of her torture, had been broadcast around the world. She had inadvertently become the face of persecuted tigran in the United States—the face of the revolution. While the council refused to let news crews into the dome again, they wanted to find ways to take advantage of her newfound fame.

Samson arranged for Taliya to record a message of thanks to her fans and supporters around the globe. That was a video she was willing to make. During the recording, she started crying, overwhelmed by the sheer emotional upheaval of the last week, but the ligran said it didn't matter. It was helpful, if anything, to show the humanity of their species. He posted her message on the website the council had set up for Taliya, and within the hour it had been viewed and shared twenty-five million times.

The next night at dinner, there was a knock on the door. Kano opened it to one of the young tigran messengers used around camp and took a note from him. Kano whoofed and froze in place as he read.

"What is it?" Taliya asked, frightened by Kano's reaction.

"An all-camp meeting has been called for tonight at seven," he said. "They're keeping the lights up until afterward. We're supposed to go to the front of camp, to the arrival area. There's news about the war they want everyone to hear."

"Good news or bad news?" she asked, glancing at the kits, though they hadn't looked up from their plates.

"It doesn't say. I guess we'll have to go and find out."

At six forty-five, their family bustled out the door, met Shreya and the boys in the street, and followed the crowd toward the front of camp. A massive screen had been set up across from the open arrival area, and creatures were being guided into a makeshift seating arrangement in rows on the ground facing it. It was a rare event to have the whole camp, all the different species, gathered in one place. As Taliya's family sat down in their spots, the kits craned their necks, trying to take it all in. Once everyone was settled, Samson stepped in front of the screen and addressed the camp in his resonant voice.

"Friends, we are so excited to share some new developments with you. As you know, since the break-in a week ago, news broadcasts around the world have been filled with stories about the plight of the tigran in the United States. But the coverage has also spread to more of the corrupt and illegal activity of the current government regime, especially the refusal to allow new elections." He paused dramatically. "It seems the United Nations will no longer tolerate this. We wanted to show you some of the footage that was shared through the media here in Canada today. Then we will go to the live broadcasts."

Samson moved aside, and the screen came to life with images being routed in from a nearby tablet. Kano reached over and took Taliya's hand. She was glad for the contact and comfort, not sure exactly what they were about to see. A blonde female newscaster, an earnest expression on her young face, brought them up to date.

"This afternoon in Geneva, the United Nations met with a firm commitment to resolve the decades-long disputes in the United States of America. While martial law has been in effect there since 2140, it is clear to all the countries of the world that this state of affairs was not meant to continue indefinitely. A resolution was passed at eleven o'clock am Central Standard Time stating that if the rule of law under the Constitution is not restored within seven days, the United Nations will send in military reinforcements to stabilize the country. Free and open elections are to be held within sixty days, overseen by delegates from the U.N. If President Kerkaw and Congress do not obey this resolution, they will be accused of war crimes and violations of the long-standing Geneva Convention guidelines."

The image shifted to scenes outside the White House, protesters with banners and posters hurling insults through the security gates. Uniformed soldiers stood guard but did not make any arrests. That, in and of itself, was remarkable. Organized protests had been quickly and violently dispersed for years. Gunning down everyone present was not unheard of. Taliya marveled at the bravery of those humans, standing their ground and demanding their rights, and someone having the courage to record and share it. A narrator described the scene, appreciating the same things Taliya was.

What will Kerkaw do? Will he yield and meet their demands or stand and fight? How much support will he really, truly have when the humans know they have backing from around the world to defy him? She'd always wondered how much of his power came from fear, not loyalty. Historically speaking, it was genuinely dangerous, downright life-threatening, to stand against him.

The newscast showed discussions at the U.N. and the passing of the resolution mentioned before. Taliya chuffed at the determination on the faces of the delegates. The broadcast also showed scenes of Kerkaw's military forces in retreat, yielding control of one city after another. Enforcers fled from the rebel army. A group of tigran in uniform gathered and smiled for the cameras, raising their guns in triumph, and the whole camp cheered in support. From all appearances, the tide had turned.

"It's amazing," Taliya whispered. "I never thought I'd live to see it."

"You almost didn't," Kano whispered back.

She imagined he was thinking of his wife, his parents, so many who had been lost along the way. *Such a waste.*

Seeing footage of Taliya and her story made the crowd whoop and cheer. Protesters in some scenes had posters with her face on them, demanding the end of the Gathering in her name. It was embarrassing to be so singled out in front of creatures who had been through as much, if not more, than her, but she could only smile at the hope that her tale had made a difference in the war.

The family watched live broadcasts for another hour, and the young ones fell asleep in their laps. Tuscan and Tyler were given permission to go home. They were excited for the promise of freedom, but there was only so much detail about it they could sit still for. When the news finally broke for a few commercials, Samson lowered the sound and spoke to the remaining audience.

"We will be leaving the screen up to follow this story, hopefully to the conclusion we have all prayed for. You are welcome to come and go during your day as time allows. If there are any huge events, I am sure you will hear word through camp quickly. The lights will be turned down for the night in one hour. Sleep well."

Many creatures took this as a signal to head back to their units, but Taliya didn't want to go yet—desperate to see it all. Marla found them and sat down next to Taliya. She scooted close and rested her head against Taliya with a sigh.

"When we played cards in the attic room, did you ever think you'd see this day?" Marla asked.

"No. I don't think I really believed it would happen. It seemed impossible."

"You should go there, Taliya," she said, lifting her head and looking at Kano. "She should go. She's the face of the tigran resistance. She should be there."

"You're right, I suppose," Taliya said. "There's not a single tigran in those crowds we see protesting. Only a handful here and there in the videos from the war."

Kano's blue eyes met hers, filled with fear. She knew he wouldn't stop her, but his concerns were justified. There were legitimate reasons for no tigran to be present in the middle of it all. The Gathering was still a very real concern. Would her newfound celebrity keep her safe?

"Let me talk to Samson about it, and the council," she said. "If Kerkaw yields to the U.N.'s demands, maybe a small group of us can go. The humans will have their own agenda that may not include ensuring our freedoms. At least not right away. Someone has to fight *those* battles."

"Does it have to be *you*?" Kano said, blinking slowly.

She didn't answer. She didn't have to.

On April 7, 2174, Taliya stood shoulder to shoulder on 16th Street in Washington, D.C., with other tigran and liran, berman, panthran, leopran, cheeman, and other genetic mixes. Tens of thousands of humans of all races and backgrounds, young and old, marched with them as well.

Kerkaw had obeyed the United Nations. Not like he had a choice. Congress and his own White House staff turned against him when the opportunity presented itself. Three days after the U.N. resolution, Drimavil Kerkaw had vanished. News reports were full of hypotheses about where he was hiding and whether he would stir up trouble some other way, but in his absence, the country moved forward like a category six bomb cyclone.

Elections had been held, and a new president was now in office: President Padme Nakobi—a woman, which Taliya was sure had chapped Kerkaw extraordinarily, wherever he was. Nakobi had been the leading voice against Kerkaw's regime for years, so the choice had been easy and unanimous across every state. No one from Kerkaw's Congress survived the elections, even if they spoke out against him in the end. Americans did not forget how they'd been complicit for decades and sent them all packing.

The new Congress faced the daunting task of bringing life in their country back under the rule of the Constitution.

Piles of legislation had been filed in the weeks since the election, including a bill giving tigran and other species their freedom. To have creatures who were part human *owned* by anyone flew in the face of the laws that had governed the United States since December 6, 1865, when the Thirteenth Amendment was passed. That day in April, Americans gathered in D.C. to show support for this bill of freedom.

Taliya led the way in the march and held the center of a wide banner declaring "Freedom For Tigran." On either side of her marched tigran she'd never met before, sent to represent their own parts of the country—finally feeling safe enough to make their voices heard. Behind them came over two million creatures and humans, filling the street with their presence, marching together.

After crossing the square to Pennsylvania Avenue, the crowd spread out into the park behind them. Grandstands, reporters, and a stage with a podium awaited Taliya in front of the White House gates. Her speech had been planned and practiced on the way to Washington from the refugee camp. She was still the face everyone, including the new president, wanted up front and center. Searching the stands, she found Marla and her mother, the boys at her side. Kano had stayed at the camp with the kits, still not confident the world was safe for them. Somewhere from the sidelines, where humans gathered, chants of "freedom" began.

President Nakobi stepped up to the podium and greeted

the crowd to deafening cheers. After some rousing words, she called Taliya up to the microphone. The overwhelming response and thunder of applause made her tail puff as she climbed the stairs and stood behind the microphone. The teleprompter magically displayed her speech in the air in front of her. Nerves fluttered in her chest, but she took a deep breath, smiled, fangs and all, and waited a moment for them to settle down. Looking out over the crowd, it occurred to her that she'd become an ambassador for her species after all.

"Thank you all for being here," she finally started. "It means so much to each and every creature who is marching today for the dignity of freedom and basic civil rights. That I am even standing here—that this is a crowd full of so many different species—none of it seemed possible not that long ago. You all know my story. Know it better than you might want to," she said with a laugh, and the crowd laughed with her.

"We have lived in fear too long. Fear of creatures different from us. You humans, you were made to fear the tigran, a species that had lived peacefully alongside you for over a hundred years. Tigran, you were made to fear humans, to see them as the enemy. I hope we are now ready to move past the lies and deceptions that led to all of this fear."

She paused to swallow and collect her thoughts, but the crowd took it as an invitation to show their enthusiasm, which they did with hoots and cheers and stomping feet. Taliya sighed and looked up at her mother. Shreya nodded slightly and smiled.

"There is much to be done to restore our nation," Taliya said when the crowd finally stilled. "Storms still batter the heartland, and floods still wreak havoc to our coasts. Fires rage and hurricanes wash away cities. We have learned to live with these horrors and avoid them as much as possible, but there is still work to be done. Congress is overwhelmed with that work. I understand their struggles and hate to ask one more thing of them, but I must. I must ask for my home back. I must ask for the safety of my young ones. I must ask Congress for my freedom, for the freedom of each and every creature standing here today."

President Nakobi led the response this time, pumping up the crowd from the sidelines.

"Freedom! Freedom! Freedom!"

Taliya's heart raced, but there was only one more part to get through.

"Just because my ancestors were created in a lab does not mean we are *less than*. Human embryos are created in labs, but when those children are born they are not *less than*. Being different does not make us *less than*. All we are asking is to stop being treated as less than."

A shout of "You tell 'em, sister!" came from the crowd, and Taliya chuffed in response.

"I am here today to address Congress and answer their questions about the bill under consideration granting tigran and other partially human, genetically created species freedom as citizens of this great nation. Freedom is all we are asking for. Freedom, for us here today. Freedom, for our young ones, still afraid to come out in public. Freedom, for the generations yet unborn. Just freedom. That is all. Thank you."

Taliya stepped away from the mic and felt a hand on her back. President Nakobi was right there, ready to stand beside her. She began the chant of "freedom" again and encouraged the crowd. Taliya felt hot tears burst to her eyes. It was suddenly all too much. The president seemed to sense this and guided her down the steps to where Samson was waiting.

With the chants and cheers of millions of creatures in the air, Taliya followed President Nakobi through the gates and into the White House.

Chapter 29
Three Years Later

Taliya flopped the damp sheet over the clothesline and tacked three wooden pins to hold it in place. The crisp spring Arkansas wind took hold and rippled it in the breeze.

"Mama," Amrita called from the house. "There's a call for you."

"I'll be right there," Taliya said, tossing the rest of the clothespins into the basket full of wet linen at her feet.

"Let me finish it," Aliania said, heading to the clothesline from across the clearing where she was spreading feed for the chickens. "You shouldn't be doing that anyhow."

Taliya stretched her back, letting her round belly poke out from under the oversized tunic. Aliania hugged her around the waist, patted her tummy, and gave her a gentle shove toward the house. Taliya waddled inside and sat down at the video table. An image of President Nakobi greeted her.

"Hello, Padme," Taliya said. "What can I do for you?"

"I'm just checking to make sure you got the notice I sent you about today's trial."

"Yes, I saw that last night. Is Carl there with you already?"

"Yes, General Thompson arrived an hour ago. He and Reynaldo are meeting with their lawyer, and the trial should begin shortly. I'm hoping you won't be required to testify at all, but a video interview should do the trick. No one wants you traveling right now. Kano would have my skin if I even suggested it."

Taliya laughed at the exaggeration, though the sentiment behind it was true.

"Reynaldo knows I will do everything in my power to help bring those men to justice. It's one of the last court cases from that attack, isn't it?"

"Yes, and we hope to wrap it up quickly. I mean, the investigators have the video of the kidnapping, found Reynaldo caged on the men's property, and have all the communications with the kidnappers. Those scumbags don't have much of a defense. I'm only sorry it's dragged on for so many years. General Thompson and Reynaldo will be glad to be done with it, I'm sure."

"Let's hope you're right, Padme. Just call if you need anything. We'll be watching the trial live from here."

"Excellent. Thanks, Taliya. I'll talk to you after."

Taliya nodded and clicked off the transmission.

"It should be starting soon," Jai said. "You can see the people getting set up in the courtroom."

Taliya glanced over at the media wall and sighed. She was glad to be free from active political life, but it was difficult to step away completely while creatures she loved still struggled through the system.

"Amrita, go get Grammy and Grampa and tell them it's starting in a few minutes."

Amrita sighed dramatically, like the four-year-old tigran she was, and headed across the field to her grandparent's house. Jai adjusted the color on the media system, reduced the image size for easier viewing, and settled in on the sofa.

"Come on over, Mama," he said. "Claim your spot before everyone gets here."

Kano came into the living room from the kitchen, a huge tray of snacks and drinks in his strong arms. Taliya was grateful to have him home with the family that day. His work on new building projects often took him away for extended periods, especially to the struggling coastal cities like Sacramento and what was left of Houston. As the only tigran to be given official status as a mason, he was in high demand, but with the new kits arriving soon, he planned on staying home for a few months. He set the tray on the coffee table and turned to his mate.

"Do you need a lift?" he said with a smile and a chuff.

"Maybe," Taliya said, chuffing back.

He helped her up and then down again into her favorite spot on the sofa. Aliania jogged into the house and flopped on a comfy chair, grabbing her lap tablet and throwing her white furry legs over the armrest. Amrita followed close behind with her grandparents, Shreya and Jai—though he was just called Grampa now to avoid confusion. Tuscan and Tyler were off with friends for the day. Many tigran families had settled in the forest around where they lived, but none of them were the same neighbors as before. Most of Taliya's friends from her youth had not survived the Gathering. Even with all of her connections, she'd never discovered her friend Anya's fate. Anya had simply vanished, like hundreds of other tigran.

As laws were finally passed granting freedom and rights to all species with human DNA, it was easier to take a step back and return to a quiet life on the family compound deep in the forests of northern Arkansas. The Enforcers had not destroyed it. It seemed like they'd never shown up there at all.

After Taliya's father returned from fighting with the rebel troops, he and Shreya built a separate house on the Arkansas land so they could be close to the grandkits. Taliya and her brood took over the main house. She'd tried to keep life as simple as her parents had wanted it to be, but there was more technology at the compound now, including an elaborate security system hidden in the forest around them—and an arsenal in the shed. Taliya would never stop fearing for Aliania and

Amrita. Kerkaw had never been found, and not all humans were happy with having him deposed, not to mention those operating outside the law with their own greedy or perverted interest in unique species. Despite the new laws, she and Kano did not let down their guard for their young ones.

For three years, Taliya had worked as the representative of the tigran cause, speaking at rallies, leading marches, debating with legislators. She had even flown on Air Force One to Geneva and met with the United Nations—Kano and the whole family in tow. One of the accomplishments Taliya was most proud of was establishing a reservation in the Colorado mountains for the handful of surviving "uncivilized" tigran. Now they had protected land to hunt and live as they pleased, wild and free. She and Kano had spent three weeks with them and had an amazing adventure, but it was not the life a creature accustomed to comfortable beds would choose voluntarily. They had, however, returned home from their weeks of wildness with a little surprise. The twins were due in two weeks.

Nobody cared what color their fur was.

The bailiff on the media wall called for everyone to rise, and all eyes in the room turned toward him, though Aliania's attention wasn't held for long. Taliya took the plate of treats that Shreya handed to her and listened while the judge rambled on about facts she already knew far too well. *The kidnappers should have just let Reynaldo free when Kerkaw was voted out.* They'd hung onto him and tried to justify their ownership of the beautiful panthran for over a year, but laws against privately owning even full-blooded tigers and panthers were established now.

As Taliya adjusted her body on the sofa, the kits wriggled around inside of her, making her stomach visibly ripple. Amrita laughed and set her hand on her mother's belly.

"Were we that floppy?" she asked.

"Oh, yes. Especially when I wanted to sleep."

As the commentator talked about the break-in at the refugee camp, images of Bunny, Coconut, Pegasus, and Polly—photos taken when the documentary crew visited the camp, before the pterodragons were stolen away—popped up on the media wall. Their training building at the refugee camp still sat empty, awaiting their return. Rumors abounded that the dragons had been smuggled overseas. Taliya smiled sadly at the pictures of Bunny on the wall and hoped that she was safe, wherever she was.

The camp had become a permanent home for many of the refugees. Dan and Kallie had stayed. It felt safe there. Marla had remained in camp for a year, but when she fell in love with a glorious tigran herself, they were married and settled down near Taliya's family compound, in an area where tigran were common and welcomed. Aunty Marla dropped by to visit at least once a week.

The TV coverage shifted back to the courtroom, and Taliya's heart raced, seeing her friends in that stressful situation.

General Carl Thompson looked handsome and official in his uniform covered in medals and ribbons, including a Purple Heart earned rescuing her. For a moment, the uniform made her think of Colonel Narlin, and a cold lump settled in her throat. Carl would use his power and authority in the right way, and she focused on that hope for the future instead.

"How can this go any other way but those guys being found guilty?" Jai said, munching on some dried venison. "I mean, this whole thing is stupid."

"The process can be frustrating at times," Shreya said, "but it's not *stupid*. Everyone is entitled to a trial and a chance to prove their innocence."

"Even if they're a pus-filled maggoty creep?"

"Yes, Jai. Even if they are a pus-filled maggoty creep. Side-stepping due process is where corruption sneaks in. No one wants to take steps backward."

"Do you suppose Carl and Reynaldo will finally be able to get married after the trial?" Aliania asked, not looking up from her tech pad.

Taliya exchanged looks with Kano and Shreya. Freedoms for same-sex couples had been quickly restored, but mixing species was another matter altogether—legally and in the mind of the American public.

"Maybe someday," Kano said.

Taliya and Kano had been legally married a year ago, making their handfasting official, but she didn't see the laws about species intermarrying changing soon. In some ways, it was a protection for the tigran and creatures like them, though Reynaldo and Carl probably didn't see it that way.

"Look, look," Amrita said, "Reynaldo is getting ready to testify."

"Samson will get it handled," Ali said, giving the broadcast some attention as he came on screen.

"I'm sure he will," Taliya agreed.

She suspected her daughter had a crush on the massive ligran, now the lawyer for the prosecution, who had continued to be a huge part of their lives and Taliya's political work. He had definitely been efficient in getting things done in court. The family settled in to watch Samson secure the conviction of the men behind the kidnapping of Reynaldo, Taliya, and the four dragons.

Taliya thought she should make some notes about the trial. She had begun recording all the events of their lives and was writing a book. She often wondered if some future creature, maybe someone not human at all but completely different, would read about her experiences—like she had read about the sadly short life of Anne Frank—and learn from it. Like Anne, Taliya wanted her voice to go out into the world and make a difference.

Taliya opened the memoir with her own thoughts on Anne's most famous words: "I still believe, in spite of everything, that people are truly good at heart."

After everything, I don't know if I believe that all humans are basically good. There were many days it was hard to believe that any humans are good. But I know that I am good—both my human parts and my tiger parts. Despite it all, I am still good at heart. Yes, I have killed, violently even. More than once. I unleashed the tiger to save what is human in me. The only regret I have is that it was necessary to kill at all. I hope that future generations, whatever their species or genetic makeup, can learn from what has gone before them. No matter how different we may seem, we are all deserving of the right to plot our own course, be masters of our own destiny.

Freedom has been called a divine right. It has been called a human right. However you want to view it, freedom is the foundation of what every mother and father wants for their young ones. What each of us wants for ourselves. Freedom is what we are willing to die for.

She would tell the stories of her own family and their struggle to survive, of Kano and his murdered wife, of Marla, Carl and Reynaldo, and so many others she had met along the way. About the nightmares that still haunted all of their dreams from time to time.

Maybe, just maybe, if she was brutally honest, the future would not repeat the horrors of the past.

The End

Author Notes

First, a gazillion gallons of thanks go out to my writing critique group, Ozark Mountain Guild of Writers (OMG), for giving me excellent feedback on so many pages of this book and helping me with the worldbuilding in the early stages. Y'all are amazing!

As always, thank you to my husband, Scott, for going through my pages, catching silly errors, and being ready to talk through my ideas as the story grew. Sorry there weren't more battle scenes. Maybe next time.

And thank you to my beta readers: Jennifer McMurrain (you can thank her for Carl getting shot), Duke Pennell (both in critique group and out), Russell Gayer (both in critique group and out), Shannon Iwanski, Katye Summers, Julie James, and

403

Callista Rose Dendler. Special thanks to Crystal Ursin for reading it twice and saying how much you loved it when I was doubting everything. Sorry I made you cry.

I try to attend as many writing workshops as I can, especially in my local area. You never know what one idea or one flash of inspiration will get you started on a new project or benefit one already in process. In April of 2018, I joined a small group of writers at the Fayetteville Library to hear Velda Brotherton speak about writing historical fiction, her specialty.

Within the workshop, she had us think of a place we had been or an event we had experienced that was really special or important to us. We should use that as our setting. I jotted down several but decided to go with my brief moments standing in the bedroom of Anne Frank in the hidden annex in Amsterdam when I was fifteen. We wrote about how that affected us and how it made us feel. Then we were supposed to shift the focus to a fictional character in that same setting. I started to go off task a bit here—that happens sometimes—and tried to imagine a character that would need to be in hiding like Anne, but in the future.

Feline characters are a favorite of mine, as is quite evident from the books I generally write, so I went that route first. Cats as aliens or cat-like creatures who are as human-like as they are feline was intriguing. I read the Chanur series by C. J. Cherryh before I was even in high school, and I loved those creatures.

Tigers, specifically, are very special to me. For many years I have volunteered at Turpentine Creek Wildlife Refuge, which houses dozens of rescued tigers. Being on the receiving end of a contented tiger chuff will change your life. I've had the privilege of watching them play from only a few feet away, rolling on their backs and rumbling in pleasure at the grass of their enclosure—or being terrified as new arrivals, snarling and spitting as we attempted to quickly build a home for them. An angry tiger is a force of nature, and the visceral reaction to that rage is not something I'll ever forget.

As I started to flesh out the main character for this workshop, Taliya jumped into my mind fully formed. A genetic experiment, like the ligers and ti-ligers I had personally seen at Turpentine Creek. I wrote her first scenes right there and then during the workshop, the opening with her in hiding. It also seemed right to have Taliya know about Anne and her struggles, her hiding. Taliya's mother giving her a copy of Anne's diary made a nice connection. She thought it would help Taliya understand they were not alone. Humans have a history of hating anyone who is "other." Could we allow another man like Hitler to rise to power, spouting hatred and sneakily working to eradicate those he felt were "less than"? Kerkaw was my answer to that.

The character of Kano and the breeding facility came much later in the process—during NaNoWriMo 2018, where I completed a huge chunk of the story—but it felt only logical.

White tigers are one of the greatest genetic atrocities forced on any animal. It's not a desired tiger coloring, except to greedy humans. Creating a white tiger cub with precision is a tricky business, and it is best accomplished by breeding white tigers who are closely related to each other and both carry the SLC45A2 pigment gene. Mothers and sons. Brothers and sisters. Nature itself does not like this kind of genetic mixing, and the offspring routinely have health and vision problems. And God help any white tiger pair who consistently produce white offspring. They will be bred as frequently as possible, the kits removed from their mother almost immediately so she will be ready to breed again. Golden tabby or strawberry tigers are a real thing, sometimes the result of this breeding as another step in the white tiger gene. They are very rare, but I have hung out with two of these beautiful creatures at Turpentine Creek Wildlife Refuge: Tigger and Khaleesi.

Since this type of aggressive breeding for profit was already a prevalent reality in 2018, I could easily imagine the fate of the tigran and what humans would do with such a creature. As a species, we are pretty revolting when it comes to the care of other life forms. A government-sponsored breeding facility didn't seem like much of a stretch. Don't even get me started on circuses that force tigers and other animals to perform. Those are being banned, and I hope the trend continues. You can avoid promoting and supporting this industry in the present day by only visiting accredited rescue facilities that don't breed, avoiding "cub petting" or handling of any kind, and supporting only ethical tourism sites.

I will be chuffed to bits if you enjoyed Taliya's story, but more than that, I hope it led you to ponder some things about life on our planet and how we respect and care for those around us: human and animal. And yes, I expect there are more stories about Taliya and her family to come.

Questions for
Book Club Discussions

1. Are genetic creations like the tigran a good idea, a benefit to society, or not? Can you envision creatures like Taliya being real in 200 years?

2. If faced with the same dangerous situation, would you be able to send your children away with strangers, like Shreya did?

3. Did Taliya get away from the facility too easily? Would you have liked it better if she had been there longer? What if she'd actually had to give away her two newborn kits? How would that have impacted her as a character going forward?

4. How did you feel when Taliya killed Narlin? Was it justified when she could have just waited for rescue, knowing the army had arrived?

5. If Taliya was not pregnant, do you think she and Kano would have stayed together after the rescue?

6. Did Taliya make the right decision to work with the dragons? What if Kano had never appreciated her work and it left

a rift in their relationship? Would you have wanted a dragon or thought it was scary?

7. How do you feel about interspecies relationships, like Marla's parents? Should they be made legal in the America of 2174? How is it a protection or benefit to the genetic creations to have it stay illegal?

8. If you had a tigran family as neighbors, would you welcome them? Would that be cool or a nightmare?

9. If you could have lunch with one of the characters, which would you choose?

10. Do you agree with what Anne Frank wrote in her diary, that humans are basically good at heart? Or do you hold more with her thoughts that humans are intrinsically violent? Why would Anne say both of those things within her diary?

11. Thinking back to the quote at the front of the book, is history always doomed to repeat itself? Do we ever learn from the past?

12. This story was edited and published in the middle of the COVID-19 pandemic and the Black Lives Matter protests, marches, and riots of 2020. How do you think these events might have influenced the author?

13. After reading this story, would you think twice about visiting a zoo or facility that allowed cub petting or breeds white tigers?

14. With the promise that there are more stories about tigran in the works, what do you hope they will be about? Are there any characters you'd love to see as the focus of a whole novella?

About the Author

Meg Dendler has considered herself a writer since she earned an award in a picture book contest in 5th grade and entertained her classmates with ongoing sequels for the rest of the year. Beginning serious work as a freelancer in the '90s while teaching elementary and middle school, Meg has over one hundred articles in print, including interviews with Kirk Douglas, Sylvester Stallone, and Dwayne "The Rock" Johnson. She has won contests with her short stories and poetry, along with multiple awards for her best-selling "Cats in the Mirror" alien rescue cat children's book series. *Bianca: The Brave Frail and Delicate Princess* was honored as Best Juvenile Book of 2018 by the Oklahoma Writers' Federation. Meg is also an editor for independent and self-publishing authors. Meg lives in Northwest Arkansas with her husband and at least one cat. Visit her at www.megdendler.com for more information about upcoming books and events and all of Meg's social media links, including how to sign up for her Reader Group.